NOVELLO

Ten Years
of Great American Writing

An Anthology

Edited by
Amy Rogers,
Robert Inman,
and
Frye Gaillard

NOVELLO festival PRESS

in association with
Down Home Press

First printing October, 2000

1 2 3 4 5 6 7 8 9

ISBN 1-878086-87-1

Library of Congress Control Number
00 133352

Printed in the United States of America

Book design by Elizabeth House
Cover design by Tim Rickard

This book was published in association with Down Home Press,
P.O. Box 4126, Asheboro, N.C. 27204

Novello Festival Press Books are published by
The Public Library of Charlotte and Mecklenburg County
310 N. Tryon St.
Charlotte, N.C. 28202

Distributed by John F. Blair, Publisher
1406 Plaza Drive
Winston-Salem, N.C. 27103

Contents

PART I — THE ESSAYS

PART II — THE STORIES

Acknowledgments

Without the support of the Public Library of Charlotte and Mecklenburg County, this project would not have been possible. We would especially like to thank Executive Director Robert Cannon, and staff members Jessica Walter, Jenny Rosenthal, Staci Falkowitz, Rich Rosenthal, Peggy Howell, Jennifer Woodford, Shelia Bumgarner; the library board of trustees, and all the supporters who have worked to make Novello possible.

Special thanks also to Barbara Solomon of Greater Talent Network who helped facilitate the inclusion of several writers.

We are grateful to Jerry Bledsoe, Pat Conroy, Clyde Edgerton, and Lee Smith, whose early enthusiasm for this project inspired us and encouraged other writers to participate. Ann Wicker, Heidi Flick and Will MacDonald, fellow writers from our home community, were a constant source of support.

Most especially, we would like to thank the writers who appear at the Novello Festival of Reading and other library-sponsored events, and those who continue through their work to enhance and sustain our literary legacy.

— The Editors

Introduction

It began just that simply, with one conversation between two colleagues who were having lunch. Neither Rolfe Neill nor Robert Cannon remembers who said it first, but both agreed it was a terrific idea: put together the best elements of a festival — the contests and games for kids, outdoor booths, and events for adults — but focus the whole celebration not on a holiday or seasonal theme, but instead on the importance of something truly timeless: reading.

A festival of reading? Cannon was intrigued by the possibility. As Executive Director of the Public Library of Charlotte and Mecklenburg County, he saw tremendous potential, not simply for on-site activities, but for outreach into schools and other venues where the public could meet authors and hear them read their work. Neill, who was Publisher of *The Charlotte Observer*, believed such an event could develop into something much more than a traditional book fair, something "as fun as sports."

And so the Novello Festival of Reading was born. Its name brought to mind books and novels, of course, in one sense. But in another, it evoked an image of something new, the first of its kind — something *novel* in the literal sense. Novello debuted in November 1991, the same year that the library celebrated a century of service.

The response was immediate. At the week-long festival's first event, a sold-out crowd gathered to hear Pulitzer Prize-winning writer David Halberstam. A few days later, North Carolina novelist and native son Clyde Edgerton told stories, played the banjo, and sang for a near-capacity group of six hundred. Author Tim McLaurin, known for his feats of snake-handling, memorably illustrated the concept of conflict in storytelling — he brandished a yard-long viper before his astonished audience and explained, "If there's no conflict, there's no story." (All three authors are contributors to this anthology.)

In 1995, PLCMC was named National Library of the Year. That year, festival attendance exceeded twenty thousand. Novello authors included Gail Sheehy, whose writings on the passages of life contributed to a thought-provoking program; and farmer-turned-novelist Dori Sanders, who satisfied audience appetites in a different way — she served cookies and sweet-potato pound cake baked from recipes in her cookbook. (Writings by Sheehy and Sanders can be found in this volume, too.)

Through its unique yet broad-based vision, and leadership that Rolfe Neill calls "galvanic," Novello has presented programs for nearly every type of audience, and the authors who take part are as diverse as those who read and relish their writing. Within the festival, WordPlay Saturday, Carolina Writers' Night, A Story Story Night, and the Business Book and Author Event are perennial favorites. And no sooner has one year's festival come to a close than phones start ringing again at the library; patrons call months in advance and ask to reserve tickets for the following year's events, sometimes even before it's been decided who will appear.

The Novello contributors in this book live and teach and write in the countryside and cities and along the coastline of the South, in the Pacific Northwest, in the Arizona desert, in New York, Boston and beyond. Whether as journalists, columnists, or war correspondents; writers of fiction, memoir, or humor, they have won nearly every award a writer could covet: the Pulitzer Prize, the William Faulkner Award, the Lillian Smith Award, the Robert Penn Warren Prize for Fiction, the O. Henry Award, the Ernie Pyle Award, the Houghton Mifflin Literary Fellowship Award, the American Book Award, and the H. L. Mencken Award, to name a few. But the appeal to readers is more than literary. At Novello, lovers of literature can see their favorite authors in person and hear them, unedited.

So far, more than two hundred authors have participated in Novello. This book is both a tribute to them and a sampler of their fine work. Some of the essays and stories were chosen by the authors themselves, and while a few pieces may be familiar to readers, many appear here in print for the first time. Still others, such as Charles Kuralt's look back at a time when old ways began to give way to modern life, could only be found regionally or in books that are out of print. Until now, only *Atlanta* magazine had published Pat Conroy's raw and wryly funny remembrance of his father, Donald Conroy, the inspiration for *The Great Santini*.

While many of the names in this anthology will be familiar to book-lovers everywhere, we're pleased to introduce to you a few lesser-known writers whose work reflects the creative and expansive spirit of Novello. We think you'll especially enjoy Chicago native Sandra Govan's memoir of her youthful "bibliomania" and the consequences of where it led. Fortunately for us, it led her as an adult to Charlotte, where she now makes her home.

The Charlotte-Mecklenburg region where Novello has flourished is rich in literary excellence of its own. No one has contributed more to this legacy than the two accomplished authors who allowed me to share this project with them; as always, it is a pleasure and a privilege to work with Robert Inman and Frye Gaillard.

Novello is now in its tenth year — its tenth "edition" as PLCMC staff like to think of it — and it is as much a part of the community's culture as our symphonies and sporting events. As we celebrate this anniversary of the Novello Festival of Reading, we hope you'll spend some time enjoying this collection of work by the authors whose dedication to the craft of writing enriches our lives, and makes Novello so memorable year after year.

— Amy Rogers

Part I
The Essays

or author Pat Conroy, his Marine Corps father, Donald Conroy, has always been the central figure in his life, a primary source of the passion in his best-selling novels. But this story is not a part of one of those novels. It is pure memory — Conroy's real-life account of a final reconciliation between father and son.

Pat Conroy

"The Death of Santini"

My father died on May 11, 1998, of colon cancer, and his children buried him in the National Cemetery in Beaufort, South Carolina, not far from where our mother is buried. When I was growing up, I thought that not a single one of his seven children would attend my father's funeral if the improbable happened, and this vital, seemingly immortal aviator actually had to die like everyone else. I used to dream of spitting on his body in the mortuary, spitting into the center of his dead, embalmed face again and again, until my mouth was dry. Those were the happy day-dreams that sustained me in the flyblown classrooms of my impossible childhood. I hated my father with my body and soul for as long as I could remember. I think I would have skipped his funeral completely if I had not accidentally built the bridge that would lead us back toward each other. I spent my childhood composing psalms of pure hatred against him, and when I was beginning to write the first sections of *The Great Santini*, I had been preparing for my entire life for that public unveiling of the ruthless bastard who raised me. My rage was the molten lava of my art.

I did not tell the whole truth in *The Great Santini* by any means. I lacked the courage and I thought that if I told the truth about Donald Conroy that no one would believe me and that no one would want to read a book that contained so much unprovoked humiliation and violence. It was not just that my father was mean, his meanness seemed grotesque and exaggerated and overblown to me. From the time he woke up in the morning until he retired to his bed at night, my father was capable of backhanding his wife and children at any time.

When my father hit, you knew he was in the room. He put me on my knees throughout my childhood. He put me on my knees until that magic year when I turned seventeen and it became dangerous for him to do so. To be honest, I do not think I was a physical match for my powerful father until I was five years out of college. But he thought so. The reason I know this is he did not touch me after my seventeenth birthday. He was not a sentimental man, but he was street smart. Also, he did not need me for a punching boy any longer. My mother had not summoned up the courage to leave his sorry ass yet, and I had four more brothers still serving as prisoners of war in his shameful household. My father slapped babies for making noise. Living with him was like being handed a grenade with the pin pulled and thrown out into the dankness. It felt like the Bataan Death March without the Japanese props. I can barely look back on my sorrowful youth, yet it haunts my every waking moment and makes me a terrible husband, father, and friend. My childhood rides me and I cannot shake it off or dull its murderous power over me. I always thought that the sight of my father's corpse would be one of the happiest days of my life. I thought I would be fawn-like and boyish as I danced on his grave and urinated on his head stone.

The character of Bull Meecham in *The Great Santini* is a greatly toned-down version of Don Conroy. I added touches of humor and generosity to Col. Meecham that my father had never displayed in his entire life. I humanized him and sanctified my mother by making Lillian Meecham an emporium of human virtue with a saintliness that would become even Carmelite nuns. My portrait of my mother rings sappy and shallow to me, but I survived both the indecencies and dependencies of those times because I idolized Peg Conroy, and I needed a flawless icon to push me through a childhood that seemed like a death camp to me. In fact, my strange, mystical attraction to the death camps of Eastern Europe that ate Jews alive and belched them out as black smoke over the mountains of Poland stem from my identification with Jews as the victims of my implacable, merciless father. Every room of every house I lived in growing up felt like a cattle car. My father ruled his house the way Mengele made his selections at the arrival stations at Auschwitz. The difference, of course, is that our lives in the family of Santini were not in danger and he would not kill us.

We did not know that then. None of us knew if my father in his great, brutal strength, would kill us by accident. The sight of my face enraged him. My eyes infuriated him every time he caught me looking at him. Don Conroy was reading my face correctly. My blue eyes served as the conduit of a rage so combustible, I can feel its savage heat as I write these words today. It burns like acid along my corneas, pulses near my retinas. I could light trees on fire with my eyes when I was a boy. Even today, I can send my children reeling for the exits when they do something that irritates or offends me. My eyes are the signal fires that can put the small nation of my loved ones on the roads that lead away from me. The father I grew up with was monstrous and unspeakable and had no redeeming features. I mean that, not one. Not as a father.

I was always proud of him as a Marine and a fighter pilot and a man who kept our country safe. I thought countries who declared war on America, places like Japan and North Korea and North Vietnam, were nuts and suicidal because guys like my father would soon be filling the air above their cities. I remain extraordinarily proud that I grew up in the Marine Corps, the toughest and most sublime of all the military services. I took enormous pride in the squadrons he flew in and the men he drank with during Happy

Hour. Their planes thundered off runways at every base where we ever lived; and in the early years, my father loved to dip his black wings over our house or school yard, the most fierce and articulate way to say hello I have ever encountered. It may also have been the way Don Conroy figured out to say "I love you" to his family, but that might be wishful, and not very convincing, thinking on my part.

If so, he never told us, or gave us a clue to its meaning. All of his family forced themselves to become the textual deconstructionists of our father's wintry, immovable demeanor. He lacked all powers of insight into his own nature; self-examination was not even a condition he valued in other people, much less something he desired for himself.

My father was a man of action his whole life, long after the jet engines quit vibrating between his legs. He was on the go and moving and ready for action from the time he rose at five every morning until the time he fell asleep watching the Atlanta Braves late at night. For his entire life, he slept like a foundling child and swore that he had never experienced a bad night's sleep in his life.

I, his insomniac son, who dreads the hours from two to five in the morning, would hear his pride in his sleep habits with something approaching despair; for it is in these early hours of the morning when the demons of my past life roll out in their caissons and artillery units and tank battalions, passing in full, maniacal review, driven not by discipline, but by hysteria and regret and an anguish that can nearly jackknife me in bed.

I draw my books from the deepest well I have. Unless the hot jets of my bloodstream connect themselves to the fingers that move my pen, I have nothing to say, nothing at all. It is a critical flaw of my writing, but it stems from the essential man I turned into after the molding took shape in my parents' house. Each day I bring the ruined, terrorized boy I was as a child and set him trembling on my desk, so I can study the wreckage of myself at leisure. If necessary, I can slap his youthful face, set in the rigid immobile defiance of bravado that he believes, quite falsely, will impress his Marine father. But the Marine sees right through the boy's most elaborate defenses, sees straight to the yellow core of him, the place where cowardice goes to pucker and hide. Cruelly, I can watch the boy's eyes fill up with tears, then watch the great internal war convulse his body as he fights with every cell of his imperiled boyhood, not to let one tear breach the spillage of an inflamed lid. I have purposefully shrunken the boy to the size of a barn owl, so I can move him around and turn him easily. As a desk ornament, he is easier for me to study by pretending he has nothing to do with me. As I watch him, the boy hiding his desperate urge to cry, I realize that all my books inch their way out of my flesh because of the million things this boy wanted to say for twenty-one years, but could not. I am simply writing down the screams that stopped in this boy's chest during the voiceless solitude he felt in his long trial by father. I am not an artist, I think. I am a recording secretary.

The boy screams my books at me. It is not the violence of his childhood that repels me; rather, it is the violence of his sensibility now, after all these years. The rage does not offend me, but its incurability does. Its acid eats away at the boy's face, but nothing fades out or drifts into memory or smokes up into time. The acid leaves neither scar nor patina; it just makes the boy's eyes glisten more fiercely with unliberated tears. Then it strikes me that the boy is a vessel of tears and nothing else.

My father did not allow his sons to cry after he back-handed us. If we did, well, then the beating turned serious and then my mother had to pull him off us and then, my father would turn to her. That was always the most killing moment. Because we wept, because we did not take our punishment like men, we drew our mother into the bloody, fiery zone of our boyhoods where she would receive her beatings for our cowardice. Those are the steps and the tune and the words of the song that framed the ruthless dance of my long-ago Southern childhood. My father could take a boy apart. It was a hobby of his that I still think he enjoyed.

Spring, 1977 — an apartment on Atlanta's Maddox Drive.

I am thirty-two years old, recently divorced from a very fine woman who had done nothing wrong except fall in love with me. The second great breakdown of my life has taken up residence along the ridges of my brain. Slowly, I am coming to the realization that each one of my books will demand a breakdown from me as extortion or repayment. Each night, insomnia comes as some minor rite of crucifixion where tiny Roman soldiers sneak into my bedroom to nail my hands against the bed board and set my brain on fire with the images of my life that offer the most torture per square inch. At dawn, a mob squad of lower life centurions pull the small nails out of my wrist, pour buckets of rancid brigade water into my ears and nostrils, quieting the brain. The first light causes me despair. Then I wait for the rap on the door.

7:00 a.m.

I hear my father's key slide into my lock and open the door. Sliding out of bed, I throw on a pair of khaki pants, a tee-shirt, then slide my feet into a pair of Docksiders. I am exhausted from lack of sleep; my breakdown is now three months old. My father knows nothing about my breakdown, nor would he be interested in knowing. Every morning of my life now, my father drops by to drink my coffee and read my copy of the *Atlanta Journal-Constitution*. He also brings me things I neither want nor need.

"Where's the coffee?" My father says as he puts two sacks of groceries on the dining room table.

"I'm making it right now, Dad," I say, as I enter the small kitchen and open the refrigerator.

"I don't want your frou-frou coffee. That panty-waist shit you and your writer friends drink," he says.

He sees me inspecting a bag of freshly ground coffee in a brown bag and says, "What's that stuff? Read it to me."

"It says, 'panty-waist shit,'" I say and begin to make the coffee.

"Whatever happened to real java? Maxwell House? Chock Full

O'Nuts? That kind of stuff."

"I don't have Maxwell House," I say.

"Ha!" He shouts and pulls the biggest can of Maxwell House coffee I have ever seen out of one of his bags. "You want it?"

"No," I say, firmly.

"You got it," he says, slamming it down on the table.

Dad lifts a hideous bottle of green dill pickles and says, "You want these pickles, son?"

"Absolutely not," I say.

Slam. "You got 'em."

Four cans of applesauce, which I loathe, go onto the table. Two cans of cranberry sauce. Two cans of orange juice. Four cans of pork and beans.

"You want it?"

"No."

"You got it, pal."

When I bring my father his first cup of coffee, he is deep into reading the morning newspaper.

"Hey, I forgot to tell you, son. Great news. I bought you a couch."

"That's the worse news I ever heard," I say, sipping my coffee. "Your taste in furniture's worse than your taste in clothes."

"Hey, this couch belonged to Mrs. Jenkins, the broad who lived down the hall. She bought the farm last week and I bought the couch for you. She was all class. I bet that couch cost three hundred big ones when it was new. Want to know how much I paid for it?"

"No."

"Are you sure?"

"Positive."

"A buck. One greenback dollar. Whatcha think about that?"

"I think you got robbed," I say.

"Lipsitz's already offered to pay me five bucks for it."

"Cash in, Dad."

"Your poor old man's just trying to help out, son. You can tell this place of yours was put together without the help of an interior fabricator."

"Decorator, Dad."

"Whatever. But I don't hear of *Southern Living* wanting to come in here to do some chi-chi fashion spread."

"They knocking your door down, Dad?" I say, looking up with mild irritation, which delights my father. His great perverse joy is to make me angry over morning coffee.

"Oh, oh, Mr. Sensitive," my father crows.

"Last time I checked, Dad, your apartment looked like the inside of a potato chip bag. Or maybe the zoo after the Dresden fire bombing."

"I'll keep the couch," Dad says. "I'll upgrade."

"You could throw a stick of dynamite in there and call it an upgrade."

"I seemed to have hit a nerve," he says. "Pass me the sports section. By the way, you know that guy I go to the Tech games with? Corrigan, real fine old gentleman? He read your crappy little book, *The Great Santini*, last weekend. He loved Santini and hated all the wimpy little whiny kids and that silly wife. That seems to be the reaction of most people I talk to."

"That right?"

"Yeh, that's the gospel truth. What do you say to that?"

"Nothing, Dad."

"He really loved the scene of me giving you the leather flight jacket," my father says. "Get me another cup of coffee."

I rise and get my father his second mug of coffee of the morning. He takes it from me and begins drinking it at once.

"You're welcome," I say, resuming my seat where I can look out on pretty, green Atlanta.

"Corrigan's wife loved the scene of me sending your sister flowers for the prom. I told her it was the least I could do. That woman eats me up with a spoon. All the ladies do."

"Dad, do you remember the night you gave me your flight jacket?" I ask.

"Your eighteenth birthday, son. I'll never forget it. It was a bew-ti-ful gesture if I do say so myself."

"I'm glad you think so, Dad. I made the scene up. It never happened. You never sent flowers to Carol at the prom. I made that up, too. You never did one thing nice for any of your kids when we were growing up. Not one. Not ever. All the good parts of Santini, I had to invent. So I tried to think if I'd had a decent father what would I have liked for him to do for me. So I made up the nice guy Santini. You were the prick Santini."

"I seem to have gotten a rise out of my sensitive son."

"You certainly have, Dad."

"I know what buttons to push, don't I, son?"

"You're still in control of the plane, Colonel," I say.

"Here's what I told Lipsitz — I said, 'I should've beaten Pat a lot more. It would've made him a better writer.'"

"You beat me much more, I'd have been Shakespeare," I say.

"Whoa! Shakespeare! My boy has a mighty high opinion of himself."

"No. Very low, Dad. Kids like me. Raised in houses like yours. We never get it right."

"Get me a violin. It's boo-hoo time," he says.

"Dad, can you name one nice thing you did for any of your kids?" I ask. "I'd like to know."

"I raised you up. I gave you a home. I fed you. You had clothes on your back. From my point of view, that's quite enough. Let me take you to India or Asia, I'll show you kids who would eat the armpit out of a rag doll they're so goddamn hungry. You kids never had it so good. Get me another cup of coffee, Shakespeare."

I return to the kitchen and pour my father the last cup in the pot. Then I fix another pot.

■■■

It was on one of those lost faraway mornings when my father and I slowly began to make up with each other. He never missed a day, not even in the middle of my worst breakdowns when every cell and fiber of my body felt electric and foreign and belonging to someone

11

else. Sometimes our fights were furious and barefanged, but no matter how pitched or harmful our battles became, my father appeared at exactly the same time every morning carrying my paper across the threshold of my sad, broken home.

Both of us were doing the repair work necessary after my novel about my family had put a nuclear missile up the exhaust pipe of his fighter plane. I had not only hurt my father with his portrait in *The Great Santini*, I had come close to destroying both of us. The blood and carnage that book drew could not be cleansed until the father and son fought their way back into some kind of concordance or agreement. It did not have to be love, but it had to feel that way to us and the other members of our family. All credit goes to Dad. He came to my house; I never went to his. We would dogfight every morning, each of us maneuvering our phantom aircraft, fighting for the proper angle, wheeling and climbing and spinning through time, trying to lock onto the other's aircraft in the six o'clock position. I had brought a warrior's heart to our morning skirmishes, but I had entered the war armed with a weapon that outclassed anything my father could turn against me: I had wounded him by deploying the great clairvoyance and fire-power of the English language against him. I put my sentences against his fists. His fists were no match and he put his hands behind his back.

During those mornings, my father and I began to talk to each other for the first time in our lives. I held nothing back and I told him exactly what I thought about him as a father and a husband. I think I was as coldly brutal as any son has ever been to a father. When a friend of my father's called to say I had hurt Don Conroy beyond repair, I confronted Dad about it.

"Col. Hamm said little Pat hurt Daddy's little feelings," I mocked my father over coffee the next morning.

"Your lies don't bother me, son," the Colonel said calmly. "I know the truth of what happened."

"Tell me that truth," I said. "I'd like to hear it."

"I was a great husband and a great father," my father said, looking at me without irony. "End of story."

My laughter was heard by my neighbor beside me and the one who lived upstairs.

"My brother, Jim, Dad. Your son. You ever talked to him?"

"Yeh, all the time. He's one of my favorites. Unlike some people I know," Dad said.

"Good, here's what one of your favorites has to say," I said, leaning toward my father, my blue eyes as mean as a cobra's. "Brother Jim claims this as his first memory. You have me by the throat. My feet are off the ground and you are pounding my head against the wall with Mom trying to pull you off me. That's Jim's first memory. Welcome to planet earth, little Jimbo. Nice Dad, kid."

"It's baloney. Must've been a bad dream he had somewhere," Dad said, turning the page of the newspaper.

"Hey, Dad," I said, the newspaper obscuring my father's face from me. "I can show you the wall."

"You write FICTION, son. Everyone knows that's bullshit," he said, unruffled. The fighter pilot is always cool under combat situations.

"The walls in the front room of that tiny house on Kees Road in Belmont, North Carolina," I said. "There are lots of other walls, but that's the one Jim's talking about."

"All my kids are fruitcakes," Dad said behind the newspaper.

"Some of us are, Dad," I said.

"You whine too much," he said.

I answered, "I don't whine enough. But no, Dad, I'm not whining. I have to tell the truth. That's all. Whining has no part in it."

"Still seeing your little therapist?" he said. "Tell her I think she's doing a piss-poor job."

"Marion O'Neill will be delighted to hear that," I answered.

"My whole side of the family thinks all my kids are whack-o," the Colonel said. "Sometimes I think they're right."

"Me, too, Dad."

"Your sisters back up my side of the story," Dad said. "Kathy and Carol say I never touched anybody."

"You did not hit the girls, Dad," I said. "Unless they happened to be married to you."

"I never touched your mother."

"Yeh, you did. I remember every time you beat her, Dad. It's branded on my brainstem."

"Tell your little therapist to bear down a little harder when she does her shrinking business on you. You're starting to hallucinate."

"I wish I were."

"Get me a cup of coffee. This frou-frou stuff tastes like piss. Get me some Maxwell House."

I rose to do my father's bidding. While I was making the coffee, my father went to two grocery bags he had put on my dining room table. He lifted a cabbage high in the air and said, "You want a cabbage?"

"No," I said, "I've got a cabbage."

"You've got another one," he said as he slammed it triumphantly to the table. "How 'bout some broccoli?"

"Not for me," I said.

"Broccoli for my son. It's got plenty of vitamins." The broccoli was beheaded into a dozen florets as it hit the table. "Carrots for my sensitive son."

"No, thanks."

"You got 'em. Good for the eyeballs," my father said, happy that he had changed the subject again. "Got any 'Arch' material?"

"None," I said from the kitchen.

Since my father's divorce from my mother, he had taken up the oddest habit, at least to his children. He took it upon himself to gather up the family archives and put them in order in multicolored and incongruous photographic albums. When any of us went to his apartment, we spent hours poring over old photographs, report cards, or newspaper articles. He was fanatical about the democratic inclusion of almost everything. Dad especially loved bad reviews of my books and he could not refrain from writing in his own editorial comments: This guy sure raked our boy over the coals. His commentaries became the prized and hilarious parts of "The Archs," and he could infuriate a daughter-in-law or a grandchild as easily as he could his own offspring. During my childhood, I did not have the vaguest clue that my father was screamingly funny. In fact, I do not think he knew it himself.

"You're lying about no Archs," he said. "I found two pieces of Arch material yesterday."

"Where'd you find them?" I asked.

"In your mailbox," he answered.

"Are you stealing my mail again?"

"It's not stealing, son. I'm the keeper of the Archs. I'm preserving history, son. A writer should be able to understand that."

■■■

On the night before my father's funeral, I awoke at two in the morning at my house on Fripp Island. My future wife, Sandra, slept beside me as I moved into my writing room to compose a eulogy for the egregiously complicated Col. Donald Conroy, USMC, Ret. My brothers and sisters slept in a house on the beach a neighbor had offered in memory of my father's life. The family and friends of Santini had gathered together in Beaufort County to bid my color- ful and famous father goodbye. *The New York Times* had called. So had *People* magazine and *USA Today*. CNN had reported the news of The Great Santini's death all over the world and flashed a picture of my handsome father on the screen.

I wanted to write my father the best goddamn eulogy ever written by an American son for an American father. I knew he expected nothing less from me. But first, I had to empty myself of the tears I had not cried since his death in Beaufort Memorial Hospital. This was the part of me my father loathed since I was a little boy, the part of me that belonged loyally and forever to Peg Conroy of Rome, Georgia. My father despised my softness, my shy, terrified face, the effeminate sweetness that ran through me like some sugary umbili- cal cord my mother had refused to cut. That was what he was trying to beat out of me when I was a boy. He raised me to be a warrior and I think it surprised him that a warrior could come screaming up from the caves of time, armed only with the dangerous, unstoppable syllables of the English language. My father's fists formed the warrior that brought his black-winged Corsair flaming to the earth.

I let the tears come and they came in floods. All my life I have been a secret crier. So again I wept alone with a house full of loved ones sleeping around me. When I finished crying, I got down to the work, the celebration of my father's extraordinary American life. I wrote from passion, from joy, from gratitude, and from pride that my father's fame stemmed from his son's telling the blazing, heart-breaking truth about his tyrannical, savage fatherhood.

In the last three weeks of his life, I went every day to my sister Kathy's house in Beaufort and interviewed my father about his entire life. My father had become a savvy protector of his own legacy and he knew what I was doing when I first set up my tape recorder beside him.

"I've always been your best subject, son."

"No doubt about it, Dad," I said.

"What'll you call this book?"

"The Death of Santini," I said.

"Hey, great title. You know how to make a guy feel swell. You sold it yet?"

"Yeh. Nan Talese and Doubleday want it badly. Julian Bach wants to have a bidding war," I lied.

"You need to get another subject, pal. I've been a cash cow for you for way too long. Any movie interest?"

"Warner Brothers. Paramount. Twentieth Century," I kept lying. "The usual suspects."

"The money any good? This should be the hottest thing these Hollywood fruitcakes've seen in years. This is Academy Award shit we're talking about here. Oscar time guaranteed. Huh, jocko?"

"That's the talk, Dad."

"The money, pal. Talk figures here. We're talking big bucks here, aren't we? Seems to me, we'd be talking millions."

"Millions."

"Any actors interested yet? Talk about a role. The guy ought to be polishing his Oscar night speech. Getting his tux cleaned. Lining up a new agent. Getting his ducks in a row. Any names in the hat?"

"Redford, Newman, Hoffman," I said.

"Too small. I'm tired of being played by midgets."

"That's a line I can promise you won't make the final cut."

"I guess this will be one of your old love-hate numbers. At first I'll be the biggest bastard who ever lived, then slowly you'll reveal the true humanity hidden beneath my rough exterior."

"Bullseye, Colonel."

"Does it bother you, Son, that you're a mediocre novelist? That's what all the critics say."

I looked at my father's face and saw the look of the trickster, the playful wisecracking imp with the touch of pure malice in his mean Irish eyes.

"They say you're not as good as Updike or Roth or Styron or even that broad from Mississippi — what's her name? Dora Delta."

"Eudora Welty, Dad," I said. "They're all better writers than I am, Dad."

He looked at me with hard eyes. "Never admit that again. That's an order, pal. You're my son and you get it in your goddam noggin that you're the best writer that ever lived. You got it, pal? There's no such thing as second best. I raised you to be the best, so you bear down and kick Updike and Roth's asses. You got me, jocko?"

He had risen to a full-pitched fury and was his old self again. It was a bravado performance. Red-faced and enraged, he had raised up on his right arm and was pointing at me with his left forefinger.

"Hey, Dad," I said. "Name me one book John Updike ever wrote."

My father roared with laughter, laughed until he hurt. He motioned for me to hand him the tape recorder, fumbled with it inexpertly, then turned it on and said, "Time to get going, pal. Hollywood's waiting for this stuff. They don't make guys like me anymore. Guess they broke the mold."

"It's your modesty that's so unusual, Dad."

"Let me tell you about Chicago. Now there's a city to grow up in," my father said.

I finished my father's eulogy at five in the morning. I let the ruined boy write it, the one I keep beside me on my desk, the one who screams my books out to me. I let his unimaginable loneliness guide my hand across the page. In his loneliness and agony all the bones of my art are laid out drying in the Southern heat. My father savaged that boy and that is the central fact of my life.

But there are other facts. When *The Great Santini* was published, my mother and father and most of my family saw it as a savage and unforgivable act of treachery and betrayal. For two weeks, my father grieved at my Judas-like betrayal of his life as a family man and Marine Corps officer. Then he remade himself and walked into his new life that I had willed and made possible for him. He returned to his children in the disguise of *The Great Santini* — the fictional one, not the real one. He became the Santini who gave his son Ben a flight jacket on his eighteenth birthday, the one who sent his daughter Mary Anne flowers at her first prom, who left his duty as Officer of the Guard when his son got in trouble. I believe my father used my novel as a blueprint to re-invent himself and make a liar out of me.

My father is the only person in the history of the world who changed himself because he despised a character in literature who struck chords of horror in himself that he could not face. My father had the best second act in the history of fathering. I hated him with every breath that I drew in my boyhood. He was the worst father I have ever heard of, and I will go to my own grave believing that. But this most immovable of men found it within himself to change.

He died a richly beloved man, even an adored one. His children were prostrate and bereft at his funeral and remain so to this day. When his funeral procession wound through the old town of Beaufort, the police stopped traffic in every street leading to the National Cemetery. My high school English teacher said at the gravesite, "They've never done that in Beaufort. Of course, today they're burying The Great Santini."

In a long-ago fight, my father said I was the meanest, most ungrateful son in history. He told me that his life's work was to make everyone think I was the greatest liar that ever wrote a book about his family.

"Dad," I said, "I'm sorry I hurt your feelings. I really am. But any hurt you feel cannot come close to making up for my ruined childhood. Got it, Marine? Got it, tough guy?"

I write this because I owe it to Don Conroy. I had no clue I would come to love him as I did or miss him as much as I have. By an act of sheer stubbornness and will, my father used my first novel to transform himself into something resembling a most wonderful man.

These are the most surprising words I have ever written.

andra Y. Govan, a scholar at the University of North Carolina at Charlotte, has been a lover of books for almost as long as she can remember. In this memoir, written especially to read at Novello, she recalls the days when her childhood obsession led her inexorably, if temporarily, to a life on the wrong side of the law.

Sandra Y. Govan

"Confessions of a Serial Reader"

Despite what some would perceive as my now privileged position as a university professor, and thus a respected and respectable (if underpaid) member of the academic community, I have in fact made close acquaintance with the intimate insides of a jailhouse three times in my life. Once when I was nine, again when I was twelve, and then again when I was twenty. On one of those occasions, I became a petty criminal, dodging becoming a convicted felon, or at least escaping the distinct possibility of reform school, by mere chance and the timely arrival of my mother. Mine is a tale of love and desire; one might even say greed, although what I coveted were not the treasures of the heart cherished by most black girls in those days.

In the spring of 1962, Chicago's Finest removed me summarily from one of the city's most eclectic and remarkable neighborhood department stores, Gately's People's Store. Gately's carried everything, from inexpensive leather purses to pots and pans, from cloth-

20

ing for the entire family to shoes, hats, and reasonably priced jewelry. Mama and I shopped there all the time; we never had to go downtown to Field's or Carson's for anything except my special order orthopedic shoes. Gately's was our favorite store and I loved it. Yet, one spring afternoon, the police hauled me away from it, embarrassed and humiliated in the back of a squad car.

I cannot now claim mistaken identity; nor will I now assert racial harassment by overzealous store security, maliciously abusing an innocent Negro child. I was, in fact, not innocent; rather, I'd been busted dead to rights for stealing. While my mother, a tall, slim, elegant, proud and proper, golden spun-honey Negro woman stood out in the street, waving down the traffic to perform her own stop and search on every Chicago Transit Authority bus heading west from Roseland in a frantic search for me, the Chicago Police Department had her small, brown, bright, but know-it-all daughter in its clutches. Moreover, they were preparing to throw the book at me because I had compounded my crime with a lie. They determined to teach me that often repeated bromide, Crime Does Not Pay.

Ironically, I was apprehended in the first place because of a book. Unlike the few kids I knew given to shoplifting (mostly the white kids I met later in high school), I wasn't boosting candy or clothes, lipsticks or cheap jewelry. I took books. More precisely, I was caught stealing the remaining volumes in a series of books I had to have, a series I had to own for my own and treasure for the sheer pleasure of reading and rereading again and then again until I knew each character as if they were neighbors or friends; I could tell by a glance at the page where the book fell open where I was in the plot. Often, I would read several books at once — one would lie open on the kitchen table, another on a living room chest, and one would be just started upstairs in my bedroom. Although I would not learn the term for my condition until much later in life, by twelve I had become an obsessive bibliophile. Borrowing and returning books from Walker Branch or Pullman Park Branch Library, the two local public libraries bracketing Morgan Park to which we rode our bikes the two-and-one-half miles during Chicago's long hot summers, no longer sufficed.

I wanted these particular books that only Gately's carried. But because they were "trash" or "commercial series" books, and not real "literature," the libraries would not buy them! The flawed judgment of librarians notwithstanding, I craved these books, required them, knew I could not rest without them. And so, I spoke to God about it. Now understand, because I had been a YMCA camper, a Brownie and a Girl Scout, a dutifully attentive child to the parental lectures on morals and values, and a regular attendee at Beth Eden Sunday School, thus privy to the precise religious instruction of the faithful Mrs. Scott (also tall, elegant, pretty, and exceedingly proper), who gave us hell about the "thou-shall-not" commandments, I knew one could talk to God about desires of the heart. "God hears all prayer," we had been taught.

I also most assuredly knew right from wrong. Desire, however, made me believe I could bargain with God. He would understand my urgent need for these books. So I prayed for His help with the pioneering retail marketing plan I originated: Buy one, take one free.

While I had some initial victories with this particular strategy (I had already successfully stolen from Gately's three times), in all probability I was stopped from stealing again by righteous wrath. I had thought my plan perfectly reasonable. It wasn't really stealing — I was, after all, spending $1.25 for one book before taking the second. And besides, after I had the complete series, I would stop.

Evidently, however, Someone Up There was not amused by my wanton use of prayer for personal gain. God, or my Guardian Angel, got annoyed by my arrogance. One of them said, "Enough is enough," and boom, on my fourth effort, having casually, but carefully, slipped my "free" book into the paper-thin shopping bag beneath the book I purchased, I was busted.

But let me digress for a moment. My first flirtation with the law came when I was a fourth-grader, a nine-year-old runaway consumed by sibling rivalry and convinced that her mother did not love her as much as she loved her older brother. The brother, truth be known, had never shown much real initiative or the actual courage to run away from home, though he had often used the threat to acquire more of our mother's attention. Typically, he only went as far as the back-door steps where he would camp for an hour, cap in hand, eyes downcast, body slumped forward to indicate profound dejection — a self-pitying, self-imposed ritualized "timeout" (a child-rearing method not practiced in my neighborhood) waiting for Mama to approach him with the "Tanny, what's wrong? Son, what happened?" attention that he craved. She could be so patient with him; he was her firstborn, and her boy, while I was just her "crippled" girl. Once I'd even overheard her say to one of her friends on the phone that she would "have to take care of Yvonne for the rest of her life."

"Oh, no, you won't," I'd vowed. "Yvonne will take care of herself."

Personally, I had little sympathy for Tanny, or with his apparent need for more notice from Mama, because he seldom did anything on my behalf without coaching. Although later, during the one of the after-the-game fights following an especially close football game ("You win the ball game; we win the fight!") between rival high schools, Morgan Park (ours) and Fenger (theirs), he did prove useful. I had stepped out of a secure niche to see where the crowd had gone when the cops arrived and started swinging their clubs. The crowd fell back and I fell down. Just as I was about to be trampled, my big brother spontaneously saved me from the mob. Suddenly he stood before me, a solid oak or maybe an elm — tall, thick, immovable, arms spread wide and feet rooted to the pavement as if magically planted. "Stop!" he shouted, "that's my sister!" And he held them back before extending a hand to pull me up.

But usually, when we were young, my big brother just liked to frame me ("Mommy, I didn't write on the dresser; Yvonne did that!"), or punch me (once hitting me so hard in the stomach I could not scream), or tell on me ("Mommy, I know where there are lots of silver dollars!"). Of course, when she asked him where, his reply came quicker than a snake can strike: "Yvonne picked the lock on your cedar chest and we found this money; not me Mommy, not me!"

At the moment of my escape from home, back when I was nine, he had told then too, calling Mama at work to report my delinquency. But fueled by the knowledge that came from my books — after all, Huckleberry Finn had successfully run away and made his way down the river on a raft, no less; and Tom Sawyer, why, he was always organizing and carrying through on a grand and wonderful plan — I knew without doubt that though he was bigger and stronger, I could outwit my brother. I could use the C.T.A. as my river to go far away and find somebody who appreciated me, somebody who wasn't always fussing about my dirty hands on her walls, straightening up after my friends, or cleaning up the mess in "that hellhole," her alternate denominator for my room.

Now to be fair, I wasn't totally influenced just by what I'd read. All my life I had also heard how my father had escaped from Arkansas by riding the rails when he was ten; how he had arrived in Chicago, making his grand entry into the city by riding atop a boxcar as the freight train he had hopped entered the train yards; how he had found his way to his Aunt Mary's, knowing only that her address was in the "5200 block of Lafayette Drive."

Indeed, what convinced me of success was the lure of adventure that came from hearing my Daddy's stories coupled to the daring exploits on the pages penned by Mark Twain and Walter Farley. Farley wrote *The Black Stallion*, a series of wonderful books about a boy and his horse, featuring redheaded Alec Ramsay, bonding with and eventually racing the bold beautiful horse he named The Black (many is the night when I became a jockey and raced The Black in Alec's place). The stories I'd heard and read really attuned me to the possibilities inherent in being on my own, making my own way in the world and proving to anybody who doubted me that, like my Daddy and other heroes, I could take care of myself; that I knew how to stage an adventure and how it should unfold.

That it did not, in fact, unfold precisely as I had planned is but another example of Bobby Burns' time-honored maxim regarding the best laid plans. True, I had deceived the school bus driver, tricked him into not stopping to pick me up for delivery to Jane Neil

Elementary School on 87th Street, the specialized school specifically geared to support children with handicaps. Back in the fifties, the Chicago Public School System did not "mainstream" such children, and so I did not go to Shoop, the neighborhood school, until the fifth grade; instead, I attended school with mostly white children who endured polio, cerebral palsy, muscular dystrophy, rheumatic fever, fragile joints, and weak hearts. Actually, despite my condition, I was in much better physical shape than most of my classmates because my "defect," being born with dislocated hips, was not life threatening; nor did we know at the time that it was degenerative.

Anyway, it was easy to fool the bus driver. When a child was sick, parents were to place a piece of paper in the window to indicate their child was too ill for pick-up that day. So I had taped a huge piece of newspaper in the storm-door window. But I had not reckoned on my brother spying on me that morning and actually betraying me at the start of my adventure. By calling Mama as he did, he forced me to act more hastily.

However, by the time he returned to the phone to report that I had moved from the house and was now hiding in the garage behind the pedestrian door, I had left my hiding place and had moved swiftly down the alley to Aberdeen; from there, it was a short half-block to 111th Street and the bus line. I had Tanny's Boy Scout canteen filled with water (which, to this day, is a beverage I force myself to drink); I had a couple of peanut-butter sandwiches tied into a neat blue-and-white bandanna; I'd even found a suitable stick to tie to the bandanna. One had to look the part, you know, and I was prepared to be a cross between the girl's version of Huck Finn and a hobo, just like my Daddy when he'd been a boy riding the rails.

To look more purposeful, I also stopped at Fillmore's Corner Store and bought a *Chicago Sun-Times*. I believed this would make me look adult, or at least like I was getting something for an adult. My mother, incidentally, was subsequently furious with old, dark, tired, arthritic and somewhat dense Mr. Fillmore; she thought that the newspaper should have been his clue — that and the time of day when I made the purchase should have told the shopkeeper something was amiss. But Mr. Fillmore seldom paid attention to the neighborhood kids who ran their parents' errands buying their milk, bread, newspapers, cigarettes, or candy for themselves; and anyway, the bus came before he thought to question me and before any general hue and cry went out. And the old, tired, white bus driver never even looked at me as I boarded his bus, paid my 12¢ fare, and rode off.

I've talked about this episode in greater detail in my writings elsewhere — how after a lengthy ride (as in perhaps a half-mile) I walked up to a white woman's home, knocked on her door, and when she opened it, demanded cookies; how, after inviting me in, she called the police; how I had nearly escaped her house and was almost back on the road again when the cops arrived to nab me — so I'll condense it here.

I was taken immediately to the Monterey Avenue police station — a squat, drab, cement-colored building that guarded the western end of Morgan Park, separating the largely black lower Morgan Park segment from the largely white upper Beverly Hills/Morgan Park section — and there interrogated by the ugliest white man I had ever seen. In his dark blue uniform with its huge brass buttons, he sat behind an eight-foot-high walnut desk placed kitty-corner in the lobby office; he peered down at me over wire-rimmed glasses, peppering me with stern questions.

"What's your name, little girl? Who are your parents? Where are they? Where do you live? Why aren't you in school, Missy?"

I ignored him and said nothing. I felt uneasy but I would not talk to him. He looked mean and sounded worse, not an Officer Friendly at all, but a man who growled questions and extended no soothing reassurance. "I asked for your name, Missy," he barked again. "Do you want to spend the night in here?"

His face was pitted; his fierce grey eyes glared down from beneath dark bushy eyebrows; his nose was huge, red, and beaked. Worst of all, not only did he look like a witch's husband, he offered me no candy bar, no cookies, and no ice cream — an egregious omission of polite concern that totally countered everything I'd heard in school, learned on TV, or read in books regarding the proper relationship between children and policemen.

I was outraged! By the time my Daddy arrived to fetch me (Mama had called him on his job and essentially said, "She's your daughter, you go get her"), my resolve to remain silent had broken; I'd begun to wail so loudly that Daddy could hear me outside the station walls. When he entered, he found me sobbing over the indignity of it all; but also licking, between breaths, at a huge vanilla ice cream cone that a somewhat kinder officer had the decency to buy for me. Someone in that station at least knew the rules.

My third encounter with the police came when I was much older. I was a senior at Valparaiso University, participating in the university's semester abroad program by studying in Cambridge, England back in the spring of 1970. But that particular tale, laden as it is with echoes of Otis Redding's "Dock of the Bay" ("I'm sitting on the dock of the bay, watching the tide roll away; just sitting on the dock of the bay, wasting time ... ") internally reverberating and inducing another adventure, an adventure that featured an encounter with my first weird sexual predator — that story will have to wait for a more appropriate time for telling. It can't be effectively condensed here. It takes too long to tell right now.

But you probably want to know the reason for my near incarceration, how it was that a proverbially good girl, a Scout, an avid reader, and a lover of all kinds of books — comic books, mystery books, crime stories, science fiction tales, books about World War II, books about adventure, books about race cars and race horses, black books, white books, all kinds of fiction — ran afoul of legal, moral, and ethical codes.

It happened the summer I was to turn thirteen, just before my spinal surgery to correct the scoliosis which, developing from the congenital hip dislocation, was slowly distorting my spine and affecting my ability to walk, run, or stand straight. Essentially, I almost wound up in jail because I would not accept restraint and could not abide romance. This is why my mother, who was anticipating returning from her job to find me clean, ready and waiting to head out to Weiss Memorial to see the orthopedist for a last evaluation before my operation, found herself instead out on 111th Street, frantically flagging down buses, searching for her errant child.

The books for girls like me were simply inadequate. The children's section of both Walker Branch and Pullman Park libraries had annoyed me to no end for years. The stuff for little kids was largely pap. The "girls' books" bored me. There were no, or very, very few, black books for black children in those days — books written by black authors or even books that featured black characters or included black girls, or boys, as the major character. I remember one that featured a Negro girl named Julia who wanted to be a ballerina; another about a now nameless Negro girl who wanted to become a nurse; and another, perhaps called *Boystown*, that featured a colored boy in the cast of characters; but overall, the pickings were mighty slim.

I was no Richard Wright, avidly reading caustic essays about the moronic American "boop-boopsie" penned by the trenchant H.L. Mencken. Nor, at that point, did I know the works of Langston Hughes, Countee Cullen, or Gwendolyn Brooks. No adult, black or white, pointed these writers out to me — not even in Mrs. Scott's Sunday school class during Negro History week. Now in Miss Perez's eighth grade class, we'd read Stephen Crane's homage to the Civil War, *The Red Badge of Courage* (which I read after I flunked her quiz!) but generally, I liked modern fiction, World War II stories, mysteries, and I still loved adventure. So, the boring dutiful Bobbsey Twins were just a cut above Dick and Jane. I had read most all of Beverly Cleary and Betty Cavanna but their formulas were wearing and dull — girl meets boy with red roadster; all is kiss kiss/hug hug. Yuck! And while I liked Beany Malone, I had finished all of those.

As for Nancy Drew, well — while she was supposedly a great model for girl readers, I found her tedious beyond belief. Miss Nancy was always getting trapped somewhere, always getting herself knocked out, always such a goody two-shoes; furthermore, and perhaps more to the rub, she was a blue-eyed blonde who only met people who looked like her and talked like her. I could not abide her insipid self over long.

Well-meaning neighbors, like Mrs. Roberts who gave me Louisa May Alcott's *Eight Cousins* and my abridged *Huckleberry Finn,* or Mrs. Purnty who gave me *365 Bedtime Stories,* would also occasionally give me a Nancy Drew. I'd read Alcott and loved her — read also *Little Women* and loved it. Huck Finn of course, even the truncated children's version, was unquestionably one of my favorite books. So I read Miss Nancy but even then had misgivings; no matter how hard I tried, something about that girl just didn't set right. In that same vein, I'd also been given, or discovered while shopping with Mama, Tom Swift and the Hardy Boys. Young, scientifically inclined Tom Swift, blond boy inventor, was kind of like Nancy Drew — did not like him; didn't find anything in him to hold on to; didn't find anything memorable or credible about the stories. The Hardy boys, Joe and Frank, were a notch or two above — and, in the fifties, we could even see them on the Mickey Mouse Club, and so there were real faces to attach to the characters. Unfortunately, seeing and hearing characters from books I knew well proved double-edged for me; voices and faces translated to the screen interfered with the voices and faces long formed in my mind's eye.

Then one day while shopping with Mama, in the long aisle fronting the notions section at Gately's, which held all the Butterick, Vogue, and Simplicity patterns, the fabric bolts, and the assorted sewing goods my mother loved to peruse, I discovered the Ken Holt Mysteries, published by Grosset and Dunlap, which led me directly to the Rick Brant Science-Adventure series, also published by Grosset and Dunlap. Possession of all of these volumes led directly to my early flirtation with crime.

That Ken Holt and Rick Brant were clearly "boys' books" is indisputable. That the heroes were sturdy, exceptionally bright, middleclass white boys is also beyond dispute. The stories usually began in the Northeast, and while later books could take readers to anywhere in the United States or in the world, the two boy protagonists — the hero and his buddy — always returned to their small-town New

Jersey homes. Each volume in the series (there were seventeen of the Ken Holt mysteries and twenty-two of the Rick Brant books), followed a distinct formula: Ken Holt, the only son of a traveling foreign correspondent, and his pal, Sandy Allen, of the red-headed Allen clan (and also the son of a newsman) initially "join forces at a time when Ken is very much in need of help." Ken moves in with the Allens at the end of book one; subsequently, while on assignment as budding journalists, the two boys go on to solve mystery after mystery through sixteen more books. In the last book, *The Mystery of the Plumed Serpent,* Ken and Sandy even receive some assistance from Rick Brant when Rick sends them three Megabuck units — miniature radio transceivers that he designed and built. Ken and Sandy have read about some of Rick's exploits. They know Rick Brant as a budding boy genius and inventor in the sciences, and as a participant in expeditions as dangerous and exciting as the mysteries Ken and Sandy solve.

Rick, and his buddy Scotty, an ex-Marine who saves Rick from a beating in the first book, *The Rocket's Shadow,* have, the dust jacket blurb tells us, "the kind of adventures all boys would like to have. They live on an island called Spindrift [off the New Jersey coast] where Rick's father heads a group of scientists working in the field of electronics. Here and abroad, the boys encounter many thrilling adventures and solve many baffling mysteries."

This was the comment that plucked the nerve raw. It wasn't just the boys who wanted those adventures! I was a girl and yet I coveted thrilling adventure, too! Despite an alleged handicap, I was not a stay-on-the-block child. I'd ridden my bike all over Morgan Park; I'd been chased out of Beverly Hills by white boys, and gone back looking for revenge. I'd faced down a strange black man threatening the neighborhood dog ("Mister, if Poogie bit your son it's because he did something to him; this dog plays with the kids on this block all the time and he's never bitten one of us!"); and, I was highly regarded for my ability to speak to any grown-up at any time. My mama, whose word was Law, had decreed: "Just because someone is an adult does not mean they are always right. If you believe you are right, you can speak up for yourself." I took her at her word.

So now you ask, just what was the appeal of these particular books to a small black girl from Chicago? Why would I be so enamored of the "kind of adventures all boys would like to have"? What was so compelling about admittedly formulaic fiction that led me to spend most of my hard-earned baby-sitting money (I regularly kept the children of a Catholic couple who had three sets of twins, all under seven years old, for 75¢ an hour!) on their purchase? My addiction was such that years later, during breaks from reading my high school texts, and still later on breaks home from college, I would take a Rick Brant down (Rick replaced Ken Holt as my favorite hero as soon as I discovered this series) from a basement shelf and secretly reread it one more time.

I don't even know that I had a favorite book from each series, though maybe I liked the ones that featured brown-skinned Chahda, Rick and Scotty's Hindu friend, the best. But, I also liked the ones that highlighted the more exotic settings, the more challenging scientific mysteries, or the more alluring titles: *The Lost City, The Whispering Box Mystery, The Golden Skull, The Wailing Octopus, The Pirates of Shan, The Flaming Mountain* (where I learned about volcanology), or *Rocket Jumper.*

Forty-something years later it is difficult to reconstruct with any certainty the urgency undergirding my peculiar compulsion. These white boys certainly looked no more like me than did Nancy Drew whom I despised; they clearly lived in worlds I should not have identified with. They lived lives of privilege, driving cars and speedboats as teens (we rode city buses in my neighborhood); they traveled nationally and internationally, and Rick Brant even flew his own airplane. On the surface I had nothing in common with them — not gender, not race, not class. So why was I entranced by these books, drawn to them, compelled to read books no one else in the world except my brother and I had ever even heard of, let alone read? It's a question I've started to probe.

In large part the attraction lay in the adventure saturating each book; in part it was also the characters (these boys were smart, resourceful, yet likable; interestingly, none of the four was blond); and in several instances it was the locale, the settings that removed me from Morgan Park and took me on expeditions to the Philippines, archaeological digs in the western U.S., treasure hunts in the Caribbean or undersea exploration in the western Pacific. I found cultural diversity in the Rick Brant series — I went to Tibet in *The Lost City;* acquired knowledge about the Philippines in *The Golden Skull,* learned about the Fulani, Hausa, and Tuareg peoples of northern Nigeria in *The Veiled Raiders* (long before there were African-American studies programs). Familiarity with the formula did not breed contempt, and the concerns and fears these boys endured — concern for the kidnapped father, or father figure, concern for the friends in danger — these were all issues I could fantasize about (how would I handle it if I were in Rick's shoes?) and empathize with despite gender. And Rick Brant had a sister, Barbie, whom he teased but did not mistreat. Barbie also craved adventure.

But you tire of this digression about my literary misdeeds, my cathartic recapitulations of a culturally suspect and politically incorrect childhood reading Jones. You want to know what happened to me in that Roseland area police station, down on 115th and Indiana. Was I sent to the basement? Did I encounter the rubber hose or the dreaded third degree?

As I told you, I got busted for boosting books, but in the eyes of the police officer who questioned me, my biggest crime was not the theft but the lies I told to cover it. The officer — white, short, and with a stocky build, dark hair and brown eyes — had rather kindly posed the usual questions.

"Tell me your name, honey. Where do you live? What's your phone number? We have to call your folks."

Having carefully thought out what I would do if caught, I pushed the envelope. I announced my name as "Yvette Jones" and claimed that I lived at "8795 West 111th Street." I even gave him a telephone number — BEachwood 4-5789 — ("You can call me up and have a date, any old time ... ") a number straight from Motown. I remember thinking, "He doesn't know me; all us colored kids look alike to

32

them. And he doesn't know the song."

The lies emerged so smoothly, as if I'd practiced them. While I had been known to cling to a good lie like Kudzu to a pine (when I was seven, while visiting cousins in St. Louis, I'd cut off a dangling front braid to create long-desired bangs; for years afterward I told everyone that a gang of girls captured me, held me down, and chopped that braid), I hadn't practiced this one. In fact, I'd only hatched it minutes before as I had walked down that store aisle. I just wanted that cop to question me quickly and then let me get back on the bus to go home — before my mother got there. She was going to be angry if I was not there. Weiss Memorial was the Jewish Hospital on the far north side and we lived far south. She was expecting me to be clean and ready to go. At that moment I was rather funky having neither bathed nor dressed in clean clothes — it was just supposed to be a quick trip to Gately's to pick up my books! I was going to take my bath and dress when I got back home.

But the moment that lie slid off my tongue, the officer's demeanor changed. His voice grew cold and distant as he informed me icily that "the numbered addresses on 111th Street do not go that high." He also added, rather coolly, that if I continued to lie to him, I could be taken away from my parents and sent away to the reform school down in Joliet for a long time. "How would you like that?" he asked. "Shoplifting," he said, "is a crime." I would go to court; I would be found guilty because the store clerks would testify against me, and I would not see home for a long time. Then he sat at his desk, tapped his pencil against the surface, and waited. "What's it going to be, honey?" His tone said it all.

I sat on the dark scratched-up wooden bench in that office, looking anywhere but at the officer; staring at the floor and then out the window and then back to the stained chipped floor. I felt my bravado seeping away; I was scared but tried not to show it; I wanted to cry but would not do that either. I was also angry at God for letting me down, angry at my Angel for letting me get caught when we'd just made a deal. I felt betrayed and as trapped as Huck Finn when Pap had him in that cabin. But there was no tool I could use to saw my

33

way out and no good buddy to come and rescue me like Scotty would do for Rick, or Sandy would do for Ken Holt. It was just me. My options came down to this: I could give myself up and let them call my mother or I could wait until she found me. Either way meant doom and destruction; as I sat there I could feel myself shrinking; I could visualize sailing out the back of our kitchen window, clear into the middle of next week, propelled by my mother's awful hand.

I suppose you know I broke. Between wiping my eyes, snuffling, and wiping my nose on the tissue provided, I confessed my real name and gave up my real phone number. The officer called my home and my brother took the call. Moments later, Mama chanced to call home to ask if I had checked in yet; she got the message from my brother that I was being held at the Roseland police station.

She came for me in fifteen minutes. I expected her to be wearing her patented "just-wait-till-I-get-you-home; I-will-kill-you" look but she wasn't. It was more a look of despair combined with disbelief mixed with fear and topped by suppressed anger. Her hard-headed, head-strong child had really done it this time and how was she to discipline me without also killing me?

But she sprang me, explaining to the officer that I actually came from a good home and was really not a terribly deviant child. She would not, however, speak to me, except to spit specific directions ("Sit still; don't you say one word"), all the way to the doctor's office. That, too, was excruciating — me in my soiled underclothes and unwashed body, forced to show all to the clean white doctor who had me parade across the room in my underwear while he checked my gait; and then, he placed me on the examining table, manipulating my legs this way and that, measuring my degree of inflexibility, while neatly-pressed Mama looked on, seeing all yet ignoring me at the same time.

Have you ever been in a space like that? Where your mother pretends you're not there? Where she looks right through you and you don't exist?

When we arrived back home and Mama finally broke the suffocating silence, her parting words were devastating. "Yvonne," she said, "I am truly disgusted. You know better and you ought to be ashamed. You know I'm going to have to tell your Daddy. He will be very disappointed."

Those last words were worse than any blow; they burned me as if I'd touched my hand to a hot iron. Failing my Daddy, letting him down, was simply not in my realm of possibilities. I was the light of his life, his baby, his star. It wasn't about fear of a spanking or some other long punishment. My father could not know I had a flaw, that I could, and would, steal and lie. So of course I begged, "Please don't tell Daddy; please don't. I won't do it again, I promise! Please don't tell!" But on this point, knowing my weakness, she was inflexible. In all things for the good of the child, my parents stood as solid as the Prudential Rock.

That night, when Daddy came in from his shift on the C.T.A., Mama talked to him in their room. Then he came next door to my room and talked to me. My Daddy, an easy-going, seemingly passive but durable brown man, was always gentle with me, always willing to be the mediator between Mama and me. In all my life he had never spanked me or raised a hand to me; and he did not, despite my sins, raise his hand or even his voice, that night. He spoke softly but sadly; I could feel my failure, hear his disappointment.

"Sweetie," he said gently, "your mama told me what happened today. You should be ashamed. You know better. You don't have to steal and you know it."

I assented to this nodding silently, for once not able to look at him or speak up for myself. "When you want something," he continued, "you ask for it; you work for it; you buy it; but you do not steal — ever. Is that clear?"

It was — crystal clear. I had never heard such pain in my Daddy's voice before; it felt like I had five pounds of sand in each shoe and I was trying to run underwater but couldn't. I never wanted to hear it again, much less be the cause of it. And I would not hear such deep pain in his voice again until we stood together at my mother's bedside as she lay dying. But that night I made my Daddy the same promise I had made to Mama — I would not ever steal again, I would try real hard not to ever disappoint him again. The skillful laying on of guilt evoked remorse like nothing else. And my parents were so good at it.

Everything with my parents was resolved by my promise. No one in our house ever spoke of my near-arrest again. My brother was forbidden to tease me about it or speak of it to his friends; and wonder of wonders, he honored his promise. Whatever they threatened him with, it worked. No one knew about my criminal activity until I revealed parts of the story as an adult.

But, there remained a problem. My obsession returned. Acquiring the rest of the volumes I still needed to complete each series preoccupied me. My criminal endeavors at Gately's had only netted me volumes 1 through 8 of the Ken Holt series; and I think I had maybe the first three books in the Rick Brant series. How to obtain the rest of the books without getting into more trouble?

To bring up the matter that I still wanted these books seemed, shall we say, unwise. So, I puzzled on it until I hit upon the solution: Having been banned from entering Gately's People's Store after the big bust, I would wait patiently until I had accumulated another $2.50 (allowance funds or baby-sitting money), then, taping the two dollar bills with the two quarters to a handwritten request on notebook paper, I sent off to Grosset and Dunlap in New York for the next two volumes in first the Ken Holt, then the Rick Brant series. Over the succeeding months, I regularly mailed the publisher that sum, or sometimes a whole five-dollar bill, until each series was complete,* thus satisfying my craving.

For the record, I still have my books. In 1993, I rescued them, my Marvel comic book collection; my Alistair MacLean World War II books; my Agatha Christie, John D. MacDonald, Rex Stout, and Helen MacInnes mysteries; and my old copies of *Huckleberry Finn*, *Tom Sawyer*, and *Eight Cousins*, when Daddy sold our house and moved away from Morgan Park.

■ ■ ■

*In doing some additional research to try to find more about the origins of each series I discovered the following: Neither Ken Holt nor Rick Brant was part of the Stratemeyer Literary Syndicate that mass produced Nancy Drew, Tom Swift, and The Hardy Boys — despite the fact that all were initially published by Grosset and Dunlap. Secondly, while I thought I had completed each series — believing there were only seventeen Ken Holts and twenty-two Rick Brants — I have since learned that there were in fact, eighteen published Ken Holts and twenty-four volumes in the Rick Brant series. The last Rick Brant volumes, which I must now obtain, are *Danger Below* and *The Magic Talisman*. Although long unpublished, this final book made it to print in 1990, just after the death of author John Blaine, the pseudonym of Harold L. (Hal) Goodwin, the creator of and author for most of the series.

s his career at CBS captured viewers from coast to coast, Charles Kuralt made his mark on the nation's backroads, telling the stories of ordinary people from California to the fishing villages of Maine. In this essay, written a dozen years before his death, the author comes back home — to the American South he knew as a boy, recalling his days on a Carolina farm, and the values and memories that never went away.

Charles Kuralt

Excerpted from
Southerners: Portrait of a People

For most people in the South, history is contained in our families. With the exception of major events that resounded all the way out in the countryside, much of history has marched past the Southerner without his even being aware of it. When you live, as many of us have, miles from the nearest town, and perhaps even more miles from the nearest newspaper or telegraph office, far-off events lose their importance. What's important is what happens where you live, to the people you know.

Even if the family's not a distinguished one — even if it's entirely undistinguished by the standards of outsiders — Southerners are interested in their families. There's much talk about whose boy managed to buy some land, about whose daughter went to school and got to be a nurse.

This intense preoccupation with the family, coupled with the famous Scotch-Irish quick temper, has often produced uncomfortable results. In the North, you're apt to get mugged by somebody who doesn't even know you. In the South, that would almost never happen. Violence down here has rarely been directed at strangers. If your life is in danger here, it's from your own cousin, or your wife. It's family. All of that dueling nonsense that went on has been consigned to history, but today it takes the form of switchblade knives in a card game, or just two friends who get drunk and fall to arguing, and one of them shoots the other.

There exists nowhere else that I know of that eagerness to do violence, and then perhaps patch it up the next day. The family feud, I think, has been much overdone; at least I never saw any evidence of it. I'm sure it did exist among certain isolated mountain families. But in most of the South it was your own family you were fighting, and you were apt to say the next day, "God, I must have been terrible drunk. I'm sorry. "

This, of course, was while you were visiting the poor fellow in the hospital.

These, then, are things that occasionally divided us, but more often were our common ground: a love of togetherness, of land, and of family; a shared language, with endless stories to be told in any one of a variety of accents and then passed by the next generation; a curious relationship to history, threaded through with our propensity for sudden violence.

In my experience, the Southerner knows who he is and where he came from. These things are one and the same. I know that my life has gone the way it has because I came from a certain people, from a place, that I'll never forget. Let me tell something about it.

■■■

I was born in North Carolina, and although my family lived all over the South while I was growing up, North Carolina was home. My father was a Massachusetts man who had come down to Chapel

Hill because he got a scholarship in geology. My mother was a beautiful young schoolteacher from Onslow County, near the coast (where Camp Lejeune is today).

We visited the Massachusetts side of the family, but life was in North Carolina.

The Great Depression was upon us, and my father found there was no call for geologists. So after working at a series of very menial jobs — creosoting telephone poles, things like that — he decided he would go back and study social work, because it appeared to him that was going to be the booming occupation of the time. Of course, it was.

My first memory is of a little town called Stedman, a crossroads near Fayetteville. My mother taught school there while my father was back at Chapel Hill. We had a black housekeeper named Rosa, whom I loved as much as my mother. Rosa took care of me when my mother was off teaching. We could see the school from the house, and we'd watch together for my mother to come home. It's Rosa I remember most clearly from that time. She made apple butter that I lived for. I could eat bowls and bowls of it, and did.

Then we lived in Washington, North Carolina, the original Washington of this country, a small city on the Pamlico River. I started school there.

By the time I was in the third grade, I was much more urbane. I was becoming interested in comic books and adventure.

Playing cowboys and Indians, we used to ride broomsticks for horses — except for one kid, named Charles, who actually had a horse. A *white* horse! He lived in a big house on the Pamlico. We hated him with the pure hatred that is born of burning envy.

One time, we secretly made a raft. (I know I hadn't read *Huckleberry Finn* yet, but perhaps someone in our group had.) We found a part of a raft that had landed on the riverbank, and we improved it so we could get out on the river.

All of us kept the secret, as if it were sacred. One day we actually floated on the river, about a hundred yards I guess, and decided among ourselves, "Okay, the thing works, now we're really going to take a trip." We weren't going to go to New Orleans, but we were going at least as far as the railroad bridge.

But Charles, the one with the horse, whom we had excluded, was a sensible boy. Because he thought it was dangerous, he told on us. Our parents came down on us in alarm. That was a disaster. We all ended up wishing we'd never thought of building a raft.

I suppose that if we'd really set out on that trip, things might have worked out as they did for Huck. We'd surely have wound up in some different place.

Our family moved to Birmingham, to Atlanta for a while, and then back to Charlotte by the time I was eleven. But all that time, I knew I had a home. Whenever there came a chance for us all to go back to my grandparents' place, my mother's old home place in Onslow County, we would go.

It is that farm I remember best of all.

■ ■ ■

It was a prosperous farm, in Carolina tobacco country terms, and we certainly weren't poor by the standard of the day. But it was a farm with no electricity or machinery or indoor plumbing. It's odd, because I was only four or five when I first saw it and never saw it again after my grandfather's death, but I remember every single thing about that place. I can see it now. A hundred-acre tobacco farm. A two-story house. A front lawn that wasn't much of a lawn, mostly sand. The side yard was too well shaded by sycamore trees to have any grass. There were chickens underfoot. Two mules, two cows, two pigs. A tobacco barn down the road, which you couldn't see from the house. A corncrib, a barn with a wagon inside, a hayloft above. A picket fence, whitewashed once upon a time.

We moved the wagon out of the barn when my Aunt Trixie came home from teaching school with her first car, a Chevrolet, which needed to be parked under cover, of course. Trixie had just managed to afford a car. So the old farm wagon got parked in the yard near the house after that.

It was an old house. It had been in the family a hundred years, I suppose, built by my grandmother's forebears. There was an addition, formal front rooms, which were themselves built well before the turn of the century. My grandfather had a great big toolbox in the shade on the back porch. There was a pump back there, where you got water for the house.

I remember the houseflies out there by the hundreds. My grandfather would do many of his chores there — fitting a new axe handle to an old axe — while he was sitting on that toolbox. He was very satisfied to sit on that toolbox and work at whatever he had to do.

My grandfather certainly never went to college, perhaps never even to high school. In his youth, he had been a fisherman down there on the coast, and so he was to me a kind of romantic character. He told stories about storms at sea and shipmates swept overboard.

And he was contrary. He wouldn't go to church, didn't have any interest in it at all. (My grandmother went, of course, for the social reasons.) He did have a suit that he could wear to church, but he hated wearing it. He was comfortable in his overalls, comfortable sitting with his back up against one of those sycamore trees. He would have a big bucket of oysters, and he'd sit right on the ground, which of course was beneath the dignity of all the women in the family. He'd just sit there in his overalls, with his bucket of oysters and an oyster knife. He'd reach in, open one, pop it in his mouth, and toss the shell on the ground. This was awesome to me. I remember thinking that was a real man, someone who could sit there and eat those things.

That was a happy half hour for him. I can see his white moustaches drooping down and that old Anglo-Saxon face that we all know — the one that Dorothea Lange photographed.

■ ■ ■

It was certainly the women who were the strong ones in the family. My grandmother, really, in my memory and the memory of many other people, was saintly. She had a gentle face. In the years I knew her, she wore her hair in a bun, tied up behind her head. She was endlessly patient. She was well educated; she was herself a teacher. And a reader, which was rare in that community. She wasn't sanctimonious about it. She just liked books. She taught a lot of children to read, I think, both in and out of schools.

She was kind, and worked terribly hard, as Southern women did. I remember her washing the laundry in the yard, in a big black pot with a fire under it. She would stir the mess of lye soap and overalls and long johns with a hoe handle — none of which suited her. She was not an elegant lady, or anything like that; she was a hardworking woman all of her life. But it was a pity, it seems to me now, that she had to work so hard at cooking and stirring the clothes instead of having a chance to do what she really wanted to do — read and teach.

My grandfather had rigged a swing for me in one of the sycamores in the front yard, and I used to swing there. Or run wild in the orchard, among the twisted-up old apple trees. Nobody ever seemed to pick the apples. They fell and rotted on the ground. Perhaps somebody did pick them and make pies out of them, but my memory is the pungent apple smell from the apples on the ground.

The farm was six or eight miles from town, and then another mile down a hot sandy road — very hot, I remember, because if you were barefoot you couldn't stand it. You had to find shade to walk in. This was white sand, and I don't care how tough you were, you couldn't walk on it. In the grass there were sandspurs. You always were barefoot, and always stepped on sandspurs, and it always hurt like hell.

In the evenings, the grown-ups sat on the front porch. That's the only use I ever remember for the porch; it was for sitting in the dark at night. To get there, you didn't walk through the house, through the parlor and all that. Nobody ever walked through the parlor, or thought much about that part of the house. You went out and walked around the house from the back.

You could count after the lightning flashes — one one thousand, two one thousand — to tell how many miles away the lightning was.

43

I remember chasing the lightning bugs and putting them in a jar with holes in the top. June bugs, you would catch if you could, tie a string to one of their legs, and let them fly around at the end of the string. I don't remember what you did with them after you tired of that.

But there was always the porch swing. I loved sitting there after dark, curled up, with my grandmother or someone else, and listening to the talk.

In the side yard there was a bell, never rung. My grandmother told me that in the old days, when she was young, they would ring the bell at all mealtimes. Not to summon hands in from the fields, because there were none. But to signal to anybody who heard the bell as he passed by on the road that he was welcome to come in and eat.

If someone came, she said, it was considered impolite even to ask his name, or to ask him questions about himself. If he were a polite person, of course, he'd introduce himself, but if he didn't — feed him anyway.

That's what a Southerner was.

■ ■ ■

The front door was never used. If anyone had ever come to the front door, the dogs would have run under the bed. The front rooms were never used, except for funerals, and weddings, and Christmas. All of life went on in the fields, in the yard, on the porch, in the back of the house at the wood stove, where my grandmother cooked the best food I can remember. Clabber biscuits, which were better, I am certain, because they were cooked in the wood stove.

She cooked always. The meals were whatever was growing at the time, and that included corn, black-eyed peas, beets, beans, cabbages, collards, and turnip greens. There was a pantry absolutely full of food in Mason jars. Everything that could be grown was put up for the winter. There was everything in that pantry, and the best of all were the spiced peaches.

Whatever was left over from dinner would still be on the table at breakfast, so it was not unusual to have black-eyed peas with your eggs and grits in the morning. The food was magnificent. They never cooked vegetables without salt pork, to give them a little taste.

Hog-slaughtering day was the day that persuaded me never to be a farmer. I hated all the squealing and blood. But I loved all the good things that followed, especially the hams. There was a smoke-house full of country hams, which smelled moldy and hammy and briny. My grandfather was really good at making hams, famous for it in that part of the country.

I don't know how old I was when I had my first hamburger. We never had beef. We had pork and chicken; the cow was for milk. Chicken, especially on Sunday. An old hen who'd stopped laying would get her head chopped off for Sunday dinner. And Sunday dinner was always — different, though it wasn't necessarily better. It was served in the dining room.

We ate all other meals in the kitchen. The meals were at six in the morning, twelve noon, and six in the evening; breakfast, dinner, and supper. You could always count on having your meals on time.

Nobody ever came close to being hungry.

The arrival of the Sears, Roebuck catalog was always a big event. I remember the thrill of looking through it. I tried not to let anybody catch me studying the pictures of actual women in their underwear.

There was a good deal of dreaming with these catalogs, but very little ordering. The catalog was a wish book, but it was useful in other ways: when we were done wishing, we used the old catalogs in the outhouse.

I don't remember ever going to the store to buy anything more than an Orange Crush. There was a store out on the highway, and we would go there sometimes, but it was always for a treat, and the treat for me was always the same — an Orange Crush in a ribbed bottle.

■ ■ ■

They didn't buy many things. They didn't have to. All they bought was what they absolutely had to spend money for, and they hated to spend money. They bought maybe salt, flour, cornmeal, and Postum, which is what they drank. Everything else came from the farm. Once upon a time, they had even fashioned clothing there. There was a loom, where my grandmother had made the cloth. Somebody was always cutting out a new blouse from a Simplicity pattern, and there was sometimes a quilt in progress.

When it's really cold, and you're in a feather bed, with your grandmother's quilts weighting you down — well, there's no place like that on this earth.

There was no Camp Lejeune then, only a little Marine outpost called Tent Camp. I used to walk there, pulling an old red wagon loaded with milk and sugar cookies that my grandmother had made for me to go sell to the Marines. I don't remember ever getting any money — perhaps I did — but mainly what I got were globes and anchors and sharpshooter medals. Great stuff like that. They would say, "Give me a bunch of cookies, and I'll give you a medal."

I probably don't have all the details right. If my grandmother were alive, you can bet she would be correcting me right now.

There were Venus flytraps in the woods, those amazing plants that digest insects. A fly flies in, and the trap closes. Something about the plant makes it close when its little hairs are tickled. I used to go through the woods, endlessly tickling Venus flytraps with a straw to watch them close. I presumed they were there for the purpose of being tickled shut by little boys.

I was told never to go into the woods behind the house. There was a logging road there, and snakes.

I was out at the woodpile one night, where I'd gone to get kindling wood. I was in the dark, and something slapped me in the leg. I thought I'd stepped on a piece of wood, but I'd been bitten by a rattlesnake.

My grandmother cured me. She did what was the accepted therapy of the day: take a paring knife, make the cut bleed, suck out some of the poison.

My leg swelled up twice its size, and ached terribly. But there was something manly about having been bitten by a rattlesnake when you were six years old — and having survived to tell the tale.

My grandparents were humane for that time and place, and decent. They never said the word "nigger," or anything bad about black people. If I came home repeating some racial slur, my grandmother would speak to me sharply about that. If someone visiting used that word, she corrected them, even if they were her friends.

Above all, we children were not to behave like poor whites. We were always to be dignified and polite. We were to call our elders "Mr." and "Mrs." whether they were black or white, and stand when we were introduced.

I can't say that I was actually conscious of class then. I knew we were better off than some. Our nearest neighbor was a poor black family, and I went over there a lot. I had a friend there, an older boy whose name was Buck.

When I was five, I got a bicycle for Christmas, which was the greatest present I ever received. I couldn't believe it. An actual bicycle! But I didn't know how to ride it. Buck was glad to come teach me to ride the bicycle, because he had never had one either. It was really a chance for him to ride mine. I learned to ride by more or less watching Buck struggling with the bike in the soft sand in front of the house. Buck would spend half an hour showing me how, then let me ride for five minutes. I finally figured out what he was doing, and resented it (though I was grateful for the instruction).

Buck's mother was nice to me. She never failed to invite me to stay if mealtime came around when I was at their house. (I often contrived to be there about then.) And I would stay to eat her delicious ham biscuits.

My grandmother would feed Buck, too, but not at the table. She'd hand us the biscuits out the door, and we'd eat on the porch. I suppose Buck knew he couldn't sit at the table, and I never thought about it. Racial discrimination was just part of everyday life, part and parcel with pellagra and tar-paper shacks — things nobody misses now.

Death was a part of life in the South. My mother's two sisters, Betty and Trixie, both died of tuberculosis. My mother, the youngest of the three, was the sole survivor. I remember Trixie's slow death. She lay dying for months and months, and I puzzled over it. I didn't understand death. Still don't, I guess. But the people of the community gathered around us, and Trixie was buried in the graveyard where I might be buried someday, down there in Onslow County. There's a move afoot now in my family to fix up the graveyard, and I'm glad.

Funerals were very cooperative things. Nobody would think of being left out of a funeral. And church, of course, was a social event. Some of the people in that county would walk to wherever there was a preaching. People went great distances to get to church, and I don't believe it had so much to do with religious fervor as with a chance to see other people.

Sometimes, now, on Sunday in the South, I see people coming out of church, or getting ready to go in, especially out in the country. They stand around outside for an hour after church, even if there's no dinner-on-the-grounds, or anything like that. Black churches are even more that way — folks get dressed up in their very best for the one day, and stand around and talk and talk. You don't see that so much in the North. When church is over up there, people go home.

There really weren't many churches in the South until the great Baptist religious revival in the 1830s. When William Byrd, the Virginia aristocrat, came through the South, he couldn't find churches anywhere until he got to Charleston. In the town of Edenton, then the capital of North Carolina, he didn't find a one. In his travels through North Carolina, Byrd remarked, "I believe this is the only metropolis in the Christian or Mahometan world where there is neither church, chapel, mosque, synagogue, or any other place of worship of any sect or religion whatsoever." It wasn't until the circuit-riding Baptist ministers came along that churches sprang up in the countryside.

But when it got going, it really got going. Today, some of the big-city churches are enormous institutions, and powerful, of course. William Byrd, the austere Anglican, would be amazed by the power of the Baptists.

Of course to me there was no event in the South so joyous as a church supper or a dinner-on-the-grounds, because it really was a bringing-together of the whole community. Women would always get together for just visiting, but usually that took place on Sunday too, because they were too busy working during the week.

■■■

I am only a little past fifty, and I have a memory of what was really a primitive farm. There wasn't any electricity, nor any machinery of any kind. Today you can't imagine a farm without machinery, but the most sophisticated machine on my grandparents' farm was probably the disc harrow that was pulled by the mule.

I remember riding the mule bareback — I guess they were indulging me because I was a little boy, but at the time I thought I was helping.

To plow, you walked behind the plow and the mule. I could do that by the time I was six. The mule knew the route so well that I just walked behind, and he knew what to do. He'd turn around at the end of the row and come back.

There was a lot of working together. The neighbors would come and help you string your tobacco and hang it in the barn for curing; then you would go down the road and help them with theirs. They would come from all the other farms, and make a day of it. I was a hander. I would take five or six leaves — I forget — and hand to an experienced stringer, who would take them, make a twist with the tobacco twine around the stick, then with his other hand reach for another handful of tobacco, so that he would end up with the tobacco hanging neatly from both sides of the stick. Then that would hang in the barn.

These were barns made of logs, squared off, chinked with mud, and heated by wood fires in mud kilns. The trick was to keep the heat even, to cure the tobacco evenly. Because I liked to, my grandfather would invite me to pull the thermometer on a pulley on a string up to the little mica window, to be sure the heat was staying even.

My grandmother used to tell me about market day. They would take the tobacco to market — in our case to Kinston, the market my grandfather preferred because he felt he got a little better price in Kinston.

Then there was the ritual of the auctioneer stopping at each pile of tobacco, and he'd stop at your pile, and there would follow this little ten- or fifteen-second auction. He'd reach down under to make sure the bottom leaves were as good quality as the ones on top. (In my grandfather's case, they were. He was a good quality tobacco raiser, he felt.) They'd have that brief auction, and right there on the spot, the auctioneer would pay in cash. And that would be all the money the family would see that year. That was it. For the year. Fifteen seconds. I don't know how much money it would have been.

My grandmother would take a little of it and go buy a dress, and maybe a hat. And my grandfather would take his little bit of it and go out with the other men and drink. I never knew him to drink any other time; alcohol was a luxury that nobody could afford. But I remember usually on market day he was sort of ... carried home. And then the next morning he was ready to go for another year, without any more indulgences of any kind.

I remember my grandmother's tales about the days when coming home from market was dangerous because there were bandits along the road, or highwaymen as she called them, who would rob you and take all your money.

So somebody literally rode shotgun. You never came back from market day without somebody up in the front bearing a gun.

Admittedly, that was a story she told me when I was a little boy, but it says something about how close we are to the days when the South was lawless and wild.

■ ■ ■

One day soon, I suppose, the little farmer will be gone. There will be enormous farms run mostly by machinery, irrigation machines, combines. Perhaps the little farmer with his hundred acres and his mule didn't have much chance against such a future anyway, but at least he could feed his family. He didn't expect to get rich.

Ordinarily, he didn't borrow against his harvest. He didn't borrow at all from a bank. His whole purpose was to make enough money from his crops to buy enough seed for next year, and to be sure his family was fed. He lived outside the money economy. He thought in terms of his pigs having pigs, and his milk cow having a calf so that he would have another milk cow. There were no balance sheets, because there was no money to speak of.

Today, the purpose of agribusiness is to turn a profit. But that farmer rarely ended the year with any more than he had the year before. It would be nice if he did, but if he wound up with a new dress for his wife and a couple of extra presents at Christmastime, he had done well.

I'll always be glad that I remember that farm, because it gives me an understanding of how life was.

I wouldn't let my child do it today, at that age, but back in the forties when I was a teenager, my folks didn't see anything wrong with letting me hitchhike around the country to see something of it. I intended one year to go as far as California, but I never got any farther west than Wisconsin. I will never forget the first time I saw a Wisconsin dairy farm — the look of it! The black earth, the green meadows. I had never seen anything like that. I hadn't imagined that farms could took so prosperous — the tidy dairy barns, everything so pretty and perfect. I thought, holy smoke! These people must be rich!

Of course, in the South we just weren't used to it. We had gullies and broomstraw, and the barn was apt not to be painted, so the Southern farm was not typically what you would call a thing of beauty. It was utilitarian in every way, no wasted motion, because the farmer was so busy that he didn't have time to paint the barn and make the place look nice, though his wife might plant some petunias in an old tire by the road, to try to dress the place up a little bit.

A mountain man in North Carolina once told me, "Oh, yes! This is good strong land we have around here. It has to be, to hold up all the rocks." All you could do, if you had a poor farm, was to make a joke about it — and to get out of it what you could.

And it's true that the Southern farmer had a harder row to hoe. The Southern farmer wasn't a particularly productive one, compared to farmers in other regions. He generally didn't have good land to work with, unless he owned a stretch of river bottom. By and large he was working with sandy soil or with red clay, and doing the best he could.

All word from the outside world came in the mail. The Raleigh *News and Observer,* the *National Geographic,* and the *Progressive Farmer* all came in the mail. I'm sure the Geographic subscription was a luxury, but the Raleigh paper and the *Progressive Farmer* seemed necessities, to me.

It's no coincidence that the *Progressive Farmer* and progressive farming came along at the same time. Progressive is not a word you would think of to describe most Southern farmers, but they became more so, thanks to that magazine.

If he could read, the farmer could find in Clarence Poe's magazine new ideas for making his farm better: how to contour his rows so the erosion wouldn't be so bad in the spring, or how it was worth it to go ahead and spend the money on fertilizer, though he had never thought so.

This coincided with all those Roosevelt programs aimed at giving the farmer a little help. At last there was a county agent to show him ways to get more out of his soil.

So times changed, and mostly for the better. I remember the first time I saw my grandmother cry. She was standing at the end of the sand road, and wiping her eyes with her apron. It was not anything alarming; they were tears of joy. She could see the rural electrification truck, the REA light poles coming up the road to electrify the farm.

From then on, we had a light bulb hanging over the kitchen table. From then on, that county always voted Democratic, because they remembered Franklin Roosevelt brought them the light.

And what that meant, the reason my grandmother wept, was not only that she didn't have to pump the water from the pump on the porch anymore, or go to the well. It meant entering modern life.

A *ward-winning political columnist Hal Crowther occasionally turns his attention to other subjects — in this case dogs, whom he says he prefers to politicians. This essay first appeared in* Oxford American *magazine in 1996.*

Hal Crowther

"THE HOUNDS OF HEAVEN"

Every newspaper in the country picked up the story. A ten-year-old boy with Down's Syndrome was lost in the Ozark Mountains for three nights, in subfreezing March temperatures. The child was rescued in remarkably good condition, except for some frostbitten toes, and his survival was credited to a pair of stray dogs who kept him warm with their bodies and attracted the search party with their barking. The boy's stepfather, who adopted the strays, calls them "God's angels."

Joe Murray, a worthwhile newspaperman from Lufkin, Texas, was inspired to write a column about some friends of his who were lost in similar rough country — and led back to the road by two mysterious white dogs.

"It would be wonderful to arrive in Heaven and find that angels are dogs," Murray wrote, "and that the dogs we had in our life on Earth had been our guardian angels."

Nice, Joe. How many newspaper columns leave us with lumps in our throats? And the idea of dogs with celestial pedigrees is catching on. In "The White Dogs," North Carolina poet Tony Abbott pictures two white Salukis — sacred dogs of ancient Egypt — who wait at the door of a Blue Ridge cabin to carry off the soul of his dying friend.

Another lump, there. I can't even read *Dog Music*, a collection of poems my wife bought me for my birthday, because I skipped through and got the impression that half of them are about dogs dying. I'm learning to cry, and I appreciate an opportunity on occasion, but I just don't have the time to sit up in my room and blubber.

If this is a weakness, it's one I share with some pretty tough customers. Take Louis-Ferdinand Celine, an anti-Semite convicted of collaborating with the Nazis, a tortured cynic who wrote novels that bare their teeth at the human race and never stop snarling. Celine saw no innocence in the world, and little virtue. But dogs impressed and moved him deeply — especially their deaths. The death of his dog Bessy inspired this passage in *Castle to Castle*, the best glimpse of his heart Celine ever gave us.

> "I held her in my arms up to the end ... really a splendid animal ... a joy to look at her ... a vibrant joy ... she was so beautiful!
>
> "Oh, I've seen plenty of death agonies ... here ... there ... everywhere ... but none by far so beautiful, so discreet ... so faithful. The trouble with men's death agonies is the song and dance ... a man is always on the stage ... even the simplest of them."

Faulkner understood perfectly. No passage in *The Bear* captures its spirit like the death of Lion, the fearless dog who matched and doomed the bear, Old Ben: " ... there were almost a hundred of them squatting and standing in the warm and drowsing sunlight, talking quietly of hunting, of the game and the dogs which ran it, of hounds and bear and deer and men of yesterday vanished from the earth, while from time to time the great blue dog would open his eyes, not as if he were listening to them but as though to look at the woods for a moment before closing his eyes again, to remember the woods or to see that they were still there. He died at sundown."

They still appreciate dogs in Mississippi. In two recent Mississippi memoirs — *On Fire* by Larry Brown and *My Dog Skip* by Willie Morris — the death of a favorite dog is the most painful thing the author can remember. There's no false stoicism, either, no tough-guys-don't-cry stuff to insulate the reader from the pain.

"Die like a dog" is a pejorative simile that turns up in action literature of a certain vintage. It was invented by a miserable observer. We should all aspire to die so well, with a dog's solemn dignity that shames all our sweaty confessions and crucifix-clutching, our theatrics. If dogs are angels, they know they're saved; if they're dumb innocent creatures, death is one more uncomfortable feeling that comes over them, like hunger or sexual heat. Either way we admire their composure, and envy it profoundly.

The worth of dogs goes unquestioned in the best Southern literature. In the fiction of Cormac McCarthy (beginning with *The Orchard Keeper* in 1965, most recently in the last scene of *The Crossing* in 1994), a sin against a dog is a paradigm of evil and moral failure.

Dogs elicit maudlin testimonials from the most unlikely sources. I'm one of them. I can't match McCarthy's pessimism or Celine's misanthropy, but no one ever confused me with Norman Rockwell or Norman Vincent Peale. I've yet to shed a tear at a wedding or a patriotic demonstration, and babies, with the exception of my own, never made much of an impression on me. Bad movies with emotional sucker-punches rarely hit me at all — unless something ugly happens to a dog.

People who reproach us for loving animals more than people are usually hypocrites who love neither. No individual incapable of baby-talking to an Airedale would ever be among my closest friends. And the very lowest rungs on my personal ladder of life are occupied by people who've mistreated a dog, betrayed a dog who loved them or even failed to love a dog who deserved it.

These prejudices are the product of experience, unaffected by any notion that I'm a red-blooded, wing-shooting, Field & Stream sort of dog-man who kicks his wife's cats. Butch, my yellow tomcat, slept under my left arm every night for fifteen years, and I wouldn't have traded him for a saddle horse. The bad blood between cat people and dog people is as phony, in my view, as animosities between universities that compete in sports.

The truth is that anyone capable of appreciating one admirable animal can appreciate another. Hating cats is an irrational prejudice, much like anti-Semitism, that boys often pick up from their fathers. It's a primitive canard that soft men love cats and hard men love dogs. Honest men respond to both. Celine's beloved cat Bebert is a major character in *Castle to Castle*. Willie Morris owned four cats.

I never had a dog all my own until I was over forty. Obviously this dog has made a great believer of me. If you asked me what sets dogs above and apart from other animals, I'd say it's a moral quality. Dogs are utterly unlike us, sharing none of our goals, preoccupations or belief systems — as the poet Howard Nemerov observes in "Walking the Dog": "Two universes mosey down the street / Connected by love and a leash and nothing else."

And yet they involve themselves in our lives, in ways that can't be explained by simple affection or canine self-interest. I hate to brag on my own dog; I'm sure her virtues are common ones. Yet I watch her break up every fight among the house cats, at considerable inconvenience and even peril to herself. She stifles quarrels between her human housemates by banging to be let out, the second one of us reaches a decibel level she finds offensive. She shames us into civility.

Who appointed her peacekeeper? Call it altruism, a sense of duty, a commitment to domestic tranquility. Call it self-righteousness. But you won't get it from a parrot or a pot-bellied pig.

The moral superiority of dogs is an easy case to argue. They come in all temperaments, from Lion who according to Faulkner "cared about no man and no thing" to my Lab, Gracie, who appears to love every man and every living thing she encounters.

But whereas human beings are continually blasting each other to pieces over traffic disputes or trivial pieces of property, I've never seen another dog fail to respond in kind to my dog's flawless amiability — unless you count this one thing so small and ugly it might have been a fuzzy rodent doing a poor impersonation of a dog.

If you condescend to dogs because they eat things we hate to step in, and resort to grooming tricks we find outré, you've mistaken your affected pantywaist hygiene for moral and intellectual superiority. There are almost no limits to a dog's potential except the ones humans have carelessly bred or trained or beaten into him.

Another poet, Lord Byron, wrote this epitaph for his Newfoundland, Boatswain: "One who possessed beauty without vanity, strength without insolence, courage without ferocity, and all the virtues of man without his vices."

It takes more than the testimony of poets to prove that dogs are angels. But anecdotal evidence is piling up. The same week the boy was rescued in the Ozarks, an Irish setter was credited with saving her owner's life by dialing 911. And a big Lab/Rottweiler mix stopped traffic — stood in the road — to get help for a boy who had fainted from insulin shock.

Next to Interstate 95 near Lumberton, North Carolina, is a billboard with a dog's picture and these words: "This dog saved my daughter's life. Now he's lost. 'Spook' — $3500 reward." Considering all the sad things that may have happened to Spook, we comfort ourselves with the possibility that he simply completed his mission, and was reassigned.

Through twelve thousand years of intimate association, humans have been a mixed blessing for their patient guardians. Lofty moral examples often provoke lethal reprisals, as Jesus, Socrates or Gandhi could testify. (A news item from High Point, North Carolina: A dog-fighting ring dumps a load of dead and maimed animals by the side of the road. One dead dog has part of its jaw missing, another has no legs.)

How can dogs square their noble mission with some of the savage treatment they receive in return?

I remember the answer, from the fantasy comic strip Barbarella, which became a Jane Fonda movie. One of the characters is an angel. Barbarella asks him why he's rescuing a villain who crucified him, in an earlier episode, and he replies, "Angels have no memory."

*J*oseph Bruchac is a story-teller and author raised in the forests of upstate New York by a grandfather, Jess Bowman, who tried to conceal their Indian ancestry — a response to the threat and reality of persecution. This recollection is taken from the book, Bowman's Store, *in which Bruchac traces the discovery of his heritage, and also offers a tender tribute to the man he loved more than any in the world.*

Joseph Bruchac

"I BE A DANGEROUS MAN"

Excerpted from
Bowman's Store: A Journey to Myself

In 1993 I was in Mexico, visiting the Lacandon Mayan people. There I learned that some of their beliefs about dogs are much the same as those of the Abenaki people. Hunting was always of great importance to those people of the jungle, just as it was to my ancestors in our northeastern forests. A good dog was more than a man's best friend; a good dog was often the difference between life and death. And a dog's loyalty goes beyond life.

"They will greet you after you leave this earth," old Chan K'in said to me.

Among the Mayan people they tell the story this way. When a man's soul leaves the body after death and travels to the under-world, that soul comes to a wide river. There he is met by his dog.

"What do you see here, master?" the dog asks him.

"I see water that is very deep," the man answers. "There is a strong current and giant alligators. I cannot cross it."

"Master," says the dog, "you always treated me well. I will help you. Lie on my back and hold onto my ears, and I will carry you over the water."

Soon another man's soul comes to that wide water. He too is met by his dog. He also sees that the water is wide and that the current is swift and that there are great alligators waiting to pull him down. He says this to his dog, and his dog answers him.

"Master," the dog says, "you cut off my tail and my ears; you drove me away from you. So I have no ears for you to grab hold of and no tail for you to grasp. I will not help you. You must cross this river alone."

So Chan K'in Viejo, who was over a hundred then and would live for three more years, told the story.

One morning, when I woke up in his village of Naha, hearing the sound of the jungle birds calling from the tall trees, I told Chan K'in about a dream I'd just had.

"I dreamt," I said, "that someone sold my little dog."

Chan K'in was silent for a while. I was surprised. Chan K'in always liked to hear people's dreams and interpret them. His usual morning greeting included the question, "Did you dream?"

Then I realized why he did not say Neh tsoi, which means, "that is good," when I finished telling him about my dream. My friend Robert Bruce, who has lived in Mexico for four decades among the Lacandones and was acting as my guide and interpreter, also looked concerned. Among the Lacandon Maya it is not a fortunate thing to dream of a dog. In their interpretation of the symbolism of dreams, a dog means that disease is coming to you. Finally Chan K'in shook his head and smiled. He spoke a few quick words in Mayan to Robert. Robert nodded and laughed.

"Chan K'in says that, though dreaming of a dog may mean illness, then again perhaps in this case it is only that someone actually has just sold your little dog."

But it was not. The sand-fly bites that I received on my ankles that morning as I went to the stream to bathe carried leishmaniasis. The wound on my left ankle grew larger and larger until, two months later, it was the size of a fist. It would take a year and six rounds of antibiotics before that wound would finally heal. The scar, which will be with me for the rest of my life, is brown, and its shape is almost that of a small sitting dog.

But here, in the land where my Abenaki ancestors hunted with their dogs for thousands of years, to dream of your dog does not mean that illness will come to you. It has only meant, for me, a reassurance that I will see again those dogs that I loved. It means only that I, like so many other human beings whose lives are brief, have dared to care for creatures whose years on this earth will always be fewer than our own.

■ ■ ■

Scotty was his name. He was a little black, short-legged mongrel who, according to the man at the animal shelter, was mostly Scotch terrier. While the other dogs hung back or yelped hysterically, he came right up to the fence and stuck his nose against the back of my hand as I held it out to him. Then he sat back on his haunches and lifted up his front paws. There was so much weight on his backside that he looked like the four-foot-tall Joe Palooka punching bag that I'd had when I was three — it was weighted at the bottom, and when you hit it, it just swung right back up to a standing position.

I laughed. Then the little black dog looked up at me and barked. As soon as he barked he fell over on his back, and I laughed harder.

I looked over to my grandfather. He was already counting out the three dollars into the hand of the animal shelter man.

"Yup," Grampa said, "he says he wants us to take him home."

Scotty was perhaps three years old when I got him, but his exuberance was always that of a puppy.

"That there is a dog with more personality than brains," said Dan Atwell, one of the loggers who often stopped by our store, as he watched me walking around the lawn while Scotty hung onto my pants leg with his teeth and growled softly.

I didn't answer that. At the age of ten I had learned there was no good answer to such remarks, whether they were about dogs or people. I just stopped walking and said, "Sit." As soon as I did that, Scotty

let go of my pants leg and swung up into his sitting position, his little front legs bent, his mouth open and his tongue hanging out.

Dan started laughing. "Well, he minds good, I'll give you that," he
said.

"You don't want to try to take ahold of me with that dog around,"
my grandfather said. "He'll come right after you."

That was what my grandfather always said about every dog we ever
owned. The strange thing was that it was true. Though I never saw
Grampa do a single thing to make any of our dogs come to his
defense, and I never heard him say "Sic 'em," all anyone had to do
was make a threatening gesture toward my grandfather to find out
that his words were not just bluff.

"Quit kiddin', you old rooster," Dan Atwell said. He reached out a
hand as if about to take my grandfather by the arm. My grandfather
didn't move, but Scotty did. In two shakes of a lamb's tail he had
jumped in between Dan and my grandfather. Front legs spread wide,
teeth bared, he growled at Dan Atwell with such ferocity that Dan,
even though he was six feet tall, jumped back.

"Jeezum," Dan said.

"Tole yuh," said my grandfather.

Although Scotty became a part of our lives, his time with us was
even shorter than Lady's. I was walking down Middle Grove Road
with him only a year later, when I heard the screech of tires behind
me. I turned to see a hopped-up Ford swerving as it squealed around
the corner in our direction. The car almost hit me as it went past.

Scotty, who had jumped between me and that car, was not as lucky.
I picked him up. There was blood in his mouth and his eyes were
open. I carried him across the driveway toward my grandparents.
Both my grandmother and my grandfather had stood up from their
chairs in front of the station and were coming toward me, but
Grampa's eyes were not on me; they were looking down Middle
Grove Road.

I heard tires squealing and the roar of a four-barrel engine growing louder; then the same Ford that had struck my dog screeched to
a stop in the driveway behind me. The driver jumped out and

slammed his door. It was Jimmy Peekpod.

"What did you —" my grandmother started to say, but Jimmy Peekpod didn't let her finish.

"Your goddamn dog got right out in the road," Jimmy Peekpod shouted, his face reddening more as he yelled. "I could of had an accident. Look at my fender there. Who's gonna pay for that?"

My grandmother's face became as pale as one of her china plates. She took a deep breath. "How can you say that? You just killed Sonny's dog."

"Hell!" Jimmy Peekpod said, stepping closer to my grandmother and poking a finger at her. "You keep that kid out of the road or I'll goddamn run him over too."

My eyes filled with tears as I put Scotty's body down on the driveway. I couldn't believe what this tall, mean-voiced man was saying. I couldn't believe the way he was treating my grandmother, a woman that everyone treated with respect. She had been town clerk for a term and she had just been elected to the school board. But Jimmy Peekpod didn't know or care about any of that.

"You hear me, you fat ol' bitch?"

I was looking for something to hit him with, but I didn't have to. My grandfather's voice spoke from behind Jimmy Peekpod.

"Don't you never talk that way to my wife," he said.

Jimmy Peekpod whirled around and lifted a big fist.

"You ol' red nigger," he said, "I'm going to —"

He never finished that threat. My grandfather's right hand came up so fast that all I saw was a blur of motion. That open palm struck Jimmy Peekpod on his left ear with a loud hollow *whop!* And even though he was a head taller, forty pounds heavier, and more than forty years younger than my grandfather, Jimmy Peekpod went down like a poleaxed ox.

"Come on," Grampa said. "Get up." He spoke in a voice I'd never heard before, cool and violent all at once. It was not a voice any man would want to hear directed at him. My grandfather stood there with his left foot forward and his right foot back, in the easy stance of a man who'd fought so many times that it came as natural to him as breathing. His hands were at his waist and balled up into fists. Out of the corner of my eye I could see Grampa's friend Jim Rollins running across the road toward us from his car. He'd seen what was happening and was coming to help my grandfather. But Grampa didn't need help.

Jimmy Peekpod scuttled away on the ground like a crab. My grandfather didn't follow him. Jimmy Peekpod pulled himself up the side of his car and held his hand to his ear, where blood was pouring out.

"You broke my ear!" he said in a high, hysterical voice. "I'm gonna get the law on you."

"Come on," my grandfather said again.

But Jimmy Peekpod was not about to come on. He fumbled open the door of his car, started the engine, and drove off up Route 9N toward Greenfield Center.

"You all right, Jess?" Jim Rollins said.

"I expect his eardrum is broken," my grandfather said. Then he turned to my grandmother. And although they were never ones to make a public show of affection — which my grandmother said was undignified — he put his arms around her that day in sight of all the world that was going by, and she let him hold her.

We were coming back up the lawn from burying Scotty, me carrying the shovel, when the sheriff's car pulled in. My grandmother was already talking to the deputy when Grampa and I arrived. Jim Rollins, who had stayed around to see what would happen and to take care of any customers that might come, remained seated in one of the chairs in front of the station. He knew better than to get in my grandmother's way when she had her dander up.

"You've got no call to get out of that car, Bobby," my grandmother said. "That boy threatened me and my husband and said he'd run over Sonny."

"I can't help it, Mrs. Bowman," said the sheriff's deputy, Bobby Bentson. "He has swore out a complaint. I got to take Jess in."

"Let him out of the car, Marion," my grandfather said.

My grandmother stood back from the door of the police car, and as the deputy climbed out, Grampa held out his hands.

"I'll go with you, all right. But I'm not going to take a step unless you put them handcuffs on me. I be a dangerous old man."

"That's right," said my grandmother.

Bobby Bentson shook his head, but he knew my grandparents. He took the handcuffs off his belt and fastened them onto my grandfather's wrists.

"Now turn on that siren," Grampa said. "Yer bringing in a dangerous old man."

Bobby shook his head again, but he did as my grandfather said. Siren wailing, the police car went up 9N.

"Sonny," my grandmother said, "you stay and watch the station. Mr. Rollins will help you out."

"I surely will," Jim Rollins said. "You give 'em heck now, Mrs. Bowman."

My grandmother got into the blue Plymouth and went up 9N in the wake of the siren, which could still be heard wailing faintly in the distance.

"Don't worry about them two, Sonny," Jim Rollins said to me. "That snotass Peekpod kid still don't know what hit him."

An hour later they were back. Grampa had been brought before Town Justice Charles Cedric Weirman, still wearing those handcuffs. Deputy Bobby Bentson never got a chance to explain that my grandfather had insisted on being handcuffed. Instead he had to fumble for his keys and get those cuffs off as quickly as he could, while Justice Weirman went up one side of him and down the other about treating an old man like a common criminal.

Jimmy Peekpod, who had sworn out the complaint to bring my grandfather in, was either too angry or too stupid to see which way the wind was already blowing. When asked what had happened he stepped forward, holding a handkerchief to his ear.

"His damn dog ran out in the road, and when I stopped my damn car that old bastard hit me with a hammer," he said. "And ... "

His testimony was interrupted by the crack of the Judge's gavel. "There will be no swearing in my court. I hereby fine you five dollars."

"What the hell?"

The gavel cracked a second time. "That is ten dollars. Would you like to try for fifteen, young man?"

"Better shut your yap, kid," said someone from the crowd that had assembled in the town hall. The ripple of laughter that went around the room subsided as Justice Weirman looked out at the audience.

Then, as Jimmy Peekpod stood there speechless, Justice Weirman turned toward my grandfather.

"Where's that hammer, Jess?" he said.

My grandfather held up his open right hand. "Right here, yer Honor," he said.

Even Justice Weirman joined in the laughter that followed my grandfather's words.

"Now, why did they bring you here in handcuffs, Jess? Did you resist arrest?"

"No sir, I reckon they figgered I was a dangerous old man for picking on that little boy there."

Justice Weirman looked over his glasses at Jimmy Peekpod. "A great lunk like you, twice the size of Mr. Bowman here, and you accuse him of assault? Is that right?"

Jimmy Peekpod thought a minute and then nodded his head.

"Then you're an even bigger fool than you appear to be, young man. Charges are dismissed." The gavel cracked down again.

Jimmy Peekpod turned away, but before he could reach the door the deputy sheriff stopped him at a signal from Justice Weirman.

"Young man," said Justice Weirman, as my grandparents left the courtroom, "have you forgotten the matter of ten dollars which you owe to the town of Greenfield?"

n this opening excerpt from his Pulitzer Prize-winning memoir, Angela's Ashes *author Frank McCourt writes about the circumstances leading up to his birth. It is, in part, an age-old tale of how his father was persuaded to marry his mother, and how, improbably, the author came to be named for a saint.*

Frank McCourt

Excerpted from
Angela's Ashes: A Memoir

My father and mother should have stayed in New York where they met and married and where I was born. Instead, they returned to Ireland when I was four, my brother Malachy, three, the twins, Oliver and Eugene, barely one, and my sister Margaret, dead and gone.

When I look back on my childhood I wonder how I survived at all. It was, of course, a miserable childhood: the happy childhood is hardly worth your while. Worse than the ordinary miserable childhood is the miserable Irish childhood, and worse yet is the miserable Irish Catholic childhood.

People everywhere brag and whimper about the woes of their early years, but nothing can compare with the Irish version: the poverty; the shiftless loquacious alcoholic father; the pious defeated mother moaning by the fire; pompous priests; bullying schoolmasters; the English and the terrible things they did to us for eight hundred long years.

Above all — we were wet.

Out in the Atlantic Ocean great sheets of rain gathered to drift slowly up the River Shannon and settle forever in Limerick. The rain dampened the city from the Feast of the Circumcision to New Year's Eve. It created a cacophony of hacking coughs, bronchial rattles, asthmatic wheezes, consumptive croaks. It turned noses into fountains, lungs into bacterial sponges. It provoked cures galore; to ease the catarrh you boiled onions in milk blackened with pepper; for the congested passages you made a paste of boiled flour and nettles, wrapped it in a rag, and slapped it, sizzling, on the chest.

From October to April the walls of Limerick glistened with the damp. Clothes never dried; tweed and woolen coats housed living things, sometimes sprouted mysterious vegetations. In pubs, steam rose from damp bodies and garments to be inhaled with cigarette and pipe smoke laced with the stale fumes of spilled stout and whiskey and tinged with the odor of piss wafting in from the outdoor jakes where many a man puked up his week's wages.

The rain drove us into the church — our refuge, our strength, our only dry place. At Mass, Benediction, novenas, we huddled in great damp clumps, dozing through priest drone, while steam rose again from our clothes to mingle with the sweetness of incense, flowers and candles.

Limerick gained a reputation for piety, but we knew it was only the rain.

■ ■ ■

My father, Malachy McCourt, was born on a farm in Toome, County Antrim. Like his father before him, he grew up wild, in trouble with the English, or the Irish, or both. He fought with the Old IRA and for some desperate act he wound up a fugitive with a price on his head.

When I was a child I would look at my father, the thinning hair, the collapsing teeth, and wonder why anyone would give money for a head like that. When I was thirteen my father's mother told me a secret: as a wee lad your poor father was dropped on his head. It was an accident, he was never the same after, and you must remember that people dropped on their heads can be a bit peculiar.

Because of the price on the head he had been dropped on, he had to be spirited out of Ireland via cargo ship from Galway. In New York, with Prohibition in full swing, he thought he had died and gone to hell for his sins. Then he discovered speakeasies and he rejoiced.

After wandering and drinking in America and England he yearned for peace in his declining years. He returned to Belfast, which erupted all around him. He said, A pox on all their houses, and chatted with the ladies of Andersontown. They tempted him with delicacies but he waved them away and drank his tea. He no longer smoked or touched alcohol, so what was the use? It was time to go and he died in the Royal Victoria Hospital.

My mother, the former Angela Sheehan, grew up in a Limerick slum with her mother, two brothers, Thomas and Patrick, and a sister, Agnes. She never saw her father, who had run off to Australia weeks before her birth.

After a night of drinking porter in the pubs of Limerick he staggers down the lane singing his favorite song.

> *Who threw the overalls in Mrs. Murphy's chowder*
> *Nobody spoke so he said it all the louder*
> *It's a dirty Irish trick and I can lick the Mick*
> *Who threw the overalls in Murphy's chowder.*

He's in great form altogether and he thinks he'll play a while with little Patrick, one year old. Lovely little fella. Loves his daddy. Laughs when Daddy throws him up in the air. Upsy daisy, little Paddy, upsy daisy, up in the air in the dark, so dark, oh, Jasus, you miss the child on the way down and poor little Patrick lands on his head, gurgles a bit, whimpers, goes quiet. Grandma heaves herself from the bed, heavy with the child in her belly, my mother. She's barely able to lift little Patrick from the floor. She moans a long moan over the child and turns on Grandpa. Get out of it. Out. If you stay here a minute longer I'll take the hatchet to you, you drunken lunatic. By Jesus, I'll swing at the end of a rope for you. Get out.

Grandpa stands his ground like a man. I have a right, he says, to stay in me own house.

She runs at him and he melts before this whirling dervish with a damaged child in her arms and a healthy one stirring inside. He stumbles from the house, up the lane, and doesn't stop till he reaches Melbourne in Australia.

Little Pat, my uncle, was never the same after. He grew up soft in the head with a left leg that went one way, his body the other. He never learned to read or write but God blessed him in another way. When he started to sell newspapers at the age of eight he could count money better than the Chancellor of the Exchequer himself. No one knew why he was called Ab Sheehan, the Abbot, but all Limerick loved him.

My mother's troubles began the night she was born. There is my grandmother in the bed heaving and gasping with the labor pains, praying to St. Gerard Majella, patron saint of expectant mothers. There is Nurse O'Halloran, the midwife, all dressed up in her finery. It's New Year's Eve and Mrs. O'Halloran is anxious for this child to be born so that she can rush off to the parties and celebrations. She tells my grandmother: Will you push, will you, push. Jesus, Mary and holy St. Joseph, if you don't hurry with this child it won't be born till the New Year and what good is that to me with me new dress? Never mind St. Gerard Majella. What can a man do for a woman at a time like this even if he is a saint? St. Gerard Majella my arse.

My grandmother switches her prayers to St. Ann, patron saint of difficult labor. But the child won't come. Nurse O'Halloran tells my grandmother, Pray to St. Jude, patron saint of desperate cases.

St. Jude, patron of desperate cases, help me. I'm desperate. She grunts and pushes and the infant's head appears, only the head, my mother, and it's the stroke of midnight, the New Year. Limerick City erupts with whistles, horns, sirens, brass bands, people calling and singing, Happy New Year. Should auld acquaintance be forgot, and church bells all over ring out the Angelus and Nurse O'Halloran weeps for the waste of a dress, that child still in there and me in me finery. Will you come out, child, will you? Grandma gives a great push and the child is in the world, a lovely girl with black curly hair and sad blue eyes.

Ah, Lord above, says Nurse O'Halloran, this child is a time straddler, born with her head in the New Year and her arse in the Old or was it her head in the Old Year and her arse in the New. You'll have to write to the Pope, missus, to find out what year this child was born in and I'll save this dress for next year.

And the child was named Angela for the Angelus which rang the midnight hour, the New Year, the minute of her coming and because she was a little angel anyway.

> *Love her as in childhood,*
> *Though feeble, old and grey.*
> *For you'll never miss a mother's love*
> *Till she's buried beneath the clay.*

At the St. Vincent de Paul School, Angela learned to read, write, and calculate and by her ninth year her schooling was done. She tried her hand at being a charwoman, a skivvy, a maid with a little white hat opening doors, but she could not manage the little curtsy that is required and her mother said, You don't have the knack of it. You're pure useless. Why don't you go to America where there's room for all sorts of uselessness? I'll give you the fare.

She arrived in New York just in time for the first Thanksgiving Day of the Great Depression. She met Malachy at a party given by Dan MacAdorey and his wife, Minnie, on Classon Avenue in Brooklyn. Malachy liked Angela and she liked him. He had a hangdog look, which came from the three months he had just spent in jail for hijacking a truck. He and his friend John McErlaine believed what they were told in the speakeasy, that the truck was packed to the roof with cases of canned pork and beans. Neither knew how to drive and when the police saw the truck lurch and jerk along Myrtle Avenue

71

they pulled it over. The police searched the truck and wondered why anyone would hijack a truck containing, not pork and beans, but cases of buttons.

With Angela drawn to the hangdog look and Malachy lonely after three months in jail, there was bound to be a knee-trembler.

A knee-trembler is the act itself done up against a wall, man and woman up on their toes, straining so hard their knees tremble with the excitement that's in it.

That knee-trembler put Angela in an interesting condition and, of course, there was talk. Angela had cousins, the MacNamara sisters, Delia and Philomena, married, respectively, to Jimmy Fortune of County Mayo, and Tommy Flynn, of Brooklyn itself.

Delia and Philomena were large women, great-breasted and fierce. When they sailed along the sidewalks of Brooklyn lesser creatures stepped aside, respect was shown. The sisters knew what was right and they knew what was wrong and any doubts could be resolved by the One, Holy, Roman, Catholic and Apostolic Church. They knew that Angela, unmarried, had no right to be in an interesting condition and they would take steps.

Steps they took. With Jimmy and Tommy in tow they marched to the speakeasy on Atlantic Avenue where Malachy could be found on Friday, payday when he had a job. The man in the speak, Joey Cacciamani, did not want to admit the sisters but Philomena told him that if he wanted to keep the nose on his face and that door on its hinges he'd better open up for they were there on God's business. Joey said, Awright, awright, you Irish. Jeezoz! Trouble, trouble.

Malachy, at the far end of the bar, turned pale, gave the great-breasted ones a sickly smile, offered them a drink. They resisted the smile and spurned the offer. Delia said, We don't know what class of a tribe you come from in the North of Ireland.

Philomena said, There is a suspicion you might have Presbyterians in your family, which would explain what you did to our cousin.

Jimmy said, Ah, now, ah, now. 'Tisn't his fault if there's Presbyterians in his family.

Delia said, You shuddup.

Tommy had to join in. What you did to that poor unfortunate girl is a disgrace to the Irish race and you should be ashamed of yourself.

Och, I am, said Malachy. I am.

Nobody asked you to talk, said Philomena. You done enough damage with your blather, so shut your yap.

And while your yap is shut, said Delia, we're here to see you do the right thing by our poor cousin, Angela Sheehan.

Malachy said, Och, indeed, indeed. The right thing is the right thing and I'd be be glad to buy you all a drink while we have this little talk.

Take the drink, said Tommy, and shove it up your ass.

Philomena said, Our little cousin no sooner gets off the boat than you are at her. We have morals in Limerick, you know, morals. We're not like jackrabbits from Antrim, a place crawling with Presbyterians.

Jimmy said, He don't look like a Presbyterian.

You shuddup, said Delia.

Another thing we noticed, said Philomena. You have a very odd manner.

Malachy smiled. I do?

You do, says Delia. I think 'tis one of the first things we noticed about you, that odd manner, and it gives us a very uneasy feeling.

'Tis that sneaky little Presbyterian smile, said Philomena.

Och, said Malachy, it's just the trouble I have with my teeth.

Teeth or no teeth, odd manner or no odd manner, you're gonna marry that girl, said Tommy. Up the middle aisle you're going.

Och, said Malachy, I wasn't planning to get married, you know. There's no work and I wouldn't be able to support …

Married is what you're going to be, said Delia.

Up the middle aisle, said Jimmy.

You shuddup, said Delia.

Malachy watched them leave. I'm in a desperate pickle, he told Joey Cacciamani.

Bet your ass, said Joey. I see them babes comin' at me I jump inna Hudson River.

Malachy considered the pickle he was in. He had a few dollars in his pocket from the last job and he had an uncle in San Francisco or one of the other California Sans. Wouldn't he be better off in California, far from the great-breasted MacNamara sisters and their grim husbands? He would, indeed, and he'd have a drop of the Irish to celebrate his decision and departure. Joey poured and the drink nearly took the lining off Malachy's gullet. Irish, indeed! He told Joey it was a Prohibition concoction from the devil's own still. Joey shrugged. I don't know nothing. I only pour. Still, it was better than nothing and Malachy would have another and one for yourself, Joey, and ask them two decent Italians what they'd like and what are you talking about, of course, I have the money to pay for it.

He awoke on the bench in the Long Island Railroad Station, a cop rapping on his boots with a nightstick, his escape money gone, the MacNamara sisters ready to eat him alive in Brooklyn.

■ ■ ■

On the feast of St. Joseph's, a bitter day in March, four months after the knee-trembler, Malachy married Angela and in August the child was born. In November, Malachy got drunk and decided it was time to register the child's birth. He thought he might name the child Malachy, after himself, but his North of Ireland accent and the alcoholic mumbling confused the clerk so much he simply entered the name Male on the certificate.

Not until late December did they take Male to St. Paul's Church to be baptized and named Francis after his father's father and the lovely saint of Assisi. Angela wanted to give him a middle name, Munchin, after the patron saint of Limerick but Malachy said over his dead body. No son of his would have a Limerick name. It's hard enough going through life with one name. Sticking on middle names was an atrocious American habit and there was no need for a second name when you're christened after the man from Assisi ...

n this haunting work of non-fiction, award-winning novelist Robin Hemley turns the writer's eye on himself and his family, searching for the story of Nola, his sister who died at age twenty-five after battling schizophrenia. This prologue from what is essentially a family biography reveals the sorrow, humor and paradox of one writer's unflinching quest for the truth.

Robin Hemley

"LARCENY"

Excerpted from
Nola: A Memoir of Faith, Art, and Madness

Admissible Evidence:

My parents seemed to believe in letting everyone do whatever they wanted until they became very good at it or died. My father, Cecil Hemley, was a poet, novelist, editor and translator of Isaac Singer's work. He was also a good smoker and that's what he died of when I was seven. My older brother Jonathan used to be good at everything, from languages to sports to the sciences, but over the last fifteen years he's specialized — in Orthodox Judaism, and lives with his seven children and wife in L.A. My sister Nola was good at everything, too, art and language, but especially things of the spirit — and that, in a sense, is what she eventually died from. My mother, Elaine

Gottlieb, is a short story writer and teacher. She's good at surviving. As for myself … I've always had a larcenous heart.

As I get older, the thief diminishes, but still there is something inside me essentially untrustworthy, someone hard and calculating and conniving, egged on by the deaths of my father and sister, who will not always accept responsibility for his actions. I remember a camp counselor at Granite Lake Camp in New Hampshire, telling me one night that he was on to me. He called me conniving. I pretended I didn't know what he was talking about, and was silent. He was one of the only people who saw through me like that, or at least one of the few who ever told me directly. I wonder about confession, this nagging need. When I confess, I make myself vulnerable. Some people will like me for it and others will arm themselves with my admissions and hurl them back. One time I told my mother what this counselor had said about me, and the next time we argued she said, "Your counselor was right. You are conniving." After that, I resolved to bury myself deeper, to hide this other person where even I wouldn't be able to recognize him. Sometimes I think it's too late, that he has already stolen away the things my sister gave me — things of the imagination and spirit that he pawned to support his habit.

Inadmissible Evidence:

I'm looking through a drawer of a desk in my room at my grandmother's house. I'm seventeen and I'm looking for something to steal — loose change would be great or an antique paper weight or letter opener.

Inside one of the drawers, I come across a legal-sized document with a rusty paper clip attached. It's titled POINT OF ERROR #1 and reads "The Finding that 'No marriage between Elliot Chess and Elaine Gottlieb (also known as Elaine Hemley) was ever entered into at any time or at any place' is contrary to the evidence and against the weight of the evidence. Appellees proved the contract of marriage." That's as far as I read. I'm not sure what this document is or how it pertains to me, but I know I have to have it, and I know that I can't tell anyone about it. It has something to do with Nola, who's been dead three years.

Discovery:

Uncovering the facts, not even the facts, but the feelings of my sister's and mother's lives, has become a detective story for me. It started out before I even knew it was a detective story, when I was seventeen and found some court documents about my mother and Nola's father, Elliot Chess, in a drawer at my grandmother's house. The remarkable thing about finding these documents was that I never told anyone I'd found them and never read them until now. For years, I kept them in a box and never looked at them. But now that I've read them, now that I understand things about my mother's life, things perhaps that she wouldn't want me to understand, the revelations follow quickly, one upon the other. And the more I uncover, the more I realize that one of these days soon I'm going to have to tell my mother about the court papers I found. Eventually, I'll confess. But the documents keep multiplying. Everyone in my family, or connected with it, it seems, has written about the events I want to write about — though not in a way that gives an overall picture of who we are. Every day, I seem to learn about new documents. I'm drowning in them. My mother tells me little by little about their existence, almost as though she's teasing me. But this is how she's always been. Rarely does she volunteer information about her life, though if asked a direct question, sometimes she'll answer. She's known a lot of famous writers and artists: Isaac Singer, Joseph Heller, Robert Motherwell, Weldon Kees, Louise Bogan, Conrad Aiken, John Crowe Ransom, but she almost never mentions any of them. Every once in a while, she'll name, almost by mistake it seems, one of these people, and I'll say, "You knew him?" "Sure," she says. It's not important to her.

My mother, for instance, has kept a journal since she was sixteen. I never knew this until I stumbled upon the fact New Year's Eve, 1994, when I asked her nonchalantly whether she'd ever kept a journal.

"Sure, I've been keeping a journal since I was sixteen."

I was stunned. She'd never told me about her journal. "Do you have anything from your time in Mexico with your first husband?"

"Sure, I have a lot about Mexico."

"I need it all," I told her.

She laughed.

"Do you know where it is?"

"I was just looking at it the other day."

"Mom, I'm always amazed how I just find out these things about you by chance."

She laughed again.

That night, she and I sat on her bed and sorted through her journal, hundreds of loose leaf typed pages dating from the '30s. She let me have whatever I wanted, but she also said, "I don't think you should know everything."

"I have to," I said, half-laughing. "I want to know everything."

I keep thinking that it's my right to know all this, that she should volunteer everything she knows, like this is some court case and she'll be accountable for what she doesn't divulge. It says something new about my relationship with my mother, that for years, everything was too painful to divulge to me, but now nothing is. My mother, since learning about my project, has been sending me steady streams of old photos, journal excerpts, letters.

The Present:

My mother is working on a novel, two novels really, a mystery about a trip we took to England when I was eighteen and another one whose subject I'm unsure of. She's been working on a novel for years, ever since I could remember — her second novel. Her first was published in 1947, the year of my sister Nola's birth. Almost every time I speak to her she's working on a new novel, having abandoned every previous one after a couple of drafts or a few chapters. Every few years she rediscovers her old novels and realizes they were pretty good. She'll work feverishly on this novel with renewed vigor until another loss of faith, and then she's off to a new project. In between she writes short stories. For many years, they were published in some of the best literary journals and anthologies.

I find myself trying to make time to read her new stories between my busy teaching schedule, doing my own writing, spending time with my own family. Everything produces guilt. I look at my daughters and realize I'm not spending enough time with them. I try to give everyone encouragement. "Just keep sending them out, Mom." "Why don't you just finish this one before moving on. I like the idea of this one."

"I'll get back to it," she tells me.

But I know that after she dies, I'll find a dozen or so novels in various stages of completion, and I won't know what to do with them. Should I find the best ones and try to edit them? Should I send them out as is? Why am I worrying about this now? It's strange to think of your family leaving you documents, but that's what my family leaves behind: stories, novels, poems. Documents. Half-truths. Fiction. It's what my family was built on, what we've always believed in. We've always been suspicious of fact, frightened of it. My grandmother, on her deathbed, delirious, asking the impossible, to just go home and sit outside for a while on her porch, started ranting, according to my mother, about a supposed case of incest in a branch of our family that happened two hundred years ago, and begged that the family line be stopped. Facts, even two hundred years old, haunt our family. "Fictionalize it," my mother says. "Why don't you fictionalize it?"

The Past:

My father has been dead six months. Heart attack. I'm spending the summer with my grandmother Ida, and she enrolls me at Atlantic Beach Day Camp a few blocks from where she lives. I hate swimming, so during swim period I organize a pickpocket ring. I don't know how I learned to pickpocket, but I'm pretty good, so I teach a small group at the camp how to do it. At first, we lift combs from back pockets, but then we start taking wallets. We're finally caught and lined up by the pool where the head counselor interrogates us.

"I know you're good kids," he says. "You wouldn't do this on your own. There's one bad apple among you. Tell me who it is and I'll let the rest of you go."

I turn to the boy in line next to me, a fat kid named Bernard who reluc-

tantly joined the ring, and who seems to think I'm cool. "Why don't you tell them it's you?" I say to Bernard, as though this would be a very good thing for him to do.

He blinks at me and tugs his hair.

"Tell them it's you," I say.

"Why?" he whispers.

"You'll be a hero," I say.

The counselor waits. He moves down the line, looking at the tops of our heads. More than anything, I don't want Ida to know what I've done. She wouldn't be able to believe it. She thinks I'm a good kid and so does my mother, and I can't bear the thought of them being told what I've done.

Bernard glances over at me and gives me an unsure and suffering look. "Go ahead," I say. "Be a hero."

He raises his hand.

"What?" the counselor says.

"It's me," Bernard says. "I'm the ringleader."

The counselor looks a bit surprised, but then a smug look replaces the other and he grins. He reaches over and yanks Bernard by the arm. Bernard cowers in front of us.

"I thought so," the counselor says. "I knew it was you."

The counselor takes Bernard away and that's the last I ever see of him. Another counselor dismisses us. No one says a word to our parents, or in my case, my grandmother, and those of us involved never speak of the pickpocket ring or Bernard again. Maybe they think they've scared us enough or maybe they don't want our parents to think Atlantic Beach Day Camp gives its campers enough idle time to organize pickpocket rings.

The next day I'm idling by one the buildings listening with a whole group of idlers to a transistor radio. We're entranced by a new Beatles song. Someone has called me over to hear it, and we gather around the radio as though hearing the first transmission from a distant universe. Across from us, the good campers, the non-idlers, the Boy Scouts, the Penny-saved-is-a-penny-earned boys, are playing softball. I glance up for a second and see something white coming down on me. It knocks me flat. The other idlers laugh at me and the softball group runs over to where I lie, mildly concussed, arguing whether or not it was a home run or fan interference on my part. I don't care. I know it's punishment. A knock on the head from Heaven.

A counselor named Herman takes me under his wing. He thinks I'm a good kid and he feels sorry for me that my dad has died. He spends extra time with me, even after the day camp has closed. With my grandmother's permission he takes me to the boardwalk one night. We ride the Ferris Wheel. He buys me cotton candy and a potato knish. It's a strange night because there's been a tidal wave the night before, and it's flooded the normally wide beach all the way to the street under the boardwalk. The boardwalk is fine, but you can hear the small waves roiling against the support beams, even catch glimpses of the water through the slats. As we're walking along he picks me up and dangles me over the railing. I see the water, the ocean right beneath me, a dark slapping sea.

He laughs. "Should I drop you over?"

"No," I say, laughing, too, confident that he wouldn't dare.

"I'm going to drop you," he says, and for a moment I can feel it. I'm lost. I'm gone out to sea, pulled far from anything solid. I scream.

Still, he holds me over.

"Don't you wish you learned how to swim?" he says.

Does he know, I wonder? Does he know that I was the ringleader? Or does it even matter whether he knows. I'm dangling over the railing by one foot. "I've got you," he says. "I've got you," and I wonder what he means by that.

The Nonfictional:

My mother returns my call on Thanksgiving. I left a message on her machine. I know she's there — probably upstairs in her study writing, but she can't hear me because she's turned her hearing aid down. One of her former students invited her for Thanksgiving dinner, but my mother declined, preferring these days to celebrate holidays by writing.

"Did I tell you I'm working on a mystery?" she asks.

"Yes." She's told me a dozen times already.

"With Nancy Cowgil," she says. "It's about our trip to England."

"I'm writing, too," I say. "I hope Jonny won't hate me when I finish this." But that's not what I really mean to say. What I really mean to say is, "I hope you won't hate me."

"Why's that?"

"I'm not holding anything back."

"You can always soft-peddle the facts," she says. "I found a photo of Nola for you, but it's from when she was twenty."

"I'm going to be writing about you and Elliot Chess."

"What do you know about us? I haven't told you much."

"But that's part of it. I've done a little . . . investigating." I think about what she said about soft-peddling. I think about the document I have that she doesn't know about, what I found when I was seventeen. I didn't even read it until this summer. I knew that someday I would, but I waited for the right moment. While preparing to write this, I remembered the papers and started searching for them, tearing through my files, coming up with nothing, thinking with despair, "I couldn't have thrown them out. Why would I throw them out?" Finally, I found them in my attic, in a corner, at the very bottom of a file box filled with assorted papers. There's so much in these papers that my mother doesn't know I know. I keep hinting that I know more than she's told me, but I just can't make a clean confession. I think about what she said the last time we spoke about this, "God, I'm going to have to become a hermit after you write this." I want to confess. I want more than anything to tell her what I have, but I know that she'd want to see it, that she'd say, "Fictionalize. Don't embarrass me." And I'd have to say, "There's nothing to be embarrassed about. It happened fifty years ago. These things happen every day now." But I know that wouldn't do a thing to diminish her pain, the pain of abandonment and betrayal. And now, here I am — am I betraying her? Do I have any right to say what I know, to tell the facts, private facts from public documents? I know that if I had grown up in a different family, a family of architects, the answer would have been no. All of my writing friends urge me to wait until the story is done before I show it to my mother. One of them tells me, "Thomas Wolfe never would have written *Look Homeward, Angel,* if he'd sought his mother's approval first."

The Fictional:

I come from a family of writers, and the pain that comes from words is not diminished, necessarily, by a fictionalized stance. I grew up as the subject or a character in my mother's published stories. I was told that I shouldn't be angered by this, that fiction transforms. And I wasn't bothered, except by momentary twinges when I saw revealed in a story, my late thumb-sucking, for instance. I still believe we have the right, the obligation, to write about the world as we see it, whether admittedly transformed or not. Of course, it's always transformed. There's a story by Donald Barthelme, "The Author," in which a famous writer uses her children as the models for all her stories, and when they come to complain to her about telling all their secrets, they ask what gives her the right, and she blithely answers, "Because you're mine." But the flipside of that is that they own her, too. The children own the mother and the father, whether they know it or not. At times, I want to cry as I'm writing. At times, I want to do wrong, knowingly, to get at what's right.

The Lies:

In Ida's room while she's in the kitchen, I open the clasp of her pocketbook and start digging for her purse. The pocketbook is stuffed with sugar packets she's taken from restaurants, salt and pepper packets, moist towelettes, tissues, combs, her compact, and finally down at the bottom, the little cowhide change purse where she keeps her bills crumpled up together in a wad. I open it and feel the bills. All of them come up in my hand together. I've done this many times. The money is for comic books. I'm fourteen. I don't plan on taking all her money, just a few dollars, maybe five, depending on how much she has and how much I think she'll miss.

As I'm sorting through the mass of wadded bills, Ida walks into the room.

"What are you doing?" she asks. For some reason, she doesn't look surprised.

"I was looking for something," I tell her.

"In my purse?"

I'm holding the wadded bills still, gently, as if I don't know what to do with them, like they're some wounded bird I've found.

"A pen," I say. "I was just looking for a pen."

There's a bit of a whine in my voice, even a threat, not physical, but emotional. I'll do whatever necessary to protect and preserve this lie. I stare at her. I hate her right now for finding out about me. And this is something she can't stand. She looks afraid for a second and says quietly, "I'll help you find one." Only then do I put the money back where I found it and neither of us say a word about this to anyone, nor to each other, nor, I'm sure, to ourselves.

The Spoken:

Nola was my half-sister from my mother's previous marriage, eleven years older than me, a brilliant young woman who graduated Phi Beta Kappa and then studied for her Ph.D. in philosophy at Brandeis. She was also interested, obsessed actually, with spiritual and psychic phenomenon and apprenticed under her Guru, Sri Ramanuja.

Sometimes I still miss Nola keenly. I miss her most when I'm with my daughters, Olivia and Isabel, and it's just us, and I wish they could know their aunt, someone who played the Irish harp, who knew Sanskrit and Greek and French and German and Hebrew, who would teach them Shakespearean songs and sing with them — someone so impractical and imaginative that nearly anything seemed possible to me in her presence.

Anything that had to do with the hidden, with the magical, Nola was interested in, and cultivated this interest in me. I was her darling baby brother, and she wanted my life to be rich with what was hidden and most inaccessible about the world. In the summer, Nola made a garland of flowers and placed them in my hair, then danced around the yard with me.

She was always telling me stories, Irish folk tales, Tolkien, Greek myths, or we sang folk songs, and even her songs, like her stories, brimmed with possibility — even to say brimmed, suggests a container, but there was none that I could see, none that she would ever tell me of. She learned to make animals out of balloons for me and birds out of paper. She loved transformation. She loved metamorphosis. Everything was changing and vibrant in her world, and she tried to show me that in all she made for me. The most ordinary earthbound thing could be made into something that could fly away.

In 1973, she died.

The last several years of her life were spent in and out of mental hospitals, where she was diagnosed with schizophrenia.

She and I had been close until her illness, but soon I started to detest her. And before I had a chance to grow up, to mature, to understand, she vanished. It wasn't suicide, I was told, though she had tried to kill herself before. It was a horrible accident, a doctor's mistake. He'd prescribed too much Thorazine and her body had shut down, kidney failure. She went into a coma and died two days later.

The Unspoken:

I've never written about my sister, except in the most oblique way. Every time I've tried head-on, I've failed. For some reason, I can't seem to recreate on the page who my sister was. The people I know the best elude me when I try to describe them. My writing friends whom I admire the most are those who seem to be able to write completely recognizable portraits of their sisters, their fathers, their friends. I've never written about my closest living relatives — never touched my brother or my mother, not even in a fictional way, even though I could avoid issues in fiction that I can't avoid in this. I wonder if you can feel bereavement for the living as well as the dead. That's close to what I feel for my brother.

Jonathan boycotted my wedding because I married a woman of Scotch/Irish/German descent, not Jewish. A couple of weeks before my wedding, a rabbi from L.A. called me and told me he was an emissary from my brother. He wanted, he said, to fly to my home and spend a day with me to "tell me the great spectacle of Jewish history."

I thanked the rabbi and told him that the spectacle of Jewish history, while interesting, I'm sure, would not affect the outcome of my marriage. Finally, the rabbi gave up, but before he left me he extracted a promise that I'd tell my brother that he'd tried. For some reason, he also seemed intent that I remember his name, which I repeated three times, like something out of Rumpelstiltskin, and promptly forgot the next day.

I know I have not always been the best brother myself. I have often been neglectful. I never bought him a wedding present when he married in 1980, for instance. I wonder if bereavement and guilt are inextricably linked, if in some way you have betrayed the memory of the one bereaved simply by continuing on your own without them. My brother, who is five years older than me, became my father figure after my father died. I always followed his lead until he chose his Orthodox path. He's hurt me as I'm sure I've hurt him. What hurt me the most was a conversation my mother reported to me last year. She said that she had told Jonny that she wished we could become close again and Jonny replied, "We were never that close." I wondered if that could be true, if my memory could be so misleading — if his version of the truth or mine is the right one, or if the years of silence between us has stolen the truth away from us forever.

Not Guilty:

I try not to feel guilty about any of this, any of these thefts. I've felt guilty in the past, but not now. In a way, I feel proud. I'm telling you, "Look what I got away with." I cheated death. I escaped madness. I stole before I was stolen. I want you to know that this is what it's really about. This is about the stories we're allowed to tell and the ones we lock away. I'm telling you this is what I've become good at. The other morning I saw that word, "Larceny," scrawled in a dream like a film title. The words scrolled in front of me like the beginning of an old movie when they want to establish a different time and place and the only way they can do it is through words, not images: "Paris, 1797. Anarchy reigned in the streets!" But these words wouldn't have made sense to a movie theater crowd, wouldn't have set any scene: "Stolen property. Your sister Nola. A search of many years ensued."

An acquaintance of mine, another writer, recently suggested that all writers should be virtuous. He was drunk at the time, but I'll assume it was an honest sentiment. I guess I don't believe it in any case, at least not in the traditional sense of virtue. Outwardly, I'd like for people to think of me as virtuous, but inwardly, I don't care. There's something inside me that still wants to be the thief, that needs it. For me, the truth is not a matter of virtue. It's something to be stolen, co-opted, appropriated — hot-button words that make the virtuous cringe and yell, "What gives you the right?" The answer is nothing, no right, but what's best about the world did not always spring from the brow of virtue. Pat your pocket. Show me the location of what you value most.

T im McLaurin has won acclaim for his novels, books such as Woodrow's Trumpet and Cured By Fire. But in this excerpt from a new work, The River Less Run, he turns to non-fiction. Setting out on a cross-country trip in a Winnebago with his mother, brother, brother-in-law and two children, he reflects on the meaning of his life — and new intimations that an enemy he has managed to hold at bay might be about to make its return.

Tim McLaurin

Excerpted from
The River Less Run

Through Rapid City, South Dakota, to Mount Rushmore to the faces blasted and chiseled and sanded into the likeness of men now dead. Makes me think of a man in Los Angeles who questioned my license to write about my life for one year; is my chief motivation the need to sculpt my own face and leave that profile in fear that people will forget I lived? Through the Black Hills where the Indians say spirits live, but in this rocking, rolling tribute to the white man, I find it hard to feel the souls of a people who mostly walked and lived in wigwams. Ma needs a Black Hills rock, and at a pull-off, one is added to the collection. We cut through the corner of Wyoming, cross rolling grasslands, cattle country. My brother-in-law Donnie is like a tour guide. Often, he talks non-stop, a monologue rolling off his tongue about where we are on the map, the history of the country we are cutting through, just about anything that happens to be on his mind. I look at Bruce and roll my eyes.

Donnie was born in Broadslab, North Carolina, a crossroads farming community in the eastern part of the state, tobacco farming country, moonshine making country; he talks in an accent that makes mine sound upscale. He is the son of parents who lived their lives as tenant farmers. He told me once that his father went to the store each morning and bought the food they would eat that day, and except for the garden and the yard chickens, no snacks ever rested in the refrigerator or pantry. Unlike most of his ancestors, Donnie graduated high school, then went on to get a technical degree in business from Fayetteville Tech.

"Somebody ought to make another pot of coffee," Donnie declares.

Yeah, somebody ought to, I think. I'm driving, and my brother Bruce just got through driving. Ma is too unsteady on her feet and the kids don't drink coffee. Who is that somebody who ought to make another pot of coffee?

Donnie stares at the coffee maker like he might will it to chug and spit and fill. "Yeah, somebody ought to make some coffee. Tim, you see some buffaloes, I want you to stop. I'm gonna catch me a baby buffalo. Take it back home and put it in the pasture. I ain't seen no buffaloes yet. Ain't seen any niggers, either. I ain't seen a nigger since we stopped for gas in St. Louis. Darlene, you want some coffee?"

Ma starts to grind to her feet, but Bruce slips up and beats her to the pot. "I'll make it, Mama," he says.

"You know, Tim," says Donnie, "that's why the Indians called niggers 'buffalo soldiers,' 'cause their hair looked the same. I don't know how they come to call them that, though, 'cause I ain't seen any niggers out here. No buffaloes either. Plenty of Indians, though."

At the end of a long day of driving, we reach the KOA located about five miles from the Custer Memorial. Hook the Winnebago up again, pitch the tent and blow up the air mattresses. As early as the dawn came, twilight drapes herself even later. Ma limps to the pay telephones to call Kelli, Donnie to call Karen; I remind the kids they need to phone their mother. I realize for probably the first time on a trip, I have no one I am obligated to report my whereabouts to — no wife back home, no steady girlfriend, my children and mother in tow with me. Standing beneath the dome of this big sky, I feel strangely small, as if the life-lines that have always buoyed my journeys have been cut, and I am adrift with only a compass in my hand.

Our campsite is in view of the Little Big Horn River. Studying the light left in the sky, I pull my fly rod and tackle box from one of the storage bins and head for the river bank.

The water is mostly shallow and slow, but I notice darker holes toward the middle of the current where fish have wallowed out vantage points from which to feed. I oil the male joint of my fly rod by rubbing it against the side of my nose, then put the halves together, thread the line through the guides, then start tying a surface fly to the leader. Circles of expanding ripples spread out from where fish are already surface feeding and I hurry trying to knot the lure until I screw up and have to start over again. Slow down, get the knot right, then strip out several yards of line and flip it out. I strip more line and whip the rod back and forth until I can feel the weight, then cast toward the middle of the river. The line lies across the water like a wave cresting in reverse, then flips the leader over and the lure lands gently on the surface like an insect lighting. That's the way it's supposed to be done. When the lure slaps too hard, it scares the fish. Twice I cast, letting the lure float over the circles of darker water.

On the third cast, the lure implodes, and the line goes taunt, and I jerk backwards on the rod; the fish runs parallel to shore. The tip of my rod is bent, and the line is stretched to where it stabs the water. I let extra line slip between my fingers. The fish leaps above the surface, writhing before smacking broadside, a big rainbow trout, his sides irradiating red and brown and ivory. He runs again and I allow him more line, but am worried he might go deep and get tangled in submerged branches or rocks. But I can't fight him in; the leader is only a four-pound test, and the fish looks bigger than any I have caught. Feels like a whale on this lightweight rod. Twice more he jumps, square tail fanning the air; six or seven minutes pass and the fish tires and I am able to land him. He is exhausted, gills heaving, wet sides fracture the sunlight and cast it back in rainbow colors. I grasp him by the lower jaw and lift, and when his mouth opens, I could put three fingers inside. This is a big one!

And I think of him gutted and scaled, sprinkled with salt and pepper and dabbed with chunks of butter and rounds of sliced onion and lemon and wrapped in tin foil and baked till the pink flesh is barely flaky. His eye is black and flat, and I look into it and think of the last squirrel I ever shot.

I was living in the cabin then, would hunt squirrels in the bottom land where the creek flowed. I hunted with a twelve-gauge Remington pump, a big gun for squirrels, but I wasn't in it for the sport. I wanted the meat. One shot would knock the varmint down, and if he still kicked, I'd snap his neck between my thumb and fingers.

I already had four that afternoon, and the fifth I shot at through branches. He fell, but ran dragging one leg into a hole in the base of a tree. I poked the rodent out with my gun barrel, and he ran squealing between my feet. I whirled and shot again, but was short and only mangled his tail. The squirrel stopped and turned to me and stood on his hind legs, silent and motionless and scalded by shot and fire as if he knew that death had come and he wanted to see it in its form. When I pulled the last time, I was only a few yards from the animal, and the blast knocked him through the air several feet and ripped him inside-out, and he was no longer good for living or eating. And I hadn't needed that fifth squirrel; I already had enough for a meal.

And I don't need this big fish in order to eat tonight. Taking a tape measure from my tackle box, I hold the trout by his lower jaw and let him hang, and the tape tips his tail fin at seventeen-and-a-half inches, by far the largest trout I have ever caught. And then I put him back in the water, and he flips his tail and is gone again among the rocks.

A pair of mallards are sitting on shore watching me. I wonder what the drake was thinking as I let that big fish go. Does he applaud me for my grace, or does he think, "You dumb sumbitch. Better fatten up now before the ice comes." I cannot know his mind or if he thinks at all, but I suspect sometimes that any intellect other than my own has more answers to the riddle of creation because my concrete knowledge is nil. Maybe the dragonfly skimming the water moved beyond clothes and cars eons ago, the duck not in need of the Internet any longer, that fish I just released a product of an evolution that has taken him beyond Cablevision and bank accounts and the need of war to ensure such luxuries. And the animals and fish and bugs and plants view humans with disdain and pity at our nakedness and ignorance, their own minds in tune with one infinite, cosmic frequency.

And Saturn shines yellow because of her chemical make-up, and black holes gobble up matter and spit it out into another time dimension, and a seventeen-inch trout will lay thousands of eggs, but maybe one grows into another big trout, and if a Methodist or a Buddhist or an Agnostic catches it, the likelihood of the fish being eaten or released depends mostly upon how hungry the man is.

■ ■ ■

Everyone is tired, and we retire early. Bruce and I talk for a while lying on our beds of air, moon and neon light mixing through the screen windows.

"This feels good, doesn't it," I say to Bruce.

"Yeah. I'm pretty tired."

"I hate you had to drive so much today. You must feel like you're at work."

"Naw. I'm enjoying this."

"I appreciate you coming. I couldn't do this trip without you to help drive and navigate. And keep me from choking Donnie."

Bruce laughs. "He can talk, can't he." He's quiet for several moments. "Donnie is just Donnie. I've learned that. He means well."

"Yeah. You gonna be able to go to sleep?"

"I'll go to sleep sooner or later."

"You want a couple of Valiums? I've got some right here."

"I'll go to sleep all right."

I hesitate a moment, then roll over to where my trousers are and get the pill vial from one pocket. Bruce will never ask for anything. He will give you his last dollar, but he would not ask for a penny even if he was hungry. "Here, take these. Ain't no reason to lay awake."

"I hate to take your Valiums. You'll need them."

"I don't ever take any except when I'm speaking. I got plenty. Here." I put two in his palm. Funny how I always carry a vial of Valium around with me, my security blanket, as if I might be stopped at a highway license check and asked to suddenly stand up and perform.

"Thank you, Tim."

"It'll be good tomorrow. The Custer battlefield is pretty impressive. That hill. Grave markers. You can see how Custer stood there, all surrounded and no way out."

They didn't make Valiums back then.

■ ■ ■

In the light of dawn, I can see against the horizon the hill where Custer and his men gathered. Steam lifts from my coffee, the pink, eastern sky stark against the dark rolling hills. I can't believe how many mornings I wasted sleeping off a pint. And since I talked to Roy, my doctor, a bit more than a month ago, I guess my appreciation of the coming of the light is tempered by my knowledge renewed that the number of dawns is finite.

The sun crests the hill where Custer died, blood red and swollen. I sip my coffee and puff on a stogie, listening to the birds chirp. I'm even more glad I let that fish go yesterday evening. He's probably enjoying this morning just like me.

A blue jay sits chirping from a nearby limb. I wonder what he is thinking or if he thinks at all, if possibly he has lost his mind in the sense of eastern philosophy, no longer ruled by thoughts, but at peace with his mere existence.

I recall a man I did not know, who died of cancer a number of years ago. He was the brother-in-law of a man Katie worked with back when she and I were still married. I heard how in his last days his wife found him each morning sitting in front of the picture window of their house, gazing intently into the world. A hard winter was upon the land, and when I thought of the man, I found the image as chilling as the frost I walked out into each morning. Limited in the sunrises he had yet to observe, the dawn frozen and gray and without colors, weeks from the flocks of robins and daffodils that would crack the ice as the sap flowed northward. He knew he would probably not live those weeks, and I imagined he lamented all that he had not touched and smelled and tasted and heard and seen when the platter had been ripe within his sight and grasp. What a cold way to go out of this world.

But this morning I realize how wrong I may have been. I judged him by the measure of what I still lacked in my life, painted his vision with the textures and colors I wished still to see. This morning I speak for him with this tongue …

■ ■ ■

… This coffee is good, the bitter blended with the sweet, and I drink it slowly and look upon the land that sleeps chilled under a blanket of rest. I have not seen the sunrise as such, the ascending light not hazed by veils of vapor, but rather crisp and crystalline and silver. What I see is not barren. History is only as real as memories, and I have stored volumes behind my eyes. The dawn is like a naked canvas that can be dressed in any cut or shade of clothing, and what I see through this portal, I can clothe with the recall of ten thousand mornings that dawned between the polar ends of chaos and calm. If I am faced with a stark canvas, let me dress it with my recall of what I did not turn from when that moment called. I am the helmsman that steered the vessel between the tides that ebbed and surged twice within each cycle of the sun. The narrow blue passage through rocks with my hand upon the wheel and

tempered with the knowledge of what is right and not right, I slipped between the shards of stone left cracked and rendered by the anger of Moses, learning that no law is etched in stone, but is scribed in a unique cursive in each man and woman's heart.

And by passing within reach of the rocks, did I not hear better the surf and see the sprays of splintered spectrum, and sail within the grasp of that person marooned and drowning? Calmer water would have given more ease of passage, but have also remained solitary and flat.

This frigid canvas is mine for the coloring, and what I bear to the grave will be the portraits of what I did not turn from when the vision of seeing hurt my eyes but held such aching beauty more treasured by the simple truth it would have been so much easier, but emptier, to have simply closed my eyes ...

■■■

This is what I now choose to believe the man saw on those white-cold mornings because I can know only my heart, and these are the pigments I would draw upon in my own last visage of dawn.

■■■

And that hill is impressive in an ignoble way, where Custer and his men fled to the high ground when they realized how seriously in trouble they were. The knob of ground isn't much higher than the surrounding hills, but the earth from it slopes down gently to the Little Big Horn River where the shallow water is shaded with willows and cottonwoods. Bruce and I broke camp and had us on the road before the rest of the troupe had gotten out of bed, and at nine A.M. I'm standing here on the crest, trying to blot out of my mind the other tourists and imagine what it must have felt like on that Sunday afternoon when the Indians were circling and yelling and soldiers were shooting and falling and the air was acrid and blue with smoke.

I never was a Custer fan. He brought death to many Rebel soldiers during the Civil War. He seems also to have caused the demise of about 230 pony soldiers on that Sabbath afternoon when he failed to heed his scouts' reports and military logic and rode into an ambush with two of his brothers and a number of civilians along. He was arrogant and brash and despite the Hollywood version of the battle, an Indian eyewitness said, "It took about as long to kill the soldiers as it takes a hungry man to eat." I do have sympathy for him, though, because he had his brothers with him, and I bet if he was any kind of man, he hated worse than losing his life what he had done to his blood.

A breeze blows up here and the river shines in the distance. A number of white grave markers dot the hillside where soldiers dropped trying to make the water. I think about the squirrel I last killed, how I was as big as an army to the creature, and when it knew there was no escape, it stood at the top of a rise of land and faced me. I like to think that's what Custer did when he realized he was not going to make the river, or the next morning, that he dropped his pistols and stood looking into Crazy Horse's eyes with the sun warm on his hair and his chest bowed out because he knew death had come for him, and he wanted to look it in the eye and not over his shoulder.

That's what I want to do if the myeloma has come back. I'll fight it again — fight it hard — but if I see that I am on a hilltop and surrounded, and the ammo has run out, I don't want to go out scrambling and clawing and lying on my back, all dignity shed and dependent on a machine for my breath.

I think about John Parker, one of my doctors before I went for the bone marrow transplant. About five years after I returned from Seattle, John was diagnosed with lung cancer at age fifty-seven. His brother had already died from the disease. John studied his case and his options for treatment and cure, and decided instead of enduring radiation and chemotherapy to add a few months to his life, he wanted to play his piano and read Shakespeare and drink good wine and die. He did, and the squirrel died facing me, and Custer dropped his guns and lifted his chin, and I ain't dying in no hospital bed. Next year or thirty years from now. Not if I see death coming.

fter graduating from Harvard in 1955, David Halberstam took a job as the lone reporter for the West Point, Mississippi Daily Times Leader. *He later moved on to the* New York Times, *where he covered the war in Vietnam, and then wrote such diverse and widely praised books as* The Best and the Brightest *and* The Children. *This story, written in 1956, was chosen by the author for inclusion here, and foreshadows a Pulitzer Prize-winning career yet to come.*

David Halberstam

"TALLAHATCHIE COUNTY ACQUITS A PECKERWOOD"

A friend of mine divides the white population of Mississippi into two categories. The first and largest contains the good people of Mississippi, as they are affectionately called by editorial writers, politicians, and themselves. The other group is a smaller but in many ways more conspicuous faction called the peckerwoods.

The good people will generally agree that the peckerwoods are troublemakers, and indeed several good people have told me they joined the Citizens Councils because otherwise the peckerwoods would take over the situation entirely. It is the good people who will tell you that their town has enjoyed racial harmony for many years, while it is the peckerwoods who may confide that they know how to keep the niggers in their place; it is the good people who say and mean, "We love our nigras," and it is the peckerwoods who say and mean, "If any big buck gets in my way it'll be too damn bad." But while the good people would not act with the rashness of and are not governed by the hatred of the peckerwood, they are reluctant to apply society's normal remedies to the peckerwood. Thus it is the peckerwoods who kill Negroes and the good people who acquit the peckerwoods; it is the peckerwoods who hang dead crows from the trees of a small town and the good people who do not cut them down.

These are troubled and tense times in Mississippi, and there has been a prevalent you-are-either-for-us-or-agin-us atmosphere. Because of this, much of the silence on the part of the good people can be traced to a reluctance to fall into another and infinitesimal group, the nigger-lovers, and run the risk of social, political, and sometimes economic ostracism. A newspaper editor who had decided to cross the line and challenge some injustices in the segregated system explained it this way to me: "There's only one thing I hate more than a nigger-lover, and that's a nigger-hater, and if it comes down to a choice of the two and I've got no other possible out, then I guess I'll go with the nigger-lovers." Most of the good people would prefer not to have to make the choice at all.

"We'd Like a Conviction"

In Sumner, Mississippi, last month the good people of Tallahatchie County convened to try the case of a peckerwood named Elmer Otis Kimbell for the murder of a Negro. Sumner is the site where another Tallahatchie jury recently acquitted Kimbell's best friend, J. W. Milam, and Milam's half brother, Roy Bryant, of the murder of Emmett Till, a fourteen-year-old Chicago Negro.

Perhaps because Clinton Melton was a native Mississippi Negro, and his death lacked reader appeal (this is the Kimbell rather than the Melton case), the flock of reporters that converged here in September had dwindled to a handful for the March trial. Only one wire service sent a staff member, and the only Mississippi newspaper that sent a man was Hodding Carter's Greenville *Delta Democrat-Times*. Cameras were barred, not only from the courtroom but from the entire courthouse property, and no press table was set up. There were none of the more obvious tensions of the Till trial, at which a defense lawyer privately asked the sheriff to integrate the white and Negro reporters at the same table because of the threatening effect it would have on the jury. "We don't want a press table here this time because the less seen of the press the better because we'd like to see a conviction," I was told by one of the Sumner lawyers who had worked on the Till defense and had turned down the Kimbell defense.

It is clear that many of the good people of Mississippi would have liked to see a conviction. The sentiment was particularly strong in the Glendora community where Kimbell shot Melton and where the deceased and the defendant were well known. Elsewhere in Tallahatchie County, of course, it tended to become the usual matter of a white man and a black man.

Elmer Kimbell, a thirty-five-year-old cotton-gin manager, shot Melton, a gas station attendant, on December 3, 1955. Kimbell claims he shot in self-defense, and displays a shoulder wound to prove it, but his story conflicts sharply with that told by the white owner of the gas station, Lee McGarrh, and McGarrh's story is supported in part by two Negroes.

Kimbell had driven up to the gas station in his friend Milam's car that Saturday night and asked for a tankful of gas, according to McGarrh. The owner told Melton to fill the tank, but a few minutes later, Kimbell, who had been drinking, rebuked Melton, saying he wanted only two dollars' worth. Then Kimbell argued with McGarrh and left, warning Melton, "I'm going to get my gun and come back and shoot you." Ten minutes later Kimbell returned and fired three shots, hitting Melton twice in the head and once in the hand. McGarrh witnessed the entire shooting from inside the store.

Despite his pleas of self-defense, Kimbell was denied bond in two preliminary hearings. At first, the racial overtones of the case were slight, and some of the good people comforted themselves with the thought that Kimbell might almost as easily have shot a white man. As a matter of fact, the case originally attracted attention because of the local reaction against Kimbell: McGarrh became the star state witness, the community raised money for Melton's widow, and the Glendora Lion's Club adopted a statement written by a local minister to the effect that:

"We consider the taking of the life of Clinton Melton an outrage against him, against the people of Glendora, against the people of Mississippi, as well as the entire human family. We intend to see that the forces of justice and right prevail in the wake of this woeful evil. We humbly confess repentance for having so lived as a community that such an evil occurrence could happen here and we offer ourselves to be used in bringing to pass a better realization of the justice, righteousness and peace which is the will of God for human society."

But if Clinton Melton is remembered at all (and already he is a fleeting memory as evidenced by the attorneys' difficulty in remembering his name and their tendency to call him Clement, Melton Clinton, or uh … that boy) it will be because the outcome of this case may have shocked the good people of Mississippi in a more profound way than the killing itself. For there is no out for Tallahatchie and Mississippi in this case.

The N.A.A.C.P., citing claims that it had distracted Till jurors from their duty, stayed tactfully away both before and during the trial. The Northern press by and large restricted its commentary on the case to praise for the progress being made. And unlike the Till case, where evidence was circumstantial and ambiguous, the state had factual authority in the person of three witnesses. Finally, whereas the Till case was seen primarily as an insult to white womanhood by a Negro who didn't know his place, this trial involved the murder of the sort of "good" Negro worker upon which the Southern economy depends.

Tallahatchie County, whose population is more than two-thirds Negro, boasts little industry, outside of an occasional company allied with its agricultural interests. Almost all Mississippi juries are made up almost entirely of small farmers, and this is particularly true in places such as Tallahatchie where there are no cities of more than three thousand. The basic ideology of what has been called the Southern Way of Life is perhaps most deeply engrained in the small farmer, who is closest to the Negro, and who would feel first and heaviest any move on his part toward a more independent life.

Thus the problem that District Attorney Roy Johnson and County Attorney Hamilton Caldwell faced when swearing in fair and impartial jurors was that they were handling a group sworn by birthright to protecting the interest and life of the white. Besides the usual questions, District Attorney Johnson asked the jurors if they could try the case without regard to color. One man rose and said, "No I don't allow as I could," and was excused. His place was easily filled by someone who allowed as how he could, but the wire-service man said he would have made a better juror because at least he was conscious of his prejudice. Ten of the jurors were farmers, one of them worked for a seed manufacturing company, and one sold insurance.

"I'm Going to Kill that Nigger"

The state for its part produced three witnesses. The main one was McGarrh, a stern little man who is a member of one of Glendora's most respected families. McGarrh stuck to the same story he had told at the earlier hearings. He said he saw Kimbell shoot the unarmed Melton. He went unshaken under cross examination. The only weakness in his story is that although Kimbell had given prior warning of his intention McGarrh stayed inside the station with his shot gun. The next witness was John Henry Wilson, a Negro. Wilson did not witness the shooting, but he damaged the self defense theory. He was standing outside the station when Kimbell returned with a gun. He asked Kimbell what he was going to do.

"I'm going to kill that nigger," Kimbell said.

"Please, sir, don't shoot that boy. He ain't done nothing to you," Wilson said.

"Get back or I'll kill you too," said Kimbell. Wilson ran to the back of the station.

The last witness for the state, George Woodson, said he was standing about ten feet away from the scene. He said he saw Kimbell walk around the side of the station with a gun, and that he did not see any gun in Melton's hand.

The plan of the defense, lacking eyewitnesses itself, was to shake the testimony of the state's witnesses. To this end its witnesses came up with only minor points. But more significant than their testimony were their positions — a sheriff, a deputy sheriff, and a chief of police. One of them, former sheriff H. C. Strider, assumed the same role he had played in the Till case as defense witness.

Carl Strider, who owns one of Tallahatchie's largest plantations on which there are seven Negro shacks each bearing one letter on top spelling out S-T-R-I-D-E-R, is not a peckerwood and certainly not a nigger-lover, and in Tallahatchie County it is hard to question him.

Sammy Kimbell, the defendant's thirteen-year-old son, like Milam and Bryant's children in the Till case — and unlike Melton's four children in this case — was seated right at the front in court, and served as a sort of unofficial Exhibit A. He was the next witness.

Now Kimbell had been hunting with his friend Milam that day, had been driving Milam's car, and said that after he was shot he went directly to Milam's house and that eventually Milam drove him to a doctor. Just how he received that shoulder wound remains as puzzling as does the question of what happened to the gun with which Melton is alleged to have inflicted it.

During the cross examination of the boy the district attorney asked Sammy whose car his father had been driving. Discarding his self-consciously slow courtroom manner, defense attorney J. W. Kellum came leaping out of his seat with an objection. Kellum did this because he was afraid that Milam had become a dirty word in Tallahatchie County, where one of the good people can tell you in one breath that that wasn't the Till boy's body they fished out of the river and in the next that Milam and Bryant were the ones who sold that information to the fellow from *Look* magazine themselves. For unlike most of the rest of the state, where William Bradford Huie's article "Approved Killing in Mississippi," drew a reaction aimed only at the magazine, around Tallahatchie and its neighboring counties there was a reaction against Milam and Bryant among the very people who had contributed to their defense fund. Because of this Kellum told me before the trial that this case would be more difficult than the Till case. This accounted for his continued objections to the stream of state questions involving Milam, and for his statement that "these questions were made for the sole purpose of prejudicing the jury." The jury, happily, was not prejudiced. It was sent out of the room, and the judge sustained Kellum's objections.

Milam paid a visit to the court at the end of the first day and I asked him if it were true that in addition to securing counsel for his friend Kimbell, he had, as one of his former lawyers claimed, given Kimbell other financial aid. He caught my meaning and answered, "He's a very good friend of mine, but I didn't get a dime for that article." And without further prompting, he added, "You can look for the cancelled check." Nevertheless, Milam is now driving a new Chevrolet and has fewer friends than he did last September when he had to pay five lawyers.

One more man damaged the self-defense theory during this trial — the defendant himself. Kimbell got up there before those twelve Mississippians and told them a story about his relations with Melton that flatly contradicts all the Mississippi mores. Kimbell told how he drove up to the station, ordered gas, and then changed his mind: "'I wish you'd make up your damn mind,' Clinton told me. I told him that kind of talk would get him in trouble, and he said, 'I'm not afraid of you or any other white son of a bitch.'" Kimbell said he went inside and told McGarrh that Clinton was getting pretty nasty and asked him to total up his account and he'd be back and settle up; when he returned minutes later someone started firing at him, hit him, and he went back to his car and got his shotgun.

Kimbell told this story to a jury which knew that you cannot provoke a Negro attendant to talk like that no matter how much you irritate him, particularly a trusted Negro such as Clinton Melton who had held his job for ten years and handled both money and credit from customers without complaint. He will not talk back, he will just turn away, and sometimes, as Melton apparently did in this case, he will go to the boss for help. And the jury also knew that no white peckerwood gin manager, the best friend of J. W. Milam, would let a Negro talk like that without doing a little whupping right there on the spot. In addition, all of this about Clinton's getting nasty was the first time Kimbell had ever mentioned the threat, and when Hamilton Caldwell, who prosecuted the two earlier hearings, asked why he had failed to mention it before, Kimbell said, "The same questions weren't asked."

Kimbell also testified under cross examination that he had complete confidence in both McGarrh and Wilson and trusted them completely, although they lied on the stand; that he knew of no reason why Melton threatened him; and that although he was badly wounded he drove past a doctor's house on the way to Milam's house, and again by-passed it when he and Milam drove twenty-five miles to Charleston.

The Summing Up

Then came the final arguments. An apologetic Hamilton Caldwell, who knew beforehand that there would be an acquittal, pointed out that he was only doing his job and told the jury that it also had a job to do. "Regardless of whether a man's white or black, you've got to be impartial. A nigger's a human being. He's got life," Caldwell said. "And you know," he added, "that no nigger would call you those things, and you would just walk away."

For his part District Attorney Johnson reminded the jurors that they were sworn to give equal credibility to the Negro and white witnesses. He reminded them that he had lived with Negroes a long time, that no Negro is going to get up there and call a white man a liar unless there is pretty good reason. He said that he was doing this for their own protection, and that it is a serious thing when a citizen of Tallahatchie County and Mississippi disregards the law. Where that happens, he said, you find a degenerated society. He knew the problem that the jurors who agreed with him faced, so he emphasized that it was important that they stand by their convictions and resist the influence of their fellow jurors and neighbors. He said he was going home with a clear conscience, and he invited them to join him.

J. W. Kellum, the defense attorney, is very tall, with a craggy sort of good looks. He would like to be eloquent, and he has a habit when he speaks of emphasizing a word that has no business being emphasized. Although he lost the runoff contest for district attorney to Johnson last August, he will probably not lose any elections for a while in the future. "You have a noble opportunity for democratic service," he told the jurors in a summation almost identical with the one he delivered at the Till trial. "You are the custodians of the American civilization." And he wound up with, "This boy was born thirty-five years ago into the land of the free and the home of the brave, and where under God's shining sun is the land of the free and the home of the brave if you convict him on this flimsy evidence?" Then he handed the jury Kimbell's bloody shirt, and the jury retired.

It took four hours and nineteen minutes to break down those members of the jury who had misgivings about the whole thing. Another case, having to do with cow poisoning, was heard while the jury was out.

The reporters sat around and talked and some said there would be a conviction, and I said there would be a hung jury, and one said he didn't know. One wonders just how deeply the jurors thought about how their decision might establish a precedent for future juries — just as they faced the Till jury precedent. I think the fifty-eight Negroes who sat quietly in the crowded courtroom were thinking about it, and I think that the few merchants sitting around were worrying about it. The merchants know that although this was a good year for cotton, business was poor in the area because the Negroes are either shopping in the hill section of the state or leaving the state completely. The merchants know what the result of this trial will be — the Negroes will not write impassioned letters to their Senators or the newspapers, but they will very quietly stop hanging around the stores on Saturdays, and business will get worse.

On the other hand, I suspect that the jurors who may have had misgivings were thinking that they had to go on living in the county, and how could they explain any other verdict to the neighbors, particularly if word got out, as it undoubtedly would, about who the two or three men were who had hung the jury? Elmer Kimbell was protected by the system whose rule of paternalism he violated. None of those jurors would kill a man, but they could not give Melton, even in death, equality with Kimbell. That would have meant that they gave credibility to the Negro witnesses, and it might have meant that they were nigger-lovers, and that they were agin us.

So the jurors walked in and announced their verdict and filed up one by one and shook hands with Kellum. Elmer Kimbell, found innocent, told the reporters that he was relieved because he had been pretty worried, and it was the first time I had heard of an innocent white man worrying about a case involving a Negro's life. Then Kimbell asked the deputy sheriff for his gun back, and now he can go hunting again with J. W. Milam for squirrel and God knows what else.

"Maybe We've Made a Start"

The immediate reaction in Tallahatchie County among the sort of people who issued the Glendora Lions Club statement was one of discouragement. "There's open season on the Negroes now," one man said. "They've got no protection, and any peckerwood who wants to can go shoot himself one, and we'll free him. Our situation will get worse and worse."

That may be true, but perhaps in the acquittal of Elmer Kimbell there is a lesson which may jar Mississippians and eventually make the situation better. I talked with one newspaperman in a neighboring county who said, "This is just what we needed for our own good. People here underwent all that criticism before, and some of it was unfair, and they hardened and became convinced that they were right and everyone else was wrong. All they could talk about was the racial problem in Chicago and Detroit, and they looked at the one new Negro school in their city and they boasted of the virtues of separate but equal. They forgot about the five or six broken-down shacks out in the county with one room and no electricity and the fact that we are a long, long way even from separate but equal. We became very defensive and stopped criticizing ourselves — our politicians and newspapers lulled us along because it got so tight you couldn't talk, and you still can't talk (don't use my name). A lot of it was the Till case when we went through a lot of undeserved attack. Well, everybody looked at this case beforehand and said, 'Here's where we show them what we're really like.' But we had forgotten what we're really like and how far we had to go, and the fact that you can't put one value on a Negro three hundred and sixty-four days a year and then raise him up equal in court. This case will hit people. It hit me. And when we look around for some place to put the blame, well, there's only ourselves. And even if we don't do our blaming out loud it will change what we think inside a lot. What's also encouraging, I think, is that a lot of pro-integration people up North who were pretty militant a while back are beginning to realize the problems involved, and that'll make things less tight. Well, if we can get them to that point and then get our own people to a point where they realize that these problems not only exist but must be faced, then maybe for the first time we've made a start. If Kimbell had been given twenty years for manslaughter we'd have been more self-righteous than ever and gone right back to our old ways of thinking."

Kimbell's acquittal may have encouraged the peckerwoods, but I'm pretty sure it has troubled a lot of the good people. And that, after all, may be a step in the right direction.

*W*riting with toughness, candor and a fundamental fairness, Gail Sheehy has made her mark during the past thirty years as one of the premier reporters of our time. In her latest book, Hillary's Choice, she explores the "complex and contradictory love story" of Bill and Hillary Clinton. This excerpt is the first chapter of her book.

Gail Sheehy

"INTO THE FLAMES"

Excerpted from
Hillary's Choice

These two people are intertwined on every level, as a man and woman, as friends, as lovers, as parents, as politicians. This is a love story.

— Linda Bloodworth-Thomason

When under siege she rises early, dresses quickly, and cauterizes her emotions. The bubble of anger rising from her gut will remain level. Head must be separated from heart. Of necessity, given her station in life, she will summon her apolitical Washington hairstylist, Isabel, to blow, wax and spray her expensively blonded hair into an unflappable helmet. She does not read the newspapers. Or watch TV. She does not want to know any more about her husband's scan-

108

dalous behavior than she absolutely has to know.

This morning, Tuesday, January 27, 1998, scarcely a week into the firestorm of accusations about a President and a dark-haired intern in an unforgettable beret, she does not worry about makeup. The *Today* show's makeup artists are able to make a tense First Lady took serene (or, a year later, a vampy intern look like a proper author). It is five in the morning and Hillary Rodham Clinton paces around her suite in the Waldorf-Astoria, priming herself for yet another crucial television appearance that will either pull Bill Clinton out of a nosedive or help ensure a crack-up. Dark smudges beneath her eyes belie her apparent equipoise. She joins her chief of staff, Melanne Verveer, and rides stoically across Fifth Avenue, arriving at NBC's Rockefeller Center studio. Anchor Matt Lauer, who was called back from vacation when the story broke, has the outlines of a scandal that already sounds like the finale of the Clinton Show.

At 6:55 A.M., between promos and airtime, Lauer dashes up to the makeup room to greet the First Lady. She is warm, though some tension is detectable in her demeanor. That's hardly surprising. In the six days since the sex-and-lies scandal broke, the face of Monica Lewinsky and a few squirmy denials by the President have occupied the first half hour of all the morning TV shows and carpeted the cable shows wall to wall. Is there anyone in America who has not heard accusations that the President enjoyed sex sessions in the White House with an intern barely older than his daughter and then told her to lie about it?

This twisted fairy tale has already captured the imagination of the public. Characters outrageous and grotesque are emerging. The plotters appear to be two older unmarried women, dead ringers for Cinderella's ugly stepsisters: Linda Tripp, an older coworker of Monica's, who coached the intern to narrate the whole sordid affair, and Lucianne Goldberg, a politically zealous literary agent who urged Tripp to tape her chats with Lewinsky in hopes of getting a hot book out of it. There are twenty hours of audiotapes.

And there are other shades of Nixon's Watergate beyond tapes, including a faithful secretary who is said to have provided cover for the President's frequent sexcapades. There are tortured definitions: Lewinsky claims Clinton wanted oral sex because he didn't count that as adultery. There is name-calling: Monica refers to the President as "the Big Creep," Lewinsky's lawyer calls the President a "misogynist." The *New York Times* reports that Monica is prepared to testify that she did have a sexual relationship with the President, provided she is granted immunity. Late-night talk shows are already lampooning the new souvenir of an Oval Office visit: a semen-stained dress.

With this flood tide of titillating and damning detail washing over Washington in only the first week, Bill Clinton's official stance is to be "outraged" by the allegations: White House insiders describe him as "freaking out." "I don't think there was a person in the White House who gave him a snowball's chance in hell, except Hillary," a former official later told *Time*. And congressional Democrats are not rushing to stand by their man.

Hillary Clinton stands alone, prepared to fight.

The First Lady tries to paint a very different scene, one in which she and Bill Clinton appear the homiest of characters. Up in the second-floor bedroom of their residence, the husband had awakened his wife the previous Wednesday morning, January 21, and said there was something he had to tell her.

"You're not going to believe this, but ..." he said, bewildered.

"What is this?" she asked sleepily.

"... but I want to tell you what's in the newspapers."

That is how Hillary describes on the *Today* show learning from her husband that their enemies were trying to bring them down with yet another preposterous scandal. She makes the dialogue sound so innocuous, it evokes images of that widely loved comic-book couple, Dagwood, the greatest victim of circumstance the world has ever known, and Blondie, who always comes to his rescue, rather than what it was — the President's first mention to his wife of explosive sex allegations that he knew were about to break in that morning's *Washington Post*. When Hillary labors to make the First Couple sound like just plain folks, there is almost always more to read between the lines.

GAIL SHEEHY

In fact, the *Post's* meticulously reported story reads like a compilation of the greatest-hit scandals of the Clintons' six years in office: reckless sex, a suicide, easy lies, cover-up, betrayal of the President's friends and aides, and a looming shoot-out at the OK Corral with his nemesis Kenneth Starr. The special prosecutor named in 1994 to investigate the collected allegations known as Whitewater, Starr was suspected of being in cahoots with lawyers for Clinton's other accuser, Paula Jones. For the past week Starr had been raining subpoenas on Clinton's people. In sum, there was enough ammunition to blow sky-high everything that these two bright stars of their generation had struggled to achieve since they had first met at Yale Law School twenty-eight years before.

On *Today*, Lauer astutely points out that the President has described to the American people only what this relationship was *not*. Has he described to his wife what it *was*?

Mrs. Clinton stammers a bit: "Yes. And we'll — and we'll find that out as time goes by, Matt. But I think the important thing now is to stand as firmly as I can and say that, you know, that the President has denied these allegations on all counts, unequivocally, and we'll — we'll see how this plays out."

During these onslaughts, the Clintons — united professionally — can hide for days behind their public faces. Even from each other. "Being in the White House when a crisis blows is like nothing else," recalls the President's former press secretary Dee Dee Myers. "This type of siege is like World War I to the Clintons," elaborates Dick Morris, the strategist who, upon Hillary's command, engineered Clinton's greatest comebacks. "They're in the foxhole. Shells are bursting all around. The two of them against the world. If your buddy does something stupid ... you allow yourself maybe a moment of 'Schmuck, what did you do that for?' But there just isn't a whole lot of time to allow yourself the luxury of reacting to things personally."

For this crucial interview Hillary has chosen the battle camouflage of a dark brown suit lightened at the neckline with a twist of seed pearls. A large presidential eagle brooch is pinned to her chest like

111

a general's medal. Her lips are precisely outlined, as are her thoughts. "Everybody says to me, 'How can you be so calm?' or 'How can you just, you know, look like you're not upset?'" she says. "And I guess I've just been through it so many times ..."

Has she become numb to this kind of scandal?

Mrs. Clinton says, "It's not being numb so much as just being very experienced."

But a couple of minutes into the interview her anger begins to simmer beneath the surface. She is asked about the gifts her husband allegedly gave Monica. She refuses to comment on "specific allegations." Her voice turns brittle. She tries to change the subject to "the intense political agenda at work here." Lauer promises to let her talk about Kenneth Starr in a moment. But first, has she ever met Monica Lewinsky? Mrs. Clinton vaguely demurs. Well, then, did her watchdogs at the White House ever come to her and say, "We may have a problem with one of the interns at the White House," and mention Monica Lewinsky?

"No," she says.

In fact, the First Lady herself had recommended the young woman for an internship as a favor to a heavyweight contributor, Walter Kaye, who was also a friend of Monica's mother. But Hillary was no fool. She had installed in the White House a handpicked Warden of the Body, the President's deputy chief of staff, Evelyn Lieberman. This short, stern, fiftyish woman, known as the "Mother Superior of the West Wing," went back with Hillary to their working days at the Children's Defense Fund. Lieberman took her role as chief enforcer very seriously. And out of the whole class of four hundred interns, she had spotted Monica early on. This one was trouble. Classic Bill bait. Fleshy with big hair and hydraulic lips swabbed with lipstick over the lines — a shoulder-baring, switch-hipped exhibitionist who came on just like Gennifer Flowers, just like Virginia Kelley, his mother, the template for most of Bill Clinton's temptresses. The Mother Superior caught Monica hanging out in the hallways near the Oval Office and reprimanded her: *Get back to your post.* But Monica was what staffers call a "clutch." She had pushed up front in every Rose Garden event and tried to cling to the President to get in the picture, and with his ready cooperation, she had. Lieberman had reassigned Monica out of the White House. But had it been soon enough to prevent an "improper relationship" with the President?

Lauer poses a hypothetical question: "Let — let me take you and your husband out of this for a second ... if an American president had an adulterous liaison in the White House and lied to cover it up, should the American people ask for his resignation?"

The question takes Hillary by surprise. She slides away from it: "Well, they should certainly be concerned about it."

Lauer goes after it again: "Should they ask for his resignation?"

"Well, I think — if all that were proven true, I think that would be a very serious offense." Suddenly she is transformed from Blondie into the chief attack dog for Bill Clinton: "That is *not* going to be proven true."

Lauer later told me, "I felt this was a woman who knew there had been trouble in the past and who was believing, and hoping against hope, *not again.*"

■ ■ ■

The story of the Clinton presidency has always been the story of the Clinton marriage. Would Bill Clinton have become President without Hillary? Would Hillary Rodham have become one of the most remarkable women of our century without Bill? Although they have been on the public stage for a quarter century, there is so much we don't know about either of them. That is the complex and contradictory love story this book seeks to unravel, and beneath it, to find the cords that have created the unique political texture and tensions of our times.

The saga of Bill and Hillary, with its echoes of Eleanor and Franklin, or Tracy and Hepburn with undertones of Bonnie and Clyde, is animated by melodrama, high passion, narrow escapes, and knock-down-drag-outs. Never more united than when they are battling adversaries and displaying their ferocious tenacity, the pair cannot resist a spitting match or all-out political war. His recklessness and her eagerness to step in and save the day have created a dynamic of crisis (his) and management (hers). They have always seemed to thrive on it.

Every time he goes down, she rears up and turns into a lioness, tearing into the political veldt to rip the flesh off their enemies. Bill Clinton, whom a former presidential adviser describes as having "the passivity of a Buddha" during a crisis, characteristically sits in a huddle of legal experts and flak catchers as Hillary lays down the battle plan. "He's like the little kid who's been told to go to his room," says a former Democratic political appointee who knows the Clintons. "Mom will handle everything. Knowing that the little kid will probably screw up again, even if she hides the cookie jar."

The costs of sustaining this volatile political partnership have been high, but the benefits over the past thirty years have also been high. Hillary's disowning of her private circumstances allows her to be First Lady, where she wields tremendous political power without electoral accountability. She is in a position to open up all kinds of private and non-governmental avenues to do the good things she believes in for children, parents, the poor, the protection of women against violence — the list goes on and on. To Hillary Rodham Clinton, these are the most important things.

And one more thing. She gets to keep Bill.

"I think she's in love with this guy" is the nearly ubiquitous refrain of their friends and advisers, although most admit that they are mystified by the dynamics of the Clintons' relationship. Until this grand episode, their friends had idealized their marriage. "Most of us have thrown in the towel," says the movie actress Mary Steenburgen, a friend of the Clintons. "These people didn't. It's exciting to be around them and to see how it can be to be a married couple." Another member of the "Arkansas Diaspora" in Los Angeles, television producer Linda Bloodworth-Thomason, is one of Hillary's most loyal intimates. "These two people are intertwined on every level, as a man and woman, as friends, as lovers, as parents, as politicians," she says. "This is a love story."

How emotionally dependent is Hillary on Bill Clinton? I asked her former mentor, attorney Bernard Nussbaum, in the Year of Monica. "I think she needs him desperately," he replied. "And I know he needs her desperately." In 1998, however, Hillary paid more than she could ever have anticipated for choosing to stay with Bill Clinton.

Now Hillary leans into the *Today* show cameras, her head bobbing for emphasis as she cleverly shifts the story line: "I do believe that this is a battle. ... The great story here, for anybody willing to find it and write about it and explain it, is this vast right-wing conspiracy that has been conspiring against my husband since the day he announced for president." She fires off a threat: "When all of this is put into context ... some folks are going to have a lot to answer for."

Lauer brings up painful history: "The last time we visited a subject like this involving your family was 1992, and the name Gennifer Flowers was in the news ..."

HILLARY: Mm-hmm.

LAUER: ... and you said at the time of the interview, a very famous quote, "I'm not some Tammy Wynette standing by my man."

HILLARY: Mm-hmm..

LAUER: In the same interview, your husband had admitted that he had, quote, "caused pain in your marriage."

HILLARY: Mm-hmm

LAUER: Six years later you are still standing by this man, your husband ...

HILLARY: Mm-hmm.

LAUER: If he were to be asked today, Mrs. Clinton, do you think he would admit that he again has caused pain in this marriage?

HILLARY: No. Absolutely not, and he shouldn't. You know, we've been married for twenty-two years, Matt.

And then, with an utter certainty that few married men or women could muster, Hillary Clinton declares that she and her husband "know everything there is to know about each other."

But this time, she didn't know everything.

Cleaning Out Closets

Ten days before her *Today* show appearance, Hillary's husband, the President of the United States, denied under oath having had sexual relations with Jane Doe No. 6 (Monica Lewinsky). That was the weekend when lawyers for Paula Jones, a low-level state employee who was suing the President for sexual harassment in an incident at an Arkansas hotel seven years earlier, at last had their chance to confront him. Paula herself would be there.

In a highly unusual courtesy, Susan Webber Wright, the federal judge from Little Rock who was presiding over this tortured case, had flown in to Washington to act as a mediator. Like just about everyone else in a high position in Arkansas, Judge Wright had a connection to Bill Clinton, having been a student in his admiralty law class at the University of Arkansas Law School back in 1974. His laxity had already come up against her astringency. Clinton had been an absentee professor, more interested in his own campaign for Congress than in monitoring his students. When he lost their final exam papers, he offered to give them all a grade of B. Susan Webber refused; she preferred to take another exam to uphold her A average.

Throughout the six-hour deposition on Saturday, January 17, the President sat eyeball to eyeball with his former student, now a stout, scholarly Republican judge with a proper southern demeanor. As described by a Little Rock public defender, "She'll tell you, in a very ladylike way, she's going to throw you in the slammer forever."

The Jones lawyers began questioning the President at 10:30 in the morning, but for almost two hours they never mentioned Paula Jones. They wanted to know about a slew of other women, starting with Kathleen Willey, a volunteer who claimed the President had groped her outside his office. Not long into the deposition, the Jones lawyers gave Clinton what friends call his "Oh, shit" moment.

One or two questions about another woman, a twenty-four-year-old White House intern from Beverly Hills, dragged out into fifty questions on an exam for which he was totally unprepared. For once words failed him. His voice grew inaudible. How did they know about the phone calls and the gifts, even the Walt Whitman poetry book and the Black Dog T-shirt, for God's sake? Had Monica talked? He thought her testimony denying their affair was a done deal, but one of the questions during his deposition left him with grave doubts:

"If she told someone that she had a sexual affair with you beginning in November of 1995, would that be a lie?"

"It's certainly not the truth," said the President. "It would not be the truth."

And then they went after him about Gennifer Flowers. Now he knew he would have to go home and tell Hillary, tell her something, before he telephoned his good-ol'-boy friend Vernon Jordan and arranged to meet his loyal secretary in the office to rehearse their story.

On the Saturday evening of the President's marathon six-hour deposition, the First Couple had planned to take Erskine Bowles and his wife out for a celebratory dinner. It was to be a special thank-you to the President's new chief of staff, who, together with his wife, had wanted to postpone their move to Washington for another year but who, of course, had been seduced by Bill Clinton. The dinner was also apparently meant to counteract any impression that the President's forced deposition had shaken up their lives.

The Clintons never made it. Except for a visit to church on Sunday, they remained in seclusion until Monday. The wind had been knocked out of Bill Clinton. He is a man who hates confrontation and who is uncomfortable in any situation he doesn't control. Monica had not been granted immunity, that he knew, but what the devil had she told Starr and his henchmen in her now-sealed deposition? It was Hillary who almost immediately went into full battle mode. She granted several radio interviews that Monday in the map room at the White House. Although garbed in a bold plaid suit, she was pale, her voice was nasal, and her eyes seldom met those of the interviewer.

"Can I ask you, uh, how difficult a day Saturday was for you and your family?" inquired reporter Peter Mayer.

It "wasn't difficult for me," the First Lady said. On Saturday "I just kind of hunkered down and went through my household tasks. Then my husband came home and we watched a movie and we had a" — she pauses and shrugs while searching for the appropriately innocuous phrase — "a good time that evening."

"And Sunday?"

"Oh, we just stayed home and cleaned closets."

Another folksy image: Hillary as the dutiful homemaker whose husband comes home on a Saturday night wanting nothing more than a good video. In fact, that was the Saturday night Hillary Clinton cleaned *his closets.*

The Dress Rehearsal

She is angry. Not all of the time. But most of the time.

Those were the notes I made after I first met Hillary Clinton. It was an earlier January morning, in 1992, the day after her famous "I'm no Tammy Wynette" appearance on *60 Minutes* to defend her husband, then the Democratic presidential front-runner, after his first national sex scandal had exploded. We met at Little Rock National Airport. Hillary was glowing. Her mother, Dorothy Rodham, had vetted me, and I was granted rare access. For several days I flew knee to knee with Hillary in her six-seat chartered plane, observing as she fashioned the strategy (as Bill Clinton later acknowledged) to bring him "back from the dead."

I watched the Hillary iconography emerge. Voters seemed to accept her take-charge confidence. But there was a shadow. Many Americans I talked to even then seemed to feel she had sacrificed something, some human part of herself, in order to persuade us to vote for her husband. There was, and there remains to this day, a nagging suspicion about Hillary's motives and her marriage. We didn't know then that she was a woman with a secret, a wife experienced at drawing the draperies around her husband's demons.

During downtime in a motel in Pierre, South Dakota, I watched as Hillary flipped on the lobby TV and was suddenly faced with Gennifer Flowers playing tapes of her steamy calls to Governor Clinton. Hillary's eyes took this in with the glittering blink of a lizard. Not a tremor of emotion crossed her face. Nothing personal.

"Let's get Bill on the phone," I heard Hillary order her teary-eyed male campaign manager. But Clinton, according to Hillary, said he wasn't concerned. Throughout the scandal Clinton behaved as if this problem were all about somebody else, not Bill. "Who is going to believe this woman?" he told his wife. "Everybody knows you can be paid to do anything." (*The Star*, a supermarket tabloid, had paid Flowers for her story.)

"Everybody *doesn't* know that," Hillary snapped. "Bill, people who don't know you are going to say, 'Why were you even talking to this person?' "

Those who encounter the Clintons are always struck by how tough Hillary is on Bill. "But the more you see them," observes a former adviser, "the more you get why she withholds the approval that he seems to need, at times desperately." Hillary, adds the source, "has never held Bill accountable" for the transgressions that have rocked their lives. "She is in a perpetual state of suspended anger because of all that she has absorbed."

An hour after giving Bill his slap on the wrist, Hillary — soft and feminine — entered Pork Producers Rib Feed in Pierre. She was all smiles until her campaign manager whispered, "All three nets led with Flowers." That's when I first saw the battle mouth. Hillary's lower lip juts out while the top one pulls tight. It is the look of a prizefighter with his mouthpiece stuffed in. In the plane I listened as Hillary rehearsed a retaliation: "In 1980, the Republicans started the negative advertising. In 1992, we have paid political character assassination. What Bill doesn't understand is, you've gotta do the same thing: pound the Republican attack machine and run against the press."

We had scarcely bumped down through the black hole of the

Dakota night before Hillary, coatless, was clicking across the field toward a shack with a sign that said "Rapid City." She demanded a phone for a conference call: "Get Washington and Little Rock on the line." George Stephanopoulos and the other baby-faced boys were about to be "inspired" by the candidate's wife: "Who's getting information on *The Star?* Who's tracking down all the research on Gennifer?"

In an earlier aside she had seethed to me, "If we'd been in front of a jury ... I would crucify her."

Her. Not him. Never him.

The Need to Know and The Fear of Knowing

So into the flames Hillary strode just as always. It was Hillary who made the first call, on the morning the *Post* story broke, to establish the line the White House would use. Her chosen interlocutor with the President was Sidney Blumenthal, a wily former journalist who had ingratiated himself with the Clintons during the 1992 campaign by writing puff pieces for *Vanity Fair* and *The New Yorker.* After the election he had "gone inside" to become a presidential adviser. Blumenthal liked to think of himself as the most trusted messenger across the often choppy channel between the President and his wife.

The First Lady told Blumenthal she was distressed that the President was being attacked, in her view, for political motives — for his ministry to a "troubled person." She said that the President ministers to troubled people all the time. She made it even more specific, saying that he had done this same thing dozens, if not hundreds, of times with troubled people (an interesting, perhaps Freudian, slip, since Clinton told Lewinsky he had had hundreds of women in the past). He was a compassionate person, Hillary emphasized. And he helped people also out of his religious conviction. "It was just part of his nature."

Those who defend Hillary believe she was given an account similar to the one that her husband gave Blumenthal later that day: The intern was going through a tough time. It got out of hand. She came on to him, but he told her he couldn't have sex. "I've gone down that road before," he said. "I've caused pain for a lot of people, and I'm not going to do that again." Monica had threatened to say they'd had an affair. She told him, he said, that she was known as a stalker.

The story Bill Clinton carries around inside his head is that of the victim. He feels like the character in the classic Arthur Koestler novel *Darkness at Noon*, he told Blumenthal, "like somebody surrounded by an oppressive environment that was creating a lie about him." That novel depicts the far more nightmarish politics of Stalin's purge trials in Moscow. Its hero is an aging revolutionary, a disillusioned Communist having an affair with his secretary; he is imprisoned and tortured and pressured to confess to preposterous crimes. He is a victim of larger political forces. And Clinton can probably make himself believe that that is he.

Hillary's friends say she believed Clinton had done something inappropriate with Lewinsky and that she would hold him accountable for it — later — but the enormity of it, the sordidness, the fact that this was a *relationship*, hadn't entered her realm of thinking at all. The most painful revelation would not come for months: Her husband had sent her out into the world to lie for him, to risk her own reputation. Not only had he betrayed her, he had used her.

One reason Hillary Clinton is able to maintain her momentum is that she imposes a PG rating on the news digests her staff prepares for her: no sex, no late-night-talk-show gibes, no facts about scandal that might distress or distract her. Hillary is not a news junkie like her husband. She would rather review reports on HMOs than wallow in tabloid or television accounts of her problems. Clinton's veteran chief of staff Betsey Wright later said jokingly to me, "Hillary Clinton is probably the only person in America you could tell a cigar joke to and she wouldn't get it."

Hillary carefully censors what she says about Bill — even with her own mother, Dorothy Rodham, who lives in a condo in Little Rock co-owned by Hillary and often listens to right-wing talk radio. She is not permitted to give interviews. I was able to engage her in a conversation in the fall of 1998.

"I don't talk to Hillary about anything deeply personal concerning her marriage," Dorothy Rodham told me. "We don't sit down and have those mother-daughter discussions about how she relates to her husband, her daughter, or anything else as far as her personal life is concerned. We don't talk about deeply personal things."

Exposed only to her own censored views, Hillary was able to convince herself that Monica Lewinsky's story was a flat-out lie. Mandy Grunwald, who had served both Clintons well during the 1992 campaign, talked to Hillary's staff before the *Today* show appearance to warn them, "Here's what's out there, for those of you who don't read newspapers." Grunwald told me her friend was "completely unfazed by it all — *at that time*. In her mind, there was no difference between Filegate, Travelgate, Paula Jones, and Monica: they were all just more of the same political charges that the Clintons have to deal with."

Why worry about this Monica Lewinsky anyway? She was obviously just another Bill-struck "rodeo queen"; that's what Hillary and Betsey Wright called all those Arkansas bimbos who came at him with the same matted hair and the same starstruck eyes when Bill so much as squeezed their arms. But given all that Bill depended upon Hillary for, they knew that no other woman could measure up.

Let the War Begin

The official declaration was left to Democratic pit bull James Carville to snarl on Sunday, January 25, on *Meet the Press*: "There's going to be a war" — a war between "the friends of the President and the independent counsel ... between these scuzzy, slimy tactics of wiring people up, of getting them in hotel bars and threatening to arrest their parents." Carville was referring to Kenneth Starr's co-opting of the Paula Jones sex hunt into Clinton's private life; the fact that Starr had used Linda Tripp to lure Lewinsky into a meeting at the Ritz-Carlton, where the perfidious friend had taped their incriminating conversation; and the fact that he had threatened to force Monica's mother to testify against her own child. But in defending the President, Carville could only repeat the President's rote denials:

"He has denied it to his staff, has denied it to the news media, has denied it to the American people, and denied it to his Cabinet and denied it to his friends."

Hillary was the one person who saw a larger story, a grand narrative in which her husband, the softhearted victim, was being persecuted by a modern-day Inspector Javert from *Les Miserables* who would pursue his miscreant into the sewer. Hillary's reasonable fury at Clinton for having jeopardized their life's work and, even worse, having handed their nemesis a silver bullet, was transmuted virtually overnight into venom-tipped arrows aimed at that mutual enemy, Ken Starr. He had been chasing the Clintons since the summer of 1994 — almost four years now. This was the Alamo. She was up against the prissy prosecutor who had challenged her integrity, had found her fingerprints on every alleged Clinton misdeed, had forced her to face a "clusterfuck" of cameras staked out to record the first appearance of a First Lady before a grand jury. However bilious the shame she had to swallow, it was nothing compared to the specter of being beaten and driven out of the White House by her personalized enemy.

She demonized Starr (with his help), transforming him into a gruesome recreation of J. Edgar Hoover by reminding people how disgusted they had been to learn, years after the fact, that Hoover had wiretapped Martin Luther King, Jr., and spread stories about his sex life. How could the country sit by and allow a right-wing political zealot to perform a sting operation on a sitting President and to hunt down every friend and relation of his from Washington to Arkansas?

Strangely enough, it seems it was something of a release for Hillary in those first weeks to have the accusations against her husband as ammunition to strike back at the man who had made her life miserable.

It was Hillary who brought back the old gang, lawyers Mickey Kantor, Harold Ickes, and Susan Thomases, who had been key figures in several campaigns; Hillary who shook up the defense team, advancing her law school classmate David Kendall over Bob Bennett;

Hillary who summoned Harry Thomason (the husband of her best friend, television writer-producer Linda Bloodworth-Thomason): "Harry, you've got to get to Washington right away — everybody around here is crying and helpless." She wanted Harry to help coach the President on how to be more convincing in his denials; he had sounded too wimpy in his first interview, with Jim Lehrer on *The NewsHour.* When Clinton looked into national TV cameras on January 26 to give his famously defiant, finger-wagging performance — "I did not have sexual relations with *that woman* ... Monica Lewinsky" — Hillary stood beside her husband, sunny in yellow, and nodded her head.

It was Hillary's idea to set up an information control operation out of the Democratic National Committee. The effort, paid for with Party dollars, would send their friends and political acquaintances "distilled information" to counter the confessions of "shock," "disappointment," "disgust," and "dismay" being offered in TV interviews by some of their closest former lieutenants, including George Stephanopoulos, who dared to use the "I" word. On Hillary's side of the White House the word "impeachment" was struck from the vocabulary. Instead, by February 1, she was saluting new polls that showed the President's popularity reaching new heights. Her surrogates warned darkly of a "day of reckoning" for foes of the President and for news outlets that ran unconfirmed reports about his private conduct.

The Family that Denies Together ...

A major soft spot in their defense remained. It was personal. It was Chelsea. Their beloved daughter, their best thing.

Little had been allowed to take precedence over Chelsea for either Clinton. When Hillary was making frequent trips between Little Rock and Washington to carry on her public service career, baby Chelsea was the girl who would wait up for the Governor. The Governor took the time to practice the piano with her. The Clintons rarely went out together alone as a married couple. And they almost never took a vacation without their daughter. They had a spectacu-larly healthy, happy, attractive, and to all appearances well-adjusted teenager to show for it. Chelsea already had her first serious boyfriend, Matthew Pierce, a champion swimmer and upperclass-man at Stanford University.

Chelsea was summoned home from Stanford on Friday, January 30, only two weeks after having spent Christmas with her parents. Who was going to tell her, and what? Hillary wanted to help prepare the nineteen-year-old girl for the rough days ahead. God knows, she had done it before.

Hillary's pastor, Ed Matthews, the now-retired minister of First United Methodist Church of Little Rock, agonized for Chelsea each time he read about another of the scandals produced by her father. Reverend Matthews had first become alarmed in 1990, shortly after Hillary had sought him out as her pastor. He came out of church one Sunday to find under his windshield a vulgar drawing of Bill Clinton's private parts. The flyer, which also implied that Clinton had sired children with black women, was affixed to all the cars out-side the church. Matthews was appalled. He had Chelsea Clinton in his confirmation class. The more he thought of the governor's vul-nerable twelve-year-old daughter and those vulgar drawings, the more puzzled he was: *How on earth do these parents explain all this? Chelsea will be going to school tomorrow.* So that night Matthews called Hillary and posed the question: "How do you help Chelsea deal with this?"

He remembers Hillary telling him how the Clintons had handled it in the past, starting when Chelsea was barely six. "The two of us sat Chelsea down and let her know that there were people who don't know the full truth of things, and they make things up and they gos-sip. But we know the truth of this story."

Matthews was not fully reassured. A reflective man who, at sixty-four, is involved in voluntary ministries building houses for low-income families, he confessed in a conversation with me in 1998 that he was mystified by how the Clintons handle all the public and pri-vate aspects of these scandals: "I've marveled at it long before all this current ugliness came to be. There is something almost superficial or synthetic that seems to be what ultimately binds this family together. It's hard for me to imagine what's bubbling underneath all that."

This time Hillary would force her husband to take some responsibility for his actions. In effect, she told the President there was no room in their White House for cowards: *You* take your daughter to Camp David for the weekend, and *you* explain it to her yourself. *I'm* going to Davos.

It was after the Monica story broke that Hillary decided to accept a last-minute invitation to address what an aide calls "the creme de la creme of the world" at the World Economic Forum in Davos, Switzerland. Davos gave her something else to think about. There, in the Swiss Alps, she would look out on an audience of two thousand global power brokers: presidents, prime ministers, CEOs of multinational corporations, Nobel Prize winners, academics, and media moguls. She was accustomed to looking powerful men straight in the eye.

While the President struggled at Camp David to find the words to keep his daughter's trust, the First Lady reminded the world of her own commanding voice. With her presidential eagle brooch clamped at her neck on a collar of pearls, Hillary Rodham Clinton delivered her vision of priorities for improving the state of the world in the twenty-first century. She challenged the leaders to invest in education and opportunities for women and to share their wealth and power. Her twenty-minute address, delivered without notes, was, according to Jim Hoge, editor of *Foreign Affairs*, "beautifully phrased" and "her manner was that of someone at the top of her game." After a standing ovation, a top Democratic Party leader from Hillary's home state of Illinois was moved to political lust. "That's our winning candidate for the Senate," he said.

Somebody else said, "Are you serious?"

The official didn't hold back: "If we could get rid of the kid [Bill Clinton], I'd run her in a minute. Nobody could beat her."

The official had the wrong state but the right instinct. A personal scandal that would have silenced most spouses in shame or self-loathing seemed only to empower and energize the President's wife. Professionally, Hillary was on top.

There was no need to tell Hillary Rodham what Hillary Rodham already knew about Bill Clinton — that her husband had a long history of reckless infidelities. But there was a great deal more that Hillary did not know at this point, that she might never have had to face if not for special prosecutors or the triumvirate of Hear Evil (Linda Tripp), See Evil (Lucianne Goldberg), and Speak Evil (Matt Drudge). The dark side of her husband's soul was not a territory she cared to explore any more closely than was absolutely necessary for their political survival.

And so, just as countless times in the past, *Hillary's choice* was not to know what she knew.

*V*elma Barfield killed her first husband by setting his bed afire as he slept in their home in Robeson County, N.C. She later killed her second husband, her mother, two elderly people for whom she worked, and her fiancé, all with arsenic. Sentenced to death, she underwent a religious reformation in prison that gained her the support of many prominent people; the fight to save her life brought international attention. On November 2, 1984, she became the only woman to be executed in the United States between 1962 and 1998. With the meticulous reporting that has become his trademark, Jerry Bledsoe recreates the last minutes of her life.

Jerry Bledsoe

Excerpted from
Death Sentence: The True Story of Velma Barfield's Life, Crimes, and Execution

Carol Oliver, captain of the guard, was in the control room when the telephone rang at 1:10. The tension was so great, the silence so eerie and foreboding that the sound startled her and she jumped before she reached for the receiver.

"You have fifteen seconds," she heard a voice say.

Oliver hurried into the death-watch area and strode determinedly to the open door of Velma's cell.

"Velma," she said, "it's time."

Velma stood. So did Rae McNamara, the director of the Division of Prisons, who had come to keep her company. For a moment nobody said anything. Then Velma turned to McNamara.

"Do you think it would be all right if I wore my robe?" she asked.

"Sure, Velma," McNamara said.

Velma pulled on her robe, and after pausing at the mirror to check her hair, she stepped through the doorway, freeing herself from prison cells forevermore.

■■■

A ghoulish party atmosphere had taken over among the death penalty supporters alongside Raleigh's Western Boulevard. Chants broke out sporadically. "Down with Velma! Up with victims!" "Burn! Burn! Burn!"

A steady stream of cars crept past, some drivers honking horns, some occupants whooping and hollering.

"Give her a shot!" came the shout from one car. "Hang the bitch!" a young man yelled from another.

"There are a lot of creeps around here," observed John Snow, a North Carolina State student who stood with the death penalty supporters. "This isn't a public hanging, but it's pretty close. She could be hanging from a tree right over there," he said, pointing to the trees on the prison grounds where the silent vigil keepers stood.

■■■

Warden Nathan Rice was waiting at the open door of the death-watch area as Velma exited her cell. Carol Oliver walked alongside Velma, Rae McNamara behind. At the door, Rice directed Velma to the small preparation room, only a few feet away on the left.

The gurney standing near the center of the room had been covered by a pale aquamarine sheet, its corners tucked in neat military folds. Velma stopped by the gurney, removed her robe and handed it to Oliver. She stepped out of her scruffy blue bedroom shoes, and Oliver stooped to pick them up.

"Thank you," Velma said.

The gurney was too high for Velma to climb onto easily, and guards reached to help her.

Carol Oliver left for the adjoining parole hearing room, the staging area where the rest of the execution team was waiting in strained and solemn silence.

Velma's friend and minister, Phil Carter, the chaplain at Women's Prison, sat beside Skip Pike, the Central Prison chaplain, each with Bibles in hand, places marked. Oliver knew Pike well and she noticed that he seemed more ill at ease than she had ever seen him. Her heart went out to him, but everybody in the room felt a professional obligation to keep emotions to themselves. Carter was nervous, too, worried about what he would say to Velma. As he fidgeted, he couldn't take his eyes off the "crash cart" parked near the door. A crash cart normally was loaded with life-saving paraphernalia and was used in hospitals, rushed to patients in crisis. But this one carried the syringes filled with deadly chemicals that soon would take a life.

■■■

One of the vigil keepers standing on the hillside in front of the prison was Mattie Lewis, a laundry worker from Winston-Salem, who had switched shifts with a fellow employee so that she could be there. "I was determined to come," she said. "I was determined. I don't think no man has the right to take another's life."

Not far away stood Wade and Roger Smith, brothers and prominent lawyers in Raleigh.

"You can't just stay home," said Wade Smith, a leader of the state Democratic Party, an attorney who had defended Green Beret doctor Jeffrey McDonald in his widely publicized trial for the murder of his family. "You don't know what to do."

Roger Smith had been among the anti-death-penalty protesters outside the capitol when Governor Jim Hunt had returned to his office Thursday afternoon.

Wade Smith looked at his watch. It was 1:35.

"I guess she's strapped on the gurney by now," he said. "She's awake, conscious. I wonder if at this point anyone is talking to her? Isn't it incredible that there's a human being in there with twenty minutes to live? Could there be anything more — more premeditated and deliberated?"

■ ■ ■

Somebody was indeed talking to Velma. Phil Carter had just begun to read to her from Romans 14: "For none of us liveth to himself, and no man dieth to himself.

"For whether we live, we live unto the Lord; and whether we die, we die unto the Lord: whether we live therefore, or die, we are the Lord's.

"For to this end, Christ both died, and rose, and revived, that he might be Lord both of the dead and the living."

His voice was breaking, and there were moments when he wondered if he could go on, but he did.

Pike had entered the preparation room first, Carter close behind. Velma was covered by a second sheet that reached nearly to her neck. She was wearing her big glasses with brown, speckled frames, and her hair was perfectly coiffed. The saline solution was already flowing into her veins in both arms from I.V. bags mounted on the gurney. Velma smiled when she saw the nervous chaplains.

"Mrs. Barfield," said Pike, "Phil and I would like to share these words from the Scriptures."

Because he'd known Velma for such a brief period, Pike wanted Carter to have most of their time. He read from Psalm 21, then prayed that God would hold Velma gently through her journey. When he finished, he later recalled, she smiled and looked him straight in the eye.

"She spoke very directly," he said. "She said, 'Thank you for the kindness you've shown me and for the times you've shared God's love with me.' She said, 'I know you are filled with the Spirit. I could tell by the way you prayed the first time you prayed for me.' I said, 'I just try to serve the Lord.' She smiled again and said, 'Chaplain Pike, God's people are the bestest kind.' It just blew me away."

Pike stepped back, and Carter moved into his place. He would never forget how fearful he was of losing control, but he kept telling himself that he had to hold together.

One look at her, he would later recall, told him he would do it. "She had a glow on her face. She looked to be at utter peace. She smiled at me. She said, 'Well, it'll soon be over. I'll be in a better place and I'm glad.'"

"The kids send their love," Carter told her.

"They're great kids," she replied.

He opened his Bible and began reading from Romans 14.

■ ■ ■

Two guards escorted the witnesses from the ground floor conference room to the elevators for the short ride up one level to the execution chamber. The official witnesses numbered eight, all law enforcement officers except for two assistant D.A.s. Four witnesses had been chosen by press organizations to represent the media. Velma's appellate lawyer, Jimmie Little, and her friend Anne Lotz, the daughter of Ruth and Billy Graham, were there as well, witnesses out of love.

The view offered by the witness room window was plain and grim. The chamber had six walls, none more than six feet long, all of them at odd angles. Against the parallel wall from the window was the dark-stained oak chair with its gruesome leather straps that had been in the service of death by cyanide gas since 1936, although nobody had died in it for more than twenty-two years.

Two rows of numbered blue plastic chairs had been set before the window for the official witnesses. Those seated on the front row would be no more than three feet from Velma.

The witnesses began entering the chamber at 1:40. With the two guards who would remain with them, the group numbered sixteen. The official witnesses took their assigned seats. The media witnesses stood behind them with Jimmie Little and Anne Lotz, who held hands.

The lights in the witness room were turned off so that the only illumination came through the window from the chamber. The effect was that of a movie theater, the chamber window serving as the screen, only the people inside would be real, and the action deadly.

Later, Anne Lotz, who did not think of herself as a witness but as a friend standing by a deathbed, would remember thinking how small and sterile the chamber seemed. She had to keep reminding herself that what she had told Velma was true: that it really was the gateway to heaven.

"It didn't look like the pearly gates," she said, "but it was. We just couldn't see the other side."

■ ■ ■

In the preparation room, Phil Carter had just finished reading Scripture. He shut the Bible and began to pray.

"God receive this our sister. We love her. Forgive her. Be with her children and comfort them and help them know the peace that only can be found in Thee ... "

He prayed at length, and when he had finished, he put his hand on Velma's shoulder and searched for the right words to say.

"You've touched a lot of peoples' lives," he told her — and felt the sudden tap on his own shoulder, telling him that time was up — "and you've changed many of those lives forever."

He wouldn't realize the double meaning of those words at the time, but he knew from Velma's answer that she understood them as he meant them, that the lives she'd changed in recent years had been for the better.

"To God be the glory," she said. "God did it all."

■ ■ ■

"We've got to go," he told her, letting his hand linger just a moment more, absorbing her warmth.

She thanked him for the worship and love they'd shared, for the times he'd sneaked her into the chapel against the rules, for the times he'd listened patiently when she'd been upset.

"I'll see you in heaven," Carter told her.

"I'll be waiting for you," she replied, and smiled for the last time, a smile that Carter would carry with him forever.

■ ■ ■

As soon as the chaplains departed, Nathan Rice stepped back into the preparation room. This time he carried a battery-powered mini-cassette recorder.

"Velma, if you would like to make any final statement," he said, "this is your opportunity."

"I would," she said, and he pressed the "record" button and held the device close to her mouth.

Her voice was strong and did not falter. "I want to say that I am sorry for all the hurt that I have caused. I know that everybody has gone through a lot of pain — all the families connected — and I am sorry, and I want to thank everybody who has been supporting me all these six years.

"I want to thank my family for standing with me through all this and my attorneys and all the support to me, everybody, the people with the prison department. I appreciate everything — their kindness and everything that they have shown me during these six years."

She paused, then said no more.

"Is that all?" Rice asked.

She nodded.

■ ■ ■

For some in the witness room the wait seemed interminable. The heat was stifling, the tension intense, the silence unsettling, broken only by the sound of somebody shuffling feet, shifting in a chair, clearing a throat, and by a guard near the door who kept nervously jangling the change in his pocket.

Then at about 1:50, the big locks on the chamber door began to turn. Slowly, the door swung outward and open, and for the first time the witnesses caught a glimpse of Velma.

A uniformed guard stepped to the end of the gurney where Velma's head lay. Velma turned her head for a quick glance into the chamber, then looked away, and the guard began to steer the gurney toward the door. A second guard appeared at the foot of the gurney, the two maneuvering it carefully past the chair into the suddenly cramped room.

■ ■ ■

Black open-ended rectangles painted on the floor marked the spots for the gurney's wheels. And as the guards guided the gurney alongside the window, Velma turned her head toward the chair and closed her eyes. The guard at the foot of the gurney stepped back. The other guard moved around the head of the gurney and took hold of a beige plastic curtain hanging from hooks on a steel rod that stretched the length of the chamber, sixteen inches below the ceiling. As he departed, he pulled the curtain out to its full length, leaving the gurney sandwiched between the curtain and the observation window. A slit in the curtain made it possible for technicians to reach through to the I.V. leads.

Velma's breathing seemed rapid and shallow. Her neck muscles looked tight. She licked her lips, swallowed a couple of times, kept her eyes closed. The witnesses saw the curtain billow as the crash cart was moved into position behind it. And in the staging area, the three executioners were given the go-ahead to take their positions in the chamber.

Velma's breathing returned to normal as the minutes ticked by and the witnesses became more uncomfortable watching her final moments of consciousness. Suddenly, the door of the witness room opened startlingly and Nathan Rice stepped inside.

"Everything is ready," he announced briskly. "I will make one call. Then the execution will proceed."

Rice went quickly to the control room and dialed the number of the secured line to the secretary of the Department of Correction.

"We are ready to proceed with the execution," Rice told James Woodard. "Are there any final orders?"

"There are none."

■■■

On the knoll outside, people kept looking at watches. At 1:58, somebody among the vigil keepers started humming. Others joined in. It was almost imperceptible at first, but it spread quickly, growing louder and louder with each new voice, and within a minute the whole crowd was in unison, and there was no mistaking what they were humming: "Amazing Grace," Velma's favorite hymn.

As the final seconds until two o'clock ticked down, the death penalty supporters across Western Boulevard began a countdown, as if it were New Year's Eve.

"Ten ... nine ... eight ... "

■■■

The curtain behind Velma rustled as technicians disconnected the lines from the saline bags and attached them to the lines leading to the three big syringes that lay atop the crash cart, then quickly exited the chamber.

The three executioners stood ready, their thumbs on the plungers. One of the three entwined lines leading from the syringes was a dummy that went to an I.V. bag hanging beneath the gurney, leaving each executioner the option, if he needed it, of believing that he might not actually be responsible for taking a life.

■■■

In the office of a deputy warden a floor below, Velma's former minister, Hugh Hoyle, who had come from Kansas to comfort her, sat in a small circle with Velma's son, Ronnie, her daughter and son-in-law, Pam and Kirby, two of her attorneys, Dick Burr and Mary Ann Tally, and her friend Jennie Lancaster, the warden at Women's Prison. Hoyle read some of Velma's favorite Scriptures, prayed for deliverance for all, gave all a chance to speak what they wanted to say about Velma, and all the time Ronnie had been watching the big round clock on the wall. He looked up in dread and fear just as the minute hand flicked to two.

"Let's all join hands and bow our heads in silent prayer," Hoyle said.

Ronnie already was holding the hand of his sobbing sister, Kirby the other, her head on his shoulder. Ronnie took the hand of Jennie Lancaster beside him and closed his eyes. He was wondering what his mother was feeling, what she was thinking. Surely, she was praying, he thought, but what was her final prayer?

■ ■ ■

Nathan Rice nodded to the executioners and said, "Velma, please start counting backward from one hundred."

"One hundred ... " Velma said.

■ ■ ■

" ... two ... one!" shouted the death penalty supporters alongside Western Boulevard, and broke into cheers.

"Kill!" somebody yelled.

"Die, bitch! Die!"

Across the road, the vigil keepers began extinguishing their candles one by one, breath by breath, front to back, their hymn dying voice by voice. As the last candle went out, a bell rang full and sonorous, the mournful sound lingering in the damp, chilly air.

■ ■ ■

In the witness room, everybody saw Velma's lips moving and several later would say they assumed that she was praying.

" … Ninety-six," she was saying, "ninety-five, ninety … " and her voice drifted away, stilled at last by drugs.

She began snoring loudly, although none of the witnesses could hear her.

The three executioners stepped back. The technicians returned, quickly removing the syringes the executioners had laid on the crash cart and replacing them with others. As the technicians exited the chamber again, the executioners picked up the new syringes and simultaneously pressed the plungers. Afterward, they returned in solemn procession to the staging area. Nathan Rice followed them out of the chamber, but he went to the control room, where Dr. E. Scott Thomas, the prison physician, sat before the heart monitor.

■ ■ ■

Velma's breathing had been deep and regular. The witnesses, not knowing when the paralyzing poison had been administered, watched the green sheet rising and falling, rising and falling, looking for a sign of ebbing life. But her breath diminished so minutely each time that it was hard to tell. Her cheeks had been rosy when she had been rolled into the chamber. But now the color faded with each breath, a pallor gradually taking its place, starting at her forehead and moving downward. A fly buzzed by her head, then disappeared from sight.

Later, none of the witnesses could be exactly certain when the green sheet rose and fell for the last time, for the movement had simply seemed to slip away, imperceptibly.

At 2:10, the line on the heart monitor in the control room went flat. Nobody made any overt movement. Regulations required a five-minute wait before the body was examined.

■ ■ ■

On the floor below, at precisely 2:10, Hugh Hoyle later would recall, Mary Ann Tally looked up at him and said, "Did you feel the release of Spirit that I just felt?"

"I did," Hoyle said. "Praise the Lord."

■ ■ ■

The vigil keepers on the hillside stood in a hush broken only by the soft weeping of a few, a whispered prayer here and there. Even the death penalty supporters across the road had fallen silent.

A *nchorman-turned-novelist Robert Inman interviewed Walter Cronkite*
at Novello and tapped into the wisdom and perspective that made
Cronkite arguably the most admired journalist of our times. Inman's
remembrance of Cronkite below is followed by a spirited conversation in
which the two journalists exchanged ideas on a variety of topics — includ-
ing the shortcomings of television news. For this anthology Cronkite reflected
on that conversation, and in this expanded version, he elaborates on some
of the issues that are most meaningful to our generation.

Walter Cronkite

"A REPORTER REMEMBERS:
A CONVERSATION WITH ROBERT INMAN"

The first time I met Walter Cronkite was in the CBS newsroom in New York
in the early '80s. My co-anchor at a Charlotte television station and I had
been dispatched to film promotional announcements with Cronkite, whose
network newscast followed ours. He was gracious and affable, willing to take
time from a hectic news day to visit with the local guys.

I was impressed by his candor about the limitations of the medium we
worked in. No one, he said, is a well-informed citizen if he or she depends sole-
ly on television for news. He gave television great credit for its immediacy, its
emotional impact, its ability to put us on the scene of events large and small,
to give us the "who, what, where, and when" of news. But, he said, it's not
so good with the "how and why."

Television depends on pictures, and pictures are usually only part of the
story, maybe even a minor part. There is a context to everything that happens,
and often, the context is more important than what happened. Walter
Cronkite tried mightily to provide context when he edited and anchored the
CBS Evening News. *He was honest enough to say that he was only partly*

successful.

Despite the limitations of television, Walter Cronkite had perhaps more impact on American life than any other journalist of the twentieth century. I think of it as the "Cronkite Century," because he lived through most of it and saw it from a special vantage point. He began his career as a newspaperman in Houston, went on to cover World War II and Moscow as a United Press correspondent, and joined CBS in 1950. He has known the famous and infamous, has been present at the great events that shaped the world we know today. Thus, he brings a unique perspective to any view of the century's legacy.

During the thirty years he covered the news for CBS, he came to be known as America's television uncle. When he reported on the news of the day, you could count on knowing what was important and why. By doing his job accurately and fairly, he built up a reservoir of trust that any journalist would covet. What Uncle Walter told us on any given night might be bad news, but we left with the impression that bad things pass and that we would not only survive but endure.

One reason Walter Cronkite was so successful, so respected, so cherished by America is that he's a natural-born storyteller. After all, that's what the news is: stories. They're about people who are doing things, thinking things, that the rest of us need to know about. Uncle Walter had — still has — an eye and a nose for the human story behind any event. He was at his best when asking penetrating questions of the people who made news, and always doing it in a civil manner.

Today, at age eighty-three, he retains the sharpness of mind and wit that he brought to the CBS Evening News *all those years. He was in rare form as we talked about the legacy of the twentieth century before a large and appreciative audience at Novello 1999.*

The Interview

INMAN: The biggest thing that happened in this century was World War II, and that's where you cut your journalistic teeth. Reflect on what that meant to you as a young man and what kind of impact the war had on the lives not only of the people who participated in it, but all of us here today.

CRONKITE: Well, personally, I have to believe that I was something of a war profiteer. I was a twenty-four-, twenty-five-year-old reporter. I was doing pretty well with the United Press. I had moved into the New York office and was working on the foreign desk at the United Press after several years of other assignments in the country. When Pearl Harbor came, I shipped out pretty quickly as a war correspondent assigned by the United Press to the Navy to cover the battle of the North Atlantic. I rode the convoys in that critical year of 1942 when it seemed we were losing the war to the German submarine packs prowling the Allied lifeline between the States and Britain. The toll they were taking of our merchant ships was terrible.

The opportunity to be a war correspondent made a career. If I had been a soldier, I certainly wouldn't have had the opportunity for all those by-lines. So in that sense I was a war profiteer as were all of us war correspondents.

As atrocious as was the war, there was a certain benefit for the country as a whole. For one thing, it was a great unifying effort for all of us, coming after the bitter years, the Depression particularly. That decade of the '30s was a disastrous period for the United States and the rest of the world. As the war came we still were not coming out of the Depression despite the Roosevelt New Deal. We were still suffering a great deal of uncertainty that the slight rise in economic activity was going to last.

World War II gave us a common purpose. We had a common enemy. We were a united nation as we seldom had been before. There was very little objection to our getting involved in World War II. There were the America Firsters, the isolationists, a tiny band compared to the conviction of the overwhelming majority that Hitler had to be put down. During the Vietnam War we were a divided people. Well, believe me that wasn't the situation in World War II.

But whatever the side benefits of World War II they were gossamer thin compared to the war's tragedy — the millions of lives lost, families disrupted, ancient treasures lost.

I realize as we come to this event, the end of one millennium and the launch of another, I have always been an optimist. I really always thought that humankind was smart enough to, for heaven's sake, get a handle on violence and conquer whatever it is in our genes that gets us in trouble.

But I'm afraid I'm turning into a pessimist as I contemplate the millennia, the thousands of years since we came out of the caves and dared to call ourselves civilized. We still believe that the best way, the final way to settle an argument is to kill each other. What kind of civilization is that? Why is it that humankind has not put as much emphasis in achieving peace as we spend in preparing for war? The U.S. defense budget approaches 380 billion dollars. How much do we spend on peace? We don't even pay our dues to the United Nations.

INMAN: There has been a lot of talk recently about a new spirit of isolationism in America, especially in the Congress. There is a lot of concern about that. Does it worry you that we seem to be pulling in, and that some of us would like the rest of the world to go away and leave us alone?

CRONKITE: Oh, absolutely. Although I don't think the last part of that applies any longer, I mean, the world going away and leaving us alone. We are accepting that we are the leaders of the world and we should, therefore, act like the leaders of the world for peaceful purposes. We should be very careful, however, exceedingly careful, of being a little too arrogant with that power we have, as the dominant nation in the world, the strongest nation in the world. The really only strong nation in the Western world today.

And I worry about the quickness with which we have begun to use weaponry to try to enforce our belief of what is right. I even worry about the strikes against Afghanistan and the Sudan and chasing down Mr. Bin Ladin, the terrorist, with Pershing missiles and guided bombs. And getting so deeply involved in Iraq. We have got a running war there. We are bombing almost every day. It is so routine we don't even report it in the newspapers or on television anymore. I am not saying that is not justified, I am just adding that to the litany of our willingness to go to weaponry to try to solve our problems.

And of course, the same is true of the Kosovar situation. It seems to me that we may be getting a little too quick in using our superiority of arms. And failing to go to the negotiating table in attempting to solve these problems.

INMAN: When you were anchoring the evening news you and your colleagues started a series of reports called "Can the World Be Saved?" which was about the ecology, the environment. And it occurs to me looking back on that, it was a real sea change in America's awareness of our environment and the threats to it. What do you think the impact was?

CRONKITE: We started it because I read Rachel Carson's *Silent Spring*, as many of us did. And I was tremendously impressed by it, and concerned, and began doing my own research on our polluted atmosphere. And I realized suddenly that there was a lot out there that we weren't telling people. So we devised this series called "Can the World Be Saved?" in which we pointed out the dangers of pollution in its many forms — pollution of the seas, pollution of the air, pollution of our food stuffs and so forth.

I was very proud of that series because I felt we helped incite the environmental revolution.

INMAN: Are you an optimist or a pessimist about the environment and about our awareness of it and what we are doing to correct some of the ills of the past?

CRONKITE: The awareness is there, I think, on the part of the American people generally. The problem is, of course, the vested interests — particularly those whose machines and factories create most of the problems. Those in the central Atlantic and northeastern states are particularly affected. Just look at the beautiful North Carolina mountains. The west side of those mountains are all defoliated by pollutants from the factories in the middle West. It's pretty evident what is happening, but the vested interests deny that. They simply don't believe it or they won't admit it. It's a little bit like the tobacco industry in some ways. They denied the poison in their product until the facts faced them down.

Am I optimistic or not? I am optimistic that we are moving ahead in all countries. The countries of Western Europe seem to be moving faster than we are. I am worried that we are not moving fast enough. I think that the terrible floods and rains you have had here in North Carolina are part of the whole global warming picture. Not all scientists agree with that, but it seems to me almost obvious. The numbers are worse than even the pessimists had predicted just a few years ago, the speed with which the temperature is going up. I think we are in some considerable danger.

INMAN: One of the big stories that you reported on, and naturally one that we were interested here in the South, the Carolinas, was civil rights. Certainly during your time at the anchor desk, you saw a lot of change in America, but it seems that we are still struggling and agonizing with this business of how we get along with each other across racial boundaries. We are particularly interested in that in Charlotte right now as we consider the future of our public schools and the post-busing era.

What is your advice to Charlotteans and Americans about dealing with the issue of how we get along?

CRONKITE: Well, I think we ought to do it.

[LAUGHTER AND APPLAUSE]

Really, I meant that to be a little amusing. But also, it is probably the answer. Just do it. I think we have come a long way in this generation, a very long way. I am proud of what we have done in America. But still we haven't finished the job. We haven't really achieved complete integration of the races. Perhaps we never shall. It is likely, I would think, that there will always be some recognition that you are different than I am and so forth.

There is growing evidence of an inclination on the part of people of each of the races to associate with their own kind first. I did a documentary with the Discovery Channel a little while ago on reverse segregation, trying to put the question of whether Martin Luther King's dream and other dreams of total integration were possible. We have seen this in quite a few communities in the United States, particularly in Washington where there are a lot of very well-educated African-Americans in our government and elsewhere. It turns out that as they achieve financial success, they start returning to their own communities and build their own suburban communities. There is a lovely African-American community in Maryland on the outskirts of Washington.

It is a reaction to the fact that they never felt that they were completely welcome in the white community. I don't know what we have to do to make them feel welcome. And I don't know whether we are welcome entirely in their community. I would like to think we were. I don't see how we ever really achieve total integration until we are comfortable with each other.

I think in business, the comfort is there. I think where there is a direct relationship, the comfort is there. It still does not seem to be totally socially comfortable. And I don't know the answer to that. I think we just keep on, getting back to my original remark, just do it. Just keep on working at it until it works.

One thing we have got to do, we have got to be absolutely sure in every way that there is equal opportunity for all in this country. We cannot in any way go backwards in that regard. It seems to me that this is particularly true in schooling. We have to be sure that everybody has the same educational opportunity. That not only applies between races, it applies between economic groups as well. I worry a great deal, a very great deal about the widening chasm between the poor and the rich in the United States, and particularly in regards to the computerization of the society.

You know, we in the more economically stable groups, our children have access, most of them, to a computer at home as well as the computers they share at school. Many of them have more than one computer at home. And yet in the poorer side of our population, they don't have that opportunity. They don't have computers at home. I am talking about the really poor. I am talking about Harlem, I am talking about Appalachia. There are not computers in many of those homes. That widens the gap of possibility. The future is, obviously, going to be locked into the computer and its successors and rapid communication.

The poor are locked out. We have got to do something about that.

I don't know what the answer is, except I would like to see the Bill Gateses of the world (and he does give computers), I would like to see him get involved with the libraries. Let him be the Carnegie of the next millennium. Establish computer centers in every under-privileged area. Maybe not just computers centers, but give comput-ers to kids in those areas.

You know, a recent speaker of the House of Representatives, Mr. Gingrich, had some good ideas that he expressed badly at times, but one of the things he said was that we should give a computer to every child in America, and he was just laughed out of court. That was a very sound idea.

He also said that children should be taken from their homes and placed somewhere where they would have a chance at life, and everybody immediately hopped all over him, visualizing the mean orphanages of old. But Gingrich wasn't so far off on that. I believe he meant that we should expand day care to the degree that every little child in the underprivileged areas of this country is taken into an establishment of some kind for a few hours a day; a loving place where they get constant attention, in an environment where they have a chance to learn, to play with educational toys, to look at nurs-ery books, even just to hear English spoken properly.

If we are going to lift our population up, we are going to have to give those people a chance as well. And it's not just a humane thing to do, it is in our best interest to do so economically and socially. If we don't do it, we are going to create a situation where revolution is not an impossibility in this country. We worry about people being armed to commit crimes; what if all those people that are armed in the underprivileged areas suddenly find a leader who directs them toward revolutionary violence to get what they would like to have, but they are not able to earn? We better be careful.

INMAN: Why has it been important for us to go to space?

CRONKITE: Because it's there.

INMAN: There had to be something in it for all of us — not just those astronauts or the people at NASA, but for all the rest of us.

CRONKITE: We originally began to think it was a necessity to go into space because of military reasons, the fear that if the Russians did it and we didn't do it, they would control the globe by being able to bomb from space and spy from space, that sort of thing. So there was a space race, which was part of the Cold War. I don't know how long it might have taken us to spend that kind of money to get into space in a peacetime situation, maybe never. But I would like to think we would have because it is a challenge. Humans, fortunately, are curious about their world. Fortunately they always want to explore, they want to look around the next corner and look over the next mountain. We want to look out and go up to space.

So under the pressure and the political advantages of the Cold War, Kennedy was able to proclaim the program that we would go to the moon. It was a terribly expensive effort. The day we landed on the moon, CBS News stayed on all day. We interviewed two or three people who were critics, even in the exultation and excitement of man landing and walking on the moon. They asked why were we spending this kind of money when there were so many demands on earth? Schools, housing, the usual things, food. And it is true the question about the priority. But I think it has paid off and I hope it continues.

I personally think that we should probably be putting more of our space money into robotic exploration today than into manned exploration, but we should not drop manned exploration. We are committed to build the space station now, and that will be highly advantageous and important — a very expensive piece of equipment out there, but one with limitless possibilities for improving the lives of us earth dwellers. We will be able to learn more about the use of space in medicine, for instance. We have never been able to create weightlessness on earth. But all the doctors agree that one of the greatest problems with seriously burned victims, is that there is no way to relieve them from having to rest somewhere on their terrible burns and these become infected with dire results.

If we could take serious burn victims out to space, for instance, into a gravity-free environment, their recovery might well be enhanced, and heart patients might find advantages to a space sojourn. The theory is that their hearts could rest with the comparatively easy work they would have to do in gravity-less space and the patients' recovery would be more likely. As well as the health advantages there are other intriguing industrial possibilities. Like making perfect crystals or ball bearings. And if you make perfect ball bearings, you can perhaps achieve perpetual motion. Yes, a whole new world certainly will open up when we can live and work in the weightless environment of space.

INMAN: But you think the greatest advantage is simply man's spirit of quest? Just because it is there and because it expands our horizons and our minds?

CRONKITE: Absolutely. And of course, it served a very definite purpose in the 1960s, the most terrible decade, the most divisive decade of this century — with the civil rights problem, Vietnam, Watergate, the assassinations. We were a divided and fairly pathetic people, really, for much of that decade. But what we had was the successes in space. And you might say it was the glue that held us together at a time when we seemed to be coming apart.

INMAN: Looking back on the America that you have seen in times of crisis and in times of plenty, what is it about us Americans, about us as a nation and as a people that gives you optimism that we might do okay in the future? What are the characteristics, the qualities of Americans that you think are our strongest points?

CRONKITE: I think that the principal characteristic is a very seldom expressed, but true belief in our democracy. And understanding that there are times when we must put aside all of our quibbles or arguments and join together in the common effort to make this democracy work. When it comes time of crisis, serious crisis, wartime crisis for instance, domestic crisis, we pitch in. We cooperate, we work together.

I hope we haven't lost that. Sometimes one gets discouraged, in peacetime, with the quarrels and quibbles that keep us from doing what would seem to be right.

INMAN: But you think we have got those kinds of qualities that, if 1941 happened today, America could respond in the way we did in 1941?

CRONKITE: Without a doubt. When we have an enemy as clearly defined as Hitler was, I don't think there is any question that we would rise to the occasion. Vietnam destroyed a lot of confidence in this country and I hope we get it back. Unfortunately, the generation that knows how we responded in World War II is passing. There are not many of us old codgers around anymore. Vietnam was a case where the motive of our being there was never fully explained to the American people. I think it was right that we went there at first to help with instructors and others, to help the South Vietnamese put together an army that could defend against the encroachment of communism. This was the last bastion of any hope of democracy in Southeast Asia. The whole rest of that part of the world had gone communist. If we were to save a foothold in Southeast Asia for democracy, we had to help the South Vietnamese create a democracy. They didn't have one.

What happened was we failed to get the South Vietnamese government to come along and do its part. And we kept sending in more and more troops, trying to defend against the ever-increasing pressure of the communist forces. Ho Chi Minh had developed a following that really believed in the communist mission. The people of North Vietnam were motivated.

The South Vietnamese had no motivation whatsoever. They were drafted, put into the army, expected to fight their brothers coming down from the north, and they really didn't understand that they hadn't had a chance to learn about democracy. They had never lived in a democracy. They were fighting for a series of monarchs, and then presumably elected but actually self-appointed generals running the country.

Here we were fighting their war for them. And it divided America. Our draft didn't operate fairly. We drafted the poor kids who couldn't get into college, couldn't afford to go to college. It was a very divisive situation.

INMAN: I remember visiting with you in the CBS news room some years ago, and you held up a copy of *The New York Times* and said the entire text of the *CBS Evening News* that night would not fill up half of the front page of the *Times*. That made a real impression on me about the role of television news. Can we watch TV news today and be well informed citizens in this democracy?

CRONKITE: No, and you couldn't when I was doing it either. I think that you could come closer doing it then. On the *Evening News* when I was doing it, the total words spoken on those broadcasts were actually just about a third of the number of words on the front page of *The New York Times*. The best we could do was try to give people a series of headlines that would perhaps entice them to go for more information to newspapers, books, opinion journals. It is true today and I think it probably would be true almost under any circumstances.

We do have all-news networks now. Of course, most of the time they are regurgitating the same headlines over and over. And that's all right, it's a service. I like that service. I use CNN, for instance.

What we did with television was to lift the floor of understanding among the people in the United States. We went into homes that had never read a book, never had a newspaper. And suddenly they were listening to the news. So we were lifting the floor, but at the same time, we were lowering the ceiling. Polls showed most of the people in the United States were getting most of their news from television. Well, in that case, most of the people in the United States were inadequately informed. They weren't getting enough information to intelligently exercise their franchise in their democracy and that's a dangerous situation. It still exists today and it is still a dangerous situation.

We have lowered the ceiling and raised the floor, we have got a little tiny crawl space of information in there in the middle and that is not good enough. What we really must do, it seems to me, is try to educate our young to read, because that is where the bulk of the information is. Television is a powerful medium, but it is almost too powerful for all of our good. We must teach people to be multidimensional, to watch television, sure. But we have got to get the depth of information from our magazines or newspapers or books.

During the Vietnam war, one reason that I was pleased to believe we were doing a good job at being in the middle of the road at CBS, is that we were getting shot at from both sides. With the same broadcast we would get criticism from those who called themselves patriotic, those supporting the war, and the objectors to the war.

The resistance people very often said, Well, you don't tell us the truth about Vietnam. You don't tell us what is really going on out there. And they would ask specific questions about specific places. I would say to them: Wait a minute, where did you hear about that? And it turned out, they had been reading books. During that time there were many books that told the full history and displayed a deep understanding of Vietnam. So the story was in the books. If it wasn't in your daily paper, if you couldn't get it all there, you could get it somewhere else. And it is important today for people to know that they should go multimedia. That is what it takes to be a well-educated voter in America.

INMAN: Reflect a little bit on the impact of the media, starting with newspapers and radio, television, now the Internet, on our political system — and the increasingly partisan nature of politics in this country.

CRONKITE: Well, I don't think the media has had an adverse effect as far as increasing divisiveness except in campaign advertising on television. I don't understand why our Senate is unwilling to go along with a reform movement on finance of campaigns. The polls show that the American people are deeply disturbed about this excessive expenditure in running for public office.

It seems to me that the question which we all probably are asking but haven't quite phrased that way, is what makes a seat in Congress so valuable? Why do congressmen have to spend two million dollars to get themselves elected to Congress? Where does this come back, the two million dollars?

But in basics, television is useful. Larry King on CNN did a very valuable thing when he finally brought, I think it was Ross Perot first to his microphone. And Perot talked at great length to Larry King about his program, and so it forced others to come in. And they began to see an advantage to that. The talk show today is a very valuable political tool for the politicians to use, but also for us to learn in some depth about them.

These things are important. They do broaden the dialogue for most of us in the United States. We know more about politics, and possibly because we know more is why we are getting more cynical about it. But that is good. We are learning and we are demanding improvement. People are demanding campaign fund reform, and eventually the word is going to seep out to the Congress that they have to do something.

INMAN: If you could spend time with any person in history, who would it be?

CRONKITE: There are a lot of people I would like to meet. There are a lot of people I would like to have interviewed through history. I would include in that modern history, Hitler. I would like very much to have had a chance to really find out what made that monster tick, as nearly as I could. I would also like to have spent more time with Churchill.

But when you say "spend time with," most of those people who I would like to interview, I would like to get out of there pretty quickly.

INMAN: It always seemed to me that there was a spirit of adventure about your practice of the art and craft of journalism. Riding in a bomber on a mission in World War II. You drove a race car at one time. You are a sailor, you have been to the bottom of the ocean, you would like to go to the moon, or at least up on the space shuttle. Is all of this spirit just part of the curiosity that goes with being a journalist? Or is there something beyond that that is essentially Walter Cronkite?

CRONKITE: Oh, I suppose there is something that is essentially Walter Cronkite. I think if I weren't a journalist, I would still want to do all those things and probably do one of them as a life work maybe. I don't think of it as adventure, I think of it as kind of broadening and informational sort of a thing. I would want to find out about these things.

You know, it's the greatest disappointment of my life that I am not going to get a space flight. But I also know that I am a fellow that very frequently sees the glass as half empty rather than half full. And if I had the opportunity to go on the shuttle today, I would go, but I would be very pouty about it because I was only going up for 220 miles and not going to the moon. I can't imagine anybody not wanting to go into space. I can't imagine not wanting to go to the moon. Could there be anything more exciting than being on the surface of the moon and looking at our globe out there from the distance of the moon? Remember those pictures of the earth rise over the horizon of the moon? The only color in the entire dark mass of the universe. All the other stars that we see are flashes of light. Here is this colored globe of ours.

What an inspiration it would be to work for world peace. Understanding we are all alone out there in that universe, how ridiculous it is that we can't preserve this world of ours and we can't feed the world of ours with all the money we spend on armaments, and house the world of ours, give its people medical aid and the education they need, and really appreciate what we are lucky enough to have, which is life on the earth.

INMAN: That is essentially Walter Cronkite and that is what we have all come to admire and appreciate over the years. We are so glad you came to Charlotte to share this with us, to talk about the American legacy. And you can tell that people still remember and appreciate what you have done for this nation. Not a single person here tonight has asked the question, "Didn't you used to be Walter Cronkite?"

CRONKITE: Let me tell you this one story before we go. Just a few months ago we were doing a documentary in Yellowstone National Park. My wife Betsy and I were in one of the little shops in the park and a little lady came up and said, "Did anybody ever tell you that you look just like Walter Cronkite looked before he died? Except I think he was thinner."

I was so overcome that I had to turn away. I was afraid I would laugh. And she turned to Betsy, my wife, and she said, "Walter Cronkite is dead, isn't he?" And Betsy said, "Yes, I think he is. He died of thinness."

Part II
The Stories

*W*hether *writing short stories, or novels such as* The Cheerleader *and* Carolina Moon, *Jill McCorkle seems to capture almost effortlessly the frank and funny voices of women — whether they are having breakdowns, breakthroughs, or an equal measure of both. This story,* "Crash Diet," *comes from McCorkle's short story collection of the same name.*

Jill McCorkle

"CRASH DIET"

Kenneth left me on a Monday morning before I'd even had the chance to mousse my hair, and I just stood there at the picture window with the drapes swung back and watched him get into that flashy red Mazda, which I didn't want him to get anyway, and drive away down Marnier Street, and make a right onto Seagrams. That's another thing I didn't want, to live in a subdivision where all the streets are named after some kind of liquor. But Kenneth thought that was cute because he runs a bartending school, which is where he met Lydia to begin with.

"I'll come back for the rest of my things," he said. And I wondered just what he meant by that. What was his and what was mine?

"Where are you going to live, in a pup tent?" I asked and took the towel off of my head. I have the kind of hair that will dry right into big clumps of frosted-looking thread if I don't comb it out fast. Once, well before I met Kenneth at the Holiday Inn lounge where he was giving drink-mixing lessons to the staff, I wrote a personal ad and described myself as having angel hair, knowing full well that whoever read it would picture flowing blond curls, when what I really meant was the stuff that you put on a Christmas tree or use to insulate your house. I also said I was average size, which at the time I was.

"I'm moving in with Lydia," he said in his snappy, matter-of-fact way, like I had just trespassed on his farmland. Lydia. It had been going on for a year and a half though I had only known of it for six weeks. *LYDIA*, a name so old-sounding even my grandmother wouldn't have touched it.

"Well, give her my best," I said like you might say to a child who is threatening to run away from home. "Send me a postcard," I said and laughed, though I already felt myself nearing a crack, like I might fall right into it, a big dark crack, me and five years of Kenneth and liquor streets and the microwave oven that I'd just bought to celebrate our five years of marriage and the fact that I had finally started losing some of the weight that I had put on during the first two years.

"Why did you do this?" he asked when he came home that day smelling of coconut because he had been teaching piña coladas, and approached that microwave oven that I had tied up in red ribbon.

"It's our anniversary," I said and told him that he was making me so hungry for macaroons or those Hostess Snoballs with all that pink coconut. I'd lost thirty pounds by that time and needed to lose only ten more and they were going to take my "after" picture and put me on the wall of the Diet Center along with all the other warriors (that's what they called us) who had conquered fat.

"But this is a big investment," Kenneth said and picked up the warranty. Five years, and he stared at that like it had struck some chord in his brain that was high-pitched and off-key. Five years, that's how long it had been since we honeymooned down at Sea Island, Georgia, and drank daiquiris that Kenneth said didn't have enough rum and ate all kinds of wonderful food that Kenneth didn't monitor going down my throat like he came to do later.

"Well, sure it's an investment," I told him. "Like a marriage."

"Guaranteed for five years," he said and then got all choked up, tried to talk but cried instead, and I knew something wasn't right. I sat up half the night waiting for him to say something. *Happy anniversary, You sure do look good these days,* anything. It must have been about two a.m. when I got out of him the name Lydia, and I didn't do a thing but get up and out of that bed and start working on the mold that wedges in between those tiles in the shower stall. That's what I do when I get upset because it's hard to eat while scrubbing and because there's always mold to be found if you look for it.

■ ■ ■

"You'll have to cross that bridge when you come to it," my mama always said, and when I saw Kenneth make that right turn onto Seagrams, I knew I was crossing it right then. I had two choices: I could go back to bed or I could do something. I have never been one to climb back into the bed after it's been made, so I got busy. I moussed my hair and got dressed, and I went to my pocketbook and got out the title to that Mazda that had both our names on it. I poured a glass of wine, since it was summer vacation from teaching sixth grade, painted my toenails, and then, in the most careful way, I wrote in Kenneth's handwriting that I (Kenneth I. Barkley) gave full ownership of the Mazda to Sandra White Barkley, and then I signed his name. Even Kenneth couldn't have told that it wasn't his signature; that's just how well I forged. I finished my wine, got dressed, and went over to my friend Paula's house to get it notarized.

"Why are you doing this?" Paula asked me. She was standing there in her bathrobe, and I could hear some movement in the back where her bedroom was. I didn't know if she meant why was I stopping by her house unannounced or why I was changing the title on the car. I know it's rude to stop by a person's house unannounced and hated to admit I had done it, so I just focused on the title. Sometimes I can focus so well on things and other times I can't at all.

"Kenneth and I are separating and I get the Mazda," I told her.

"When did this happen?" Paula asked, and glanced over her

shoulder to that cracked bedroom door.

"About two hours ago," I told her and sat down on the sofa. Paula just kept standing there like she didn't know what to do, like she could have killed me for just coming in and having a seat in the middle of her activities, but I didn't focus on that. "Just put your stamp on it and I'll be going." I held that title and piece of paper out to her, and she stared down at it and shook her head back and forth. "Did Kenneth write this?" she asked me, like my reputation might not be the best.

"Haven't I been through enough this morning?" I asked her and worked some tears into my eyes. "What kind of friend questions such a thing?"

"I'm sorry, Sandra," she said, her face as pink as her bathrobe. "I have to ask this sort of thing. I'll be right back." She went down the hall to her bedroom, and I got some candy corn out of her little dish shaped like a duck or something in that family. I wedged the large ends up and over my front teeth so I had fangs like little kids always do at Halloween.

"Who was that?" I heard a man say, frustrated. I could hear frustration in every syllable that carried out there to the living room, and then Paula said, "Shhh." When she came back with her little embosser, I had both front teeth covered in candy corn and grinned at her. She didn't laugh so I took them off my teeth and laid them on her coffee table. I don't eat sweets.

"I'm sorry I can't talk right now," Paula said. "You see . . ."

"What big eyes you have," I said and took my notarized paper right out of her hand. "Honey, go for it," I told her and pointed down the hall. "I'm doing just fine."

"I feel so guilty, though," Paula said, her hair all flat on one side from sleeping that way. "I feel like maybe you need to talk to somebody." That's what people always say when they feel like they should do something but have no intention of doing it, *I feel so bad,* or *If only.* I just laughed and told Paula I had to go to Motor Vehicles and take care of a piece of business and then I had to go to the police station and report a stolen car.

"What?" Paula asked, and her mouth fell open and she didn't even look over her shoulder when there were several frustrated and impatient knocks on her bedroom wall. "That's illegal."

"And you're my accomplice," I told her and walked on down the sidewalk and got into that old Ford Galaxy, which still smelled like the apples that Kenneth's granddaddy used to keep in it to combat his cigar smoke. If there'd been a twenty-year-old apple to be found rolling around there under the front seat, I would've eaten it.

■ ■ ■

I didn't report the car, though. By the time I had driven by Lydia's house fourteen times — the first four of which the Mazda was out front and the other ten parked two blocks away behind the fish market (hidden, they thought) — I was too tired to talk to anybody so I just went home to bed. By ten o'clock, I'd had a full night's sleep so I got up, thawed some hamburger in the microwave, and made three pans of lasagna, which I then froze because mozzarella is not on my diet.

The next day, I was thinking about going to the grocery store because I didn't have a carrot in the house, but it was as if my blood was so slow I couldn't even put on a pair of socks. I felt like I had taken a handful of Valium but I hadn't. I checked the bottle there at the back of the medicine cabinet that was prescribed for Kenneth when he pulled his back lifting a case of Kahlua about a year ago. The bottle was there with not a pill touched, so I didn't have an excuse to be found for this heaviness. "When you feel heavy, exercise!" we warriors say, so before my head could be turned toward something like cinnamon toast, I got dressed and did my Jane Fonda routine twice, scrubbed the gasoline spots from the driveway, and then drove to the Piggly Wiggly for some carrots. It felt good being in the car with the radio going, so I didn't get out at the Piggly Wiggly but kept driving. I had never seen that rotating bar that is in a motel over in Clemmonsville, so I went there. It was not nearly as nice as Kenneth had made it sound; I couldn't even tell that I was moving at all, so I rode the glass elevator twice, and then checked into the motel across the street. It was a motel like I'd never seen, electric finger massages for a quarter and piped-in reggae. I liked it so much I stayed a week and ate coleslaw from Kentucky Fried Chicken. When I got home, I bought some carrots at the Piggly Wiggly.

■ ■ ■

"I was so worried about you!" my buddy Martha from the Diet Center said, and ran into my house. Martha is having a long hard time getting rid of her excess. "I was afraid you were binging."

"No, just took a little trip for my nerves," I told her, and she stood with her mouth wide open like she had seen Frankenstein. "Kenneth and I have split." Martha's mouth was still hanging open, which is part of her problem: oral, she's an oral person.

"Look at you," Martha said, and put her hands on my hips, squeezed on my bones there, love handles they're sometimes called if you've got somebody who loves them. "You've lost, Sandra."

"Well, Kenneth and I weren't right for each other, I guess."

"The hell with Kenneth," Martha said, her eyes filling with tears. "You've lost more weight." Martha shook my hips until my teeth rattled. She is one of those people who her whole life has been told she has a pretty face. And she does, but it makes her mad for people to say it because she knows what they mean is that she's fat, and to ignore that fact they say what a pretty face she has. Anybody who's ever been overweight has had this happen. "I'm going to miss you at the meetings," Martha said, and looked like she was going to cry again. Martha is only thirty, just five years younger than me, but she looks older; the word is matronly, and it has a lot to do with the kind of clothes you have to wear if you're overweight. The mall here doesn't have an oversize shop.

I went to the beauty parlor and told them I wanted the works — treatments, facials, haircut, new shampoo, mousse, spray, curling wand. I spent a hundred and fifty dollars there, and then I went to Revco and bought every color of nail polish that they had, four different new colognes because they each represented a different mood, five boxes of Calgon in case I didn't get back to Revco for a while, all the Hawaiian Tropic products, including a sun visor and beach towel. I bought a hibachi and three bags of charcoal, a hammock, some barbecue tongs, an apron that says KISS THE COOK, and one of those inflatable pools so I could stretch out in the backyard in some water. I bought one of those rafts that will hold a canned drink in a little pocket, in case I should decide to walk down to the pool in our subdivision over on Tequila Circle. Summer was well under way, and I had to catch up on things. I bought a garden hose and a hoe and a rake, thinking I might relandscape my yard even though the subdivision doesn't really like you to take nature into your own hands. I had my mind on weeping willows and crepe myrtle. I went ahead and bought fifteen azaleas while I was there, some gardening gloves, and some rubber shoes for working in the yard. Comet was on sale so I went ahead and got twenty cans. I bought a set of dishes (four place settings) because Kenneth had come and taken mine while I was in Clemmonsville; I guess Lydia didn't have any dishes. Then I thought that wouldn't be enough if I should have company, so I got two more sets so that I'd have twelve place settings. I figured if I was to have more than twelve people for dinner then I'd need not only a new dining-room set but also a new dining room. I didn't have any place mats that matched those dishes so I picked up some and some glasses that matched the blue border on my new plates and some stainless because I had always loved that pattern with the pistol handle on the knife.

They had everything in this Revco. I thought if I couldn't sleep at night I'd make an afghan, so I picked out some pretty yarn, and then I thought, well, if I was going to start making afghans at night, I could get ahead on my Christmas shopping, and so I'd make an afghan for my mama and one for Paula, who had been calling me on the phone non-stop to make sure I hadn't reported the stolen car, and one for Martha that I'd make a little bigger than normal, which made me think that I hadn't been to the Diet Center in so long I didn't even know my weight, so I went and found the digital scales and put one right on top of my seventy-nine skeins of yarn. I bought ten each of Candy Pink, Watermelon, Cocoa, Almond, Wine, Cinnamon, Lime, and only nine of the Cherry because the dye lot ran out. It made me hungry, so I got some dietetic bonbons. By the time I got to the checkout I had five carts full and when that young girl looked at me and handed me the tape that was over a yard long, I handed her Kenneth I. Barkley's MasterCard and said, "Charge it."

It was too hot to work in the yard, and I was too tired to crochet or unpack the car and felt kind of sick to my stomach. Thinking it was from the bonbon I ate on the way home, I went to the bathroom to get an Alka-Seltzer, but Kenneth had taken those too, so I just took two Valiums and went to bed.

■ ■ ■

"I feel like a yo-yo," I told the shrink when Paula suggested that I go. All of my clothes were way too big, so I had given them to Martha as an incentive for her to lose some weight and had ordered myself a whole new wardrobe from Neiman-Marcus on Kenneth I. Barkley's MasterCard number. That's why I had to wear my KISS THE COOK apron and my leotard and tights to the shrink's. "My clothes should be here any day now," I told him, and he smiled.

"No, I feel like a yo-yo, not a regular yo-yo either," I said. "I feel like one of those advanced yo-yos, the butterfly model, you know where the halves are turned facing outward and you can do all those tricks like 'walk the dog,' 'around the world,' and 'eat spaghetti.'" He laughed, just threw back his head and laughed, so tickled over "eat spaghetti"; laughing at the expense of another human being, laughing when he was going to charge me close to a hundred dollars for that visit that I was going to pay for with a check from my dual checkbook, which was what was left of Kenneth I. Barkley's account over at Carolina Trust. I had already taken most of the money out of that account and moved it over to State Employee's Credit Union. That man tried to be serious, but every time I opened my mouth, it seemed he laughed.

But I didn't care because I hadn't had so much fun since Kenneth and I ate a half-gallon of rocky-road ice cream in our room there in Sea Island, Georgia.

"Have you done anything unusual lately?" he asked. "You know, like going for long rides, spending lots of money?"

"No," I said and noticed that I had a run in my tights. After that, I couldn't think of a thing but runs and running. I wanted to train for the Boston Marathon. I knew I'd win if I entered.

■ ■ ■

Lydia was ten years younger than Kenneth, I had found that out during the six weeks when he fluctuated between snappy and choked up. That's what I knew of her, ten years younger than Kenneth and studying to be a barmaid, and that's why I rolled the trees in the yard of that pitiful-looking house she rented with eleven rolls of decorator toilet paper. My new clothes had come by then so I wore my black silk dress with the ruffled off-the-shoulder look. Lydia is thirteen years younger than me and, from what I could tell of her shadow in the window, about twenty pounds heavier. I was a twig by then. "I'd rather be an old man's darlin' than a young man's slave," my mama told me just before I got married, and I said, "You mind your own damn business." Lydia's mama had probably told her the same thing, and you can't trust a person who listens to her mama.

I stood there under a tree and hoisted roll after roll of the decorator toilet paper into the air and let it drape over branches. I wrapped it in and out of that wrought-iron rail along her steps and tied a great big bow. I was behind the shrubs, there where it was dark, when the front door opened and I heard her say, "I could have sworn I heard something," and then she said, "Just look at this mess!" She was turning to get Kenneth so I got on my stomach and slid along the edge of the house and hid by the corner. I got my dress covered with mud and pine straw, but I didn't really care because I liked the dress so much when I saw it there in the book that I ordered two. The porch light came on, and then she was out in that front yard with her hands on her hips and the ugliest head of hair I'd ever seen, red algae hair that looked like it hadn't been brushed in four years. "When is she going to leave us alone?" Lydia asked, and looked at Kenneth, who was standing there with what looked like a tequila sunrise in his hand. He looked terrible. "You've got to do something!" Lydia said, and started crying. "You better call your lawyer right now. She's already spent all your money."

"I'll call Sandra tomorrow," Kenneth said, and put his arm around Lydia, but she wasn't having any part of that. She twisted away and slapped his drink to the dirt.

"Call her?" Lydia screamed, and I wished I had my camera to catch her expression right when she was beginning to say "her"; that new camera of mine could catch anything. "What good is that going to do?"

"Maybe I can settle it all," he said. "I'm the one who left her. If it goes to court, she'll get everything."

"She already has," Lydia said, sat down in the yard, and blew her nose on some of that decorator toilet paper. "The house, the money. She has taken everything except the Mazda."

"I got the dishes," he said. "I got the TV and the stereo."

"I don't know why you didn't take your share when you had the chance," Lydia said. "I mean, you could've taken the microwave and the silver or something."

"It's going to be fine, honey," Kenneth said, and pulled her up from the dirt. "We've got each other."

"Yes," Lydia nodded, but I couldn't help but feel sorry for her, being about ten pounds too heavy for her own good. I waited until they were back inside before I finished the yard, and then walked over behind the fish market where I had parked the car. There wasn't much room in the car because I had six loads of laundry that I'd been meaning to take to the subdivision Laundromat to dry. Kenneth had bought me a washer but not a dryer, and I should have bought one myself but I hadn't; the clothes had mildewed something awful.

■ ■ ■

Not long after that all my friends at the Diet Center took my picture to use as an example of what not to let happen to yourself. They said I had gone overboard and needed to gain a little weight for my own health. I was too tired to argue with Martha, aside from the fact that she was five times bigger than me, and I just let her drive me to the hospital. I checked in as Lydia Barkley, and since I didn't know how Lydia's handwriting looked, I used my best Kenneth imitation. "Her name is Sandra," Martha told the woman, but nobody yelled at me. They just put me in a bed and gave me some dinner in my vein and knocked me out. As overweight as I had been, I had never eaten in my sleep. It was a first, and when I woke up, the shrink was there asking me what I was, on a scale of one to ten. "Oh, four," I told him. It seemed like I was there a long time. Paula came and did my nails and hair, and Martha came and confessed that she had eaten three boxes of chocolate-covered cherries over the last week. She brought me a fourth. She said that if she had a husband, she'd get a divorce, that's how desperate she was to lose some weight, but that she'd stop before she got as thin as me. I told her I'd rather eat a case of chocolate-covered cherries than go through it again.

My mama came, and she said, "I always knew this would happen." She shook her head like she couldn't stand to look at me. "A man whose business in life depends on others taking to the bottle is no kind of man to choose for a mate."

I told her to mind her own damn business, and when she left, she took my box of chocolate-covered cherries and told me that sweets were not good for a person.

■ ■ ■

By the time I got out of the hospital, I was feeling much better. Kenneth stopped by for me to sign the divorce papers right before it was time for my dinner party. His timing had never been good. There I was in my black silk dress with the table set for twelve, the lasagna getting ready to be thawed and cooked in the microwave.

"Looks like you're having a party," he said, and stared at me with that same look he always had before he got choked up. I just nodded and filled my candy dish with almonds. "I'm sorry for all the trouble I caused you," he said. "I didn't know how sick you were." And I noticed he was taking me in from head to toe. "You sure look great now."

"Well, I'm feeling good, Kenneth," I told him and took the papers from his hand.

"I'm not with Lydia anymore," he said, but I focused instead on signing my name, my real name, in my own handwriting, which if it was analyzed would be the script of a fat person. Some things you just can't shake; part of me will always be a fat person and part of Kenneth will always be gutter slime. He had forgotten that when he *had* me he hadn't wanted me, and I had just about forgotten how much fun we'd had eating that half-gallon of ice cream in bed on our honeymoon.

"Well, send me a postcard," I told him when I opened the front door to see Martha coming down the walk in one of my old dresses that she was finally able to wear. And then came Paula and the man she kept in her bedroom, and my mama, who I had sternly instructed not to open her mouth if she couldn't be pleasant, my beautician, the manager of Revco, my shrink, who, after I had stopped seeing him on a professional basis, had called and asked me out to lunch. They were all in the living room, mingling and mixing drinks; I stood there with the curtains pulled back and watched Kenneth get in that Mazda that was in my name and drive down Marnier and take a left onto Seagrams. Summer was almost over, and I couldn't wait for the weather to turn cool so that I could stop working in the yard.

"I want to see you do 'eat spaghetti,'" my shrink, who by then had told me to call him Alan, said and pulled a butterfly yo-yo like I hadn't seen in years from his pocket. I did it; I did it just as well as if I were still in the seventh grade, and my mama hid her face in embarrassment while everybody else got a good laugh. Of course, I'm not one to overreact or to carry a situation on and on, and so when they begged for more tricks, I declined. I had plenty of salad on hand for my friends who were dieting so they wouldn't have seconds on lasagna, and while I was fixing the coffee, Alan came up behind me, grabbed my love handles, and said, "On a scale of one to ten, you're a two thousand and one." I laughed and patted his hand because I guess I was still focused on Kenneth and where was he going to stay, in a pup tent? Some things never change, and while everybody was getting ready to go and still chatting, I went to my bedroom and turned my alarm clock upside down, which would remind me when it went off the next day to return the title to Kenneth's name and to maybe write him a little check to help with that MasterCard bill.

I could tell that Alan wanted to linger, but so did my mama and so I had to make a choice. I told Alan it was getting a little late and that I hoped to see him real soon, *socially*, I stressed. He kissed me on the cheek and squeezed my hip in a way that made me get gooseflesh and also made me feel sorry for both Kenneth and Lydia all at the same time. "A divorce can do strange things to a person," Alan had told me on my last visit; the man knew his business. He was cute, too.

"It was a nice party, Sandra," my mama said after everybody left. "Maybe a little too much oregano in the lasagna. You're a tad too thin still, and I just wonder what that man who calls himself a psychiatrist has on his mind."

"Look before you leap," I told her, and gave her seventy-nine skeins of yarn in the most hideous colors that I no longer had room for in my closet. "A bird in the hand is worth two in the bush."

"That's no way to talk to your mother," she said. "It's not my fault that you were overweight your whole life. It's not my fault your husband left you for a redheaded bar tramp."

"Well, send me a postcard," I said and closed the door, letting out every bit of breath that I'd held inside my whole life. I washed those dishes in a flash, and when I got in my bed, I was feeling so sorry for Kenneth, who had no birds in his hand, and sorry for Mama, who would never use up all that yarn. I hurried through those thoughts because my eyelids were getting so heavy and I wanted my last thought of the night to be of Alan, first with the yo-yo and then grabbing my hipbone. When you think about it, if your hipbones have been hidden for years and years, it's a real pleasure to have someone find them, grab hold, and hang on. You can do okay in this world if you can just find something worth holding on to.

n novels such as Raney *and* Walking Across Egypt, *Clyde Edgerton revealed the inseparable blend of humor and sadness in the lives of everyday people. This short story, chosen by the author for inclusion in this anthology, was published originally in* The Carolina Quarterly. *Once again, Edgerton creates characters who are not only funny, but lovingly familiar as well.*

Clyde Edgerton

"LUNCH AT THE PICCADILLY"

We're in the nursing home parking lot. Aunt Lil and me. She's behind her walker. She pushes it way out in front of her. Arm's length. Humped way over and all fell-in the way she is, and weighing less than ninety pounds, her arms look longer than brooms. To see where she's going she has to look up through her eyebrows.

"Is that my car?" she says.

"Yea ma'am. I washed it."

"Well, it looks good."

She's wearing a striped jacket, Hawaiian shirt, tan slacks, gold slippers, silver wig, and a couple of pounds of make-up.

"I'll let you try to drive it after we eat," I tell her, knowing damn well she ain't able to drive. I've been putting it off — letting her practice her driving, that is — by driving my truck when I take her to lunch instead of her car. She keeps asking me when she can practice her driving and I keep putting it off. Because for one thing, as far as when she's going to get out of this place, I don't think it's going to happen. And she won't be able to drive again in any case, and it's my job to tell her. I'm it. It's one of the most worrisome things in my life because I'm about all she's got left, as far as people. Everything is pretty much up to me.

But today we've got her car, and after I let her try to drive after lunch, in the mall parking lot there at Piccadilly's, for just a minute or two, I'm going to tell her she can't drive any more. It's past time to just break the news.

I get her walker fitted in the back seat, get her in the passenger seat — her head about as high as the button on the glove compartment. Her car is a 1989 Oldsmobile, kind of a maroon color, with a luggage rack on the trunk lid. She drove it seven years before her problems and it ain't got but 21,000 miles on it. She's always had something kind of sporty in cars. Back in '72 she had a 1967 two-door Ford Galaxie with fender skirts. White with red interior, and she let me drive it to my prom.

We park on top of the two-deck parking lot at the mall. It's mostly clear of cars. I tell her that after lunch I'll let her drive around up there a little. Mainly, I'm simply going to let her prove to herself that she can't. Can't drive. That will make it lots easier for her to take the news, which I will probably deliver as soon as she makes her first mistake, which might even be before she cranks up.

We get inside Piccadilly, and since it's only 11:30 there's not a real long line, but on the way past the food toward the trays and silverware where the line starts she wants to stop and take a look at what they're serving today. Right here I want to say, Aw, come on Aunt Lil, you'll get to see it in a minute. But I'm thinking, Be patient. Be good. She's in the hardest time of her life.

We get the trays, silverware. She gets a bowl of Chinese stuff without the rice. I get it with the rice. I'm trying not to help her. Let her do what she can. It's going to be bad enough when she sees she can't drive. Aunt Sara, before she died, said stopping driving was the worse thing she ever went through, including Uncle Stark's death.

Down at the cash register a small black man, maybe sixty years old, takes Aunt Lil's tray and leads us to a table. She wants the smoking section. She smokes Pall Malls. He puts her tray down. She says thank you and starts getting all settled in. She can't figure out where to put her walker. I move it over against the wall.

All she's got on her tray is this bowl of Chinese stuff and a biscuit and iced tea and a little bowl of broccoli and cheese sauce. I got the Chinese stuff over rice, fried okra, string beans, fries, cucumber salad, pecan pie, and Diet Coke. She reaches for my little white ticket slip and puts it with her own. She'll get me to pay with her Mastercard.

She says, "That was Larry," talking about the man that brought her tray over. "Let me get him a little something," and she starts looking around for her pocketbook.

I'm thinking, Oh no, the quarter tip.

"You know," she says, "he's lost some weight." She finds her pocketbook, but can't get it open. I help her.

"He'll be back," I say.

"He's been working in here for twenty years at least," she says.

Here comes Larry, walks right by before I can say anything. I check his name tag. It says LEWIS CARLTON. "There he goes," I say. She raises her hand, misses him. "His name tag said Lewis," I say. "Lewis Carlton."

"No, it didn't."

"I think it did. 'Lewis Carlton.'"

"Then it's Larry Lewis Carlton," she says. She sort of twists around in her seat, like a buzzard in make-up looking over its shoulder. "There he comes back. Larry! Larry, come over here."

The man, Mr. Carlton, comes over.

"Here, I want you to have this." She hands him a quarter.

"Thank you, thank you." He steps back a couple of steps, starts to turn.

"You've lost some weight, ain't you?" says Aunt Lil.

He frowns. "Oh, no ma'am."

"You've lost at least twenty pounds."

"No ma'am, I, ah, been at one-sixty for quite a few years now."

"Well, I remember when you weighed a lot more than that."

He looks at me, kind of smiles and backs off.

"He's been here a long time," she says. "I don't know if they want you to tip them or not, but I always do."

Yeah, I'll bet he's glad to see you coming. "Say he's lost some weight, huh," I say.

"Oh yes, he used to be a great big old thing."

So we eat along, and talk about the normal things.

Last time we were in here, a woman named Ann Rose wanted to carry Aunt Lil's tray from the cash register. Aunt Lil saw her coming and said to me, "Lord, she'll talk your head off." Aunt Lil shunned her, but Ann Rose took the tray anyway, said she'd saved Aunt Lil a table, but Aunt Lil don't want no part of it. Said she wanted to sit someplace else. So Ann Rose looks at me with this nod of understanding. I'm staying out of it. Later at the end of the meal, Aunt Lil says, "Go tell Ann Rose to come on over here. I don't want to make her feel bad." So Ann Rose comes over, sits down and starts right in about how she worked 44 years at the cigarette factory — American Tobacco — and they'd all told her that whenever *she* finally left they'd have to close it down, and sure enough she left in June of '91, and then in *July* they announced they *were* closing it down, and then there was a woman had been working there got cut loose, then joined an accountant firm that came right back and was doing an audit of the very people who'd just let her go, and, "I want you to know they lost 100 retirement checks and only one showed up and that was at somebody's P.O. box and nobody knows how in the world that happened, that all the ones with regular addresses got lost," and blah blah blah blah blah. Like to drove me crazy.

Just about every other time we come in here, somebody comes over. Because Aunt Lil made all these friends, coming up here all these years. I like it when they don't come over.

■ ■ ■

It's one of those giant two-decker parking lots, about the size of a football field, with a couple of ramps going down to the ground-level deck below it.

We drive to the far end of the lot, where it's away from the mall and empty. I stop, get out, get her out of the passenger side, the walker out of the back seat, and she plods around the back of the car in her walker.

This all started when Aunt Lil fell in her tub, twice on the same night, same bath, a couple of years ago. Then not long after those bathtub falls her back started breaking on its own — from gravity, you know, just broke and broke, then broke some more and the awful thing is that you could see so clear and fast the way it bent her right over. The worst thing was the pain it caused her. She cried a couple of times, and I'll tell you she is not the crying sort. The first few minutes in the nursing home, after she got off the van, she was following her walker — real slow, you know, with it ten feet out in front of her, and it hurt her just to walk. She sat down in her little room with her roommate — I helped her — and she said I don't know what I'm going to do and she started crying right there. It was almost like one month she was standing as straight as an arrow, walking as classy as a model, one foot in front of the other — eighty-seven years old I'm telling you — and then in a few months there she was with a walker and all bent over like that, crying.

I got my own business and can get off work when I need to, and this was say, three o'clock in the afternoon and when she finished crying, she said to her roommate, "Don't you wish you had a nephew who'd do for you like this one?" and her roommate, name of Melveleén, says, "I got two nephews. *They* both work." Melveleen.

So, anyway, I help her in. I get in the passenger side, hand her the key, she puts it in the ignition, turns it, starts the car right up, and kind of looks around. I'm feeling a little sad about it all. This is it. This is the last time she'll ever do this. I'm about to break the news. She will not like what I have to tell her.

"Where's the exit?" she says.

"We're just going to drive around up here on top for a few minutes and let you get the feel of things."

"I got the feel of things."

Yeah, you got about one minute left in your driving history on earth, Aunt Lil. And I'm the one about to break the news.

She pulls it into drive and we're off — in a little circle.

"Where's the exit?" she says.

"We're going to stay up here on top, Aunt Lil. You can drive over toward those other cars if you want to. Maybe a little slower." We do.

All of a sudden, she says, "There's a exit!" and swings the car to the left, right down this down ramp. Because the sun was so bright up top, I can't see. I assume she can't either. I'm straining to see straight ahead, one hand on the dashboard. Then I see the curb on each side of the car — about two feet high, thank goodness. Aunt Lil is drifting left. I think about pulling the hand brake, but decide against it. She needs to see, to prove to herself what she can't do. We scrape the curb with the front left tire, or bumper, I can't tell which. She slows to a stop.

"We drifted left," I say. "Let's pull on straight ahead, on down there beside that column and I'll take her back over." This is all the proof I need. The proof I want her to know for herself: She is unable to drive anymore — the time has come. I will have to break the news to her — as soon as we stop.

The top of her head is even with the top of the steering wheel. She starts out slowly, drifts left, and runs against the curb again. "What's wrong," she says.

"You keep running up against the curb."

"Oh," she says. She looks over at me, her hands up on the steering wheel. "Am I driving?"

"Yes, yes. You're driving. Pull straight ahead there and I'll take back over."

"I need a little more padding under me," she says. "I'm too low in this seat."

"I don't think that's the basic problem, Aunt Lil."

"And I need a little more practice. That's all." She pulls straight ahead and stops. We sit there. This is the time to tell her, I think, but I'll just wait until I'm back behind the steering wheel with everything under control.

"Okay," I say. "Put it in park."

She does.

Then for some reason she presses her door lock switch and locks us in.

"It was unlocked, " I say. "Now it's locked. You need to unlock."

She touches the window button and her window starts down. "That's the window," I say. "Press where you just pressed it."

"'Where?"

"Right there where that lock button is — the top part of what you just pressed on the bottom. You locked it. Now you need to unlock it. Right there, above where you pressed it."

She looks up into the ceiling, her hand in the air like she's waving at somebody.

"This one right here." I point to my lock button.

Finally, she gets it right, unlocks the doors, then opens hers. I get out to go around and help her out. I'm sort of preparing my speech. I want to make it as easy as possible, to kind of set it up so she might make the suggestion herself, set it up in a way that if she doesn't take the bait, then I can say, Aunt Lil, I think you're just going to have to give up driving. And then I'll say something like, That way you won't have to pay car insurance and all that. That's costing you over a thousand dollars a year.

I open the back door, get out her walker. As I pass around the back of the car, I see her head leaning into the middle of the car, looking down at something. As I come around to her side I see her feet hanging out the open door. I can't remember if she put it in park.

"Be sure it's in park," I say.

This is where she pulls the gear shift from park down into drive, and off she goes, them gold slippers hanging out the door. There she goes, very slowly, at about two miles an hour, her door and the passenger door wide open. I open my mouth. Nothing comes out.

She's going in a big wide circle, missing one of those big columns, then another, circling around. I see her head now. I think she's steering. I decide to just stand and wait, because it looks like she might come on back around. All I have to do is wait. Something tells me if I holler at her she'll try to get out. She's not going fast. I must remain quiet.

She's now traveled one half of a large circle, missing everything. There are about five or ten cars in this area and many thick concrete columns. If I stand still I think she'll be back around. She must be holding the steering wheel in one position. I hope she doesn't straighten it out. But if she does, maybe she'll start up the ramp and the car will choke down — that thought crosses my mind. But then she'd roll backward. Her foot is not on the gas because I can see those two little gold slippers. She misses another column, then another. I will wait.

Here she comes. I believe she's steering. I move so that I will be on her side of the car when she comes by. Both doors are wide open. I see those gold slippers. I see her eyes above the steering wheel. Here she comes. I start walking beside her; fairly fast walk. "You need to put it in park," I say. I put my hand on the door. She's looking straight ahead, frozen. The passenger door hits a column and slams shut. "Put it in park, Aunt Lil."

There is a tremendous explosion and pain to my body and head. I've walked into a column. I stagger backwards, catch myself, and head out after the car. By God this proves she can't drive anymore. I run to the passenger door, open it, jump in, grab the hand brake between us, and pull it up slowly and firmly. We stop. I put the gear lever in park. Because her feet are out the door, she can't turn her head all the way around to see me, but she tries.

"Is that you, Robert?" she says.

"Yes ma'am. It kind of got away from you there, I believe."

"I was doing okay," she says.

God Almighty. "Let's get you out, and I'll drive us on back."

"I would have got out," she said. "But I couldn't reach that seat belt thing."

"What would have happened to the car, Aunt Lil — if you'd got out?"

"You could have caught it. Just like you did."

I figure that as soon as we get back and sit down in her room and kind of recover and eat a couple of Tootsie-rolls, I'll break the news to her. She keeps Tootsie-rolls for everybody that comes in. I buy them for her, along with bananas and other stuff. It's not going to be easy, but I'm just going to have to tell her like it is. Her driving days are done and over. Ka-put. End of story.

F red Chappell, born in Canton, is the Poet Laureate of North Carolina. While his work is closely identified with the place of his birth, it also transcends that place and moves beyond Southern nostalgia, occasionally reaching as far as the realm of science fiction. The story which follows was chosen by the author for inclusion in this anthology; it appears in print for the first time here.

Fred Chappell

"THE ENCYCLOPEDIA DANIEL"

Yesterday *cows* and the day before that *clouds*, but today he had skipped all the way to *fish*.

"What about *dreams?*" his mother asked. "What about *dandelions* and *dodo* and *Everest* and *Ethiopia?*"

Danny's reply was guarded. "I'll come back to them. *Fish* is what I've got to write about today. Today is fish day."

"Do you think that's the best way to compose an encyclopedia? You're twelve years old, now. That's old enough to be methodical. You were taking your subjects in alphabetical order before. When you were in the B's you didn't go from *baseball* to *xylophone*. Why do you want to jump over to *fish?*"

"I don't know," Danny said, "but today is fish day."

"Well," she said, "you're the encyclopedia-maker. You must know best."

179

"That's right," he said and his tone was as grave as that of an archbishop settling a point of theology. He rose from his chair at the yellow dinette table.

"I have to go think now," he announced.

"All right," his mother said. "Just don't hurt yourself."

Her customary remark irritated Danny. He didn't reply as he tucked two blue spiral notebooks under his arm and headed toward his tiny upstairs bedroom. Going up the steps, he found his answer but it came too late: "It doesn't hurt me to think, not like some people I know."

■ ■ ■

He closed his door tight, dropped his notebooks on the rickety card table serving for a desk, and flung himself down on the narrow bed. Then he rolled over, cradled his hands behind his head, and watched the ceiling. It was an early May dusk and the headlights of cars played slow shadows above him.

He tried to think about fish but the task was boring. Fish lived dim lives in secret waters and there were many different kinds and he knew only a few of their names. People ate them. People ate a lot of the things Danny wrote about in his Encyclopedia: apples, bananas, beans, coconuts. Cows too — Danny had written about eating cows in a way that distressed his mother. "Slaughterhouses!" she exclaimed. "Why write about that? You don't have to put that in." He had explained, with a patient sigh, that everything had to go in. An encyclopedia was about everything in the world. If he left something out, it would be like telling a lie. He wrote what was given him to write.

Yet today he had skipped from cows to fish, leaping over lots of interesting things. He would come back to *daredevil* and *Excalibur,* *eclipse* and *dentists,* but it wouldn't be the same. His mother was right. It was sloppy, zipping on to *fish;* it was unscientific. He said aloud: "This method is unscientific."

Then another sentence came into his mind. He could not keep it out. It was like trying to hold a door closed against someone bigger and stronger and crazier than you. You pushed hard but he pushed harder, swept you aside and came on in, sweaty and purplefaced and too loud for the little bedroom. This sentence was as audible in his mind as if it had been spoken to him in the dark and lonely midnight: "He tore the living room curtains down and tried to set them on fire."

He sat up on the edge of the bed and gazed out the window above his table. The dusk had thickened and the lights made the houses on Orchard Street look warm and inviting. But that was only illusion. They were not inviting, all full of people who whispered and said ugly things. They lived happy lives, these people, you could tell from the lights in their windows, but you were not to be any part of that. Those lives were as remote and secret as the lives of fish in the depths of the ocean.

He turned on the dinky little lamp with the green shade and sat down in the creaky wooden chair. Dully he opened a notebook and began to read what he had written in his encyclopedia about cars:

The best kind of car is a Corvette. It is really flash. Lots of kids say they will buy Corvettes when they grow up but I don't think so. You have to be rich. Billy Joe Armistead is not going to be rich, just look at him. Anyway by the time we grow up Corvettes won't be the hot car. The hot car will be something we don't know about yet, maybe it has like an atomic motor.

Danny flipped the page. He had written a great deal about cars; that was his favorite subject. He had learned all about them by looking at magazine photos and articles and talking to the guys in the neighborhood. Corvette, they all said.

He turned through the scribbled pages until he came to a blank one to fill up with the facts about fish. Except that he didn't know any facts. Well, a few maybe — not enough to help. And then while he was looking at the page with its forbiddingly empty lines another sentence sounded in his head so strongly that he reached for the green ballpoint: "Then he vomits a lot of red stuff, yucky smelly red stuff." But he couldn't write and dropped the pen.

The house began to tang with kitchen smells and Danny understood they would have spaghetti for supper, he and his mother chatting at the dinette table. He understood too that he had better write at least a paragraph about fish because it would soon be time to go down. With a heartfelt groan, he began:

■ ■ ■

Fish have gills so they can breathe water. They are hard to see but fisher men find them anyhow with radar they have. Some fish are real big like whales but most are not as big as people. When the police men come he tries to hit them all and then they put hand cuffs on him and drive off.

■ ■ ■

Three times he read the last sentence and then slowly and with close deliberate strokes marked out the words one at a time. Then he used his red ballpoint to make black rectangles of the canceled words. Red on green makes black.

■ ■ ■

He had interpreted the smells correctly. Supper was spaghetti and meatballs with his mother's pungent tomato sauce. She offered him a spoonful of her red wine in water but he preferred his Pepsi. There was a green salad too, with the pasty raw mushrooms he would avoid.

His mother raised her glass in his direction. "So — what is your schedule tomorrow? After school, I mean."

"Baseball practice," Danny said. "I'll be home about five."

"Homework?"

"I don't know. Math, probably. Maybe history."

"How about tonight?"

"None tonight."

"So you can go back to writing The Encyclopedia Daniel. How is *fish* coming along?"

"Not so hot."

"That's because you skipped," she said. "You were going like a house afire when you wrote the entries in order. Now you've lost your rhythm."

"I'll come back," he said. "I'll pick up *doors* and the *Dodgers* and *elephants* and *engines* and *farming* and *falcons*. I'll do *fathers*."

Her eyes went wet and she set her glass down as gently as a snowflake. "*Fathers*," she said. "That's what you skipped over, isn't it? You didn't want to do that part."

"I don't know. I guess not."

"Maybe you'll be a writer when you grow up," she said. "Then you'll have to write about sad things whether you want to or not."

"No. I'm not going to be a writer. Just my Encyclopedia. When I get it finished I won't need to write any more."

"Maybe I could be a writer." His mother spoke in a murmur — as if she was listening instead of talking. "When I think about your poor father I believe I could write a book."

"No," he said. His tone was imperious. "Everybody says they could write a book but they couldn't. It's real hard, it's real real hard. Harder than anybody thinks."

"Are you going to finish your Encyclopedia?"

"I don't know. If I can get past this part. But it's hard."

"Maybe it will be good for you to write it out."

"It makes me scared," he said. "Stuff comes in my mind and I'm scared to write it down."

"Like what? What are you scared to write?"

New sentences came to him then and Danny couldn't look into her face. He stared at his cold spaghetti and recited, "He said he would kill her no matter what and she said he never would, she would kill him first. If that was the only way, she would kill him first."

"Oh Danny," his mother said. "I didn't know you heard us that time. I didn't realize you knew."

"I know everything," he said. "I know everything that has already happened and everything that is going to happen. When you write an encyclopedia you have to know everything."

"But that night was a time when we were both pretty crazy. I wouldn't hurt your father. You understand that. And he's never coming back. They won't let him. You understand that too, don't you?"

"Maybe. Maybe if I write it down I'll understand better."

"Yes," she said. "Why don't you write it all down?" But it was coming too fast to write down. Already there were new words in his head, words that spoke as sharply as a fire engine siren:

"Then in August the father got away and came back to the house. It was late at night and real dark. He didn't come to the front door. He went around back. He was carrying something red in his hand."

*I*n 1996, with the publication of her first book, The Distance From the Heart of Things, *Ashley Warlick at age twenty-three became the youngest recipient of the Houghton Mifflin Literary Fellowship. This excerpt opens her award-winning novel, the story of Mavis Black, a young woman who is the wise and confident backbone of her family.*

Ashley Warlick

Excerpted from
The Distance from the Heart of Things

Edisto River starts somewhere up about Batesburg, South Carolina, starts itself up like a forest fire or a thread of cancer, pulling down through the flats and the orchards, through the hogs and the Herefords and the smell of rotten peaches in the sun. It will be cancer that finally puts my grandfather Punk in the ground, cancer like fine barbed wire they'll keep pulling from his cheek and jaw for too many years of tobacco. He used to grow his own in the back parts of the pastures, down where the river snakes over his land. He cured it himself with burning cow dung.

What he'd do was harvest the stalk when the leaves were full and green, leaves enough to dress a child head to toe, and he'd bundle them by the dozen in the rafters of his smokehouse. He'd rub each leaf with ash from the last cure, set fire in the floorboards with cedar kindling laid to tent a cow pie and shut the door up tight. Those leaves would smoke until his fire sweated itself out, three, four days. But all that was when he had his cows, back when he'd send us into the pastures with feed sacks to collect up those cow pies, dry as wasps' nests.

After the cows, he bought his tobacco at the Dixie Home Store, like everybody else. He'd buy it and complain about how sweet it was and how they used maple syrup and tonka beans as additive, and how good tobacco didn't need additive to make it smooth. He'd complain the Redman was stale, aged too long, and the grind not fine enough. He'd complain, but he chewed it anyway.

■ ■ ■

The bus I ride lists back and forth slow over the asphalt, crossing the river bridge just at sunset. A spread of light cuts through my window and across my face, warms my skin from temple to collarbone, and I watch as this same light blooms on the river, reflects back to me in yellow and gold and strokes of heat. Punk's farm starts here, right where this water and this highway lope across each other. It's no longer Herefords and Black Angus, chicory and pokeberries and pastureland, but miles and miles of vineyards making rhymes across the hills. It's June, and the grapes are still hard and green on the vine.

Punk sold fifty Herefords for Niagara and Scuppernong vine stock when I was still in grade school, up and did it one afternoon without sign or signal. Miss Pauline, Punk's wife and my grandmother, gave him a piece of her mind, cussed him in such a way as no other soul on earth could and still draw breath.

She said, "Punk, you are a flat-crazy son of a bitch," and there was more, but I'll not tell it here.

Miss Pauline, herself, is an entrepreneur. She has her own business, Miss Pauline's Boutique, and she understands things that make sense and things that don't and where exactly they overlap in her husband. The day Punk picked up his stock shipped down from the nursery, hickory posts and cables for trellising all in the back of his truck, he pulled by her store like he was head of a parade. He threw open the front door to the Boutique and set foot inside for the very last time.

He said, "Hey, Miss Pauline, it's your crazy son of a bitch come to roost on your own slat porch."

He's a caution. His was the first vineyard in South Carolina, and even as Punk Black was Punk Black, more than a few people shook their heads and laughed.

Two years later, he brought in sixty thousand dollars selling his grape to Taylor Winery in Fredonia, New York. Nobody laughed then. He expanded, planted Concords and Catawbas to fill out the season, and when I was in high school and still at home, there wasn't a summer's day I couldn't head out to his barn and find a camp of migrant fruit pickers, tussling over something. These are the facts of his business, the figures, the moments I'll have to remember when I keep books for Punk.

Punk says, "Mavis, honey, you're gonna make me a fine book-keeper one day. Yessir, this fancy education will return to me ten-fold."

It was Punk who paid my four years at Appalachian State. He gave the money willingly and never once did he ask me about my grades, ask about my studies. Five thousand dollars a year, every year in my bank account.

He'd say, "Most of that's for the school, a little extra for your pretty self."

Punk's that kind of man.

Appalachian is the school Miss Pauline graduated from and the school my mother might have gone to if she'd not had me. There is a certain weight to this, a legacy of sorts to carry out. It's like knowing you're the only son in a family line and having only daughters of your own. Thoughts like that can be heavy on a body, can make a person see their situation as a part of something bigger, something older and wiser and testing of themselves. I liked that feeling when I was at school, liked knowing I was connected up to larger workings, a lash in a long chain, part of a constellation. I like weight placed on me. It feels good.

■■■

This bus comes out of the Appalachian Mountains, the Blue Ridge Travels Line. It's old, silver, chugging, and yesterday broke down in the rain, left me and twenty others on the berm of the highway with our bags over our heads, raspy and worn down. The kindness of Blue Ridge Travels put us up for the night at a roadside stop near Bessemer City. I've been in roadside motels before with my boyfriend Harris and by myself when I would travel here or there. I've come off a bus tired and anxious with wait or destination, and I've crossed my arms 'neath my head and slept like the dead called home. But last night I was beside myself, alone and fidgeting and walking the floor in my new high-heeled shoes.

It was dark when we checked in, but too early in the evening to go to sleep, that time that's both day and night, when all I wished for was a deck of cards, a good book, or a dog to walk. I was tired with myself, tired with standing up, so tired of stretching my legs out beneath me it almost hurt. I wanted to be still, but I couldn't. I wanted to run the whole rest of the way home, but I couldn't do that either.

My motel room was red, and the carpet was shag, a picture over the big bed of a girl with eyes like blue spades. I walked that room, stretched out my legs, and opened all the drawers, the closets, and the bathroom. There was a Bible in the nightstand, a body hair on one of the towels, a roach in the ice bucket, which made me cringe in spite of myself. I've seen dirt and crawling things before. I've found bugs in my lunch bag or pressed between my books, skittering 'round the toolshed when the light comes on. But those were roaches at home, bugs in familiar places, and this was different. Anybody could have been here before me. I considered standing up the whole night through, but my body got the better of me.

I laid myself out on the big bed fully dressed in my best, folded my hands at my rib cage, and tried to make my limbs go dead still so as not to wrinkle. I'm making this trip in good clothes, careful clothes, new stockings and a short black dress, high heels I walked in for a week to get it right. I'd planned on coming back to Edisto looking polished, like a new penny, smart about myself. I'd planned on coming back sooner; it just didn't happen that way.

I closed my eyes and tried not to be disappointed at my delay. I tried to fall asleep so that the night could pass quickly and I could wake to the same bus, the same chugging engine taking me closer and closer to home. But it wouldn't happen; I couldn't sleep, and there were still hours and hours of wait ahead. When I took off my dress, I ironed it on a clean towel across the bureau top for a board.

Then I rinsed out my underwear in the sink, my stockings too. I'd brought no change of clothes with me in my canvas bag, so I made a pastime of undressing piece by piece and fixing myself to dress all over again when the time came and the bus was ready to go. I ironed and stacked and shined and rinsed. Finally, I stood naked in that motel room with nothing left to take off, stood naked as if I were comfortable there and this was a just fine way to spend the night I'd been waiting on for so long. If I could have gotten my hands on a chambermaid's cart, I would have cleaned that entire motel room, sheets to shower.

I wasn't going to pout. I was going to stay busy.

I propped my feet on the edge of the bed and smoothed lotion on my bare calves, cupped my knees and ran it down over my ankles, under the arch of my feet. My fingertips tapped at my shins, played that ridge of bone. This was not my lotion, but a bottle from Harris's apartment I'd packed up with my things. Maybe I took it by mistake, or maybe I saw it every day and began to think of it as belonging to me, or maybe I took it because it was Harris's and I wanted it to belong to me. They all come from the same place, these mistakes and thoughts and wants, and it doesn't really matter which turned my mind at the time.

Harris had taken me to the station to catch my bus home, watched me board, and even stood on the platform and waved as we left

Boone. But there was no kiss, no tears or flowers or promises to write every day. We had words in his car, minutes before leaving; not a fight really but something that passed over us and cast things off balance like a great gust of wind. He doesn't understand why I'm coming home, and I don't understand why I must explain myself. I thought of him last night like a tickle in my throat, something that needed soothing, and a phone call might have done just that.

But instead I called home. I told Miss Pauline not to wait up for me, told her to make sure my mama didn't worry, but we didn't talk long or about anything other than me and my broken-down bus. I don't want to talk to her on the phone anymore. I've been two years away from Edisto at school, two years without seeing my mama or Miss Pauline or Punk or anybody in my family. I was unable to hush my fluttering brain, let-down and restless and full of thoughts that would not lie quietly.

I could say I'd kept away from home. I could say I'd been kept away, and in some sense both would be true. There have been things for me to do without that place, those people, in my foremost mind. But what I'd not thought about once I finally steered myself toward home was the sheer amount of time it would take me to get there.

And so last night, with the sound of Miss Pauline's goodbye still in my ears, with my wistful, anxious self about to set to flight or shatter, I realized something. I am about to enter a moment in burgeon, wide open and flat out. I am traveling back home to my family, sprawling and uncommon and longed for as they are, and those hours in that bare red room were to be my last in harbor with myself.

It was enough reason for quiet, almost enough for content.

I slept in the middle of that big red bed with all four pillows, two under my head, one to my side, and one in my arms held close.

It was a calm and dreamless sleep, and in the morning I dressed carefully all over again, made up the bed, and left that motel room neater than I'd found it. Parts arrived from Shelby and the bus was repaired. We left Bessemer City in the afternoon.

I keep thinking of my two years gone and it doesn't seem that long, just a breath of busy time. Harris tells me as we get older, each year seems shorter, because it's a smaller part of our lives, and once we reach sixty it really is all over in a heartbeat. He says time is relative, and I know he's right. But I want to come home with my time away marked on my face and my body, my expressions and my carriage changed for their distance from Edisto, as if I know a secret or two that I'm not telling. It's in the way that I've dressed myself up, in the care I've taken with my hair and my makeup. It's a simple change I feel the need to show, and I want it to be simply obvious.

My freshman year I came home for my holidays, for a few weeks at Christmas and around Eastertime. But in the summer, I got a job at the Mast General Store on King Street because I liked Boone, its mountains and its coolness, and staying up there made sense. Everybody thought so. I was glad to take my free days and spend them how I liked, especially after I met Harris. There were long lazy weekends in his apartment, whole hours watching TV or reading magazines and knowing we had nothing more important to do. Harris and I found the trails back along the ridge, the quarries that had flooded up to be swimming holes, the banks of meadow grass that held the sun best. I taught myself how to bake in his kitchen, and Harris would eat my sweet things until his stomach ached and then he'd drink a glass of milk and lie on his sofa and pull me down on top of him.

Before we knew it evening would come, and then the night, cool and starry, and Harris would lead me out of doors and we'd wind down the streets of Boone for coffee and a newspaper. It would be like we were the only two people in the world and our waking and our sleeping was enough event to set time by. I know it was not always this way. I know we both had jobs and work to do, and sometimes I didn't bake for weeks, but when I think back, those summers were sweet like cake and fine naps and there was always night coming on and on and on.

Those summers with Harris were magic, and I loved them.

Even so, something could sweep across me like cool shade and I'd want to see my mama, want more than her voice on the phone or her words in a card, and plans would get made, tickets purchased, and I'd be packed for Edisto. It could happen all that fast.

It seemed always something would come up. Last Christmas I got the stomach flu and stayed in bed until New Year's. There were exams and papers that took longer than I thought they would, and in the spring, I was walking out the door to meet the bus, and I just sat down. I found a chair and sat down and was still for a while. It was important to me that I could do that, that I could change my mind and not go and be still. It was important that the plans were mine to change.

Then there were the times too that I'd be walking out the door and Punk would call, ask me instead to run up to New York State and look in on an old friend at Taylor Winery, get an answer to this or that delicate question, pose this or that proposition. These were in-person errands, things he'd want to do himself, but I was closer or packed already, and it was an honor to be trusted this way. Plans are Punk's to change as well and I've been to the winery in Fredonia for him and to Texas where they grow grapes in the dirt, to Minnesota where they develop stock, and up and down, across and over the state of North Carolina. I'd always go alone and I've come to love the travel.

I'd call Punk when I got back to Boone, tell him what I'd learned, and he'd thank me. He'd always ask if I'd gotten myself a souvenir for my trouble.

■ ■ ■

Of the twenty passengers who spent the night in Bessemer City, there are only a spare few left on the bus. Most got off in Columbia, here and there along the way, with their trails of bags, armfuls of things. I have the feeling the bus is lighter and faster now, feel as though I'm all alone, but I know I'm not.

Across the aisle from me there's a woman huddled into herself as if she's cold, as if she's trying to keep something inside her blouse from escaping. She is Asian and slight of form, her face thin-edged like a piece of porcelain, her clothes crisp as if fresh unwrapped from plastic. She has creases to her, the posture of paper. She looks as though she's been dressed and set in place and told to stay put.

I think how this woman is still, like me, but not like me at all. She rests in two dimensions, still without the want of motion in the near or distant future, like a fallen feather or a stone, and me, I am swelled full and at rest, all things stored up. It's then I see a bead of water skein from her hair to her lap, her skirt blue and bluer yet in places, her face wet with tears.

She makes no sound. No sound at all.

The tears roll down her face, some falling from her nose, her chin, her lips, and some catching in the wisps of hair about her face and glistening there in the warming light, like late ice in treetops.

I reach into the canvas bag on my lap, sift through the contents for a tissue or a handkerchief to give this woman, but I have nothing like that. In fact, I know I have forgotten something, something left in the motel room for the chambermaids to find, like a silver earring, or a cake of powder, a photograph I might miss later. Last night in my pacing, I emptied this bag across the bureau, spilling pots and jars and tubes over the veneer. Something could have slipped away from me then. Something I won't know how much to care about if I can't remember now.

I prop my elbow on the window ledge, train my eyes out the window. If I can't give this woman anything for soothing, anything to dry her tears, I don't want to stare her down and make her uncomfortable or feel the need to stop. I feel so for her my tongue's gone salty. I've been on this bus so long, it's a taste in my mouth.

I watch the roadside quicken, the bus picking up speed to make the rise to town. Punk's farm fades behind us, giving way to other pastures, other land full of burdock and ragweed breaking to bloom, dry grasses, horse nettle forcing up through the crackish clay. The land at school is so different from here, verdant and wet. In springtime it rains up there for weeks at a time and I like the rain. I used to sit in the library, waiting for Harris to finish researching this or that. I'd just sit and listen to the rain on the skylights, listen to the rain on the thin roof, a spread sheet across my lap.

Edisto is a simple ratio of water to dust, water like the river that moves and tangles, water that glasses in the heat and pales under white dust. My mama got this idea that she's allergic to dust, and when she tells me about it, she holds her hand over the mouthpiece as if to make sure her words sift clean through the jammed-up air.

She'll say, "All this dust comes from someplace. It comes from ash, little bits of things far away. I swear as we sit here, we're probably still breathing in parts of Pearl Harbor and forest fires in the Northwest, that great quake of 1910."

That's Elsbeth. She's my mama. She thinks about the things that make up dust and send it way up into the atmosphere, like fires in distant places, fires in Oregon, Sweden, and Tasmania, volcanic eruptions in Hawaii, fires at the center of the earth, strip mining in Utah, coal mining in West Virginia, land mines left over from World War II, the A-bomb, the H-bomb. All those women all over the world, beating out rugs they've hung on clotheslines.

I turn in my seat to watch the Edisto dust billow out behind us.

And when I turn back around, my eyes sweep over the woman sitting across the aisle. She's not moved, her tears coming and coming, and all this dust and land passing by her window unseen. I wonder where she's going, who sent her on this bus and where she will get off. She has no luggage with her on the seat, no bags above her head. I get the idea that she might just ride this bus forever, for something to do or be or seem to be doing. If this were a vacation or a homecoming, she would have luggage.

I carry two suitcases with me underneath the bus, and the rest of my things I sent on ahead. Over the weeks I'll receive the boxes I shipped. They'll come from New York and Arizona, Jackson, Mississippi, and Jackson Hole, Wyoming. One will come from Thailand and one will come from my next-door neighbor. But I don't know that yet. What all I do know is I graduated a week ago with a degree in business, and I come home now, a few days before my Aunt Hazel's wedding.

Hazel is my aunt, Aunt Hazel. She's thirty-three, too old to be a bride. I'm twenty-two, old enough to know when a woman is clutching at straws. I know this because I know how to audit assets and liabilities, to prove they're properly valued, incurred, recorded. I know there are fifty-two busts on display in the Accounting Hall of Fame in Cincinnati. I know how to draw up books and balance the balance sheet. I know loss is inevitable. I know clutter is a sign of despair and I know the furniture in Harris's apartment is arranged according to the forces of entropy, that red wine should be stored on its side, that the heart travels the body, and that blood is thicker than water. I know that men like to have love in the morning and lunch in the afternoon. I have a liberal arts education, but a degree in business. I think, therefore I am.

I got that degree only a week ago, but I didn't go to the ceremony. Nobody came up from Edisto either and I didn't send down invitations as there was no reason, no circumstance in which I would have needed them. This degree was only what was set before me. What all I took went beyond paper and lawn chairs and champagne, and such learning doesn't hold audience.

But I can tell how it came about. I saw all these things at college I'd never see in Edisto. I saw a very famous Irish poet read his poetry, but now I can't remember his name. I do remember leaving the reading room and hearing two girls talking. One girl said, he is the most handsome man I've ever seen. The other said, yeah, except for my father. Then they twined their arms about each other and kissed on the lips, and I must admit I could not look away. They were pretty, holding each other like that, or at least I like to think of them that way now.

I've developed my own tastes too, things I appreciate and things I don't. I like good coffee and long skirts. I like the smell of old books, old papers, manuscripts in the library that haven't been opened in thirty years. I like things you have to go places to get, apples from a roadside market, fish from a lake, beer from a bottle in a bar, and men too, men with long ropy backs and sweet shoulders, men who are smarter than I am, and you might find such men in the library, or smelling old books, or wherever you least expect it. I like the unexpected. I like thinking those two women were pretty, even as I wouldn't trade my place for theirs.

■ ■ ■

Owen is to meet me at the station in town. He was to meet me yesterday, and he will be there again today, I'm sure of it. Two weeks ago he told Punk he was headed for Saudi or South Africa or someplace else; he was heading out at the end of the summer to do it on his own. He'd had enough of the small town, the small time, and he'd been learning Arabic from tapes he'd ordered through the mail. This was it; this was his life that was coming around. He was going to have a big time.

Owen is my uncle. He's six years older than me and we'd play together when we were kids. He had these plastic handcuffs and he used to cuff my hands behind my back and see how long it took me to turn a doorknob. Then I'd cuff his ankles together and see how far he could walk.

We talked on the phone days back, but you don't talk much to Owen. You mostly listen and you don't make much effort to understand.

He kept saying, "Let's see how long this one lasts. See how long this one lasts."

Owen used to meet me after school when I was too little and too scared to ride the bus home. We'd walk down Main, by the Rexall Drugstore, crowded with older kids, kids Owen's age, but he'd want to be with me. We'd go by Boyd's Tire and Tool, by the Edisto Bank and Trust. At the Dixie Home Store he'd give me two quarters for a Coca Cola.

He'd say, "Here, getcha that Co-Cola."

Then he'd move on ahead, knowing I'd catch up, find him at Miss Pauline's Boutique, sticking his face in double-D bra cups. In Edisto, it'd still be hot in the fall in the schooltime, and the ashen dust from the road settled in our throats.

Up at Appalachian in the fall, it was cool, and I was older. The leaves turned a thousand colors, and the ground frosted as early as October. It was October when that Irish poet came. It was like he had a word for every color.

And when those colors were bright, Harris used to take me over to Blowing Rock to see how the mountains turned like fire. We'd toss maple leaves off the edge of the outcropping and catch them as they rose back up, sometimes for hours on end. There's a Cherokee legend about Blowing Rock, something about a brave and his woman being in love, and him jumping over the edge of this rock to avoid her father's anger, to kill himself for her love. She, this Cherokee woman, wept at the edge of the rock and the winds bore him back up to her. If you love something, set it free and all that. And maybe it's true.

But Harris says the velocity underneath the outcropping is of the magnitude, and the direction is of the angle, to create an undercurrent spiral, allowing something like a leaf to fall to the basin of the wind and be swept back up toward its point of release in the undercurrent. He says it would never work with a whole body, says it all at once like that, and it is the way he's now come to speak in the fall-times when he is serious and working on his papers and his manuscripts.

So, I will admit I am more in love with the way Harris is in the summer, the way we would eat 'til we were full and sleep when we were tired and not ask much else about why or how. It's easier to love a person that way, simply, plainly, and with belief. How you love is how you love, and you can't help that.

■ ■ ■

Outside Edisto we pass by the carnival grounds. They're all grown over now, green and viny with kudzu that bodies the Ferris wheel like a hide, like fleece, a few cars short of full. Its frame is rust-old, like the carousel that still turns and chimes in the wind, and looming over all is the roller coaster, Thunder Road, a trestle of plank and rail, the sun settling in behind it every night.

I was too young to remember this carnival as ever working. But Owen knew about it, the reason it up and left its pieces here, on a dry lot at the outskirts of Edisto.

You know why they shut this sucker down, don't ya, Mavis? That boy lost his leg on Thunder Road. I saw it happen. Nothin' between his ankle and kneecap but gristle and blood. You never seen blood flowing like his, not in your life.

He'd pause, draw off his cigarette, and I'd sit on his lap in a Ferris wheel car, the great bleached remains of the coaster highing up in front of us. The cars were stuck at the top of the highest track, just thousands of feet in the air, like floaty black tubs filled with rusty rainwater.

His thick fingers tracing the veins in my wrist.

The only girl I've ever loved, her name began with the letter M.

He'd whistle low in his throat, make that M on my wrist, his palms smoothing down my skirt, over my bare calves, fingertips tapping at my shins.

Yep, tried to get him down from the tracks, that boy, but his bones hung up underneath and each pull cracked 'em and splintered 'em; you could hear his bone snappin' like twig in an empty forest. They say he died up there, long before any doctor ever saw him.

He'd turn his face to mine, make that low whistle.

He'd say, *You wonder about things like that? Like dying on top of a roller coaster, or underneath a combine, or in a car. Maybe in a airplane or chock full of buckshot. To be twisted up in metal. To have metal twisted up in you.*

I'd shake my head, no, never. Maybe other ways, other ways to die I might have wondered about, like in water, or in fire, or coming out of the air, getting sucked up by the earth. I wondered what it would be like to die in my own bed. I was six years old. What did I know?

I'd whisper to him and we'd whisper even as there was no one else around, no one else to see and sit and listen. I'd ask if he'd ever climbed up on that thing, looked for any pieces or parts of that boy.

He'd say, *And fall through all that rotten wood? I'd rather kiss my own ass.*

And then he'd cup my knee and sigh, run his hand under the arch of my foot. He'd look me flat in the eye, make me hold his stare.

He'd say, *I saw the thing that happened here, I saw what happened.*

And with a jerk, he'd open his legs and I'd fall through in the direction of down, toward the floor of the Ferris wheel car, before he'd catch me. I'd know all along it was coming and I'd wait for the scare.

He'd tell me to get on home now, and he'd start off the lot, his steps heavy and loud on the gravel path, the kudzu licking at his ankles. He'd go off 'til dinner, sometimes even into the night, and he'd do things I'd never know about.

I'd sit back up in the Ferris wheel car and watch him go down the gravel path, into the trees, slowly Owen, then the sound of Owen going away. Even at twelve, he could disappear like that.

A lthough *Dori Sanders' best known novel,* Clover, *has been translated into six languages, the author still considers herself first, last, and always a farmer. In this excerpt from Sanders' second novel,* Her Own Place, *war bride Mae Lee Barnes faces the challenges of caring for her five children, her aging parents, and a farm of her own — with little more than her own determination and grit to guide her.*

Dori Sanders

Excerpted from
Her Own Place

Even with the help from Hooker Jones and his wife Maycie, keeping the farm going wasn't easy for Mae Lee. Hooker's wife was in poor health. And, although she rarely complained, so was Mae Lee's mama. She had kidney trouble. Yet she was always there, helping out on the farm and with the grandchildren.

"The farm is too much for you," Mae Lee's mama would moan. "You need help. To be married. Besides," she'd add, "you've got the hip set for more babies." Then she would hint. "I don't reckon you'd fuss too much if Howard Jamison would drop by for a few minutes or so Sunday. It's been a while since that wife of his died. He'd make some lucky woman a mighty good husband."

Then her mama would look at her hard. "You need to start wearing your straw hat more and protect your smooth, light skin and get some rest. A man's not going to want some woman that's worn herself to a frazzle. As soon as we get caught up with our hoeing, I'll come and help you out with yours."

Every time her mama had come to help, however, there had always been someone there to pull her away. On one occasion, after it had rained for days and the grass was about to take over Mae Lee's cotton crop and poor Maycie was sick, her mama left off her own hoeing and came over to help.

Just then, who drove up in her fine car but Liddie Granger, Church's wife. "Don't look up, Mama," Mae Lee urged, but her mama had already stood her hoe up and was walking over to the car.

Liddie Granger leaned over and rolled down the car window on the passenger side. Mae Lee could hear a baby crying. Liddie sounded as if she was crying too, "Vergie, Vergie, my baby is crying and I can't get him to stop. My mama is away. Oh, Vergie, please help me. I don't know what to do. I really don't."

Vergie looked over her shoulder at her daughter leaning on her hoe. "Go on, Mama," waved Mae Lee.

Vergie took off her shoes, knocked them together several times to shake off the soft dirt, and got into Liddie Granger's car. Mae Lee watched them leave with the crying baby. What a pair they made, Liddie Granger with every strand of hair in place, face powder on, and her mama barefoot, in old field clothes and a frizzed straw hat.

"If my baby was sick I don't think I'd take time to put all that stuff on my face," she thought, but shrugged it off. "She probably already had it on."

Mae Lee's daddy always said he'd never think too hard of the young Grangers. After all, they sold her the land she owned, something very few white landowners in Rising Ridge would do. He made her promise to hold on to it.

Watching the car disappear down the road, Mae Lee was jealous of the fine life Liddie Granger lived, terribly jealous. Liddie was so rich. In her jealousy she had forgotten all about her own children, happily playing in the shade from the trees at the edge of the woods.

Mae Lee never ever carried her children into the cotton fields, because her mama always said, "If small children play up and down the cotton rows while their parents work, they will grow up to be cotton pickers. And if they pry open a green cotton boll with a boll weevil inside, they will have a short, tragic life." Her mama always spoke of her regrets over letting her play in the cotton fields while she worked. But Vergie Hudson had made sure Mae Lee would be so afraid of the boll weevil inside a green, unopened cotton boll, that she'd never pry one open.

■ ■ ■

It had been fine for her mama to tell her when she returned that Mrs. Granger's baby was all right. She'd gotten it to sleep. But when her mama kept on talking, Mae Lee hoed furiously. "Mama, I don't want to hear about the new things in that house, the presents her husband bought her, the good supper Lula Jane is cooking for her tonight," she said. "Why couldn't she take care of the baby?"

"Lula Jane don't know nothing about no children, look at how she messed up with hers. When it comes to mothering she is as bad as some cuckoo birds. Well anyway, as I was saying —" "Mama," she cut her short. "I don't believe I want to hear any more."

"Oh, good, then," her mama grinned, waving a crisp five dollar bill in her hand. "I thought you wanted to hear how I was planning on splitting what I made on that little short trip."

Mae Lee threw her hoe down and chased her mama up and down the cotton rows.

The two women sat down at the edge of the field to rest. Vergie Hudson pulled sprouting grass from around the cotton plants on nearby rows. Her face grew serious. She looked across the field at Hooker and her husband plowing the land he loved so much. She listened to him calling out "gee," "haw" to the mules. She pulled a crumpled letter from her shirt pocket. "Your granddaddy's going down fast," she said. "Mama wrote and asked if I could come down and help out for a while. It'll be hard on your daddy for me to pull up and go down to the Low Country right in the middle of the farm season, but I'm going to have to go. You know, Mae Lee, that your grandma is in no better shape than your grandpa." Vergie had stopped short of saying that due to her own poor health it would be hard on her as well.

Mae Lee stood up and reached for her mama's hand. "I'll take care of Daddy," she promised. "You go and get Grandpa and Grandma ready to come to Rising Ridge so we both can take care of them."

■ ■ ■

The year was 1955. A troubling fear swept into the farmhouses, fanning out like a plague of bees, each family imagining their own stings. It was the year that Emmett Till was lynched in Mississippi. Mae Lee wept for him, just a young boy murdered in cold blood.

There was also a home problem she had to face. Her mama's eyes had brimmed with tears when she told her that the day they'd feared had indeed finally come. She and Mae Lee's daddy had decided they were going to have to leave Rising Ridge and move to Low Country South Carolina to take care of her mama's aged sick parents, rather than the other way around. Her grandmother, a diabetic, was rapidly losing her eyesight, but she was still caring for her grandfather who had suffered a stroke. Vergie's efforts to get her parents to move to Up Country and live with her had failed. Her mother stubbornly refused to move. "We won't be taken from our home, not while we can lift a finger to hold on to the doorknob." And the children had to look out for the parents, even if it meant moving away to the Low Country. "Mae Lee, we will have to leave as soon as the fall harvest is finished," her mama said. "Your daddy's already made arrangements for Hooker Jones to farm his land on the halves. Hooker and his wife claim with you helping out so much, the three of you can run both farms. You and your children can move into our house, so they can live in yours."

Mae Lee and her parents finished the fall harvest early. The last bale of cotton was ginned two days before the November eleventh Veterans Day parade, a big event in Rising Ridge. Since most of the crops were harvested there was always a Christmas float included in the parade to get people in the buying spirit, with a Santa Claus tossing candies and small gifts into the crowds. On the day of the parade, dressed in warm mittens and tasseled knit caps, and under the watchful eyes of their mama and grandparents, Mae Lee's children eagerly scampered about gathering the goodies. Inside one of the stores, Mae Lee and her mama showed the children the pretty dolls and toys. The children wanted them all.

Before they left, Mae Lee's parents put all the Christmas presents they bought for the children under lock and key in the big chifforobe in their front company room. Mae Lee's mama reminded her over and over that she wouldn't be with her this time, so she mustn't forget to wrap the things they'd bought in the child's personal clothes. That way, even though they didn't have name tags, fancy wrappings, and bows, the children could tell which presents were theirs even before they could read. Vergie Hudson had already put the baseball she bought for Taylor in one of his socks, and wrapped a baby doll in Annie Ruth's little pink dress. She reminded her daughter of some of the good hiding places she used to search out on Christmas morning when she was a little girl. For Mae Lee's children, Christmas was like an Easter egg hunt.

A couple of days later Mae Lee's mama and daddy packed up the few things they were taking with them, and with help from a few neighbors, moved Mae Lee and her children from the little house she'd bought, back into the house where she had been born and grown up.

Mae Lee looked about the rooms, now crowded with her furniture as well as her mama's. She loved the new things her mama had. A Kelvinator, and an electric cooking stove and oil circulator to replace the potbellied wood-burning stove that had been in the kitchen. She step-measured enough space in a corner for Taylor's little bed, then measured with an outspread arm how much cretonne material it would take to run a drawstring curtain across. Poor little Taylor would still have to sleep in the kitchen, she thought. She looked at the nice front and back porches, but it was having a larger bedroom for her daughters that pleased her most.

It was late in the day before her parents were ready for departure. They hated to leave fully as much as she hated to see them go. Her mama reminded Mae Lee once again that her cousin Warren would always be there for her to go to in case of need. "Remember, Warren is a porter on the Southerner," she said, as if Mae Lee didn't know that very well, "so he can hold true to his promise that there'll always be food and a place at his table for you and my grandchildren. Warren will see that the family sticks together."

Her parents urged their grandchildren to be good, and showered them with candy, little gifts, hugs and kisses, which seemed to take away their sadness. Mae Lee fought to hold back tears. For her, there was no comfort.

Outside, before he climbed into his truck, her daddy put his hands on her shoulders. She dropped her head. "I'll do my best to keep things going until you all get back, Daddy," she said softly.

"Oh, you'll keep things going, Mae Lee. Just remember you are not going to be alone," he said. "You'll have help."

After they waved good-bye, Mae Lee's children went back inside the house, but she stayed out alone under the dreary fall sky. She thought of her daddy's parting words, "You'll have help." She wondered if some surprise awaited her, if there was something her daddy knew that she didn't. Maybe her husband was going to come back home. Perhaps her daddy felt that it might no longer matter to her what people might say if she took him back. She had been a grass widow too long, faced too many lonely nights alone in her marriage bed.

The feelings and desires for her husband that she thought were dead and buried were briefly very much alive, she realized, springing back like drought-parched corn coming back to life after soaking rains.

She felt the evening chill, and turned to go inside.

■ ■ ■

It was early on a cold winter day when Mae Lee's cousin Warren came by. Mae Lee had already started cooking. "It's too cold to do anything but eat," she said.

"And keep warm," her cousin added. "I brought you some kerosene."

Warren spent the day hauling wood for her fireplace and fixing up the chicken coop. He put a new wick in the kerosene heater that she used to keep the chicks warm, and fussed at her for ordering baby chicks during the winter months. "Your hens will start hatching their eggs come spring," he argued.

"Yes," she agreed, "and my chicks will be plump young fryers by spring."

Her cousin shook his head. "You work too hard for a woman, Mae Lee." He glanced out the window. "I see Hooker heading out to feed the mules. They're getting pretty old for farming, Mae Lee. Especially Maude. Hooker said she barely finishes eating her bundle of corn fodder at night."

"I know," Mae Lee said. "Old Molly's started to limp. Since Daddy left she hasn't been shoed right. Both mules are going down. First it was Starlight, and now the mules. I guess I'll just have to let go of the mules." She turned to face her cousin. "There's talk that a lot of farmers are buying new tractors. Warren. I wonder what they'll do with their old ones?" Mae Lee asked.

"Either trade them in or sell them," Warren answered. "That's a mighty big step to take, Mae Lee. I know your daddy will understand if you don't farm the land for a year or two. They'll probably be back sooner than that anyway."

Mae Lee wasn't listening. "If I scrape up what I've saved back and take the money Mama's going to send for the children's new Easter clothes, I might can make a down payment on a used tractor."

Warren got up to add kerosene to the oil circulator. "You'd better hold on to that money, Mae Lee. With little children in the house it never pays to take out the last piece of money you have in your shoe.

Besides," he added, "you never want to be forced to have to buy your seed and fertilizer for spring planting on time. Come fall, Mr. Kingsford can charge you whatever he wants to. Remember, with Hooker Jones working the land on the halves, you've got to put up all the money up front — to buy all the supplies."

Mae Lee pursed her lips. "Seems like the landowner puts up too much," she said softly.

Warren inserted a funnel into the heater tank and poured kerosene in. "The sharecropper carries a full load. He puts in all the labor and still pays half the expenses at harvest time."

"And gets half the profits," Mae Lee added quickly.

Since he had a few days off from his job, Warren promised Mae Lee he would ask Church Granger if he knew of a used tractor in good condition for sale. And to spare her from having to go to her parents while they were dealing with sickness, he would loan her what he could spare for a down payment on a tractor.

■ ■ ■

Later in the winter Mae Lee and Hooker set out together to check on a used tractor. It was a cold, windy Saturday. Hooker slowed his truck for the ruts in the dirt road. "Church Granger said this tractor is a good buy. I don't guess he would steer me wrong," Hooker said. "He never has before."

Mae Lee didn't know what she was looking for when she walked around the tractor. She merely duplicated every look Hooker Jones made. Somehow she felt she should. She nodded her head in agreement when Hooker Jones told the seller he thought the asking price seemed right much, but she didn't like it when he added that he'd be hard pinched to pay that much. It was her money, she thought, not his, that was being paid out. The least he could have done was say it would be hard for her. She said nothing, however; Hooker was old enough to be her father. Perhaps it was best that she'd remained quiet. The seller knocked one hundred and fifty dollars off the asking price.

In the cold truck with a nonworking heater, Hooker was gleeful. "We've got us a tractor and it's a fine one. Hardly broke in. I didn't let on how good it is."

Mae Lee pulled her scarf around her face. The cold air that blew in through the ill-fitting cardboard in the old pickup window chilled her to the bones. She was hungry. There would be nothing much for the Saturday supper, but she planned a really good dinner for Sunday. It seemed to her that if she could just scrape together a good Sunday meal, Saturday night didn't matter so much.

Before Mae Lee opened her front door, the smell of fried pork chops greeted her, but inside there wasn't a scrap of food in sight. The kitchen was clean and warm. She had only to read her children's faces to know they were hiding something from her.

Nellie Grace pulled her mother to a chair and put her hands over her eyes. "Don't look, Mama." Mae Lee didn't look, only listened to her children set the table and put out the food they'd hidden. When she opened her eyes she was truly shocked.

Her daughter Dallace had prepared her very first meal. She had cooked the food that Mae Lee had bought for Sunday dinner. She watched her son, Taylor, roll up his sleeves to his little elbows and wash his hands in a washpan on the wooden kitchen bench. "We didn't eat a bite of nothing all day long, Mama," he said excitedly. "We just all pitched in and helped cook." Mae Lee forced a weak smile and tried to appear happy. What the children didn't know was that they wouldn't be going over to their cousin Warren's house for dinner the next day. Not after what happened last Sunday, when Warren was away on duty and his wife Lou Esther had said what she said.

Last Sunday she'd done just like she'd done ever since her parents had gone — gathered up the children and headed for her cousin's house for Sunday dinner. Warren was what was called well-to-do. He wore his shoes shined, and a suit to work. He had taken Mae Lee and her children under his wing. Even when he wasn't in the area, the Sunday dinner was prepared for her family by his wife, Lou Esther. It was tradition.

Mae Lee had always felt welcomed and right at home for the weekly dinner, until last Sunday when her cousin was away working and Taylor, her fourth oldest, had asked for another helping of food, a single piece of chicken. There had been a platter still piled with fried chicken and more on the stove, even after everyone was ready for dessert.

Mae Lee had said no. "One piece is enough," she'd said.

"But I'm still hungry, Mama, bad hungry," Taylor said.

The hunger of a growing boy was in his eyes, so she gave him another piece. Lou Esther made no attempt to hide her displeasure. Her husband was away, and she was free to speak her mind. Her remarks were cutting and unkind: "Children who are fathered by worthless men are the hungriest children in the world."

Mae Lee didn't wait for her children to have the usual Sunday's two desserts, one of which was always a delicious nutmeg egg custard. Ignoring their pained, silent pleas not to have to miss dessert, she ushered them away from the table and straight out of the front door. As she marched her crying children home she made a sworn oath that she would never set her feet under Lou Esther's table for a meal for as long as she lived.

■ ■ ■

Now, the morning of the Sunday after the episode, Mae Lee stirred and sleepily opened her eyes. It was still half-dark outside. She reached out from under her warm layer of quilts and fingered the source of the cold wet thing pressed against her face. It was her littlest girl's nose. Her face and hair were dotted with melting snowflakes.

"It's snowing, Mama, snowing like crazy," Amberlee whispered excitedly. She slipped under the warm covers.

Mae Lee bolted upright. She had planned to be out of bed bright and early to gather a few turnips for dinner, before other farmers started passing her fields, going to church. Like her mama, so many of them felt it was a sin to harvest on the Sabbath. Now she would never find the turnips. It was probably just as well. Her children hated them anyway. She made a roaring fire in the fireplace and turned the oil circulator down. She needed to save oil. She scooped up the wild hickory nuts her son, Taylor, had hidden in the wood box and gave them to him to crack open and pick for brown sugar hickory-nut fritters.

By midafternoon, the children were hungry again. When the snow stopped, they begged to be allowed to go back to their cousin's house. They didn't say why; they didn't have to. Besides the food, there was a TV set at Warren's. Mae Lee felt regret over her rash vow. She shook her head sadly. Never cut off your tongue to spite your lips, she thought.

She was sifting the words of her vow through her mind again and again when Warren came to the door. He was not his usual self. "Well, what's the excuse?" Warren asked. "Dinner is almost on the table." He looked at the empty wood box. "I'll bring in more firewood from the porch while you get the children ready."

Mae Lee suddenly realized that her rash solemn vow not to eat at Lou Esther's table again had not included her children. She had only spoken for herself. She had vowed, "As heaven is my witness, I will not set my foot under Lou Esther's table for Sunday dinner again" — nothing about her children. They were free to go.

She didn't have to lie to make an excuse for herself.

Dallace, her oldest, held her head high as her mama buttoned the top button on her coat. "Mama, tell Taylor not to eat up everything on the table this time. I hate it when Cousin Lou Esther's face turns into sour milk because he wants more chicken or something."

Mae Lee dropped her head in shame when she saw that Warren, standing in the doorway, had heard. She wished he hadn't.

"Oh, good Lord," he groaned, "so that was the fire that started the kettle to boil. I should have known Lou Esther said or did something. I still can't believe that my own cousin wouldn't at least tell me, though. Try to overlook Lou Esther, Mae Lee. You know how she is. She says things without thinking. She didn't mean no harm."

Taylor looked at his mama. "They better hold my hands then, Mama, 'cause I'm mighty hungry."

His mama pulled him close. "Eat all you can hold, son, and tote home all you can't." With a hug and the whisper "Eat, eat" to each one, she waved goodbye.

Afterward she scrounged for food in her kitchen. There had been more than enough for breakfast, even some leftovers. As always her son had been hungry, hungry, and had eaten every scrap of food in sight. Her mama had always said, "If there is a hungry child, a mother's hunger pain leaves." But Mae Lee's hunger pains were rising, increasing like the chill factor of winds that multiply the cold. She had a strong craving for fried chicken. It seemed that if it was Sunday, you should have fried chicken or fried something. They may not have had it during the weekdays, but nearly always for Sunday dinner. She thought briefly of her brood of young chickens in the small henhouse, feeding on cracked-corn mixture, warm in the dull glow of a smoky, slow-burning kerosene heater. All she had to fry was one of her biddies. The very thought of a fried biddy doused her taste for chicken. She glanced at the almost empty Coca-Cola jug in the kitchen corner. There was enough kerosene to last the night, but she'd have to head for the general store the next day. Monday was her day to deliver fresh eggs and shop for her week's groceries.

She made a batch of hot-water cornbread pancakes and loaded them down with homemade butter and sugarcane molasses. The homemade butter was from Mrs. Whitfield's house. After Starlight had died, she never owned another cow. She always got a week's supply of milk and butter in exchange for her children feeding and watering Mrs. Whitfield's cow. Her children wouldn't eat the butter at first; they claimed they saw her cat in the butter. Mae Lee told them cats didn't ever go near butter, but in the future Mae Lee made sure she was at Mrs. Whitfield's house from the time the butter-making started until she got her share. "I'll get the churn ready and churn the butter for you, Mrs. Whitfield," Mae Lee would offer, and would then use the wooden press to make a fancy mold.

"Why, Mr. Whitfield is going to be tickled pink when he sees this on the dinner table," Mrs. Whitfield had said once. "Mae Lee, I know you always say you don't have time to cook for anybody but your family, but you don't suppose you'd have time to make up a fresh batch of those good buttermilk biscuits of yours? Daddy —" she paused and smiled, "that's what I call my husband sometimes — loves fresh buttermilk biscuits. But I can't seem to make good ones." Her eyes saddened. "I actually can't make any kind at all, Mae Lee. My mother didn't cook. And 'Cook' didn't want me fooling around in 'her' kitchen, as she called it, when I was growing up."

She sat nearby on a high stool while Mae Lee made the biscuits. She had a couple of dollar bills sticking out of the eyelet-trimmed pocket of her pink housedress. Mae Lee hoped they were for her. She was fresh out of sugar and coffee.

Mrs. Whitfield traced her fingers lightly across the smooth countertops. "My husband," she began softly, "would be glad to pay you whatever you'd charge if you'd agree to come in the late afternoon just to cook." When there was no immediate reply from Mae Lee, she hurriedly went on. "There would be no cleaning whatsoever. I just love to clean house."

Mae Lee glanced about and thought to herself, If you love to clean so much, why in the world don't you do it?

"Even Daddy says you work too hard on that farm," Mrs. Whitfield volunteered. "Farming the land is too hard for a woman — too hard."

At least you won't ever have to do it, Mae Lee thought. Mr. Whitfield was the county solicitor, but everyone knew that she was the one with the money. Ellen Whitfield didn't want for anything.

Mae Lee rolled out the biscuit dough. Her body rocked as though the rolling pin needed an extra push. "Farming is not too hard when it's your farm, your land, Miss Ellen. You see, that farm is mine, so it's not too hard at all."

She didn't offer Mae Lee the money in her pocket. Mae Lee had, after all, turned the cooking job down. Anyway, her butter was good, and she needed the milk for her children. In a small way, Mae Lee kind of thought that one reason why the Whitfields kept the cow was to make sure her children had milk.

Over a steaming hot cup of sassafras tea, Mae Lee envisioned what her children might be doing right now at her cousin's house. Maybe dinner wasn't ready when they got there. Perhaps they were sitting in the warm company room with the fancy doily-laden, deep wine velvet davenport, looking through Sears catalogs and watching TV. Lou Esther would most likely be in the same room, juicily licking her fingers to flip the catalog pages, sticking torn paper bag pieces between the pages to mark something she was sure to order. Mae Lee thought of the identical rose-colored butcher linen dresses they'd both ordered once. Looking through the wish-filled pages together, each had been careful to seem disinterested in the smoothly pleated skirt and rosy pearl buttons that fastened the simple top, lest the other decide, too, that it would be perfect for Sunday church. And that was exactly where they'd met, with their shocked faces greeting each other from opposite ends of the pew.

Her cousin's wife was probably getting up and down to make the few steps to the small kitchen to stir the trays of homemade ice cream freezing in her Kelvinator, and taking her time to put dinner on the table, not in the least concerned that Mae Lee's poor children would be starving. With fresh snow on the ground it would be quicker to make snow cream. Her children probably would have preferred it. Eventually the food would be ready, however, and with Warren home that Sunday there would be plenty for them.

■ ■ ■

The following spring Mae Lee realized how very right her cousin had been about the need to hold on to what money she had. She had to write and ask her mama for some money for seed, plants, and fertilizer. She didn't tell her mama that she'd had old Hooker Jones plow up every foot of clear farmland and plant produce. She knew all too well that her mama would once again urge her to try and find some good man to marry before she wore herself out working. Her mama would also fuss that Hooker Jones was too old for such a heavy work load. Once the farm work was caught up, she and Hooker planned to sell the corn, beans, okra, tomatoes, watermelons, and other field-fresh vegetables from his pickup in the back lot behind downtown Main Street.

Then near the end of summer, poor Hooker's wife Maycie fell sick again and was unable to help gather the crop. Half the time Hooker had to take care of her, and when the cotton picking season started Mae Lee was forced to help. As soon as she got her children off to school, she made a daily morning trip to the little house where she used to live to take food to Maycie, before heading to the cotton fields to pick.

The warm sunshine from the mid-October sun streamed down through the clear skies. It was midafternoon. Mae Lee stood and stretched her aching back. She took off her sweater and tied it around her waist. She glanced at her half-empty burlap cotton poke. If she stuffed the cotton into it well, she wouldn't have to empty it until she reached the end of the long cotton row. Next year, she thought, I'll ask Hooker to shorten the cotton rows.

Mae Lee worked alone, her hands moving from one cotton boll to the next as fast as they could go. At the rate she was picking, before the end of the week she'd have another bale of cotton ready to be ginned. The entire cotton crop would be finished before it was really cold, because once again it was a poor crop. It had rained almost every day during the late summer and early fall. The cotton was damaged and wouldn't bring a good price. Cotton was at its best if there was dry weather in the weeks prior to harvest. She remembered the years before DDT, when the boll weevil wiped out her daddy's cotton crop. Her daddy tried growing tobacco. The boll weevils didn't like it, but the young boys in Rising Ridge sure did. They stripped the leaves and smoked the green tobacco.

Even though the poor cotton yield meant little profit, Mae Lee didn't mind too much. She and Hooker had made good money with the summer produce crops, and with the profit from the cotton, though small, they would both come out all right. Best of all, Mae Lee would be finished picking cotton sooner. She hated to pick in the cold, and the fall days would soon be getting really cold. She hated it most when she had to brave the frosty mornings. The cotton work gloves, with the fingers cut off so her bare fingertips could grasp and pull the cotton from the bolls, were usually wet from dew or frost. They did little to keep her hands warm, and nothing at all to keep the hard, pointed, knife-sharp outer bark of the open bolls from puncturing and piercing her stiff, bleeding fingers.

From a distance Mae Lee watched her children walk up the narrow dirt road home from school. Taylor carried his baby sister's little primer. Little Amberlee was a year younger, but taller than her brother. Her older girls walked behind. She waved and called out to them. They didn't hear her. She was a little concerned that Taylor had not rushed to the cotton field where she was, the way he usually did, but instead had waited to see her at home.

Afterward, while she finished preparing the supper that Dallace had started for her, she watched Taylor slide into a chair. Mae Lee wanted to cook at least a part of the supper every night. Her daughter wasn't quite thirteen years old, too young to have to be the head cook in the house.

Mae Lee hugged her oldest daughter, "Smells good, Dallace. Now you go get your schoolbooks and study your lessons."

Taylor propped his elbows on the table and cupped his small face in his hands. He was small for an eight-year-old. "Mama," he blurted out, "where's my daddy? I wish my daddy would come back home, Mama."

At all times Mae Lee hated that question, but she hated it most at night. She poured cornbread batter into a large, black cast-iron skillet and slid it into the oven. She was in no hurry to answer her son's question. She closed the oven door, and looked directly at Taylor. "I don't know, baby, I really don't know." She lifted his little face upwards. "I'm going to go and feed the chickens, and when I come back inside I want to hear you helping your little sister read from her primer." Outside, Mae Lee fed her chickens and cried. When she went back inside Taylor was asleep in his chair.

At the supper table Taylor asked to be excused when he finished eating two wedges of hot buttered cornbread and a glass of buttermilk. He didn't eat any vegetables. Mae Lee thought he was too tired and sleepy to eat, so she made a little pallet for him on the floor near the new oil circulator, so he could rest until time for bed.

Mae Lee washed her children's socks and underwear and hung them on the backs of chairs to dry. She didn't want the dirty clothes to pile up. She was still feeling a little guilty about doing the washing the Sunday before. Her mama wouldn't have washed clothes on a Sunday no matter what. But it had been such a bright warm day. Mae Lee would have picked cotton that day if there had been no one to see her and think she had no respect for the Sabbath.

She had fallen asleep, and forgotten to move Taylor into his bed, when she heard him call out to her. "Mama, Mama, I hurt, I hurt, Mama." She rushed into the next room. Her son looked at her as if he was afraid. She felt his forehead. He was burning up with fever, and was talking crazy, out of his head, jabbering like a two-year-old.

She glanced at the clock. It was after twelve, the middle of the night. She covered her sleeping children, her little stair-steps she called them. She gently shook her oldest child. "Dallace, honey," she whispered, "Taylor is sick. I've got to get him to the doctor. I'm going to Church Granger's house. Take good care of your sisters and don't open the door for nobody but your mama."

She pulled on her pants and field boots, tied a belt around her cotton flannel gown and pulled it up under her heavy sweater and coat. She wrapped her sick child in blankets from his bed and hurried through the chilly October night to the Grangers'.

The bright moon cast eerie shadows from trees alongside the narrow path. She could feel the warmth of her son's feverish body. He was breathing harder. Her brisk steps quickened into a slow steady trot.

It seemed that, almost before she knocked, the front porch was flooded with lights and Church Granger was at the door. Maybe the dogs had barked. She didn't remember hearing them.

"My baby is sick," she cried. "I've got to get him to the doctor!"

Church turned quickly, walked to the foot of the stairs and called up to his wife. "It's Mae Lee, Liddie. Her son is sick. I'm taking her to Dr. Bell's."

"Wait," Liddie called back, appearing seconds later at the top of the stairs. Mae Lee watched her pull her robe about her as she hurried down the steps. She looked at the sleeping child in Mae Lee's arms. "Oh, Mae Lee," she moaned, "you had to carry him all the way here." She peered beyond Mae Lee. "Where are your children? I'll go get them and bring them here."

"No, no," Mae Lee hastily responded. "My Dallace won't open the door. Theyll be all right. She'll take care of her sisters."

Liddie turned to her husband. Her eyes were anxious. "Hurry, Church, hurry."

Church Granger tried to take the heavy child from Mae Lee's grasp, but her hold on her son was firm. The child felt almost weightless in her strong arms.

He drove faster than Mae Lee had ever ridden in her life. She held on to her son and pressed imaginary brakes to the floor every time he rounded a curve, but she didn't ask him to slow down. Instead she studied the moon that seemed to travel along with them, and tried to think about setting out to find her son's daddy. He had asked about his daddy. Taylor needed his daddy. She nestled her chin against his warm head. "I'll find your daddy," she whispered. The long country road seemed to stretch forward forever into the moonlit night, like the sometime worries of motherhood, long roads with no end.

As they drove on, Mae Lee thought about how concerned Liddie Granger had seemed over her little Taylor and her little girls at home. She remembered the day Liddie had been so worried over her own crying baby, she'd driven down to the cotton field where she and her mama were hoeing to ask for help. Mae Lee'd been furious seeing Liddie Granger drive her fine car down from her big fancy house on the hill. Now she couldn't believe that she had been so angry with Liddie for causing her mama to stop hoeing and go check on a crying baby.

At Dr. Bell's house, Church remembered he should have telephoned so he'd have been waiting for them. He called out to the doctor's barking dogs. "Be quiet, Duke, now, now, Trouble. Duke, Trouble, calm down, hush up."

"It's me, Bland," he called out, banging on the door, "Church Granger."

Dr. Bell took one look at the sick child. "Get me some cold water, Church," he said. "There is ice in the refrigerator." He put cold cloths on the boy's forehead and an ice bag at the back of his neck. He slid a thermometer under Taylor's tongue. When he pulled it out he shook his head. He didn't reveal the temperature. "Taylor's throat is really inflamed, Mae Lee. Nothing to be alarmed about, but I'll give him an injection of penicillin and keep an eye on him for a while." He took a small bottle from his medical bag and broke the snap seal. Tears rolled down Taylor's cheeks as the doctor injected his behind, but he didn't cry out. His mama obliged on that.

Church watched with Mae Lee as Dr. Bell changed the cold compresses once the heat from the child's body had warmed them. "Mae Lee," Church said, "I'm glad you came directly to me without waiting. I wish you had a phone so you could have just called us. With your parents gone, don't you struggle with those children alone. When you need help, call on me or Liddie."

"I did," she whispered, "and I will. Thank you."

After some time it was evident that Taylor was cooler and less restless. The ice packs had started to work even before the penicillin. As Dr. Bell took the child's temperature again, a relieved look crossed his face. He turned to Mae Lee. "The fever is going down," he said, then added, "but that doesn't mean it might not come up again. Be sure to keep him home a few days, and try to get him to take as much fluid as possible."

"I'll keep an eye on them," Church told Dr. Bell.

Once Taylor was well, he seemed to have forgotten about wanting to find his daddy. Mae Lee was grateful. The episode had finally confirmed in her mind what her divorce had put on paper, that she didn't want ever to lay eyes on Jeff Barnes again. Her child had been sick, and she had had to turn to a neighbor for help. If it hadn't been for Church Granger's willingness to oblige, Taylor might have died. She didn't know where Jeff Barnes was, but whatever the children might believe, he had spurned them, left his family to get by on their own without his help or caring or even, so far as she knew, curiosity. Biologically he might be their father but that was all. The children owed nothing to him but the fact of their birth, and she wasn't ever going to feel guilty again about them not having their father around, no matter what they might say. They would just have to get along without him.

*T*he time is 1963 and young Denise Palms leaves Virginia, where she has been raised by her grandmother, and returns to Detroit to live with her mother, Margarete, as they await the arrival of Margarete's baby. "Neesey" is expected to take her place cooking and caring for her extended family, but an influential teacher has higher aspirations for the girl.

A.J. Verdelle

"THE LANGUAGE OF MASTERY"

Excerpted from
The Good Negress

Miss Gloria Pearson tried to help me bury my backwater bad habits. She'd be there in the mornings: sweatered, straight-skirted, and wearing perfect stockings. Unmarred by any hurry, or anyone's baby, or a struggle to get a stroller out of doors. She wore gloves every day, cotton in the spring and fall, and some other smooth material in winter, no heavy, scratchy wool.

She would fill up all three blackboards, writing with chalk. She started at the left, and progressed to the right. She erased one board at a time, starting with the left. If you daydreamed — and I did — then when you got your mind back in place, you wouldn't know the sequence of the boards. So, what I copied would occasionally be jumbles of things. When the first blackboard I copied was the center, but she was actually at the center having started on the right, so right was first and center was last and the left was the middle of the lesson, I would have center first, right second, and left last, hurrying to catch up. So what I got, early on, was in segments not in sequence. This was before I learned to turn my mind to a subject like a flashlight. Miss Pearson had me practice doing that. "Concentrate," she'd say.

Doctor Dew Boys. Now he was her hero. I knew I spelled his name wrong and got none of the zillion initials in front. But Gloria Pearson could talk days about him and did, in the five years I did everything I could to learn from her. She got elated when she talked about him, her eyes shining like Margarete's when Margarete and Big Jim were having their parties, and they had beer after beer after beer.

I didn't quite understand all she said about him, but then when did I ever understand all she said? Miss Pearson said it was very important for me to understand about heroes, and to always have one chosen for my own. It's like having a star to follow, she said. I wish that then I could have made my way through my stumbling, faltering English to tell her I already had a hero in her. But I couldn't. I find out in this hero process that some things she expects me to get, and some things she doesn't. I hadn't known that; I thought I was supposed to understand everything, which is why I tried.

She said I seemed overwhelmed by Doctor Dew Boys. And so she introduced me to Doctor Carver. She said I might understand him better, me being from the country and all. Since he is a farmer who turns into a scientist, she thinks maybe I can follow him from tomato plants to the laboratory. She told me he looked into the peanut and the sweet potato with a microscope. We had one microscope at the school, and she showed me what it does. Out of his own curiosity and initiative, she said, he picked up the crops from the ground. He took them inside to a laboratory, where he made new compounds. He invented things. She said he ground up both the peanut and the sweet potato. Remind me of a kitchen. Made things this country had a need for, but that no one else had figured out how to get. From her voice, you could tell, she is proud of Dr. Carver. "Yes, I am proud of Dr. Carver," she answers me; "he is a Negro of great genius." According to Miss Pearson, This Country needs to see that there are many Negroes of great genius.

According to Miss Pearson, We need to pluck genius Negroes from the farms, and the railroad flats, and shotgun houses. And We all need to know that We have our geniuses too. That if We look at what We do closely, We too will Invent and Discover and Be celebrated. Many more of us Negroes can be heroes, she believes.

Dr. Carver started out working with the soil. In farming, there is so much to do, the demands of the land and the weather make you work, and notice, and understand. But, she says, she thinks that Dr. Carver — who was at that time just George — was paying close attention. He was practicing turning his mind to a thing because what he ended up noticing and what he ended up going after was specific and small. With studied attention to the specific and the small, he revolutionized science, she said.

Gloria Pearson got in the habit of being able to tell when I was vague about what she said to me. "I'll slow down," she said once or twice, and that gave me a minute to breathe in and start concentrating fresh. Once I learned to breathe in and concentrate fresh, then I could also do it for myself, in the times she didn't say she would slow down.

Missus Gloria Pearson went to Livingstone College in North Carolina. She told me. I guess that's why she know so much about how to fix my English speaking. I wrote to Granma'am about Missus Pearson and Granma'am say ain't no reason I cain't go to college, Livingstone or Hampton Institute, when I gets to be woman enough. Granma'am say Hampton Institute cause she want me to come back to Virginia. I want to too; me and Granma'am feel the same about this. Granma'am say she got a little piece a money stored up in the house she can draw on when the time come. I don't exactly know how all that business happen but Granma'am say it's a grown folks' question. Granma'am say learn as much as I can in Detroit, and then we can see about me going to college.

I do all my work on the big kitchen table. In fact, the whole kitchen is mine. Nobody comes in to turn on the hi-fi, killing my quiet sound. Luke edward will not plop down on the couch, shaking it underneath me, or stretch his feet across to the coffee table so that I have to move my papers. In the kitchen, I don't have to use my back to bridge between their divan and the surface where I can write things down, what with all the papers I am stacking and restacking, writing on and reading through to learn.

The kitchen is also where I know everything going on. I know whether there are leftover chicken legs for Luke edward to snack on when he comes. Luke edward always goes to the icebox when he comes in the house. Big Jim says Luke edward holds the box door open like there's a hungry woman inside. I don't quite know what he mean, but I don't like the tone of it. What Luke edward really does is come in late at night, and check out the stores; he picks what he wants, and then eats it, all. We don't have no rules in the house about leftovers. Big Jim and Luke edward and all us know, first to the leftovers, first to the leftovers.

When it's time to make the next meal, I just get up from where I'm sitting and move into my next set of things to do. I can look up words and write down definitions while the kidneys are parboiling. I keep a clean dish towel hung across the chair so I can wipe my hands from the cooking to my books and back again. I can hear anybody who calls me, or anybody calling anybody else. Margarete has to call through the kitchen for David or Luke edward. Sometimes they answer, sometimes they don't. When they don't answer, I can help things out and say, "Luke edward. Margarete is callin you." I can even see the front door opening and closing from the place where I sit at the table.

Missus Pearson pushed up her sweater sleeves. After some of the other kids start to leaving, she kept me and Josephus late as we could stay. Her arms write everything neat and lined up on the board.

Missus Pearson's interest in me, and Josephus's present pride, made me want to shine. I didn't have the time I could see it would take to prove myself to Gloria Pearson, but I worked with a fever, racing Margarete's baby to life.

It's funny and sad how I saw everything in terms of Margarete's child then. I think I thought there would be no life for me afterwards. I worked hard, hard, hard at Missus Pearson's lessons. At the same time, I resisted Margarete's.

Margarete said she wanted to clean out a drawer and look at my things. She had me clear out my grip on her and Big Jim's bed while she rearranged. She said she wasn't wearing much of nothing anyway, big as she was getting.

"Where the rest of your things?" she asked me.

"This is all I got."

"What you mean, Neesey?"

"This is all I got."

"You ain't got no clothes to wear to school?"

"Yes I do." I pointed to my blouses and skirts. "Four skirts and six blouses."

She picked up my two dresses and held them up to my shoulders. Then my skirts. "These skirts look mammy-made," she said, "and besides they too short. These dresses ain't much better. I can't believe this is all the clothes you got. What you do, leave the worst things at Mama's?"

"Yes," I answered, but I hadn't left much.

"Somebody hand these things down to you?" she went on.

"Yes. Lantene," I told her.

Margarete looked sad. "After I have the baby and get back to work steady, I'm gonna have to buy you a thing or two," she said. "I don't want you to be embarrassed about what you have to wear."

Missus Pearson say she will teach us all the rules. She say English is governed by rules of grammar, and the rules, she say, go special with nouns and verbs.

Missus Pearson don't do exactly what she said. She don't tell us no rules. She start to asking us questions and wanting us to say the answers or write them down. I want to know about the rules. I don't have much time. I ask her, "Missus Pearson, which a these is the rules?"

Missus Pearson say, "Say, Which *of* these."

She waited, looking at me. So I say, "Which of these," and I remember the rest of my question, "is the rules?" She takes a deep breath, and that usually mean we got a lot to do yet. Shoot, I could of clocked myself on the head for making whatever mistake I made, but I didn't. Miss Pearson say I must express myself with English, not with gestures.

"Say, Which *of* these *are* the rules?"

"Which *of* these *are* the rules?" I repeat very carefully.

"Which *of*, two *of*, one *of*, six *of*."

"Which *of*, two *of*, one *of*, six *of*."

"On account *of*."

I am surprised. "On account *of*," I repeat very slowly.

"Can you think of other examples?"

I hesitate.

"Can you think of other examples when you might use the word *of*, Denise?"

"Could *of*, should *of*," I say, looking up at her.

She blinks. "No, Denise." She picks up her chalk and says come up here to the board. She draws a swift line down. She writes:

Could have Should have Would have

Copy these phrases thirty times each, she says. I start to write, very slowly, so as not to screech the chalk.

She put up on the blackboard Rules of Agreement, with fast and level lines under the words. Missus Pearson explain that the subject have to agree with the verb, and you use a different verb depending on your subject. I want to look at Josephus, see do he know what she talking about, but I also don't want to look away since Missus Pearson is talking right to me. I wonder will she explain it some more. "For example," she continues, "I is is not correct."

She ask us to repeat what she say, and we both repeat, "I is is not correct."

225

Don't make the first bit a sense to me. Then she ask us what is correct, and I think I need to know what what is, before I can even try to tell what is correct. I think we both just look at her. She wearing a pink sweater and gray skirt. She wear black T-strap shoes every day with stockings look like they fresh out the package. When she move round I smell counter-bought talcum. Her hair has loose waves and skirts her shoulders.

I wake up; her long chalk is writing on the board again. I look at what she is writing, and I wonder did I miss something important, like what this is on the board now. I had been wondering where she got her clothes from, see could me and Margarete go. The writing on the board say:

I am	We are
You are	You are
He or she or it is	They are

"Do you know these are verbs and pronouns, the present tense of the verb to be?"

Aw God, it's getting worse. I don't answer. "Say, I *am*," she tell us. We both say it. She ask me to read all the pronouns and verbs off the board, just as they are written. I read: I am. You are. He or she or it is. We are. You are. They are.

I can read pretty good. Granma'am had me read out loud all the time. I like the way I sound in the classroom, though, reading out loud with the big windows all round. Josephus don't read good as I do. I wonder if she know the "you are" is the same on both sides. I wonder what is the rule to help me understand this when it's not up on the board.

"Denise," Missus Pearson call me; "Josephus," she call him too. "I want you to start hearing these words." She tugs at her ears, and then points to the words on the board. "These are where you make your worst mistakes," she say, leaning toward us. "We will go over this, and over this." She go on, "You both must concentrate." She say, "Remember to form the ends of words, not just the beginnings.

These words, and all others. Denise, say I am-m." Sound like I am-uh, and my mouth is screwed shut because she been leaning to me talking about my worst mistakes and I thought I done good reading out loud. "Denise," (clap) "say I am-m."

"I am-uh," I say.

"Josephus?" she call his name.

"I am-uh," he answers.

"Now, listen," Missus Pearson go on. "The next time you hear yourself say I *is*, know that that is wrong. Wrong. Wrong. Stop right then and say I am-uh. I want you two to really start listening carefully to how you talk. Listen to what you say when you talk and correct yourself immediately. This is so important.

"Again, be very attentive to the ends of words. If you say only the beginning of a word, that is only half the word. And since so many words begin so similarly, you could be misinterpreted. Don't say fo', say for-r. Don't say a, say of-uh. Don't say gone, say go-ing-uh. Don't say 'gwon, say go on-uh. Don't say mah, say my-y. Don't say ah, say eye. Eye. Eye." She making me tired she think so fast. I don't really know what misinterpreted means but I guess it mean somebody cain't hear what I'm saying. "Don't say iss," she still talks, "say it is."

Dog. These is the rules and I ain't ready. I'm trying to get out my pencil and get my book open to a clean page. She say, "Don't say ast. Don't say ax. Say ask. As-suh-kuh." I don't get no rules writ down cause after that she clap on my name again with her voice.

Gloria Pearson has given me ten years' worth of spelling words — I go from one set to the next, and I am never idle. I am so grateful that she taught me to try to match the English language to what I was trying to say. Making a match between what I wanted to say and what is permitted in English is the closest thing I had then to religion. Although the whole of what she is showing me has yet to come clear, it's something I trust that she knows. I don't doubt what she tells me. So I open all my books, and get familiar with the red marks on all my papers. I check and recheck my spelling and try to make sure that the nouns and verbs have the *s*'s in the right places.

The walk from our flat to my school building was my time to examine my mind about things. I raked over my mind plenty, most every day. Lord knows life been kind as grace to me, allowing me to come up from down home and go to school all these months, learning about geography and maps, and math and English, and reading some poetry out loud. Here I am concentrating on proper English, and if I was still down outside Richmond, I never would of had a chance to learn it. And Missus Pearson, she such a fine teacher. She start to teach us the important things soon as she get in the classroom. Not like with Missus James, all us country kids sitting in the back and wishing half the time we was back home.

Missus Pearson taught me to diagram sentences. Put the subject and predicate on a straight line to themselves. Slant other words underneath the line of the word it modifies. In language, one thing precedes and another follows. That's what Miss Pearson said. Even though precedes seems like predicate to me, Miss Pearson say it is the subject that precedes and the predicate follows. When she said something that subject and predicate I could understand, I would reach out my hand, try to snatch it, and try to paste it correctly in my composition book. Late at night, while I waited for Big Jim and Margarete to come in, I would take apart the nouns and adjectives, verbs and adverbs, and get straight the words that had capital letters. By the end of all our time together, she had taught me appositives, and subordinate clauses, verbs of action and of being. She amazed me what she knew and saw in things.

I diagrammed the sentences she shot at me aloud. I wrote down the things I remembered that she said, and I would put them on their grammar lines. Do your homework. Purse your lips. Repeat what I say, Denise. Try harder.

The subject lines were mostly blank, and when I asked Missus Pearson about it, she was pleased to grinning by my question. She talked forty minutes about implied subjects and imperatives.

At home in our apartment, I wrote and wrote. At our kitchen table, or hunched over the coffee table, sometimes while I rocked Clara's bassinette swing. I looked up words in the dictionary, wrote their spellings and definitions ten times. Like formula, dismissed, perturbed, precipitation, barometer, proprietor. Used my dictionary for spelling and for meaning. I might put the baby to sleep, and then spread all my things out on the single bed I slept in in the room with the sleeping child. Or I might put the baby down and go back into the kitchen where I could smell that the kidney beans and neck-bones were still cooking, about done, needing salt, or just about to burn. Me and Granma'am never ate as much neckbones as Margarete and Big Jim, Luke edward and David seem to. But I try to keep up with the tastes they have for things.

I filled a composition book a month studying on my own. The thick pages with my handwriting gave me something to show to myself for my days.

Missus Pearson said that it was my not knowing the English lan-guage that cut me off from a bigger world. But it was Margarete's baby that kept me in the house, that cut me off from outdoors, even. Well, I figured if I could feed and wash the baby, douse her with pow-der and lay her down, clean and sweet, then I could look up all the words I didn't know and write them down in my school notebooks and try to reach to somewhere.

I find other things to do besides cook, clean, buy meat, wash bot-tles, and diapers. I practiced how to write answers to questions. Every time I went to school, I took in extra I had done.

At the end of the school days, I said, "Good afternoon," to Missus Pearson longingly. On the days I got my extra back, I felt better. The extra would be marked across the top: Look up Charleston (atlas). Look up Corsica (encyclopedia). Who is Valentine Kinsey? (your memory). Who is Lawrence and what about those brooms he made? How many times have you been to Richmond Center, and what did you do each time you went? And the bottom: Good. Very Good. Six, seven, eight, two wrong verbs. Correct and bring back. We got to the place where she stopped circling the wrong verbs for me. Just a note of how many, and I had to find my own mistakes.

Some days I walk with the carriage to meet Missus Pearson after she has finished the after-school work with other students but me. After me and J left, she stopped the after school at four when all the kids said they had to leave. I roll the buggy and she carries her papers and we go back to the flat where she lives. That's one thing Clara did for me, made Missus Pearson more than my teacher, also a kind of friend, for a time.

When there's time she invites me in, I mean, us in. I have made tea on her stove. Her stove is a small and friendly fixture in her kitchen, which is small too. Clara sleeps like the little exhausted baby she is; she sleeps in her stroller like it's a good bed. Missus Pearson's flat is quiet like a blanket that surrounds it. Missus Pearson lets me help her with whatever it is she has to do. The first summer I was out of school, I cut up two hundred and twelve paper bags and covered fifteen crates of school books for Missus Pearson's next year. The bag paper dried my hands out so bad. And it took me days because when Clara would wake up and start to bawl, Missus Pearson would not let me walk her up and down and shake her. Instead, Missus Pearson told me, the first time I tried to quiet Clara in her flat, that when Clara needed to play or cry or romp and grow, I should take her home and let her do it. She prefers children who can speak English and who are old enough for discipline, she said. I think I heard some amusement in her voice. I know I always hoped I did. Anyway, she left whatever I was doing — this time, the books, covered and uncovered — for me to finish the project on my own. Wasn't that nice?

She also gave me lots of things to write about, insisted I write about raising the baby. She read every page of my composition books, and marked them up with red ink. Never said a word about what I wrote:

> Margarete does not seem interested in the baby. Clara threw up on my new sweater today. Big Jim wakes Clara up too late in the night. Clara doesn't seem to be full of Margarete's anger, not like Big Jim about Luke edward, not like I worried she would be, what

with them arguing and the baby living in her belly. I am glad. Clara loves Luke edward like milk. Clara and me are the same in that way.

Missus Pearson was trying to cheer me up by letting me visit her apartment, and she tried to continue to teach me by letting me sit in the back of her class whenever I could come. Going to her house, I couldn't help but think: what must I look like, young, and with that carriage. I must look fast, and ruint too. Beyond myself. People must wonder where is my spoiler. They must think he gone.

I n 1993, author *Reynolds Price gathered into one volume fifty short works of fiction, representing a career that spanned five decades — and is now entering its sixth. From the many pieces varying in tone, style, and setting that are contained in* The Collected Stories, *Price chose for inclusion in this anthology the short but powerful story that follows.*

Reynolds Price

"An Evening Meal"

Sam Traynor had got the reprieve two days ago — the five-year cure of his stomach cancer — and he'd spent both days in quiet pleasure, not unstrung but high on a joy he'd hardly known since boyhood. Because his parents were long dead though, and he'd lived alone since chemotherapy made him reckless for weeks on end, he had no close friend to tell the news. A woman who worked at the next desk over and the doorman in his apartment building seemed at least to notice a change. The doorman remarked on the tie Sam spent thirty dollars for, in celebration; the woman said "Sam, are you wearing blush?" (it was healthy color). And that was all, for human response. Sam wouldn't phone his aunt or her sons; they'd offered so little when it would have counted.

So after work that pleasant Friday, he walked ten blocks to eat at a diner he'd last visited the week before surgery, not even sensing a near ambush. It was not his favorite restaurant, then or now; but he'd planned this evening in further celebration — or the risk of one. That last visit he was also alone; but a new waiter was working the counter, a boy just off the plane from Amalfi and as good to see as any face that rushed toward Sam too fast to use, in his early days. The boy had accepted his invitation, turned up after the diner closed and — through a whole night — lent Sam his stunning body and smile, free as air.

And never again. When he left at dawn, he thanked Sam, saying "I liked you, sir." Sam stopped him there with a silent hand and fixed the moment in his mind where he knew it was safe as long as he lived. Five years later though, the boy wouldn't be there — surely not. His name was Giulio, called Giuli; and still his memory seemed worth the risk.

But there he was after all at the grill end when Sam took a stool up near the cash register. A few pounds thicker but lit with a heat that spread from inside him, the generous fearless eyes of a creature better than humankind anyhow. He was talking intently with an ancient woman in a genuine cloche hat, stained pink velvet. The one other worker in sight was a girl who served the counter and the booths by the street wall. Final daylight was strong at the windows, colored green by water-oak leaves.

Right off, Sam knew he'd give no sign. If Giuli glanced his way or walked by, Sam would look right at him but not speak first. That would test many things — how much the wait had changed Sam's looks, how deep his face had registered on Giuli that one dark night, what Sam's whole life might hold from here out: a whole new life. He was calmer than he'd expected to be and was halfway through a bowl of good soup before Giuli passed to ring the woman's check.

No look Sam's way; and once the woman passed back of Sam, blowing a dry old kiss at Giuli — and Giuli had actually turned to Sam and asked if the crackers were fresh enough — still no door swung open between them. Giuli grinned but in a general direction.

Sam knew it was strange, but he wasn't disappointed. The most he'd hoped for was some shared memory and the chance of Giuli's pleasure in the news. It was plain anyhow that Giuli's forgetfulness was real when their hands touched to exchange the crackers. The skin was warm as before and tougher. On the right ring finger, Italian-style, was a wedding band.

By the time his turkey sandwich was ready, Sam had agreed they'd touched near enough. They'd silently proved they were still alive and had asked for no more; but then Sam's mind set off on its own, watching a clear line of pictures that came from the night they'd shared nearly all they had. The same pictures had been a main help through the six hard months after surgery and X-ray — Sam's old skill as a home projectionist of well-kept memories. In lucky hours he could shut his eyes and play through a useful number of scenes, from minutes to days, in keener detail than when they were new, tasting individual pleasures and thanks strong as ever. There were twenty-some scenes from his adult years, eight of which were masterworks of time and light; and the scene that centered on the early Giuli contended for best. In the next half-hour, through his sandwich and tapioca pudding, Sam had again everything Giuli gave him and needed no more.

He believed that at least till he asked for his check and Giuli brought it, clearing the dishes in graceful ease — not a clink or scrape. But one more time their hands brushed; and Sam was startled by the wash of gratitude poured out in him — an unexpected need to say his own name, then allude to their meeting and tell Giuli what that memory had meant to a man condemned by a ring of doctors to die in a month. *It hauled me back;* Sam knew that much. At first a cold-scared hunkered patience of constant pain; then slowly an easier slog through time, dense at first as hip-deep seaweed.

Terrified and then edgy as the wait was, it came to feel better than what went before; and the new years turned out, of all things, celibate. In eighteen hundred ominous nights, however often Sam ran the scenes, he'd never once felt compelled to reach for another man near him. A bigger surprise by far than his cure; and he sometimes wondered if the X-ray had done it, burning out some nerve for longing. Or was it simply fear of more sickness? Whatever, Sam took the world through his eyes now. With no real blame and no regret, though he'd sometimes wonder *Am I dead and punished? Or maybe it's Heaven.* Alone on his stool he actually laughed.

Giuli turned from cutting a blueberry pie and seemed to nod toward a table beyond them — a nod and a frown to hush the air, then a dark-eyed sadness.

Sam hushed and tried to see a reflection in the glass pie-cabinet; it curved too sharply. So when he'd sat another two minutes, dawdling through the last of his coffee, he laid a small stack of bills on the check, caught Giuli's eye and said "Keep the change," then turned on his stool.

Four yards ahead — close to the door in a four-seat booth with the low light on him — a single man was huddled inward on himself as tight as if a blunt pole had pierced him, threaded his chest and bolted him shut. He might just weigh a hundred pounds; his rusty hair was parched and limp. His eyes hit Sam's a moment, then skittered.

It's Richard Boileau, already dead. Sam guessed it that fast; but since the man's eyes wandered to the window and watched the street, Sam stayed in place and tested his hunch. He'd last seen Richard in '78, the November morning after they'd proved through a long bleak night how well they'd learned each other's least weakness and how they could each flay the other with words. Then as daylight had streaked the roof, Sam suddenly found the one path out. He stood from the bed they'd shared for three years, picked up a few good things from the bureau — his father's gold watch, a comb of his mother's, his wallet and knife — and said "All right, the rest is yours."

The rest had literally been the rest — Sam's clothes, books, records, two years of a diary, a few nice pieces of furniture he'd more than half paid for. All well lost and Richard with it, the dazzling tramp hungry as any moray eel, cored-out by a set of monster parents. Through the years Sam heard second-hand of his whereabouts, always in town at a new address; but the two had never collided till now, if this was Richard.

For whatever reason, of Sam's old loves — vanished or lost — it was only Richard he'd thought of as dying, purple-splotched with

Kaposi's sarcoma or drowning in lung and nerve parasites. Each day he'd read the obituaries, crouched against the name on the page; and while he chalked off friend after friend, Richard stayed inexplicably free. Even in Sam's own worst days though, when radiation seared his gut in third-degree lesions, he somehow knew he'd outlast the havoc inside his skin while Richard Boileau would certainly die in this new plague. And not from an endless hunger for bodies — scrupulous Sam could have picked a killer any calm night — but from some cold rage in Richard's mind to leave a string of his riders appalled.

But is this helpless scarecrow Richard? In two more seconds Sam all but knew. The worn blue shirt that swallowed the long neck was one Sam had left — a red *S.T.* still edged the pocket, sewed by Sam's mother. Had a stranger bought it at the Salvation Army? Sam turned away to steady himself.

By now Giuli was back by the grill, laughing with a cook that had just turned up, a rangy boy with a knife-blade profile.

Sam thought of quietly walking their way and asking if they knew the man in the booth — was he a regular; what was his problem?

But the young cook met Sam's eyes, gave a wave with his spatula, then kissed Giuli's jaw — their eyes were identical; they had to be brothers. Giuli called out "Grazie," smiled at the whole room, took a short bow and scrubbed at his neck.

Sam stood up and faced the booth. The man was still pressed close to the window, though Sam could see there was nothing to notice, nothing Richard would have spent ten seconds on. The fact freed Sam; he stepped across, took the opposite bench two feet from the man's head and said "See anything good out there?"

The man turned gradually and, at close range, the skin of his upper face was transparent — that thin and taut on the beautiful skull.

Sam thought he could see a whole brain through it, a raddled mind, whatever it knew or had lost for good. But Sam stayed still till he'd drawn a direct look from the eyes — they'd kept their color, an arctic blue. Then he said "Is it Richard?"

No move or sign from the frozen face.

Sam tried a new way. "Bertrand? Remember?" In the early days he'd sometimes called Richard "Bertrand Le Beau" when nothing yet had dulled the shine.

At first the name seemed to penetrate. The eyes widened and the dry lips cracked.

But then a quiet voice said "You know him?" The waitress was there with a dry slice of toast and a cup of milk that gave off smoke. She set it by the man's right hand and spoke to him gently, "This'll warm you fast. "

Sam took the risk and looked to the girl. "You know his name?" The man might have been on the moon, engrossed.

The waitress smiled. "I know he's been bad off a long time. I know this is what he eats every night. But he's gaining strength now — aren't you, friend?" She touched the wrist that was nearly all bone.

The man faced her, his smile a ruin. He managed to lift the cup of milk though and drink a short swallow.

The waitress tapped Sam's shoulder lightly. "Sit with him some. He never sees people; make him drink his milk." As she left, she asked Sam if he was still hungry.

He shook his head No; but when she was gone, he saw she'd left an idle fork and spoon on the table, bound in a napkin. He took out the clean spoon, stirred the milk, drank a spoonful himself; then slowly over the next ten minutes, he fed Richard Boileau the whole cup.

rowing up in the South in the days before the civil rights revolution, C. Eric Lincoln came to understand the dynamics of his region. Producing such ground-breaking works as The Black Muslims in America, *he emerged as one of the leading black scholars of his generation. But he was always drawn to the place of his birth, and this story, taken from his novel,* The Avenue, Clayton City, *is deeply rooted in the ironies of that place.*

C. Eric Lincoln

"COLEY'S HAND"

Excerpted from
The Avenue, Clayton City

Coley lay on a low iron cot next to the window. He could see a good piece down the road without much trouble, and if any of his regulars should be coming, he could just reach under the bed and have his order ready by the time he got up to the window. On weekdays most people just wanted half-a-man to get them through the day. Beginning late Friday evening, business stepped up right nicely, and sometime Coley really had to exert himself to keep from working. But today was Monday, and business was slow. Coley knew just about everybody who would be calling at the window at the side of his house. Jay Dee had already come by to get himself a taste to go

to bed with. Jay Dee worked all night at the ice plant, and since
Monday was his day off, he always stopped by Coley's on his way
home to get a little something to help him sleep. It was about seven-
thirty when Jay Dee was there. A little after that Velma Ray woke him
up bamming on the front door as though she thought she was somebody important. As a matter of fact, she was. Velma Ray could ask a
favor of most any of the white men downtown and get it. She could
help you, or she could hurt you, depending on how you treated her.
That was why Coley didn't say too much about her waking him up
bamming on his door, even though she knew perfectly damn well
that he didn't do no business inside his house. Only at the window.
He just didn't want any trouble with any woman that close to white
folks nohow. It could be bad for his business. But he let Velma Ray
in, and after she'd had a toddy, she'd gone to the kitchen and fried
up some salt pork and potatoes. Coley took a plateful and set it on
the floor beside the iron bed. Velma Ray ate what she wanted and
left after reminding Coley she had other fish to fry, an' she didn't
mean no wore-out ol' crawfish like him! "I hear you, Boss Lady!"
Coley grinned, waving her through the front door. "You know I need
you, Baby, but I jest don't have the price!" He turned over on the
iron cot to watch Velma Ray strutting on off down the road toward
town. "She got to have a whole lot of poontang," he said aloud,
" 'cause she got a whole lot of box to tote it in." All ass and no class,
he mused. Nothing like Queenie. Queenie got it all. Still, he admitted to himself, Velma Ray did look good going away; it was coming
toward you where her equipment broke down.

Coley was glad she was gone. He had a lot on his mind, and having a woman around, especially if she's not your woman, interferes
with hard thinking, and hard thinking was what Coley wanted very
much to do this particular Monday morning. Coley had his eye on
The Avenue, but he was being messed up by a shitass named
Roosevelt. He was thinking hard about Roosevelt and how he could
get him out of his way. Not only was Roosevelt messing up his plans
for The Avenue, but Roosevelt was ahead of him to the tune of $8,
and try as he might, Coley hadn't been able to figure out a way to

get any of his money or to keep Roosevelt from taking further advantage of him. Just thinking about Roosevelt made his head ache. His feet, too. In the first place, Roosevelt had made him violate his business principles. Coley didn't do no business on credit; that's how he had gotten where he was. Roosevelt knew that. Why, then, would he put him in a position which required him to break his own rules! Every one of those $8 Roosevelt was owing him was a dollar against everything Coley imagined himself to be. He was a businessman. If you want a man, or half-a-man, then pay your $3, or your $1.50, and get your whiskey. That's the way to do business! But no, Roosevelt had to take advantage of the fact that Queenie was his sister, and Queenie was the one woman in the world right now that Coley wanted to be his woman.

Coley's bitter reflections on Roosevelt were interrupted by a sharp rap at the front door. He glanced at the Waterbury clock on the mantel. Ten-thirty. He had been so absorbed in the trouble Roosevelt was causing him that he hadn't even heard the car drive up to his door. But he knew who would be in it, and when Velma Ray left, he had left the latch off the door in anticipation. Someone knocked again, this time with authority.

"Come on in," Coley shouted. "This here is Coley's house!"

The Clayton City Police Department, consisting of the chief and his deputy, strode through the front door and on into Coley's bedroom.

"Coley," jibed the chief, looking down at the iron bed where Coley languished, "I hear tell you been sick."

"Yes, suh, Chief," Coley strained himself to reply, "I've been right po'ly. Right po'ly. And I'm sho' obliged y'all come out here to see ol' po'ly Coley. Sho' is, suh!"

"I also hear," continued the chief with a grin and a wink, "that you been selling whiskey!" At that all three men burst into laughter and Coley swung his long bare feet to the floor, the better to slap his skinny black thighs.

He reached under the bed and brought out a quart jar of lethal-looking clear corn whiskey and handed it to the chief. "Well, this here's to prove Coley ain't selling nothing." He grinned. "Ol' Coley's giving it away, white folks. Giving it away!"

The two white men sniffed at the jar and bobbed their heads in approval. Then they headed for the front door. On the way out the chief paused long enough to run his fingers into the brown faded Limit Life Insurance Company envelope hanging on the wall near the door. He removed the ten-dollar bill Coley always left there for him and stomped across the wooden porch after his deputy.

Lots of folks called Coley a "nigger" because of his white-mouthing to the police, but that didn't bother him too much. After all, he was a bootlegger, and bootlegging was his business. And if you're gonna do business, you have to do what the trade demands. A man had to make a living, and the less strain involved in the process, the sweeter life was bound to be. Life was a matter of energy. "Juice," Coley called it, and if you put all your juice into working, there wouldn't be any left for enjoying what you worked for, and that wouldn't make sense. No sense a'tall. The trick was to put out a little juice, decorate it with a little bullshit, and set back and let nature take its course. That way your back wouldn't be aching, your bones wouldn't be creaking, and you wouldn't have any knots on your head when it came time to enjoy yourself. Now the white man had the right idea, Coley thought: Get the niggers to do the work, get the niggers to dejuice themselves on your projects while you lay back in the shade and prosper.

Coley never denied that he was a nigger — that'd be mighty hard to sell, him being both black and humble — but Coley always believed that he was a nigger in a class by himself. He knew he was smarter than the average colored man he'd ever seen, or heard about, and half the white folks who thought he was a coon were going to wake up someday and learn he was a fox. For all his smartness, the average white man is still stupid. All you have to do is call him "boss" and cut the fool for him, and he'll give you the gravy off his grits. Coley had a way with white folks. Most of the ignorant niggers in Clayton cut the fool for nothing, but every time Coley cut the fool, it was another dollar in his bucket. That's business.

It was 10:38. Roosevelt would be coming as soon as he got off for lunch, and just as sure as his name was Roosevelt he was going to try to put the arm on Coley for half-a-man. It wasn't the money so much, but Coley just didn't like for anybody to owe him. He didn't do no business on credit. Roosevelt knew that. He didn't like for anybody to put anything over on him either, especially a chickenshit punk like Roosevelt. That just naturally made him mad. Roosevelt had somehow managed to make things hard for him. If Roosevelt had the guts to get married or just go on Up North, or something, Queenie wouldn't have to look after him and do his cooking and washing. If Roosevelt would go about his business like a grown man ought to, maybe Queenie would cook and wash for Coley. Yeah. He could move his business over to Queenie's house on The Avenue. Yeah. True, Queenie wasn't going to have any and everybody coming to her house buying whiskey. You see, he could understand that, he could live with it. He could fix things up to get around that problem. He could build him a little place out in the backyard, off a piece from Queenie's brick house. She got a big yard. Yeah. And a big behind, he remembered with satisfaction. He could fix it.

Now Queenie thought a lot of herself. She didn't have much education, but she had class. She knew how to wear her clothes and how to furnish a house off nice, to bring out the best. When Queenie came back to Clayton City when her mama died — she'd been off living in Chicago and big-time places like that — when she came back to Clayton to get young Roosevelt and take him with her back to Chicago, the white folks up and bought their old home place out in Fairmont for cash money and put up an electric station there. When she got the money, Queenie changed her mind about going back to Chicago and built her and Roosevelt a brick veneer house right smack on the Upper End of The Avenue! Right there with the McVeys and the Goddards and all the other Big Niggers. That's one of the things that made Roosevelt such a pain in the ass. Roosevelt thought that because he *lived* on The Avenue, he *belonged* on The Avenue. Shit! Who the hell was Roosevelt — a grown-ass man driving a silly-looking goddamn three-wheeled motorcycle around picking up cars for Jack Romine's automobile laundry! What made it so bad was that he dressed up in a leather cap, big black goggles, and leather gloves and all that shit like he thought he was a speed cop, or something. Putting on his funky airs! Smoking a big cigar! Ain't that a bitch? He better watch out; one of these days one of them crackers up there around Courthouse Square might snatch him off that motorcycle and kick his ass 'til it ropes like jelly. Coley figgered to do it himself if it wasn't for Queenie. Roosevelt wasn't shit and he wasn't worth a shit! He was just a two-bit hustler, and right now he was hustling Coley, and there ain't been no nigger born who could hustle Coley and get away with it. Mighty few white folks — and no niggers at all — could take Coley for his money.

Yeah! White folks got their hustle, too. Ol' Chief Evans and his po'-assed deputy came there every Monday morning like clockwork. Looking for whiskey. Looking for money. They always find a quart of corn and they take that away for "evidence." But long as Ol' Chief find ten dollars in the insurance envelope, the evidence always disappears before him and that dumb-ass deputy he got get back to town. One of these days the insurance man might get there first and get the money and Ol' Chief might have to *present* his evidence. "But if he do," Coley mused aloud, "they'll have to pump it out of his belly. Won't that be a bitch! But that Roosevelt. He's gon' be a pain in the ass long as grass is green and shit stinks. Roosevelt got to go."

Coley's thoughts were broken off by the sound of somebody marching down the road to a brisk military cadence. The approach was from the other side of the house from where Coley lay looking out of the window, but he knew that in a second or two Shelly Mahaley would march into his line of sight. Hut! Hut! Huh-Won-Who-Free-Four! Hut! Hut! The cadence grew louder, and he could hear Shelly's boots crunching the loose gravel at the edge of the road. A moment later he popped into sight, swinging along the road, looking to neither right nor left. He was in full battle dress, from canteen to gas mask, all of 1918 vintage, except that over his shoulder he carried a Civil War musket complete with bayonet affixed. The world war uniform was his own; the musket he had found on one of his forays into the trenches at the fort where he went to dig almost every day. Shelly was a casualty of the war. Shell-shocked in the trenches of Argonne, he was mustered out a corporal and sent home. His experiences in France remained his last consistent contact with reality, and over the years people had gotten accustomed to seeing him marching up and down the road counting cadence or singing the war songs of 1918. This morning was like any other. Shelly was going to the fort to dig for the money he believed the Germans had buried there. Probably he would not find any, and even if he did, it would more likely be Confederate money than German. But there were other treasures he had taken from his years of digging — cannonballs, muskets, arrowheads, bayonets, helmets, and even an occasional skull.

Coley watched Shelly march on down the road, and the germ of an idea creased his black, shiny forehead. Suddenly he leaned as far out the window as he could and yelled: "Shelly!"

Shelly Mahaley continued to march. Coley yelled again, his hoarse voice cracking with the effort.

"Shelly! Hey, Shelly!"

Shelly gave no sign of hearing. The crunch, crunch, crunch of his boots remained steady and determined. Coley cursed him and spat his disgust through the window. Suddenly it came to him that since Shelly thought he was still in the army, he might respond to an army command.

"Corp'al Mahaley! Halt!" Shelly took two steps and stood stock-still. Coley grinned with satisfaction. Now ain't that a bitch? "About face!" he ordered. "Now march on over here to my front door!" he commanded. Up to now Coley had not had time to figure out just what he wanted Shelly to do, although he was certain that his luck had sent Shelly to be the answer to his problems with Roosevelt. "Po" Jip always said, *If money lasts, luck has got to change!* And Coley believed in luck. Some people had it and some didn't, and some who had it didn't know how to take advantage of it. But Coley always knew he had a good hand, and he expected to come out on top ninety percent of the time, whatever it was he was after. He was lucky with the women. He managed to stay out of jail most of the time. And he had a molasses bucket full of money buried under his house — all of which was proof that he had a hand. Now his luck was rising again. He could feel it. He was going to get rid of Roosevelt and move into that big house with Queenie. On The Avenue.

Shelly was turning into the front yard. Coley could hear him still counting cadence: A-hut! Hut! Huh-Won-Who-Free-Four! When he heard Shelly come clomping up on the porch, Coley got up off the bed and yelled through the door; "Detail, halt!" Shelly stomped to a standstill, and Coley made some effort at hurrying about preparing for his reception. He slipped his long, bony feet into a pair of old shoes with the heels cut out, put on a wrinkled white shirt, and rummaged in the closet for an old chauffeur's cap he used to wear before he went into business for himself. He then ordered Shelly in through the front door, being careful to look up and down the road to make certain that no one had seen him enter.

Shelly Mahaley was a small, wiry man, in his middle forties now, but with muscles still as powerful as spring steel, conditioned no doubt by daily calisthenics and digging in the trenches of the fort. His uniform, though somewhat tattered by years of wear, was clean and neatly patched, and his ancient musket glittered from the meticulous care of the professional soldier. Shelly had been a volunteer, one of the first men to leave Clayton when the United States finally joined the conflagration of 1914-18. In the early days of the war he had fought under French command, as many American officers at the time considered it demeaning to be assigned to officer black combat troops. As the war neared its end, Shelly was a seasoned combat veteran, and he was transferred to a regular American army unit along with hundreds of other blacks who had fought under the French. Shortly afterwards, following three months of exposure to sustained enemy bombardment, he was shipped home suffering from extreme battle fatigue. Shell-shocked. Coley, too, had been briefly in uniform, but after ninety days of training he had been discharged "for the good of the service." Now the military experience he had hated so much more than twenty years ago was finally about to become very useful to him. At the moment Coley was about to feature himself as an officer of the United States Army. He savored the thought, and for the first time ever he wished he had kept his uniform. But, no matter, the chauffeur's cap was enough. It would do. His hand was bound to hold, and in a few hours he would be on his way to new levels of personal success.

Coley was tempted to tell Shelly to sit down on the old overstuffed sofa by the door, but then he realized that that would be unbecoming to an officer-enlisted man relationship. Instead, he ordered, "Parade rest!" and Shelly set the butt of his musket on the floor, tilted the bayonet forward, and spread his feet eighteen inches apart. Coley was ecstatic. He had a one-man army under his control. He had power. He reached under the bed for a pint bottle he kept handy for his personal use and took a long swig from it. The corn whiskey was hot. Raw. It coursed like fire through his frail body and shook him like a small clap of thunder. Then a warm, tingling sensation flowed over him, and suddenly he felt very wise. The secret of a man handling his whiskey rather than being handled by it is in never drinking enough to make you stupid. A man's whiskey ought to serve him. If whiskey is going to be the boss, a man ought to leave it alone. Right now Coley knew he was boss. He slipped the pint bottle into his hip pocket, wiped his mouth on his sleeve, and looked sidelong at Shelly. If the old soldier had any thoughts about Coley's behavior, no sign showed on his face. He stood rigidly at parade rest, his gaze transfixed on some point in space far beyond the walls of Coley's house. Coley adjusted his chauffeur's cap and moved directly into Shelly's line of vision.

"Corp'al," he said in as grave a tone as he could muster, "Corp'al, we army men have to stick together. We got to fight for each other. That's the law. You listening at what I say, Corp'al?"

For the first time Shelly seemed to look directly at Coley. There was a dull gleam in his eyes that startled Coley for a minute. After all, he remembered, Shelly was not all there. Shell-shocked. Coley straightened his chauffeur's cap and tried to assume an air of military authority. His hand felt nervously for the pint bottle in his hip

pocket, but upon being reassured that it was still there, Coley resisted the urge to strengthen his confidence with another drink. Shelly
was saying something. He seemed to be looking through Coley
rather than at him.

"The krauts are our natural enemies," Shelly announced simply.
Coley was immensely relieved. He had gotten Shelly to say something. Now he was ready to proceed with the plan taking shape in his
mind. He looked at his watch. It was 11:47. Roosevelt would be there
in thirty minutes or less. Shelly was talking about krauts. Germans.
That was the angle he ought to push. The shortest distance between
two trees is apt to be through the bushes. He cleared his throat and
rocked back on his heels the way he imagined a general would do.

"Krauts. You got to be right, Corp'al. Them krauts is our natural
enemies. They's downright hard on colored people. They don't 'low
no colored to even live over there! You got to be right."

"We are Americans," Shelly announced. "The Yanks are here to
make the world safe for decent people to live in. Safe for democracy. We will destroy the Germans. God is on our side. God is for the
right!"

"Yeah. Yeah!" agreed Coley. "Them goddamn German krauts got
to go! We gon' kill all of 'em. Roundhead bastards trying to take our
democracy. God sho' don't like no ugly, do he? Naw, sir. He sho'
don't! Now looka here, Corp'al, you an' me can stop them krauts
cold, see? They out here every day. They got spies riding around on
motorcycles — you know, like them German officers do in the
movies — course, you don't have to see no picture shows 'cause you
done been there for yourself. But you know what I mean? They
come out here on them damn noisy-ass motorcycles messin' with our
democracy every day. We got to put a stop to that shit!"

"We defy their bombs and their warplanes," Shelly cried, his voice
now rising with a strange anxiety. "We ain't scared of their bombs.
We ain't scared of their planes! We will shoot their warplanes out of
the sky!" His face was contorted and strained as though he were reliv-
ing the scream of artillery shells and the whine of aircraft on some
far-off battlefield. He brought his musket sharply to his right shoul-

der and began to march rhythmically in place to some ethereal cadence. Coley's apprehension increased. His inclination was to put as much space between himself and Shelly as he could, but his annoyance with Roosevelt made him stick it out.

"Jest be cool! Papa," he said to Shelly, "be cool! We got them krauts by the short hair. If you listen to me, you gon' be a big hero. Now listen: You see them German pilots bail out of them warplanes wearing them black caps and them big goggles so you can't tell who they is? Well, they right here sneaking around trying to get back to their units across the lines. Now here's what: when they come 'round here today, we got to stop 'em. If you help me, you'll git one of them medals. I'll see to it." He led Shelly into the kitchen and pointed through the back window. "You see that well out there? Well, them kraut bastards gon' come sneakin' 'round that well there. They lookin' for secret guv'ment documents to steal and to take back to them roundhead generals. Now if you lay down in the grass behind the woodshed over there, you can guard the whole area. You can stop 'em cold. When you see one of 'em trying' to pull something out of the well, or somethin', Corp'al, do your duty! Do your duty! We got to destroy them German krauts. God don't like ugly, and God despises them roguish krauts. When you hear one of 'em on his motorcycle, get ready. It'll be your time to win that medal and wear it on your uniform. Now, detail, take cover!"

Shelly trotted across the backyard and flattened out on his stomach in the weeds behind the woodshed. He spread his legs apart and trained his musket on the well where he expected the enemy to appear. But from time to time he swept the weapon back and forth, covering the whole pie-shaped space between himself and Coley's house. He was ready.

Coley went back into his bedroom, took off his shoes, and lay down on the iron bed by the window. He had been lucky. Shell-shocked Shelly was like a letter from home. In about an hour now Coley would have to go and tell Queenie about how Shelly went crazy all of a sudden and killed Roosevelt. Soon as the funeral was over, he'd move into her place on The Avenue to keep her from being so lonely all by herself in that big house. Business ought to pick up if he was on The Avenue. Luck is a funny thing. When he woke up this morning, all he had was trouble. Now his troubles were about over, and all he'd had to do was to be smart enough to use his luck. It's one thing to have a hand. It's another to know what to do with it.

The crunching of gravel and the squeak of dusty brake linings let him know that a car had pulled up in front of his house. He looked anxiously at his watch: 12:12. Roosevelt would be due any minute now, and whoever it was out front was going to be in the way. The car door slammed shut, and Joe Jipson came around to the window. Joe was one of Coley's regular customers, but Joe liked to joke too much and carry on a lot of stuff all the time. It got in the way of business. Sometimes Coley would exchange gibes with Joe, but he wasn't in the mood for a lot of foolishness today. He hoped that Joe Jipson would just get his man and go on about his business.

On seeing Coley's head protruding from the window, Jipson broke into laughter. "Well, if it ain't Po'ly Coley, the crummy mummy! Your head looks like an eight ball on a black toothpick, and if you don't get back in the window, a passing breeze could cause you to sneeze and break you neck! What say, my man!"

"Stuff's here!" Coley answered. "This is Coley's house, an' we got what you got to have! If our stuff can't drive your blues away, you may as well dig a hole and send for Ferdy Frost! How come you so sharp today? This here's Monday."

"I'm hip to your liver lip, but don't you try to jive po' Jip!" Jipson said. "If you plan to be seen, then you got to be clean, an' that ain't just on Sunday. If you're good-looking, you ought to be looking good. Every day. You owe it to your public. But then, I doubt that you ever need to worry, since you have missed the first requirement."

"I hear you, Bossman," Coley said with an exaggerated deferential nod. He didn't want to swap gibes with Joe Jipson all morning. Best thing to do was to let him win and maybe he'd get on out of the way before Roosevelt came up on his motorcycle.

But Jipson was not going to be put off so easily. He twirled at the toothpick he wore in the corner of his mouth and laughed again.

"Bossman? If I was your boss, I'd have you in a cotton field with rows so long folks behind you'd be plantin' before you got through pickin'! And if you complain, I'd put a bull ring in your nose, and hook it to your toes, and roll you 'round like the spare tire off a Hupmobile! Let me have a man."

Coley fumbled quickly under the bed and withdrew a pint of corn whiskey. "With all the stuff you got," he told Jipson, "you don't need a man, you need a jug to burn your mouth out. You full of shit as a Christmas turkey!"

Jipson grinned with satisfaction. He knew he had wounded Coley, and he was waiting for the next cue. He took the pint bottle and placed it carefully in the inside pocket of his jacket; then, holding on to the windowsill with both hands, he peered past Coley into the semidarkness of the bedroom. Coley eyed him suspiciously. Now that their transaction was complete, he was ready for Joe Jipson to move on.

"What the hell you looking for? Ain't nothing in here belongs to you!"

" 'Pears to me ain't much in there that belongs to you either," Joe retorted. "If you had to go by the furniture, you couldn't tell what lived in there — people or possums. If you ever cleared out that rat's nest, I'll bet your dear old mother would roll over in her grave in natural disbelief!"

Coley raised himself to a rare sitting position. As Joe withdrew hastily from the window, holding his nose, Coley pointed a long, bony finger at him and warned: "You can leave my mama out of this. You know damn-good-and-well I don't play no dozens. Jiving around is one thing; talking 'bout my mama is something else. I can joke with anybody, but enough is enough and too much stinks!" He was angry, and the words tumbled out so fast that he was sputtering and spraying spittle in all directions. "Now, while you carryin' on all that foolishness, don't forget to pay me for that man you have put in your pocket." He hoped desperately that Jipson would give him the money and go. Talking about his messy housekeeping hit a sore nerve. And besides, Roosevelt was due. But there was a day coming when neither Joe Jipson nor anybody else could talk about the way his house was kept, because somebody else was gonna be keeping house for him, and it wouldn't be in the little shotgun shanty he was living in now.

Joe Jipson retreated across the yard in mock fear. "Don't spray me, Po'ly Coley. You'll poison me for sure!" he pleaded. "I'd heap rather have you break my leg. But if you think you're a polecat, you shootin' from the wrong end. That ain't legal unless you shave off your mustache!"

Having delivered himself of that information, Joe Jipson stepped delicately back toward the window and paused to flick an imaginary fleck of dust from the front of his spotless jacket. He then dusted the toes of his glistening two-tone shoes by buffing each in turn against the back of the leg of his flawlessly pressed trousers and reached for his wallet. Coley's eyes followed him without moving. He dreaded these sessions with Joe Jipson; at the same time he could hardly conceal his admiration for Joe's stinging wit. Joe always had a comeback, but he liked to play too much to be a grown-ass man. A man ought to act like a man. But then, on the other hand, Joe Jipson always had money, and he was sharp. His clothes always looked nice on him. To have money and to be sharp, that's part of what it took to be a man. *If you ain't got no money, you ain't got no business here!* That was Joe Jipson's byword, and Coley had made it his gospel.

The staccato sound of a motorcycle throttling down interrupted Coley's flow of generous feelings about Joe Jipson. Damn! Coley thought. It was that chickenshit Roosevelt now, and Joe Jipson was still hanging around the window. He grabbed the five-dollar bill offered him by Jipson and pushed two crumpled singles at him with an air of dismissal.

It was too late. Roosevelt drove the three-wheeler into the side yard directly opposite Coley's window, revved it up a couple of times, and cut the motor off. In addition to being annoyed by the noise — he'd told Roosevelt a dozen times not to drive that damn thing up under his window — Coley was in a near state of panic. Shelly was back there layin' for Roosevelt, and nobody could predict exactly what he might do. Shelly was shell-shocked. Nobody had counted on Joe Jipson being there in the way when Roosevelt came. Now Jipson was already sounding on Roosevelt. He might never go away.

"Twiddle-dee-dee and twiddle-dee-dum," Jipson was saying, "you mash one bug and his brother'll come! Oh, but excuse me, peoples, if you please, it's brother-in-law, in this case."

Roosevelt sat on the motorcycle, his legs spread apart, his black leather cap and goggles still in place. He rolled a cheap, cold cigar around in his mouth and looked at Joe Jipson. "I don't reckon you talking to me," he said. "I ain't got no kinfolks over this way you coulda' been mashin', in law or outa law!"

"Why don't you mind your own business?" Coley said to Jipson. "You jest like a big ol' catfish, all mouth and no brains. Roosevelt and me is friends. We don't claim to be nothing else. An' if we ever do, that will also be our business. Ain't that right, Roosevelt?"

"Right," Roosevelt said, thinking about the hype he aimed to put on Coley for half-a-man.

Joe Jipson twirled his toothpick and looked critically at Roosevelt while he burnished his fingernails against the lapel of his sports jacket. Roosevelt looked helplessly off into space, waiting for Jipson to demolish him.

"Booker T. Washington Frederick Douglass Robert E. Lee Roosevelt Jones," Joe Jipson began, circling Roosevelt to get a better look at him. "My good man, aside from having the same name as the president of the commonwealth, just what is your claim to fame anyhow? You don't stand on the corner, you don't score with the wimmin, and you don't have the price of a Coca-Cola, so tell me, my man, just what do you do for sport?" Roosevelt swallowed hard and began digging a hole in the gravel with the toe of his shoe. He couldn't get any comeback words to come into his mouth; it was too dry. Jipson stepped back for a different perspective. "Uhmm," he continued. "Now it comes clear to me, my man. When you on your motorcycle and got your big goggles on and a champ cigar resting on your tonsils, you's the biggest sport of all! All you have to do is go poot-poot-poot up The Avenue and I bet the wimmin run out in the street to clip your fingernails for souvenirs!"

It was not because of Roosevelt's discomfort that Coley interrupted Joe Jipson's needling. There were bigger things at stake. Shelly was out there in back somewhere, and Jipson was just getting warmed up. Things had gone too far for Coley to call it off now, and he probably couldn't call it off if he tried. How do you stop a crazy man from being crazy if he decides to do something? If Joe Jipson didn't have sense enough to leave and go on about his business, then maybe it was meant for him to stay. Coley knew he had a hand, and his hand was smoking. He had to move while his luck was with him. As a matter of fact, maybe Jipson was a part of his hand. He could be a lot of help in case anything went wrong. Yeah. If you got a good hand, play it.

"Roosevelt!" Coley broke into Jipson's monologue as though his sole interest were to rescue Roosevelt. "Roosevelt, if you tired of Joe Jipson, tell him that how you run your business ain't no business of his. And listen here, I got me some good home brew cooling in the well out in the backyard. You go git a bottle for me, and one for you and one for Ol' Big Mouth Joe. As usual, he got his bowels in his mouth, and maybe some home brew'll dry him up."

For once Roosevelt was glad to hear Coley call his name. "Where you say that beer is, Coley?" he asked gratefully. "I'll go get it for you. Right now." He started removing his leather gloves. Coley was dismayed. It was important that Roosevelt keep his regalia intact.

"I got it in the well back there," Coley said hastily. "I got it tied up in a croker sack an' hangin' on a long ol' chain. You better keep your gloves on so you won't mess your hands up. That ol' chain is rusty."

"The world is got to be coming to an end," exclaimed Jipson. "Coldhearted Coley is going to give away somethin' besides bad breath and body odor. There's got to be a catch to it."

Roosevelt's first inclination was to ride his motorcycle right on around to the well. He loved the commanding throb of the engine between his legs, and he seldom walked where he could ride. But he knew he'd be criticized by both Joe Jipson and Coley if he should start up the motor again. He didn't care about Coley, Coley could go to hell, but Joe Jipson could make you feel like a fool sometimes. He didn't want to give Joe any more ammunition than he had to. In fact, when he got back with the home brew, if he could somehow get Joe's attention focused on Coley, Coley would be so frustrated he'd more than likely turn loose the half-pint Roosevelt intended to ask for on credit without too much trouble.

He climbed off the motorcycle and pushed it carefully to one side of the driveway; then he tugged at his black leather gloves, glanced down at his shiny black leggins, and sauntered toward the rear of the house. The gloves and leggins and the leather cap and goggles he wore all contributed to his sense of importance. He was short and not too big, and whenever he wore regular clothes, like on Sunday, nobody seemed to even see him. But when he was riding his motorcycle, everybody heard him and saw him and knew it was Roosevelt. Whenever he passed somebody on the street, he always threw up his hand and they always waved back. He was Roosevelt. In his fantasies he was a speed cop patrolling up and down the highway like he'd seen at the picture show. If he ever really got to be a speed cop, he'd sure as hell pull a raid on Coley. Coley was stingy as hell. There he was, calling hisself liking a man's sister and too damn stingy to credit her own brother for a drink now and then. To tell the truth, he didn't really drink Coley's white lightning — Queenie'd put him out of the house if he did — but every pint he got from Coley, he sold to some of the boys working around Courthouse Square for a little change to keep his motorcycle looking good. Trouble was that when it came time to pay Coley, he'd already spent the money. But Coley thought he was trying to deadbeat him just because Queenie was his sister. Maybe he ought not to even worry about paying him. Coley was so damn conniving and stingy. And if Queenie was to marry him, which he hoped and prayed she wouldn't, he'd get his money back with interest.

Roosevelt turned the corner and sauntered over to the well. It had a brick housing shaped like a barrel standing about three feet above the ground. The housing was once topped by a wooden frame from which there had hung a well wheel or pulley in times past. Now only a single two-by-four upright remained, and to this was fastened a rusty chain secured by a bent nail. The other end of the chain was lost in the darkness of the well itself. Roosevelt leaned over the housing and peered down into the gloom. The well was quite deep, and he could see nothing. He tugged at the chain. Whatever was on the other end of it was heavy. Coley must have a dozen bottles of beer in that sack, the cheap bastard. But he was glad Coley told him to wear his gloves. He leaned over the well and started hauling in the chain.

Behind the woodshed Corporal Shelly Mahaley lay concealed in the tall grass and weeds. He lay on his stomach, his legs spread apart, his rifle ready. He checked his gas mask. It was ready if he needed it. He had heard the motorcycle drive up several minutes ago, and he watched carefully as the uniformed kraut came down the side of the house and headed for the well. He could have shot him then, but he wanted to see if there were others. Shelly couldn't exactly tell whether the man he was about to kill was a downed pilot trying to get back across the lines or a courier trying to get some message through to his superiors. But he was a kraut, he was sure of that. And Corporal Mahaley had him in his sights. The German peered into the well. His back was to Corporal Mahaley, so he waited for his target to straighten up. He aimed at the base of his skull and squeezed the trigger.

"Zap!" The old musket misfired. Corporal Mahaley squeezed again.

"Zap!" Corporal Mahaley checked his bayonet. Suddenly he was on his feet and in a half crouch. "C-h-a-r-r-r-ge!" he screamed, and hurtled across the yard toward the well.

Roosevelt was hauling the sack of beer up from the bottom of the well, hand over hand, when he heard the blood-chilling scream. Instinctively he let go the chain as he saw the madman charging toward him with fixed bayonet. The sack of beer plummeted to the bottom of the well, followed by the long chain wrenched loose from the rusty nail that held it to the rotting two-by-four. Roosevelt was frozen with fear, his back against the well housing. But even in his fright he recognized the figure charging down on him as Shelly — shell-shocked Shelly, gone completely crazy! He screamed and tore off his black leather cap and goggles.

"Shelly! For God's sake, man! It's me — Roosevelt! Shelly! Don't kill me, man!" It was too late. With a second cry of "Ch-ar-r-rge" Shelly was already at the well. He twirled his rifle, and the butt caught Roosevelt squarely under the chin, lifting him from the ground and sprawling him backwards across the mouth of the well. A split second later Roosevelt caught the full thrust of the bayonet in the left side of his chest. As the bayonet was withdrawn, Roosevelt's body shuddered for a brief moment and then slipped into the well. A long second later there was a splash, and then silence.

Joe Jipson rounded the corner of the house just in time to see somebody in an old soldier suit stick Roosevelt with a bayonet and disappear in the weeds beyond the woodshed. It looked like Shelly Mahaley, shell-shocked Shelly. Both he and Coley had heard screams a moment before. When neither Roosevelt nor Joe came back after several minutes, Coley put his shoes on and went to the back door. Jipson was peering down into the well and calling Roosevelt.

"What happened, man?" Coley wanted to know as he hurried across the backyard, stuffing his shirttail inside the wrinkled, dirty pants he had on.

"Roosevelt's in the well," Jipson said simply. "I think he's dead. Shelly Mahaley went crazy and stuck him with a bayonet."

"Goddamn!" Coley said with convincing disbelief. "Now ain't that a bitch? I always said that crazy-ass Shelly was gonna kill somebody! Now he's done it. We better git the Law, 'cause he'll probably kill somebody else if they don't catch him. He still fighting them Germans in the war. You know that?"

"I always heard he was shell-shocked," said Jipson.

"We better git the Law," Coley urged. "You git in your car an' go on downtown and git the police. And if you don't mind, stop on by Queenie's and tell her. I'll stay here with the body." Jipson was halfway to the street when Coley called out to him, "Say, man, which way old Shelly go?"

Jipson shook his head. "I don't know. I don't know which way he went. He just sort of disappeared." He got in his car and drove off to get the police.

Coley said aloud, "He sure is shook up over Roosevelt. First time I ever saw him let five minutes go by without a lot of foolishness."

A sudden silence descended on Coley's place as the sound of Joe Jipson's automobile traced around the corner a half block away and faded into the distance. What started off as a routine day for Coley had developed into a busy morning. A lot of things had happened, and his hand was holding. He walked toward the well where Roosevelt was supposed to be. Spying Roosevelt's black leather cap on the ground, Coley picked it up and let it hang from his finger. "Now ain't that a bitch?" he said half aloud. "The way he loved this cap, and he couldn't even take it with him partway. Now ain't that a bitch?" He examined the cap, snapping and unsnapping the goggles attached to it. Finally, he put it on and pulled the goggles down over his eyes and fastened them. This was the way Roosevelt liked to look, but Roosevelt was gone now. Coley leaned over the well and peered in to see if he could see anything through Roosevelt's goggles.

"Ch-a-r-r-r-ge!" came a cry that sounded like some demon from hell itself. Coley turned just in time to see the wild, piercing eyes of Shelly Mahaley zooming at him through space. He caught the full thrust of the bayonet in the pit of his stomach. As he lay slumped and dying on the well housing, he managed to pull off the leather cap that used to belong to Roosevelt. It hung from his finger for a moment and then dropped off into the darkness.

n this excerpt from a novel in progress, Nanci Kincaid writes about grief, loss, secrets and the search for forgiveness in a family of otherwise ordinary people, including a heroine who has kept her life on hold for a decade as she relived the loss of her husband. Now, it appears, her life might be about to take a different turn.

Nanci Kincaid

Excerpted from
It's Not Cool To Be a Fool

Lord, Eddie had gotten tired of watching his mother, Bena, sit in the yard in a folding chair with all the mismatched laces unraveling, just sit there with a cup of coffee in her hand and contemplate the sorry shape of her life, her head bowed low in something that looked like defeat — or prayer, since the two can look the same from a distance. But Eddie had a pretty good idea that no prayer was going on out there. He figured it was more like an endless question-and- answer session with a God she had once believed in — and tried to make them believe in — a long, long time ago before everything got so messed up and she got so tired.

It was just in the last year, when things should be back to normal, that Bena had begun to sit alone in the yard, drinking her morning coffee and waiting for the sun to come up before going off to work over at the school administration building where she spent the day filling out government forms. She waited for the sunrise the way a person waits for a big disappointment and then is not surprised when it comes because it proves the ongoingness of disappointment — like one thing in this world you can count on.

■ ■ ■

The rest of them had more or less bounced back, you know, the flat way a ball with not much air in it bounces. They had stopped looking behind them and started looking ahead into that magic place everybody was always talking about — the future — where everything was not only possible, but likely. Hadn't his mother spent the last decade trying to make sure they all believed in that? The future. The future was her God, wasn't it? And now, here she was, giving up. When she got home from work in the evening she microwaved a cup of leftover morning coffee and sat right there again in that same damn chair, this time turned to face the sunset. It was like she got some kind of weird satisfaction from watching the sun disappear and the world go black. Sometimes she sat there long after dark, until Eddie, her youngest son, called out to her. "What are you doing out there, Mama? Are we going to have any supper or what?"

Bena would rise like a zombie and come inside and bang around in the kitchen until she had produced plates of eggs and toast or spaghetti or a couple of chicken pot pies. Gone were the days when Bena used to clip recipes out of the Sunday paper and try out strange but delicious casseroles on the family as if they were a bunch of Guinea pigs. She had the pig part right, Eddie thought. He could not remember a time when he wasn't hungry. With five kids in the family and him the youngest, Eddie had learned to grab and gobble. "Slow down, Eddie," his mother used to say. "We got plenty, son." But Eddie had never been sure of that.

Now, Bena cooked exactly the same way a person fell asleep. She just got in position and let herself go and before she knew what was happening, she had supper on the table. It was both totally predictable and also a little like magic. And then she and Eddie sat down. Eddie asked the sing-song grace he had memorized as a child, the only real poem he knew by heart, and they ate whatever food Bena had caused to appear before them.

Eddie had plans to go off to college in the fall. He'd surprised everybody and gotten a track scholarship. Up until then Bena had thought Eddie was more or less lazy. She knew he liked to run but thought that got started because he always wanted to go places and was too young to drive, then later he was old enough, but didn't have a car. So he would just set out on foot. And now all his running was going to take him off to college. Still, Bena didn't think of running as something good to do with your life. In fact, it bothered her, seeing Eddie run so much, like he was trying to get away from something, but couldn't. Bena knew he counted the days until he could leave home and move into a tiny eight by eight dorm room with some strange boy he didn't know, perhaps a long distance runner, one of those skinny boys from some exotic land, and start — at last — to be really, truly, happy for a change. Bena wondered when exactly happiness had started to be something that happened far away from home, something you had to leave home to go get. And how had all Bena's children managed to figure that out when Bena hadn't?

"Too much thinking is not good for a person, Mama," Eddie said.

"I'm not exactly thinking out there, Son," Bena said. "I'm meditating. They say you should sit quiet and meditate to start your day out and to finish it up."

"Who says that?"

"All the people on the talk shows. All the health books. They say it's a good coping strategy."

"So how's it going then? All your coping?"

"My mind just wanders over the same stuff when I meditate as it does when I think. It feels like I've got a broken record going around in my head."

"I think you need to forget about meditating and take up a hobby, Mama. It's good to keep busy."

"I wish I had a dime for every hobby I've taken up over the years. Remember when I used to make all those Christmas decorations out of egg shells?"

"Heck yes, you used to make me and Joe suck the egg out first."

"You were supposed to blow," Bena said, "not suck."

"Yeah, now you tell me."

"They sure were pretty, weren't they? All those sequins and the little deer I used to glue inside. Remember that?"

"I thought you were going to kill me and Joe when we fell into the Christmas tree and crushed those ornaments. I never seen you go so crazy. First you were screaming, then you were crying."

"Y'all shouldn't have been rough-housing in the living room. It might be funny now, but at the time it almost broke my heart to see you knock that tree over like that. I'd worked so hard on that tree, staying up late at night after all you kids were asleep, trying to make everything just right, you know. The perfect Christmas. It was the first Christmas after your Daddy died. I guess I was a little crazy then."

Eddie didn't like to talk about his Daddy dying. He hardly even ever thought about it anymore. And if it weren't for the pictures his mother saved in the photo album he would have already forgotten what his Daddy looked like. It seemed like a long time ago that his Daddy had tried to ruin all their lives. Maybe his sisters still liked to discuss the matter, but he didn't.

"I still say you need a hobby, Mama," Eddie said.

"Lord knows I need more than a hobby, Son."

"Like what?"

"I don't know exactly. Some good reasons or something."

"Well, I can't help you there," Eddie said, "I'm fresh out." He stood up and rinsed his dishes and put them in the dishwasher and kissed Bena on the cheek. "I'm out of here for a while," he said. "Going to Anna Kay's."

Anna Kay was Eddie's girlfriend. She was the kind of girl who was so cheerful that it was a wonder nobody had killed her yet. But if anybody ever did kill her it wouldn't be Eddie. That was for sure. He loved Anna Kay's cheerful ways. He wished everybody would take a lesson from Anna Kay's positive attitude because then, to his way of thinking, this would be a better world. He had made a personal decision never to voluntarily become involved with a woman who was not cheerful. His mother and sisters had almost run him crazy with all their moods and heartache and bouts of moral outrage. He liked happy women better. He liked Anna Kay, who as far as he could tell, woke up happy and went to bed happy and experienced nothing but happiness in between. He was real lucky to find a girl like that.

■ ■ ■

When Bena's husband, Bobby, had been killed ten years ago it had put her life on a path that she had not chosen and didn't know how to get off of. Looking back, it seemed Bena's life had more or less belonged to her right up until Bobby died and took it away. With Bobby in the grave Bena's life had quickly become about doing what Bobby wasn't there to do, like keep the lawn mowed, keep the car running, pay off the mortgage and raise his kids right so that they would all turn out decent, reasonably athletic and basically honest — which she had done. Not a criminal among them. They were serious children, maybe that was true. When Bena looked back she thought probably they hadn't laughed enough or ever found the pleasure of pure out-and-out silliness. But on the other hand, not a one of them was mean.

It was years ago now, but sometimes it still seemed like yesterday. *The news* — which is how they talked about it still. *The night we got the news. When he told Mama the news. When the news hit school,* etc. For Bena and all her kids *the news* would always be something that happened ten years ago, not something they tuned into nightly on TV or read about in the newspaper. That stuff was just a bunch of current events most of which barely had a thing to do with any of them. But *the news* was and always would be personal.

"Bena, honey. There's been an accident. It's Bobby. Killed in a rollover. And Bena, he was not alone. There was a woman." The news had come at

once like that, packaged in sentence fragments, and even after all these years Bena had never really sorted it all out and made sense of it.

She had been at home with the kids that night, the five of them. Eddie, the baby, was just eight and Sissy, the oldest, was a senior in high school. The TV was on and every radio and stereo in the house was blaring out some pounding noise. Bena was grading papers at the kitchen table. She had the kind of mind that could cut right through the distractions of life and stay focused on her task. She was a sixth grade teacher then, a good one. That was before she found out they would pay her better money to fill out government forms than they would to teach the children anything about the government. That was back when she still believed certain things were worth doing.

And then there came the knock on the door that changed everything and the police car with its blood-red flashing light parked in the yard making the dog, Elvis, howl like all get-out, as if he knew exactly what had happened by pure instinct. And all five of her golden children wild-eyed and frozen at the news that Bobby Eckerd, their daddy, was dead.

Two afternoons earlier Bobby had told Bena he was going to a meeting in Montgomery. His company was trying to get a bid in on paper supplies for Maxwell, the Air Force base. He said it would take him a day or two and kissed Bena good-bye. And she had let him go off being believed.

■ ■ ■

The police said his car went off the embankment up on that twisty part of Highway 82. They said it just looked like he forgot to take the curve like maybe he thought for a minute his car was an airplane and that it would just lift off and sail him through the air, like he was a pilot, like he could take wing and fly. There were no skid marks, the policeman said. No signs of braking. Car rolled over six or eight times. Bobby was killed instantly.

They found the woman in a ravine with her skull mostly crushed. She was still breathing. They took her to Jackson Hospital and called all her next of kin. "I'm sorry, Mrs. Eckerd," the policeman kept saying to Bena. "I'm real sorry, ma'am."

■ ■ ■

The day after the accident the newspaper ran the pictures of Bobby and the woman together, side by side, like a pair. *Accident Takes Local Man's Life,* the paper said. *Woman in Critical Condition.*

Bena's daughter Ellie, who was ten, had brought the newspaper into Bena's bedroom to show it to her. "Mama," she said, "you want to see what the woman looked like?" Bena sat up in bed and studied the picture of the woman. Her name was Lorraine Mayfield. She was only twenty-eight. Bena had never laid eyes on her before. Her hair was dark and curly and Bena remembered thinking she probably dyed it to get it so dark looking. Bena searched her face and decided that she might be foreign or something. Mexican maybe. Or Puerto Rican. A stranger just passing through on her way someplace else. It was clear she was not someone who belonged in Bena's, or Bobby's, life.

"She's not as pretty as you, Mama," Ellie said.

"Pretty is as pretty does," Bena said.

"I bet she's not as nice as you either," Ellie said.

"There's more important things than being pretty or nice, Ellie. You remember that, okay?"

"Yes, ma'am," Ellie said. "Like what?"

"I don't know for sure right this minute," Bena said. "You'll have to ask me later, okay?"

"Like being alive," Ellie said. "It's more important to be alive. Right?"

■ ■ ■

Bobby's funeral was well attended because nearly everybody loved

Bobby Eckerd. His children were all well scrubbed and good looking and behaved in a way that would make any father, even a dead
one, proud. His wife, Bena, was composed and gracious. Anybody
that pitied her was wasting time, at least that's what she liked to tell
herself. Bena had entered the church with her two sons and three
daughters flanking her like clear-skinned, blue-eyed soldiers, and
she had felt strong in the midst of them. What Bobby Eckerd had
needed with Lorraine Mayfield, Bena might never know. But she was
not going to let her children become ashamed of their father. She
was going to insist that they look beyond the obvious. That's what
she had always tried to do herself.

It rained when Bobby was laid in the ground. Black umbrellas surrounded the grave like so many gnats clustered on a wound. It was
muddy and messy and the coffin slipped and sank while the men
tried to steer it into place. Amen, people kept saying. Bena had
watched it all like she was a person in the audience at a really sad
movie.

That night her son Joe said, "Daddy ruined everything, didn't he,
Mama?"

"No, Son," Bena said. "He changed everything. But we're not
going let everything be ruined."

■ ■ ■

It was two weeks after Bobby was buried that Bena got the phone
call from Lorraine Mayfield's mother. "Mrs. Eckerd," she said,
"please forgive me for intruding on your terrible grief."

Bena had been too stunned to speak.

"I'm calling to ask you something," Mrs. Mayfield said. "It's very
hard for me and I hope you'll forgive me."

"What is it?" Bena asked.

"It's Lorraine," Mrs. Mayfield said. "She's not doing so good. The
doctors say it's only a matter of time until everything, you know,
shuts down. She needs the Last Rites. Her brain, you know, is … "

"I'm sorry," Bena said.

"So, what I am wondering is. I was thinking if you might. I would like Lorraine to die in peace, you know. Do you think you might be able to, maybe, forgive her?"

"Forgive her?"

"I didn't raise Lorraine to be off with somebody's husband. I know in her heart she is so sorry. It's just that, if you could forgive her, then maybe she could go, you know. Die. I think she's lingering until she gets the forgiveness."

"What do you want me to do?" Bena asked.

"Can you come to the hospital?"

■ ■ ■

It sounded to Bena like the woman must be Catholic or something, all that talk about forgiveness and Last Rites. Bena was a Baptist. She knew nothing about all the rigmarole the Catholics put their dying loved ones through. She had no idea what they expected from her. *Forgiveness,* Lorraine's mother had said.

Bena drove to Montgomery without telling anyone where she was going. She could not have said why she was doing this exactly, except that she had been asked to. For the most part, when she could, Bena tried to do what people asked her to.

Mrs. Mayfield, Lorraine's mother, didn't look any older than Bena. She looked like she could just as easily have been the woman in Bobby's car. A woman, maybe like her daughter, so compelling that Bobby would be unable to keep his eyes off her and on the road. "Thank you for coming," she whispered.

"It's okay," Bena said.

"I'll show you where she is." Mrs. Mayfield took Bena's arm and led her down the intensive care hallway and into a cold, well-lit room with a roll-up bed in the middle of it. A bandaged, wired Lorraine Mayfield lay in the bed looking as small as a child. "She can hear you," Mrs. Mayfield said. "The doctors might think she can't, but she can." Mrs. Mayfield leaned over the bed and whispered, "Lorraine, honey, Bobby's wife is here to see you. It's okay. She's not mad."

Then she kissed the bandaged head and stepped away from the bed. "I'll give you a few minutes alone," she said. "I'll wait outside the door."

For an instant Bena didn't want to be left alone with this small, dying woman. She stared at the swollen face of a person she did not know at all. Lorraine's eyes were sealed closed and her face was purple and distorted. It occurred to Bena that the dark, curly hair in the newspaper picture had been shaved so that the doctors could try to stitch her head together in some hopeless gesture only they understood.

Bena pulled a tall hospital stool to the bedside and sat on it. She touched Lorraine's hand, but it was dry as paper. "This is really strange, isn't it?" Bena whispered. "Your mother called me," she said.

For a minute Bena just sat and stared at the tiny figure in the bed. She could be one of Bena's daughters. Sissy maybe. Sissy was a child with a wild streak too, wasn't she? She tried to imagine Bobby in a car with this woman but she couldn't think of it, what they would say to each other, where they might be going, what Lorraine had been wearing or planning. It was all dark and impossible.

"Okay," Bena took a deep breath. "So, here goes. Your mother says you can hear me. I don't know how you knew Bobby — how long or how well. But, look, Bobby was an easy guy to love. You should have seen his funeral. Everybody came. Practically the whole county. So you shouldn't feel bad because you loved him too, okay?"

■ ■ ■

Even as she spoke Bena wondered if she meant a word she was saying. Words just came to her like she had been rehearsing for this scene all her life. She would have laid hands on and healed Lorraine Mayfield if she could have. She would have commanded her to rise from her bed and go forth and sin no more. It was odd how connected she felt to this woman, the one whose hand she kept instinctively touching. Later she would accuse herself of simply being curious to see what she looked like, this woman who had been with

Bobby when he died. This woman who, dead or alive, had altered Bena's life forever.

As Bena was leaving the hospital Mrs. Mayfield said, "If there is anything you'd like to ask me — you know, about Bobby and Lorraine, their relationship. I'll tell you what I know. If, you know, that would make things any easier for you. Knowing the truth."

"No, thank you," Bena said.

■ ■ ■

Some of the teachers at school told Bena that lots of times a dead loved one will appear in the night to have a last word with you or maybe, in Bobby's case, explain things and beg for understanding. They said, "You'll think you're dreaming, but you won't be." One teacher's mother had appeared in a white nightgown at the foot of her bed and touched her foot. It was as real as anything. And another's son had waked her up to say he loved her. He had shot himself in the face with his father's gun, but wanted her to know it wasn't her fault. She swore it gave her the only moment of true peace she'd known since the accident.

Lord, Bena hoped this was true. She was ready to believe it because she needed a last word with Bobby, to know for sure that his sin had not backfired so bad that he had completely lost his salvation. Bena herself had witnessed his being saved. He had walked the aisle for Christ and the preacher shook his hand and patted him on the back and everything. There was no doubt at the time that it was for real, too. Some people even said they could see a change in him afterwards. Bena had never been a very religious person, really. It was just that now that Bobby was gone, the afterlife seemed her only hope of ever seeing him again. It made her want to truly believe in all the things she had only pretended to believe all these years.

Now, Bena went to bed at night in a state of waiting, praying that Bobby's spirit would come to her just once. She would say, "Bobby, is heaven real?" She would say, "Look what you've done!" Some nights she fell asleep imagining Bobby and Lorraine both appearing together, sitting on the edge of her bed, holding hands and glowing, their wings fluttering like a couple of lovesick angels.

■ ■ ■

It wasn't until Bena got the call from Mrs. Mayfield less than a month later, saying that Lorraine had died without ever opening her eyes, that a merciful God had taken her home at last, that Bena began to comprehend death, the finality of it. It was only then, when she knew that Lorraine was buried more than sixty miles from where Bobby was buried, that she finally stopped looking for Bobby to come up the drive at the end of the day, blowing his horn like a public service announcement, or a warning to any children who had a talking-to coming, that he was home.

Now, when Bena looked back over her marriage she couldn't remember a single time when she hadn't been glad to see Bobby Eckerd come home. For real. He would sling his briefcase on the dining room table and walk across the room in his wilted white short sleeved shirt, unclip his necktie along the way, give her a little automatic kiss on the cheek and say, "How's the Queen doing?" That was what he had called Bena: *the Queen*.

If it was summer, he would head for the bedroom and change into shorts and a tee shirt and he might mow the grass. If it was winter, he might rake the pine straw into mounds and cushion the flowerbeds with it. Or throw the ball with Eddie and Joe until Eddie got frustrated and started to cry. Or watch Sissy practice her baton twirling, figure eight after endless figure eight. Or talk Leslie into letting the turtle she'd caught go, convincing her that life in a cardboard box was not worth living, no matter how loved one was. And if Leslie could not be convinced, then it was Bobby who dug the turtle's grave and put the dogwood blooms on it.

Bobby might fill up all the birdfeeders with sunflower seed or pour kerosene on the fire-ant beds dotting the yard or spray the deck with water repellent to prevent rot or put sand on the oil spills blighting the carport floor. Bobby was always doing something, with

Elvis trailing him every step he took. Bobby claimed he had gotten Elvis for the kids, but Elvis had never belonged to anybody but Bobby. It was Bobby who picked him out of the litter. And it was Bobby who named him. Bena had protested, "Elvis?" she'd said. "No way." To her it was like naming a dog *War Eagle* or *Roll Tide* — something corny and cliché like that. But Bobby had insisted, saying, "Look how black his fur is. So black it's blue. Like Elvis' shoe polished hair."

■ ■ ■

Bobby had always loved the story about Elvis putting black shoe polish on his hair for dramatic effect and then getting rained on on his way to school and all that black just washing down his face and staining his clothes and everybody laughing at him and thinking he was totally weird. It was sad stories like that that made Bobby love Elvis Presley. He loved him as much as any girl ever did, maybe more. It sort of embarrassed Bena too, having a husband that worshiped Elvis like that. She wished Bobby would get more current. Some Sunday nights Bobby put Elvis' gospel music on the stereo and played it full blast and when the kids came and gawked at him in horror, saying, "Daddy, stop it!" he would smile and say, "The Catholics, now they may have the Pope with that crown on his head. But us Baptists, we got Elvis. We got the King." He would actually get tears in his eyes when Elvis sang "Amazing Grace," like that was the one song in the world that made Bobby believe in the Holy Spirit for real. Bena had asked the preacher to play Elvis's "Amazing Grace" at Bobby's funeral too, which he did. After which she never could stand to listen to it again.

■ ■ ■

Bobby was ordinarily not the kind of man who let himself get bored, although on rare nights Bena remembered that he might just sit in the den and watch the news like he was in a trance, waiting for her to get supper on the table. Bobby had been a casserole man, too. Chicken casserole was his favorite — the one with the spaghetti noodles, cheddar cheese and almonds. Most men are meat and potatoes guys, but Bobby was different that way. He liked everything all mixed together from the beginning.

After supper sometimes Bobby sat in the yard with Elvis under his chair and smoked a cigar. "The cigar stink keeps the mosquitoes away," he said. But it did not keep the children away. When the children were little they practiced their headstands and backbends in the grass where he sat, saying, "Watch this, Daddy," and Bobby watched them tirelessly, his cigar smoke settling like a gray cloud around his head. Sometimes he'd send the children to the kitchen saying, "Go tell the Queen to come out here. Tell her there's a handsome traveling salesman out here who is craving her company." Minutes later the children would run back to him, saying, "Daddy, Mama's coming as soon as she finishes cleaning up the kitchen." But sometimes it took longer than Bena expected and Bobby would come inside before she could make her way outside. She regretted that now.

Bena had re-lived their early life from a million different angles since Bobby died. She remembered him the same way you remember a magic trick: all the pleasure is in the bewilderment.

But she knew this. It used to be when Bobby had walked through the door at the end of the day, Elvis panting at his heels, Bena's life had made perfect sense. The meatloaf she was slapping into shape made sense. The laundry she would rotate from washer to dryer to dresser drawers all evening long made sense. The children arguing and telling on each other and all their lamentations and denials made sense. The car payments made sense. Her menstrual cramps made sense. The toilet whose handle had to be jiggled just right to stop its whining made sense. Even her students who, try as she might, she could not quite reach, who would leave her class still unable to read a standard paragraph and make sense of it, even they made a sweeter, gentler sense. Bobby had had a way of putting the sense into everything. That had been his gift to Bena. Marriage to Bobby had kept her very sane.

■■■

For the first few months after Bobby was killed in the car accident, Happycat McKale, their mailman, had walked up the long drive and delivered the mail to Bena by hand so that she wouldn't have to make her way down to the mailbox just to get a fistful of overdue bills and rhyming sympathy cards. "Anything I can do to help out?" he asked her nearly every day in the beginning of her widowhood. Later he got bolder and said, "You'll get over this, Bena. It might not seem like it now, but time is a great healer."

"I haven't noticed time healing Sue Cox," Bena said. Sue Cox was Happycat's wife. It was as hateful a thing as Bena had ever said to anybody, especially somebody who was trying to be nice to her. Happycat had just stood and looked at her like she had slapped his face. Afterwards he stopped hand delivering her mail, just stuffed it in her mailbox the way he was required by law to do.

Sometimes Bena wouldn't take in the mail for weeks at a time just because she couldn't stand to. She thought people should not be allowed to intrude on her life simply by licking a thirty-cent stamp. Depending on the feel of the mail, she might just dump a whole handful of it straight in the trash and never so much as glance at the return addresses or the penmanship. All summer long she did this. It was good when school started up again and she was forced back to work. For some reason it seemed easier to make the transition from wife to widow while she was at school where it was part of her job to be mature and appropriately distant.

But at home she remained a wife for the longest time. A wife with no husband, but with five of his children to concentrate on, which she did. She watched her children for signs of lingering sadness or loneliness or anger or any of the other sorts of things that were natural by-products of grief or normal rites of passage of adolescence. It seemed to her that every one of them took at least one turn to do something crazy that might get them killed or mess up their lives forever if Bena hadn't been around to prevent that from happening. Their daddy might be floating around somewhere right now like a re-tread angel of some kind, but his children were no angels. They were real. No mood of theirs went undetected or unaddressed, not until Bena was sure they had weathered the worst of things. By the time she was sure the children were going to survive and go on to thrive, a couple of years had passed and they had started teasing her about needing to go out on a date.

■ ■ ■

Bena didn't think about Happycat for a couple of years. She sometimes saw him go by in his U.S. Mail van, but she didn't wave or honk her horn in recognition the way she once would have when Bobby was alive. Bobby and Happycat had been friends in high school. Happycat had been a big-time athlete and Bena supposed it was only when he was required to wear his postal uniform that he had finally given up wearing his letter jacket. He had played college ball until he hurt his knee. As far as she could tell he had been one of those boys who was cursed with the great expectations of others. Including Bobby. Bobby, who had never been an athlete, was an admirer of Happycat's and had never stopped being disappointed for him, for the way his career had failed to materialize. "Tough break," he used to say to Bena whenever they saw Happycat. "He was one of the best."

The one notable thing Happycat had done was marry Sue Cox Miller. She was a year younger than Bena and had been the girl that other girls assumed all the boys had wanted to marry. She was rich, for one thing. That would have been enough by itself, but she was beautiful too and there was nobody anywhere who would ever say different. Even now when middle age had her in its clutches, it was gentle with her. As a girl she had always been free-spirited in a way that had set her apart from most all the other girls who had more or less set their sights on going to heaven and hooking up with Jesus in the afterlife. Obviously this had not been part of Sue Cox's life plan. It wasn't just the drinking and the partying that she did better than anybody else, but it was her bold, unladylike style that made her so universally appealing to almost everyone. Like getting arrested for suggestive dancing on the roof of Happycat's car and spending the night in jail for disturbing the peace and public drunkenness. Or like cutting her hair short when everybody else's hair was long and she was drunk and somebody dared her to. Even with her head half skint and her dark hair in little butchered tufts she was still beautiful. Everybody knew that Mr. Stein, the math teacher, used to take Sue Cox out to lunch during his planning hour on school days and simply write her a pass to get back in class afterwards. There were rumors that they didn't really go to lunch at all, but to his apartment, which had mirrors on the ceiling. In her purse she carried a whole book of passes that he had signed for her just in case a need ever arose. She was good about giving anybody who needed one a signed pass. Nobody ever said she was a stingy person.

In those days, Sue Cox's drinking had seemed rebellious and full of style. Something she would look back on someday and be happy about, while most of the other girls would be full of regret over how careful they had been, how worried about their imaginary reputations and what "people" would think. Even in high school, Bena had understood the sorts of regrets that would come later about having played it too safe and been too sweet. She knew those regrets lay in wait for her. But even so, she had been unable to set herself free the way Sue Cox could. She both admired and hated Sue Cox for this. It was the kind of hatred good girls feel for the wild girls who get away with what the good girls are secretly afraid to try. It is an early form of jealousy, when jealousy is the poison of choice for so many girls frightened of life. Like Bena had been.

That Sue Cox would choose to marry Happycat didn't really surprise anybody. That he married her was even less of a surprise. The surprises had come later when Happycat ended up without the pro career everyone was counting on and instead became a civil servant, just like any ordinary federal postal employee earning his government check. And Sue Cox had discovered for herself — and revealed to all — that she was not, after all, just a bold and beautiful party girl who was simply sowing the wild oats to which she felt entitled and with which she thrilled everyone around her. But she was, instead, a relentless and chronic drunk, referred to by those who loved her as an alcoholic who suffered an insufferable disease. Booze had kept Sue Cox from holding a job or having any babies or, after three DUIs, driving a car. There was debate about whether or not the accident was really Sue Cox's fault, but there was no debate about the fact that it left the other driver so mangled that her left leg had had to be amputated in order to get her out of the smoldering car. The only reason that Sue Cox didn't go to jail was because the woman with the amputated leg had had a higher blood alcohol level than Sue Cox and she had been the one who sped through a stop sign and smashed headfirst into the rear end of Sue Cox's car.

Afterwards there was no glamour left in Sue Cox's drunken escapades. The thrill was gone. Besides, drinking was the old-fashioned way to lose your mind and forget what you needed to forget. Now they had slick new designer drugs to do that for you. Drugs with catchy little names that you could buy from behind the Texaco station from boys in sunglasses who lived in the housing project and whose baggy pants were falling off their behinds. Or you could buy from that lawyer up at the courthouse. Or people said there were two interns out at the hospital who could sell you a little bliss or insanity, either one.

Part of Sue Cox's drunk driving sentence was public service. She had to speak to the kids at the high school about the evils of alcohol. She'd titled her talk, "It's Not Cool to be a Fool." They put an article in the newspaper with a picture of Sue Cox talking to students. It looked like she was a preacher behind the pulpit. But people knew better.

The same people who used to find Sue Cox exciting and interesting now found her borderline pitiful instead. Her life was a series of trips to rehab where she would dry out and explore the depths of her heart and history in search of some reason why or some evidence of an indestructible soul from which she could draw strength in the future, after which she would be sent home to slowly forget all that she had unearthed. In a matter of months, as a matter of course, she would begin to self-medicate again: just one beer at a ballgame, just one sip of champagne at a wedding, just one shot of vodka to get her going in the morning.

It was generally agreed that life had been cruel to Happycat and Sue Cox, first by blessing them so singularly, making them the envy of all. And then by allowing those same blessings to sour on them and become curses. Now they were reduced to living lessons for the young people in the county. Their lives provided perfect examples of why it is better to study than to be popular. As adults, they caused most of their friends to feel lucky in comparison. But nobody ever really thought badly of either Happycat or Sue Cox. It was like they were living examples that life might actually be fair after all.

■ ■ ■

So when the doorbell rang late one afternoon, too late for a mail delivery, Bena was not expecting to see Happycat McKale standing there, smiling. "Hey," he said.

A few years ago, newspaper reporter Jody Jaffe turned her attention to writing murder mysteries, the first three of which blended her affinity for journalism and horses. This story, published here for the first time, represents the beginning of still another mystery, told from a very different point of view.

Jody Jaffe

Excerpted from
You Gotta Have Heart

I've never been lucky at love. Until now. You should see the way this man gazes at me, stares at me as if he's trying to drink in every detail of my being so when we're apart he can remember everything. Where my waist curves down to meet my hip, how my knees turn in, the slightest bit uneven, even the small wart on my third finger. How gently he runs his fingers over my face, like a sculptor, building me feature by feature in his mind, until I am there with him always. At least that's what he keeps telling me.

"You are inside me now, Jane," he says. "So when you're not next to me, you're in me."

It makes me giddy. All this attention. Someone that loves me so much. It's hard to believe his words, his stares, his adoration, that they're all directed to me.

I know this disbelief comes from self-esteem issues, because I didn't get enough love or attention as a child. God knows I'd spent enough on therapy to figure it out.

I thought it happened once, I thought my lucky time had come. All the signs were right and the words too. He promised me the moon, the sun, but in the end, he gave me darkness.

We were to be each other's safe havens, protected by one another from the scary things in the world: betrayal, abandonment, confusion. In the end, he turned out to be my emotional landmine and why I'm in this predicament now with Edward, my new suitor.

But before his abrupt change of heart, this man stared at me the same way my new man does. He ran his fingers across my face the same way, stopped at every feature to make sure he had it right. Always, he said. Always.

Too bad always never lasts beyond the shelf life of strawberries for me.

Oh, shhh, here he comes. My Edward.

"Jane, Jane, my love," he whispers in my ear. "I'm so sorry I'm late. I know I promised I'd be here earlier, but you wouldn't believe the traffic, an accident on the Beltway, a back-up as long as the horizon. Forgive me, love?"

Of course I forgive him. What's not to forgive? He is a kind, gentle and generous man, always caressing me with just the right words. One time he even prayed over my body, giving thanks. How many men do you know who would do that? Even the last one, Peter, the one I thought was to be my lucky time, hadn't done that.

I gaze at Edward too, drinking in his features so when we are apart I can have him inside me. He's not a particularly good looking man. In fact he's not my type at all. He's bald with a short fringe of yellowish hair that circles his shiny head like one of Saturn's rings. He does something that poufs the hair up on top — blow dry? curling iron? hair spray? — and I haven't told him, but it does make him look a little bit like the Mayor of Munchkin City. He has brackish hazel eyes and a nose that swoops down hard and from the side almost looks like the bottom half of the letter C. Like I said, he's not a good looking man and he's very pale. I wonder if he gets outside much. But I guess in his job, he wouldn't.

It's not his looks that make me love him. It's his words and his promises and his reassuring touch. This, I think, is finally a man who won't abandon me.

Like the last one.

■ ■ ■

The last one. Where to start. I guess from the beginning. Over dinner. I sat next to him. We'd never met, but soon he was brushing his arm against mine, his leg accidentally grazing mine. He said "Good" when I'd ordered my filet still mooing as if he had a list of requirements for women. Women who like rare beef — check.

Women who liked *Remains of the Day* — check. He'd read it three times, myself twice. "Unreliable narrator," we said in unison.

Women who were short — check. I'm five feet two.

Women who were effervescent — check. I could always carry a conversation.

Soon the telephone conversations started. Long, winding roads of words with many detours.

Women who talk with digressions — check.

Then the emails, followed by face to face meetings. Tentative at first, but not for long. One time we escaped to a phone booth, just to be alone, to hold each other, to whisper in each other's ears how much we meant to each other. Within two weeks, he used the L word. He said it first. Not that I am a cautious woman. I am a careless woman who holds nothing back and no amount of pain can seem to teach me any differently.

"Jane," Peter said with such passion in his eyes that I believed him. But truth be told, I'd have believed him even if his eyes had been flat pools of pond water, "I love you."

Love in two weeks? Could that be possible? Why not? You read about those kinds of things in women's magazines, stories of fifty-year marriages that start with love at first sight. Why not me?

I held nothing back. He told me that later. As if I should have held something back. As if I should have known that in love you're supposed to keep some of your currency liquid, so if the big investment doesn't pay off, you've got something left at the end that's not tied up in the crashing stock.

I did push hard, but I thought, no harder than he was pushing at me. Maybe I shouldn't have made the joke that I intended to marry him. Men, I've finally learned, don't find that kind of thing funny. But how was I to know, especially the way he was talking to me.

"Do you think we'll ever want to go out to a restaurant to eat?" I said to him after a day in bed so long I watched the light covering our bodies move from the crisp yellow of a new day to a soft blanket of darkness.

"Oh, maybe in about thirty or forty years," he said.

The last time I spoke to him he'd said, "Can you meet me for lunch at the Mill House?"

■■■

"God, Jane, you're beautiful." Edward is talking to me. He's sliding his index finger down the left side of my throat, over my clavicle — I am learning medical terms — over my left breast and onto my nipple.

I'd thought Peter was lying when he told me he preferred women in their forties because they have something to talk about.

"Yeah," I'd said, "And then next thing you're going to tell me is you love small boobs."

Peter smiled. "I do," he said. I thought he was kidding until the first time we were together.

He opened my blouse and seemed to collapse in happiness on top of my chest. "I know this sounds weird," he'd said and I swear he was quivering, "but small breasts and big nipples … .that's exactly what I like."

It did sound weird. But I believed him. Just like I believed everything he said to me. As it turned out, his stated preference for small breasts and big nipples was the only truthful thing he'd told me.

"So beautiful." It is Edward talking now. His hand has moved from my nipple down the center line of my stomach. Flat.

Women in shape — check.

In the end, all the check marks in the world wouldn't have mattered with Peter.

I'd never have the big one.

Was she Nina? — no check.

I would always be Jane.

"I'm sorry," Peter had said at that final lunch. "I thought I was over her. But I'm not. I still love you, but I realized I love her more. I can't lose her. Can we slow down a little? That's all I'm asking, slow down until the dust settles?"

Tears spilled from my eyes onto the linoleum table in the Arlington Hospital cafeteria. He was there to have his moles photographed. We'd agreed to meet there, instead of the Mill House. When I'd first arrived I felt guilty for being so happy in a place of misery. I wrapped my arms around him and kissed his lips. They were dry and scaly. Then he said, "We have to talk; it's not bad."

"It's not bad?" I said after he told me. "How much worse could it be? Last time I saw you, I was your life. Now you still love Nina, she's married, won't leave her husband, but she loves you and you're willing to wait for her forever and choose her over me because you love her more. What was all that stuff about love you told me? You told me I was your safe haven, your love, your life. What was that all about?"

"I'm sorry," Peter said.

I looked at him. It was like I was underwater and he looked so far away through my tears. "*I'm sorry's* for being fifteen minutes late to dinner. *I'm sorry's* not for telling me that all those times you told me you loved me, wanted me forever, that was all a mistake, that you were confused. I cried in your arms, I told you my biggest fear is opening my heart to you and you leaving. You said you wouldn't hurt me. *I'm sorry* doesn't cover that."

"I'm so sorry," Peter said.

■■■

I made Peter go over and over it again and again. I was trying to understand the words, but I couldn't. Finally I asked him if he thought Nina and he could be happy together. He said yes and didn't hesitate in his answer.

I stood so fast the chair clattered to the floor. I was crying, but it was a hospital where people are supposed to cry. Another death.

I ran to the hallway, hid behind a partition and shook. Then I went back to look for Peter. He was gone. Of course. He'd said what he had to say and he could now go back to his strange arrangement with Nina.

I stood there dazed for a few moments and no one even noticed me. This was a hospital. People stand dazed, crying, lost, all the time.

My car. It seemed I should get to my car and drive somewhere. Home.

Finding the cafeteria from the parking lot hadn't been easy when I'd thought it was my lucky time, when I still thought this man loved me, wanted me, always. The path was labyrinth-like with twists and turns and glassed over tunnels. That's one of the reasons I'd been late to hear his it's-not-bad news.

Finding the parking lot from the cafeteria seemed impossible now. So much had changed in twenty minutes, it altered my already wobbly sense of direction. I meandered around halls, looking for parking lot signs or signs of Peter coming back to find me to tell me he'd changed his mind again. I found neither.

Finally I saw a door I thought I remembered. I opened it and followed the steps down. I couldn't tell if it was familiar or not. At the end of the steps was another door, I opened it. It was an underground something. Parking lot?

It was darker than I would've liked. But I didn't care. What could hurt me more?

"Too bad," the man with a mop and bucket was talking. "This one was a looker. I wouldn'ta minded seeing her when she had the red stuff going through her veins. Look at the bod on her. Bet she spent some time pumping — not only iron."

I watched as Edward did his best to ignore him.

"Know what I mean, doc?" the man with the mop said to Edward like they were Thursday night bowling pals and rocked his hips back and forth. "Get it? Pumping iron? Pumping?"

Edward smiled and I knew it wasn't because he thought it was funny, but because he wanted the man to leave and he knew that was the only way to get him out of there.

"Yeah, I bet she did," Edward was saying, edging the man toward the door. "I think I've got everything under control here. Why don't you see if they can use you up in ER?"

The man shrugged his shoulders. "Sure doc, no prob. Call if you need any more help." He took his mop and bucket and left.

I heard Edward sigh, follow the man to the door and lock it behind him. Then he walked back to where the orderly had made his lewd comment.

"I'm sorry about that, Jane," he said as he leaned down to me, "some people have no respect for the dead."

■ ■ ■

Oh, that's the one thing I left out. I'm dead.

I know it seems a little strange, you know, finding love now. And it certainly isn't the way I would have planned it, if I could have. But at least this one I can't scare away with my big emotions, my not holding anything back, my dumb jokes about marriage.

And he does love me. You should see the way he gazes at me, croons to me, tells me how perfect I am just the way I am. That's not anything I ever heard when I was breathing — and talking. My shrink, Marge, would have a field day with this, or just maybe she'd be happy for me that I had finally found someone to adore me. She's pretty liberal in her ideas about love.

I'm not sure how I wound up this way. Dead, I mean. I know when, though. It was that dark, underground place I knew I shouldn't have entered. But if you'll recall, I wasn't thinking clearly.

My friend Abbie says she always looks to Jane Austen for help. And I think in this case, she would be right. Bounder, that's what Jane would have called him. But any way you look at it, Peter was a cad. A bounder. A dickhead in disguise. An excellent disguise — he was all charm, enthusiasm and words of enduring love — but a dickhead all the same.

Having just been dumped by him, after a month of promises he'd love me forever, a month of believing, I'd lost my moorings. Under normal conditions, I'd have never walked in a darkened underground space, especially after hearing the footsteps.

That's the other thing I didn't say. As I was going down the stairs, I did hear someone behind me. Insistent steps. But I was so upset, I'd lost my sense of vulnerability. That's a dangerous thing to happen to a woman. It lets her guard down, lets her go into stupid places, disarms her natural radar.

Any other time, hearing footsteps that determined would have snapped my head around. I'd have altered my course, screamed, something. I just kept walking into the darkness.

I didn't even have a chance to turn around. The only good part about dying, other than meeting Edward, is that it's painless. Everyone worries about what it's going to feel like. Wham, before I knew what happened, it was done.

The next thing I knew I was lying on this shiny steel table that looked like it should've been cold, especially since I wasn't wearing anything. And there was Edward, gazing down at me. Dressed in a blue scrub gown.

He'd been reading from a chart. It must've had my name, little bits of my history. Blood type — AB; weight — 105; height — 5'2". Age — 41.

Time is all mangled when you're dead. At least in the beginning. A minute could be an hour or a day could be a second or the other way around. So I can't fix how much time passed before he knew more than little bits about me.

One moment we were strangers, the next he knew more about me than anyone has ever known, or cared to know.

He picked up my left hand — see, he knew I was a southpaw — and brought it to his cheek, stroking up and down. "Is this how your hand moved when you painted? Did your wrist make a little break like that or was it stiff?"

Actually, it was neither. I painted in short, staccato strokes. But that is something even he could not have known.

I do wonder how he could know so much about me. So much more than is written on a medical report or a police report. The police report. That's why I'm still on this shiny table. To find clues. To find out how I got this way. To help the man in the wrinkled and ill-fitting suit solve the crime. He's been here about four times so far, pestering Edward for this and that.

I wish I could tell him, "Go arrest Peter. I'd have never gone in that damn place if he hadn't had his it's-not-bad news to tell me."

But the man in the bad suit can't hear my words, plus it's not against the court's laws to rip out someone's heart, at least not metaphorically. I am hoping, however, it is against some celestial law and Peter will get his someday.

■ ■ ■

The first time the man in the bad suit came was when Edward was looking at my chart, right after the orderly left. He went to the door to let him in and together they walked towards me.

"Got anything on her yet?" he said. He was middle-aged, with bushy grayish hair, big suitcases under his eyes and coffee-stained teeth.

Edward picked up the chart and read out the details. "Just what you know so far," he said. "I'm really backed up. Don't know when I'll get to her."

The cop, of course he was a cop, looked down at me. He was wearing that same too-bad expression that had been on the orderly's face. So all those hours at the gym had paid off. I was one buff stiff.

The other nice thing about death is you don't lose your sense of humor. In fact, some things seem even funnier.

"Too bad about her," the cop said. "See if you can work her in sooner rather than later. A killing in a hospital's not good. Reporters love this kind a thing. Know what I mean? It's bad for everyone — especially her."

He chuckled. Maybe I should've been ticked, him making a dumb joke at my expense. But I wasn't. I know about dumb jokes and where they come from — nervousness, trying to cover pain and insecurity. Too bad Peter couldn't have known where dumb jokes come from.

Edward nodded. "I'll see what I can do. Maybe things'll ease up a little and I'll see if I can squeeze her in."

The cop was looking around, distracted like he was trying to figure what to say next.

"I got a bad feeling on this one," he said. "This is the second time I'm looking down on a woman like her lying on one of these shiny tables. No blow to the head, no stab wounds, no nothing but a needle hole in her back."

So that's what got me? A shot of something. I hate needles.

The cop was still talking. "I'm running a check on slight women with long, dark hair, see if it's more than two killed this way. See if we're not looking at a Ted Bundy kind of thing. I got nothing to base it on, just a bad feeling right here."

The cop rapped his fist on his stomach and it made a soft and penetrating thudding sound. This is a man who could've used some time in the gym.

"All right," Edward said, "I'll see what I can do. It's probably just a coincidence. A bad coincidence."

The cop nodded. "Yeah, maybe. I hope so."

He was back before I knew it. I wanted to be alone with Edward and this beefy man in the bad suit kept popping up like toast before its time.

"Hey doc," the cop said. "Anything on the girl yet?"

Edward was at the other end of the room, working on a body. Cutting, weighing, measuring organs, recording his findings on tape.

I can't say I was looking forward to him doing that to me, but since

I couldn't feel any pain, what would it matter? In a way, it was the ultimate act of intimacy, to know someone from the inside out.

"I just got a rush order on this one right here," Edward said. "Sorry, haven't had a chance to get to her. I can't say what killed her until I look inside. I promise, next."

The cop was wandering around, checking out all the bodies, me included. Did he like small breasts and big nipples too? Is that why he was looking at me like that?

"My bad feeling turned out not to be my wife's cooking," the cop said. "Though Jesus only knows that's enough to turn anyone's stomach. The other night she serves me something the dog wouldn't even eat afterwards. She says she's too busy studying for her real estate exams to get creative in the kitchen. Creative? I'm just looking for something that tastes and looks a little better than Alpo."

God, this guy was a talker. Just cut to the chase, buddy. Am I some sicko's dream date, do I have sisters in murder that I don't know about?

"So anyways as I was saying," the cop said. Yeah, come on, just say it and then please leave. I've always been impatient and death hasn't improved on that aspect of my personality. "This bad feeling turns out to be right. Someone's out there looking for short, athletic women with long, dark hair. He's not in a big hurry. Not so far. She's the fourth one in two years. So far I checked the east coast, but who knows how much he likes to travel. If it turns out she was killed the same way, I think we got us something bad here, a serial killer."

A serial killer got me? Did this mean one day a little, boxed picture of me would appear in *Time* magazine? Along with four, five, ten — however many he got before they caught him — pictures of similar looking women, all smiling, looking like we had a life to look forward to? Which picture of me would they use? The one with ...

There I go digressing. Well, Peter had liked it, or so he said. Maybe it had been another one of his lies. Was Nina a digresser? I should've been listening, watching the cop and Edward. It was me, after all, they were talking about.

Another thing about death is this new laissez-faire attitude. I didn't really care who did it to me. I know I should have, but I was here and there was nothing I could do about it now. And I have to say, it was good to stop hurting. I don't mean physically. I've always been able to deal with physical pain, I will my attention away from it. My dentist was always amazed.

I've broken bones before — an arm, a few toes — I'm sure Edward would discover that soon — but neither broken bones or dental work compares to a broken heart. That's not anything I've ever been able to will myself away from: the raw, aching edges of a pain so deep you can't get to it.

"A serial killer?" Edward was saying; he'd stopped his weighing and measuring of my morgue mate's organs. "That's certainly bad news. After twenty years on the job you'd think I'd get used to it. But some cases are harder than others. Women like her, you can tell she was full of life, when they turn up in here, those're the ones I take home with me. The ones I can't forget about when I go to sleep at night."

Ones? Plural? Am I hearing a faint alarm bell in the way back of my mind? The same small noise I ignored when Peter asked me the first, second, third, fifth time if I was sure I didn't mind that he and Nina had to take research trips together and spent their weekends going to Civil War reenactments because they were both ardent history buffs. No, I assured him, you've already told me how much you love me and that it's over between you two, why should I care? I'm friends, business associates, pals, whatever, with lots of men.

"You're a special woman," Peter had said gratefully.

Specially stupid.

"Yeah," the cop said. "I hate these myself. Only thing worse are kid cases. Anyways I see you've got your hands full here. I don't want to take up anymore of your time. Let me know as soon as you get to her."

The cop put his hand on my shoulder and it lingered there for longer than it should've. What, I turn up dead and now two men can't get enough of me? I'd told Peter the gods were nasty.

■ ■ ■

Now I remember how Edward knew so much about me. He worked the phones, as Peter would say. Peter was a big-time thriller writer, whose main character was an agoraphobic investigative reporter. In all his books, there was always a riff on how this guy had to work the phones because he couldn't leave the house.

I'd see Edward hunched over his desk, his head craned to the left, cradling the telephone between his ear and shoulder. Ouch, I wanted to tell him, you'll give yourself a cramp that way and I won't be able to massage it out from you. Too bad I can't touch you, make love to you. Peter had told me it was the best sex of his life, what went on during those long, wonderful days in bed watching the light change. I wonder if he and Nina ever consummate their union will he tell her that, too? Will I be bumped to the second-best sex of his life? Or was it all a lie? And maybe he really likes big breasts after all.

"Jane Fishman," Edward was saying. "Right, uh-uh; Yes, that's the one. This is the Stillman Gallery, right? Doesn't she exhibit there? I have one of her paintings and I'm crazy about it and I'd like to know a little more about the artists I collect. Do you know her? ... Oh no, that's horrible. That's terrible. How well did you know her? ... Oh really, mind if I ask you a few questions ... "

Edward, working the phones. By the time he was finished with Claude Stillman, who could outtalk even me, Edward could've written a biography on the late Jane J. Fishman. Not that it would sell; I was an artist of minor import. I painted red-headed women with aquamarine skin flying through the night skies of people's dreams.

"Quirky, bold and spunky." Those were the kind of reviews I'd get. A critical success of sorts, but not a commercial blockbuster.

Claude must've given Edward the names of my friends because he spent the longest time on the phone, calling and talking about me. Once again I was watching the light change from the crisp yellow of day to a falling blanket of darkness with a man who had my heart in his hand.

Every so often he'd break from the phone, come back to me, run his fingers down my body and caress me with soft words, telling me new things he'd learned about me.

"You had two cats? Scratch and Sniff? What funny names. Did you make everyone laugh?"

I made Peter laugh. That's one of the things he said he loved about me.

Edward knew about Peter. Claude must've told him. Or Diane, my best friend.

"Your boyfriend's name was Peter," Edward was saying. Was that a look of jealousy on his face? No need for that, I wanted to tell him. "Was he good to you? Did he treat you the way you deserve to be treated?"

No and no. Well, maybe no and yes. That was my dwarfed self-esteem talking. Definitely no and no. No one deserves to be treated the way Peter treated me.

Edward was gazing down at me again. What a look on his face.

"Jane," he said, "you are the most beautiful one I've … "

Before he had a chance to finish his sentence there was another knocking at the door. I bet it was that cop in the bad suit again, here to press poor Edward to cut me open and find out what happened to me.

"Be right back," Edward said to me as he grazed the back of his fingers over my cheekbones. I watched him walk to the door, unlatch it, open it.

The voice. I knew who it was before I even saw him. The voice with the flattened out *a*'s of his Buffalo childhood; it would've sliced right through to my heart, if I hadn't have been dead.

Peter. It was Peter. To see me. Like this. For a flash, I wondered if my hair looked OK. He'd always loved my hair, or so he said.

" … friend of hers and I have a few questions," Peter was saying. His voice was getting closer. My heart would've been pounding against my chest now.

Peter was standing over me now, looking down. Looking sad. Good.

"From what I hear you were a lot more than a friend," Edward said.

A surprised look washed across Peter's face.

"Well, I guess you could say that. Sort of … "

Sort of? You cad. You bounder. You dickhead. Tell him. Tell him the things you said to me. Tell him how you cradled me in your arms and told me not to be afraid of love. "How'd you know that?" Peter said.

Edward picked up the chart, as if all the answers were there.

"It's routine. Nothing really. Whenever there's a murder I try to find out what I can about the victim, it helps the police. You know, the man you write about is an investigative reporter."

An even more surprised look on Peter's face. But this time he didn't say anything. I knew that expression, he was filing something away in his mind.

"So what can I do for you?" Edward said.

"I don't know, I don't know," Peter said. Now he looked shaken. "I just found out about it. Her friend Diane left a message on my machine. I was out of town. Maybe I shouldn't have left, maybe I should have stayed, to see how she was … ."

Edward raised an eyebrow. "See how she was? Was something wrong?"

Peter was rambling now. My death had rattled him. Maybe a few of the things he'd told me had been true, after all.

" … wrong? Something wrong? Yeah, you could say that. The last time I saw her she was kind of upset. I, ah, I'd given her some bad news."

Edward's face hardened. I could tell he was getting angry. "You hurt her?"

"I didn't mean to," Peter said. "It's just that things moved so fast, too fast. I kind of got swept away by her. She's very captivating."

Edward's back was to Peter now, he was facing me. "I know," he whispered. Peter didn't hear him, but I did.

"She's all energy. In the beginning she was all I could think about. Being with her was like riding a roller coaster. It was so exciting, I couldn't think straight. Intoxicating is the word. It was like I was drunk on her. And I probably said some things, more things than I should have."

Edward turned to face Peter. "Like what?"

Peter was looking out the window now. He had a distant look in his eyes. What was he seeing? The first time we were together? Or when he'd told me he loved me? Or the last time, when my eyes were red from crying? I wondered if they were still red.

Edward's hand was resting on my shoulder, his fingers moving back and forth as if to assure me. Of what? That he would take care of me, keep me from getting hurt again?

"What'd I tell her?" Peter said. "Things, stupid things now that I think about it. It's just that it seemed so real at the time, then one morning I woke up in a panic. Took some Ativan, tried to figure out what was going on in my mind. No, really my heart."

Peter turned away from the window and walked back to me.

"Look at her," Peter said. "I know you can't see it now, but you wouldn't believe what she was like. I don't know, maybe I made another mistake, maybe ...."

Now he's changing his mind? As if we could go back to where we were?

Edward was looking angrier and angrier. "What'd you say to her? Did you break her heart?"

Peter walked over to me. Edward had moved to the window where Peter had been standing. Now another hand was on me. I remembered the touch well. "MMMMMMM," I'd write to him in my emails. "I love it when you purr," he'd write back.

"I told her I had some news, that it wasn't bad. That was probably the stupidest thing I've ever said in my life. But I was nervous, I hadn't slept for two days thinking about telling her what I had to tell her. I couldn't even brush my teeth that morning. I told her I loved someone else more than I loved her. But the worst part was I'd been telling her for a month how much I loved her and not to worry about getting hurt, that I wouldn't hurt her."

There were tears in Peter's eyes.

"I told her I wouldn't hurt her, then I hurt her as badly as anyone could."

OK, maybe he wasn't a total cad. Edward didn't look as if he was feeling quite as forgiving. His face was red and hard. Like some weird stone from the Amazon or some other exotic place where stones are red. This was a new side to Edward. I didn't like it. It was scaring me. His eyes, those soft green eyes of his looked like chunks of frozen river now. There was a small tic working at the corner of his right eye and his jaw was clenched hard enough for me to see the outline of his lowers.

Calm down, Edward. It's done. I'm fine now. He can't hurt me anymore.

"It was stupid," Peter said. "I was stupid. What can I say? I wish I could change things, I wish ... "

Peter didn't finish his sentence. The tears were running fast from his eyes, falling on my chest. He took his hand and wiped them into me. Oh, that touch of his. Then he leaned down and pressed his head against the tear stains and stayed that way for the longest time, with his arms around my shoulders and his eyes closed and his tears falling.

Edward had walked over to his cabinet. I heard him rummaging around.

Peter was mumbling something about being sorry.

And what was I feeling? Who knew.

Edward still looked mighty angry. I wanted to tell him to lighten up, live and let live.

"So you hurt her? You broke her heart?" Edward was saying and the tic in his eye was going faster and his jaw was clenched tighter.

Peter was too lost in his sorries to either hear Edward or see what he was carrying.

But I did.

Peter, Peter, move. Move. Get out of here.

But Peter couldn't hear my words anymore than the cop could. Or Edward, for that matter.

"So you hurt her? You broke her heart?" Edward was still saying. "Why would you do something like that to her?"

I saw the silver of the syringe catch a beam of light from the fluorescent tubes overhead just as it came down into Peter's back.

Wham, he never knew what hit him. Just like me. He collapsed on my chest, much like he had done the first night we were together.

Edward's face had changed completely. It was hard and mean.

"He hurt you, my love, he broke your precious heart. I couldn't let him get away with that. You understand, don't you?"

He lifted Peter off my chest and placed him next to me on an empty shiny table. I know the corners of my mouth didn't turn up. But they would've, if I'd been alive. It would've been the wriest of smiles. Together at last. I wish I could let my shrink in on this ultimate and final irony.

"Now it's time, my dear. It's time."

Edward folded back the blue sheet and doubled it over my legs. On a tray next to me I saw his tools. Then I knew what it was time for.

I watched as he lifted the scalpel and brought it to my chest. With a quick and sure movement he ran the sharp blade down my center line, as if he were slicing pastry dough in half. Next he took the chest spreaders — I'd watched him do this earlier and listened as he talked into his microphone. He placed the spidery tongs underneath my ribs and turned the crank again and again until I was as open to him as I've ever been to any man.

Then he reached deep inside me. I could feel nothing, but I could see his hands working, separating, looking for something.

Suddenly he stopped. His hands froze. He closed his eyes, took a deep breath and shuddered, much like Peter had shuddered that first night he'd placed his hands on my breasts. I waited. For how long? It's that time thing again. I don't know.

Then his hands started moving, out of me, away from me. And I saw what was nestled in the palm of his hands. It was the size of a big pear. It was my heart.

The mean Edward was gone. His face was back to that sweet, soft man who'd uttered so many words of love to me. Except now he wasn't looking at me. He wasn't gazing at me or running his fingers down my face, telling me how perfect I was. He was looking at my heart. He was running his index finger around and around, over, across. Caressing it with his hands. Calling it "Jane, my love."

No, I'm over here on the table, I wanted to say. But what good would it have done? How many times could I grovel before a man to please love me?

I watched as Edward took my heart and placed it in a jar. Then he walked over to a cabinet, took out a key, unlocked it, opened the top shelf. Inside there were six identical jars with floating hearts.

"Good-bye, my sweet Jane," Edward said. "You're here with me now, always, whenever I want you."

Then he walked back to the head of my gurney, leaned his hips against the edge and pushed. I heard the soft, swoosh of sliding metal and realized I was moving. Moving into something. Inside the wall where all the other bodies were. Click, I heard behind me, and the door shut tight. It was dark. I was alone, once again.

Like I said, I've never been lucky at love.

A s a renegade Baptist preacher from Mississippi and supporter of the civil rights movement, Will Campbell traveled the dusty backroads of the South from one trouble spot to the next. He saw the triumph, but also the ironic toll, as the region sought to come to terms with its past. In this short story from his book, Covenant, Campbell envisions a character with a strong resemblance to one of his friends in the hills of Tennessee.

Will D. Campbell

"BILL JENKINS"

Excerpted from
Covenant

My son wadn' hardly nothin' more than a boy when he got into the Move-ment. Nawh, wadn' hardly more than a boy. His mama didn' want him mixed up in all that mess. Me neither. But nothin' would do him but to get right there in the middle of it. 'Course, we knowed he was right, even at the time. Colored folks couldn' vote then. Couldn' go to town an' buy a hamburger 'ceptin in some colored juke joint where we didn' want him hangin' out. Couldn' go to school where the white chirren did. Couldn' ride on the bus lessen they set in the back. All kinds of things. It wadn' that we blame him so much. It was jes we didn' want him gittin' in no trouble. None of our folks never been in no kind of trouble. Many atime I had to bite my tongue to keep from gittin' in trouble wid the white folks. But me and my brothers, six of 'um, we never been in no trouble.

He wadn' gone six weeks 'fore we heard he was in jail up in Tennessee. Preacher here, he preached agin it. At first he did. Later on he change though. Said them younguns runnin' off, tryin' to eat in places wid the white folks, where they wadn' wanted in the first place, wadn' nothin' but triflin' niggers. He said it just like that.

We wadn' gone set there an' listen to nobody talk about our boy that way. Right or wrong, be our own flesh and blood. We didn' go back to church for the longes' time. 'Course, we shamed of it too. Him being locked up in some ol' jailhouse. Folks say that be on his record from now till doomsday. Say he wouldn' be able to git no job, git in the army or nothin' cause he been a criminal. Like I say, the preacher change later on, but that 'uz the way he talkin' at first. His mama jes a squallin'. Hollerin', "We lost our baby. We lost our baby." In our family, far back as we could trace, it always been a disgrace to git put in jail.

But the boy, he kep writin' to his mama. Tellin' her he doin' it for our sake. For the colored people everywhere. That what we was called back then, wanted to be called: Colored people.

Later on, the boy, when he come home to visit, tole us not to say colored no more. He said we was Ne-groes. Back when I was comin' on, you meet up with somebody and he call you a Ne-gro, well, lot of folks didn' know how to say that word and it sound too much like nigger. And no colored person ever wan' hear that word. That 'uz when I had to bite my tongue, when somebody call me or one of my chirren nigger.

Wadn' long, my boy say we ain't Negroes no more. We black. Black and proud. We was proud all right but it took some gettin' use to for me and his old mama. Back when we was comin' on, somebody call you black, almost as bad as callin' you nigger. But we done best we could to go along. Now days, the younger people tellin' us we ain't black. We African-American. I reckon we'll get use to that too. But they's only so many changes a body can take in one lifetime. When I was a lil' boy, folks plant the crop with oxen. And pick it by hand. Now they plants it from a airplane. Fertilize it that way too, and pick it with a machine half big as my house. That's a lots of changes. Lots of changes to get use to. Put that on top of not knowin' what to call yoself or what you gone be called next. From nigger to African-American. Lots of changes. Ox team to jet airplanes. Lots of changes.

Back to the boy you askin' 'bout. Next thing we knowed, he back in jail. Us thinkin' he off in college. Freedom ridin'. On a bus from Nashville to Birmenham. Back in jail. And Bull Connor done let him get beat half to death to boot. Picture in all the papers. On the TV. We seen him layin' there bleedin' in the bus station. Six white men standin' over him. Kickin' at him. Police just a-watchin'. Doin' nothin' to stop um. His mama screamin' agin. "We lost our baby! We lost our baby!" Him twenty, twenty-two years old by then. 'Course he was the baby too. Him bein' the youngest and all.

All the time though, he kept writin'. And visitin' too when he could. Tellin' us we raised him right. Raised him to do the right thing. Next thing we knowed, he workin' right here in the county. Registerin' folks to vote. Tryin' to anyhow. Most the time jus' gettin' turnt back. Yessir, we was worried. Plumb worried sick. Scared he gone get killed. White feller from up north did get killed. Our boy been with him that same day. Later on, a white lady too.

Next thing we knowed, it was that big march. Boy say they gone march from Selma to Mister Wallace's place in Montgomery. Boy say they gone pass right by our house. White man say, he catch any of his niggers out there they might as wells to pack up. Say he wadn' gone put up with no more foolishness.

We seen um comin'. 'Bout half hour by sun. Our boy right up in front of the line. His mama jerk her apron off, put her Sunday hat on and lit out, me right behind her, tryin' to pull my overhalls on. Didn' even tie my shoes. We hadn' even talked about it. Both of us so proud of that boy by then we 'bout to bust. "My baby leadin' the Move-ment! My baby leadin' the Move-ment." They wadn't no sad tears. Both of us blubberin' for joy. That boy, he stopped the whole line. A mile of folks stoppin' when our baby stopped, and him huggin' us like he wadn' never gone turn us loose. So full he couldn' even say a word. Dreckly he commence to march agin. Me and his mama right solid behind him. I reckon we musta marched till midnight. Everybody singin', "Keep on a-walkin'. Keep on a talkin'." When they bedded down for the night we turnt aroun' and head for the house. Boy walk with us for the longes' time. Then he say, "Mama, I got to leave you now. Got to git on back. It's cause I love you, Mama. It's cause I love you." Course, by then we already knowed that. Me and her both.

You know where that boy is right today? Detroit City. Yessir. That's him awright. That's the very one you got his picture there. He made a lawyer. Then made a judge. Fed'ral judge. Lots of changes I seen in my day. Lots of changes.

We don' hardly ever see the boy no more. I know he awful busy. Makin' them laws work right and all.

Sometimes, late at night jes 'fore she goes off to sleep I hear his mama sayin', "We lost our baby. We lost our baby."

In a way, I reckon we did.

n this previously unpublished excerpt from a novel in progress, Lee Smith once again exhibits her gift for scene-setting and the deft sketches of character that she displayed in such earlier works as Oral History *and* Black Mountain Breakdown. The Last Girls *opens as a small group of classmates — women who are no longer young — are gathering in Memphis to relive an adventure.*

Lee Smith

Excerpted from
The Last Girls

Wasn't it William Faulkner who said that the South begins in the lobby of the Peabody Hotel? Waiting to check in at the ornate desk (gilt, cherubs, the works), Harriet can well believe it. The great hushed lobby, vast and exotic as the Taj Mahal, stretches away forever with its giant medieval chandeliers, its marble floors, its huge palms, Oriental rugs and central fountain and little islands of big comfortable furniture (conversational groupings, she thinks they're called), graced by gorgeous blond heiresses showing a lot of leg as they lean forward toward each other confidentially telling secrets she will never know and cannot even imagine, not our sensible down-to-earth Harriet who has no business being here in Memphis at all, no business in this exclusive lobby, no business going on this trip down the river again with these women she doesn't even know any longer (thank God!) and has nothing in common with, nothing

300

at all. As if she ever did. As if it were not entirely a coincidence — proximity, timing, the luck of the draw, whatever.

Harriet has read that they assign roommates now strictly by height, a system that works as well as any other. And in fact she and Baby were exactly the same height (5'6") and exactly the same weight (125) — though Lord knows it was distributed differently — when they were paired as roommates at Mary Scott College in 1963. They looked like sisters, blue-eyed brunettes; they could wear each other's clothes perfectly. Harriet remembers pulling on that little gray cashmere sweater set the minute Baby took it off, Baby coming in drunk from an afternoon date as Harriet rushed out for the evening. She remembers how warm and soft the cashmere felt slipping down over her breasts which no boy had ever seen. That was freshman year. *Oh this is all a dreadful mistake,* Harriet realizes now as her heart starts to pound and she tries to breathe slowly and deeply in the freezing fragrant air of the Peabody Hotel. "Air conditioning saved the South," Baby wrote once in her rounded prep school hand, years ago, from Mississippi.

■■■

Harriet tries to anchor herself by looking up the nearest enormous column, so massive, so polished. Really, she is quite insignificant here beside it. Insignificant, in all her unseemly heaving and gasping and emotional display. Harriet gazes up and up and up the slick veined column stretching out of sight into the dark Southern air of the mezzanine at the top of the marble staircase that leads to all those rooms above where, even now, cotton deals and porkbelly futures are being determined and illicit lunchtime affairs are still in steamy progress. Oh, stop! What is *wrong* with her? Everything Harriet has worked so hard to get away from comes flooding back and she has to sit down on a pretty little bench upholstered in a flame stitch. She really can't breathe. She's still getting over her hysterectomy, anyway. She breathes deeply and looks around. The walls are deep rose, a color Harriet has always thought of as *Italian,* though she has never been there. The lighting, too, is rosy and muted, as if to say, "Calm down, dear. Hush. Everything will be taken care of. Don't worry your pretty little head … "

A black waiter appears before her with a silver tray and a big grin (doesn't he know how politically incorrect he is?) and asks if he can bring her anything and Harriet says, "Yes, please, some water," and then he says, "My pleasure," and disappears like magic to get it. The big corporation that runs this hotel now must have taught them all to say "My pleasure" like that. Harriet is sure of it. No normal black boy from Memphis would say "My pleasure" on his own. It is all a corporate scheme. The New South is all about money.

But *was* it William Faulkner who said, "Mississippi begins in the lobby of the Peabody Hotel"? Or did somebody else say it? Or did she, Harriet, just make that up? At 53, Harriet is experiencing a Senior Moment. She can't remember anything these days; sometimes, of course, it's a blessing. But for instance she can't remember the names of her students five minutes after the term is over. She can't remember the names of her colleagues at the community college if she runs into them someplace unexpected such as the Pizza Hut or Home Depot, as opposed to the faculty lounge or the library where she has seen them daily for thirty years.

Yet suddenly Harriet can remember Baby Ballou's face as if it were only yesterday, that blindingly beautiful face on the day she married Charlie Mahan in the biggest wedding Harriet has ever seen, to this day, and they were all bridesmaids: Harriet and Anna and Courtney, suite-mates (sweet mates) forever, the Big Four, and now they are all gathering again, oh it is too tragic. It is too much! Just because Harriet took care of Baby Ballou in college does not mean she has an obligation to do so for the rest of her life.

Harriet cannot remember why she ever consented to do this anyway, why she even called Charlie Mahan back when he left that message on her voicemail months ago, considering it was probably all his fault anyway. Yet Charlie Mahan is still charming, clearly, that deep throaty drawl that always reminds Harriet of driving down a gravel road, the way she and Baby used to do when she went down to

Alabama visiting. Joy-riding, Baby called it. Harriet has never been joy-riding since. Just driving aimlessly out into the country in Baby's convertible, down any road they felt like, past kudzu-covered barns and cotton fields and little kids who stood in the yard and silently watched them pass and would not wave, just drinking beer and listening to Wilson Pickett on the radio while bugs died on the windshield and weeds reached in at them on either side, towering goldenrod and bee-balm, Joe Pye weed as tall as a man. Like everything else in the Deep South, those weeds were too big, too tangled, too jungly. They'd grow up all around you and strangle you in a heartbeat, Harriet felt. A Virginian, Harriet had always thought she was Southern herself until she went to Alabama with Baby Ballou. And now here she is again, poised on the lush dark verge of the Deep South one more time.

Harriet thinks of the present the bridesmaids gave Baby the night before her wedding, sort of a joke present but not really, not really a joke at all, as things have turned out: a fancy evening bag, apricot watered silk, it had belonged to somebody's grandmother. EVERYTHING YOU NEED TO LIVE IN THE DELTA, they had printed on the accompanying card. Inside the purse was a black silk slip and a bottle of gin. Harriet could use a drink of gin herself, just thinking about Baby's sweet flushed face with those cheekbones like wings and her wide red mobile mouth and huge pale startled blue eyes and the long dark hair that fell into her face and how she kept pushing it back in the same obsessive way she bit her nails and smoked cigarettes and did everything else.

"Here you are, Ma'am," the waiter says, coming back with a beaded crystal goblet of icewater. But when Harriet fishes in her purse for a tip, he waves his hand grandly and glides off singing out "My pleasure!" in a ringing gospel voice. Harriet fights back an urge to laugh because she knows that if she does, she will never, ever, stop.

A scholarship student all through school, Harriet often identified more with the blacks she worked alongside in the college dining room than with some of her classmates who had never worked one day in their privileged lives. A black person will tell you the truth, as opposed to rich white Southerners who will tell you whatever they think you'd like to hear. They will tell themselves this, too, before they go ahead and do whatever it was that they wanted to do in the first place. ("The whole South runs on denial," Baby wrote from the Delta.) *You ought to know,* Harriet thinks.

A beautiful coffee-colored nurse presided over the examination which decided Harriet's recent hysterectomy, shining a flashlight thing around inside Harriet while three white male doctors stood in a row and said "Hmmm" and "Humn" gravely and professionally. One of them, apparently their leader, appeared to Harriet to be about twelve years old. When did doctors get so *young?* Harriet has already forgotten his actual name, thinking of him only as Doogie Howser, M. D. The doctors were looking at her reproductive tract on a television screen set up right there in the examining room. Harriet, feet up in the stirrups and a sheet wrapped primly around the rest of herself, was watching this television, too. It was truly amazing to see her own uterus and ovaries and Fallopian tubes and everything thrown up on the screen like a map. It was a miracle of modern medicine and so, oddly enough, it was not personally embarrassing to Harriet at all. In fact, it was like she wasn't even there. The doctors discussed the mass on her ovaries, which they couldn't actually see, due to the fibroid tumors in her uterus. *"Hmmmmm,"* Doogie opined significantly. Then the doctors withdrew, walking in a straight white line out the door to consult among themselves.

The nurse, who had said not a word during the entire examination, turned to Harriet. She cocked her head and raised one elegant eyebrow: "Listen here, honey," she announced, "in my line of work, I've seen about a million of these, and I want to tell you something. If I was you, I'd have the whole damn thing took out."

Harriet did this. She'd been bleeding too much for years, anyway. (Somehow, the phrase "bleeding heart liberal" comes into her mind.) But a person can get used to anything and she had gotten used to it, used to feeling that tired and never having much energy and having those hot flashes at the most inopportune times.

"Didn't all these symptoms interfere with your sex life?" Doogie had asked her at one point.

"I don't have a sex life," Harriet told him, realizing as she spoke that this was true. It has been true for years. Once she had dates, boyfriends, she liked men ... When did this stop? The phrase "use it or lose it" comes into her mind.

Well, the truth is, she didn't mind losing it. In many ways, it has been a relief, though Harriet always thought she'd have children eventually. She always thought she'd marry. Harriet is still surprised, vaguely, that these things have not happened to her. It's just that she's been so busy taking care of everybody — first Jill, then Mama, then starting the COMEBACK! program at her school, sponsoring the newspaper and the yearbook; and of course, her students have always been her children in a way. She sees them now, sprinkled all across the Shenandoah Valley, everywhere she goes. "Hello, Miss Holding! Hello, Miss Holding!" their bright voices cry from their strangely old faces. She can't remember a one of them. Time has picked up somehow, roaring along like a furious current out of control ...

And yet, how odd that Harriet never had children of her own, after all. How odd that she never married. She always thought she'd get her Ph.D., too, and publish papers in learned journals while writing brilliant novels on the side. Why, even Dr. Tompkins wrote "Brilliant" across the top of her term paper once — now, whatever was it about? "The Concept of Courtly Love in ... " *something*. So why *didn't* she ever get her Ph.D.? Why didn't she ever marry? These things strike Harriet now as a simple failure of nerve. Of course she's always been a bit shy, a bit passive, though certainly she's a *good* person, and loyal ... Oh, dear! These things could be said of a dog, she realizes. She's never been as focused as other people, somehow. She's never had as much energy, and energy is fate, finally. Maybe she'll have more energy now, since she's had this hysterectomy. Maybe all that progestin was just confusing her, messing things up. Now she's on estrogen, *"unopposed estrogen,"* Doogie called it, writing out the prescription in his illegible script. "Go out and have some fun," he said.

Instead, Harriet is experiencing another failure of nerve here at the desk in the freezing lobby of the Peabody Hotel, the entrance to *Mississippi*. Harriet writes her name on the line, she hands over her Visa card and her driver's license. She takes the massive gold room key which pleases her somehow. She's glad they haven't gone over to those little electric card things. Standards are slipping all over the South.

"Oh, yes, a package arrived for you this morning, Federal Express," the frail clerk says in an apparent afterthought. He plucks the red and blue cardboard box from the shelf of packages behind him and pushes it across the counter toward Harriet, who steps back from the desk involuntarily. "El Destino, Sweet Springs, Mississippi," reads the return address. The clerk hesitates, watching her, watery-eyed. Has he been weeping? He slides the package a little further across the counter.

"Shall I take that for you, Ma'am?" the bellboy asks at her elbow with her luggage already on his cart. Dumbly, Harriet nods. Then it's over and done, it's all decided, and it is with a certain sense of relief that she follows the back of his red and gold uniform through the lobby toward the elevator, past more ladies drinking in their high fragile chairs at the mirrored mahogany bar. Baby should be here too. She was raised to be a lady though she didn't give a damn about it. Actually, Harriet hates her. To have everything given to you on a silver platter, then to just throw it all away ... if anything is immoral, Harriet believes, then this is immoral. *Waste.* Harriet follows the bellboy past the fountain where the famous ducks swim round and round.

Soon, she knows, the ducks will waddle out of the fountain and shake their feathers and walk in a line across the lobby and get into an elevator and ride upstairs to wherever they're kept. The ducks do this every day. What would happen, Harriet wonders, if somebody shooed them out the door and down the street and into the river? This is what's going to happen to Harriet.

For here is the great river itself, filling up the whole picture window of her eleventh floor room. Unable to take her eyes off it,

Harriet absentmindedly gives the bellboy a five-dollar bill. (Oh, well, that's too much but she's got a lot of luggage; indecisive as ever, she just couldn't decide what to bring, so she brought it all.) The bellboy puts the FedEx package down on the glass coffee table next to a potted plant and a local tourist magazine with Elvis on the cover. VISIT THE KING, the headline reads. Harriet moves over toward the window, staring at the river. She does not answer when the bellboy tells her to have a good day, she does not turn around when he leaves.

Across the lower rooftops, past the Memphis Business Journal building and the Cotton Exchange and the big NBC building blocking her view to the right, across the street and the trolley tracks, that must be Mud Island with its pyramid and its scale model of the entire Mississippi River ending in that pool to the left. Harriet can't even *remember* Mud Island, but now it's a major tourist attraction. She's read all about it. Oh, but the steamboats have not changed! Frothy and improbable as something out of a dream, two of them sit placidly at anchor like dressed-up ladies in church, flags flying, smokestacks gleaming, decks lined with people as small as ants. While Harriet watches, one of the paddlewheelers detaches itself from Mud Island and steams gaily out into the channel, heading upriver. The ants wave. The whistle toots and the carousel is playing, Harriet knows, though she can't really hear it, it's too far, and you can't open these hotel windows. But she imagines it is playing "Dixie." Now the steamboat looks like a floating wedding cake, its wake spread out in a glistening V behind it. Its progress up the channel reminds Harriet of a fat lady moving through a crowd of people. Can this be the Delta Queen herself, the boat Harriet will board in the morning? Probably not. Probably this is just one of the day cruisers, maybe the sunset cruise or the evening dinner cruise mentioned in the brochure. Harriet checks her watch. My goodness, five o'clock. It probably is the dinner cruise already leaving.

Harriet certainly doesn't have much time to get herself together before dinner, when she is supposed to meet Courtney in the dining room. Now, why did she ever say she'd do that? Married, organized, and rich, Courtney is everything Harriet is not. Every year she sends Harriet a Christmas card with a picture of herself and her family posed before larger and larger houses. Two sons, two daughters, a cheery husband in a red vest. Tall. All of them very tall. Harriet can't remember why she ever said she'd come.

The river is brown and glossy, shining in the sun like the brown glass of old bottles. Here at Memphis it is almost a mile wide; you can barely see across it. The Hernando de Soto bridge arches into Arkansas, into oblivion, carrying lines of brightly colored cars like so many little beetles. Light glints off them in thousands of tiny arrows. The great sun hangs like a white-hot plate burning a hole in the sky all around, its beams leaping back from the steamboat's brown wake and off the shiny motorboats flashing by. Harriet is getting dizzy. She's glad to be here, up so high in the Peabody Hotel, behind this frosty glass. Across the river, along the low dreamy horizon, huge clouds stack themselves like pillows into the sky. A thunderstorm in the making? Too much is happening too fast. At her window, behind the glass, Harriet is insignificant before this big river, this big sky. Surely it will not matter if she leaves now, quickly and inconspicuously, before Courtney finds out she's here. Oh, she should lie down, she should hang up her dress, she should go back home.

The river ... it all started with the river. How amazing that they ever did it, how they ever went down this river on that raft, how amazing that they ever thought of it in the first place.

God, they were young. Young enough to think why not when Baby said it, to think *why not* and then to do it, just like that. Just like Huck Finn and Jim in *The Adventures of Huckleberry Finn,* which they were reading in Mr. Gaines' Great Authors class at Mary Scott, junior year.

Tom Gaines was the closest thing to a hippie on the faculty at Mary Scott, the closest thing to a hippie that most of them had ever seen in 1965, since the Sixties had not yet come to girls' schools in Virginia. The Sixties had only happened in *Time* magazine so far, and on television. Life at the hazy fairytale Blue Ridge campus was proceeding much as it had for decades past, with only an occasional emissary from the changing world beyond, such as somebody's long-haired folk-singing cousin from up North incongruously flailing his twelve-string guitar on the steps of the white-columned Administration Building. And Professor Tom Gaines, who wore jeans and work boots to class (along with the required tie and tweed sports jacket), bushy beard hiding half his face, curly reddish-brown hair falling down past his collar. Harriet was sure he'd been hired by mistake. But here he was anyway, big as life and right here on their own ancient campus among the pink brick buildings and giant oaks and long green lawns and little stone benches and urns. Girls stood in line to sign up for his classes. *He is so cute,* ran the consensus.

But it was more than that, Harriet realized later. Mr. Gaines was passionate. He wept in class, reading "The Dead" aloud. He clenched his fist in fury over *Invisible Man,* he practically acted out *Absalom, Absalom,* trying to make them understand it. Unfortunately for all the students, Mr. Gaines was already married to a dark, frizzy-haired Jewish beauty who wore long tie-dyed skirts and didn't shave under her arms, her dark armpit hair curling out from her sleeve-less sundresses. This armpit hair gave Harriet nightmares. Well, they were all hairy — Mr. Gaines and his wife and their little hippie baby, Maeve. They carried her with them everywhere in something like a knapsack except when Harriet, widely known as the most responsible English major, came to babysit. Now, people take babies everywhere, but nobody did it then. You were supposed to stay home with your baby, but Sheila Gaines did not. She had even been seen breast-feeding Maeve publicly in Dana Auditorium, watching her husband act in *The Cherry Orchard.* He played Uncle Vanya and wore a waist-coat. They had powdered his hair and put him in little gold specta-cles, but nothing could obscure the fact that he was really young and actually gorgeous, a young hippie professor playing an old Russian man. Due to the extreme shortage of men at Mary Scott, Mr. Gaines was in all the plays. He was Hamlet and Stanley Kowalski. His wife breast-fed Maeve until she could talk, to everyone's revulsion.

But Mr. Gaines' dramatic streak was what made his classes so won-derful. For Huck Finn, he adopted a sort of Mark Twain persona as he read aloud from the book, striding about the old high-ceilinged room with his thumbs hooked under imaginary galluses. But even this jovial approach failed to charm Harriet, who had read the famous novel once before, in childhood, but now found it surprisingly disturbing not only in the questions it raised about race (ah, you could see Mr. Gaines' not-so-hidden liberal agenda here) but also in Huck's loneliness, which Harriet, caught up in the great adventure, had overlooked the first time through. In Mr. Gaines' class, Harriet got goosebumps all over when he read aloud:

"Then I set down in a chair by the window and tried to think of something cheerful, but it warn't no use. I felt so lonesome. I most wished I was dead. The stars were shining, and the leaves rustled in the woods ever as mournful; and I heard an owl, away off, who-whooing about somebody that was dead, and a whippoorwill and a dog crying about somebody that was going to die, and the wind was trying to whisper something to me and I couldn't make out what it was and so it made the cold shivers run over me. Then away out in the woods I heard that kind of sound that a ghost makes ... "

This passage could have been describing Harriet. It could have been describing her life right then. Mr. Gaines was saying something about Huck's "estrangement" as "existential," as "presaging the modern novel," but Harriet felt it as personal, deep in her bones. She believed it was what country people meant when they said they felt somebody walking across their grave. For even in the midst of college, here at Mary Scott where she was happier than she would ever be again, Harriet Holding had these moments which she had had ever since she could remember, as a girl and as a young woman, ever since she was a child. Suddenly a stillness would come over everything, a hush, then a dimming of the light, followed by a burst of radiance during which she could see everything, truly, *everything,* each leaf on a tree, in all its distinctness and brief beauty, each hair on the top of somebody's head, each crumb on a tablecloth, each black and inevitable marching word on a page. During these moments Harriet was aware of herself and her beating heart and the perilous world with a kind of rapture that could not be borne, really, leaving her finally with a little headache right between the eyes and a craving for chocolate and a vast sense of relief. Still, she was prone to such intensity. There was no predicting it, either. You couldn't tell when these times might occur, or when they might go away. Her mother called it *getting all wrought up*. "Harriet," she often said, "You just get too *wrought up*. Calm down, honey."

But Harriet couldn't help it. She felt everything too intensely, that was the problem. You were supposed to be cool in college, but Harriet was not cool. Another day, Mr. Gaines read from the section where Huck and Jim are living on the river: *"Sometimes we'd have that whole river to ourselves for the longest time. Yonder was the banks and the islands, across the water, and maybe a spark — which was a candle in a cabin window; and sometimes on the water you could see a spark or two — on a raft or a scow, you know; and maybe you could hear a fiddle or a song coming over from one of them crafts. It's lovely to live on a raft."* His words seemed to ring out singly, like bells, in the old classroom. Harriet could hear each one in her head. It was a cold pale day in February. Out the window, bare trees stood blackly amid the gray tatters of snow.

Then Baby said, "I'd love to do that. Go down the Mississippi River on a raft, I mean." It was a typical response from Baby, who personalized everything, who was famous for saying, "Well, *I'd* never do *that!*" at the end of *The Awakening* when Edna Pontellier walks into the ocean. Baby was not capable of abstract thought. She had too much imagination. Everything was real for her, up close and personal.

"We *could* do it, you know," Suzanne St. John spoke up. "My uncle owns a plantation right on the river. My mother was raised there. She'd know who to talk to. I'll bet we could do it if we wanted to." Next to Courtney, Suzanne St. John was the most organized girl in school, an angular forthright girl with a businesslike grownup hairdo who ran a mail-order stationery business out of her dorm room.

"Girls, girls," Mr. Gaines said disapprovingly. He wanted to get back to the book, he wanted to be the star. But the girls were all looking at one another. Baby's eyes were shining. *YES!* she wrote on a piece of paper, handing it to Harriet, who passed it along to Suzanne. *YES!* This was Baby's response to everything.

Harriet shivers. She hangs up the new navy dress with the match-ing jacket she'll wear to dinner tonight, the khaki skirt with the striped knit shirt she'll wear tomorrow when they board the Delta Queen. Harriet orders all her clothes from catalogues; it confuses her too much to shop. (Back in college, she usually wore Baby's clothes, and usually did her laundry, too, laundry being something which never occurred to Baby until she ran out of blouses about a month after school started.) Harriet unpacks a jumble of cosmetics and medications (vitamins, cold cream, calcium, Advil, lipstick, the alarm-ing estrogen) and tosses the old envelope of clippings onto the bed. She steps out of her sensible flats and takes off her denim jumper and white tee shirt (Lands End) and hangs them up in the closet along-side the navy dress and the khaki skirt. All these clothes she might have owned in college, she realizes, confirming her suspicion that whatever you're like in your youth, you only get *more so* with age.

She remembers believing, as a girl, that wisdom would set in some-how, sometime, as a matter of course. Now she doubts it. There are no grownups — this is the big dirty secret that nobody ever tells you. No grownups at all, including herself. She cannot think of an excep-tion — except, she's afraid, *Courtney*, the suite-mate she'll be having dinner with later tonight. The very thought of Courtney makes Harriet feel like her bra strap is showing or her period has started and she's got blood on the back of her skirt. But this is ridiculous! Harriet has had a complete hysterectomy and now she has to lie down. She's still under doctor's orders: Doogie has prescribed a daily rest for the first four months after surgery, and in fact, Harriet cannot imagine doing without it. She' s so tired ... They say that for every hour you're under anesthesia, a month of recuperation is required. Maybe that's an old wives' tale.

One thing which is perfectly clear is that Harriet Holding will *never* be an old wife. It's too late now. Though she doesn't look *old* ... Harriet slides off her slip to stand before the mirror in her white cotton underwear. The only real difference is that her brown page boy is cropped below her ears now instead of at her shoulders. But her hair is not grey yet, only a softer, duller brown. Flushed in the sunset's last glow, which illumines the whole room now, Harriet could still be a girl, the girl who went down the Mississippi River on that raft so many years ago. She's still trim, almost slight, her skin pale and softly freckled and luminous in this odd peachy light. Her stomach is flat, her breasts are small and firm. Children have not worn her out.

But suddenly Harriet can't breathe. She leans forward, clutching the dresser, staring into the mirror. The light flares up behind her somehow, throwing her face into darkness. Now Harriet is a black cut-out paper doll of a woman before the glowing rectangle of sky, not a woman at all, nobody really, a dark silhouette. No children, no parents, alone in the wide, wide world. Tears sting her eyes; she gropes for the lamp switch and turns it on. The room comes back. Harriet throws herself down on the bed, heart beating through her body like her blood. Here it comes again: she's all wrought up.

She has not looked through these clippings for years. She picks the envelope up and fishes out a faded newspaper entry from the Paducah, Kentucky, newspaper, dated June, 1966.

"We can't believe we're finally going to do it!" were the parting words of 10 excited Mary Scott College students about to begin their "Huck Finn" journey down the Mississippi River on a raft.

The adventuresome misses weighed anchor at 1:15 p.m. today, bound for New Orleans, 950 miles south. Their departure was delayed when one of the "crew" threw an anchor into the river with no rope attached, necessitating a bikini-clad recovery operation, to the crowd's delight.

"Hey, New Orleans is that-away!" shouted local wags as the ramshackle craft finally left land, hours later than planned.

Their skipper, 74-year-old retired riverboat captain Gordon S. Cooper, answered an ad that the girls had run in a riverboat magazine, writing them that he would pilot their raft down the river for nothing. He plans to make 8 or 9 miles an hour during daylight, tie up at night, and reach New Orleans in ten or twelve days.

"I've carried more tonnage, but never a more valuable cargo," said the captain.

The raft, named the Daisy Pickett, was built by a Paducah construction *company under Captain Cooper's supervision. Resembling a floating porch, the Daisy Pickett is a forty-by-sixteen-foot wooden platform with plywood sides, built on 52 oil drums and powered by two 4-horsepower motors. It cost $1800 to build. The raft has a superstructure of two-by-fours with a tarpaulin top that the "sailors" can pull up over it, mosquito netting that they can hang up, and a shower consisting of a bucket overhead with a long rope attached to it.*

■■■

Harriet smiles. They'd named the raft for an early Mary Scott College alumna from Paducah whose sister, Lucille Pickett, had entertained them for tea in her gingerbread family home on the bluff several days before the launch. Harriet remembers that tea as if it were a scene in a play, the crowded musty parlor like a stage set, the old lady sitting up ramrod straight on one of those terrible tufted horsehair sofas, referring again and again to "Sis-tah Daisy," whose photographs lined the walls. A dark-haired beauty, "Sis-tah Daisy" had been a concert pianist, they were told. After her graduation from Mary Scott, she had performed in "all the grand capitals of Europe," settling at length in Paris where her brilliant career continued until a personal tragedy forced her to return to Paducah. Miss Pickett had said "personal tragedy" in such a way that no one, not even Baby, dared to ask what it was.

"Here she gave private lessons at that very piano until her untimely death," Miss Pickett continued, pointing at the piano with her cane. (Catherine Wilson, on the piano bench, jumped up as if shot, then sat back down shamefaced.) "But I must say," Miss Pickett continued, "after her return from Europe, a certain luster was lost. A certain luster was most assuredly lost." She seemed lost in thought herself for a moment, then began banging her cane on the floor with such force that everyone was startled.

A tiny black maid who looked as old as Miss Pickett herself came scurrying out of the kitchen bearing a tarnished silver tray piled high with slices of fruitcake, of all things, and passed it around. Harriet ate hers dutifully, though she got the giggles when she happened to catch, out of the corner of her eye, Baby slipping her own slice of fruitcake into her purse. Of course it was left over from Christmas! Of course it was. Or maybe the Christmas before *that*.

Standing in the vestibule waiting to shake Miss Pickett's icy blue hand as they left, Harriet was startled to turn her head and come face to face with the ill-fated Daisy herself, staring out of her ornate gold-leaf frame with such urgency that Harriet was shocked. What did Daisy Pickett mean, beseeching Harriet so intensely across all these years? What did Daisy Pickett want? For clearly she wanted something, and wanted it so badly that she would have done anything, anything at all, to get it. Harriet was relieved to come back out into the bright sunshine, the ordinary June day, to run down the sidewalk toward the nondescript motel near the dock where they were staying, laughing all the way. (Who could even imagine how old that woman was! And what about the *fruitcake?*) By the time they reached the river, they'd named the raft: The Daisy Pickett. Harriet felt that they had cheapened the memory of the mysterious Daisy by doing so; she hoped that Miss Lucille never knew it, but of course this was impossible. They were celebrities in Paducah for the next four days as they bought provisions and made commercials to finance the trip. Everything they did was on the news.

Living provisions are piled in corners of the raft, with Army cots around the walls for sleeping. Some girls will have to sleep on the floor each night, or on land. A roughly-lettered sign spelling "Galley" leads into a two-by-four-foot plywood enclosure with canned goods, hot dog buns, and other odds and ends of food supplies. The girls will take turns on "KP duty" and have a small wood-burning stove in one corner.

The Daisy Pickett left flying two flags, an American flag and a hand-painted flag with a huge yellow daisy on it. The girls wore white T-shirts with yellow daisies painted on them and sang, "Goodbye, Paducah," to the tune of "Hello, Dolly" as the unusual craft pulled into the river, after a bottle of champagne was broken across its "bow" — or porch rail, in this case.

■■■

In fact, in Harriet's memory, they sang relentlessly, all the time, all the way down the Mississippi. They sang in spite of all their mishaps and travails: the tail of the hurricane that hit them before they even got to Cairo, sending the temperature down below forty degrees and driving them onto the rocks; a diet consisting mostly of tuna and doughnuts; the captain's severe sunburn; mosquito bites beyond belief and rainstorms that soaked everything they owned. If anything really bad happened to them, they knew they could call up somebody's parents collect, and the parents would come and fix things. They expected to be taken care of. Nobody had yet suggested to them that they might ever have to make a living, or that somebody wouldn't marry them and look after them for the rest of their lives. They all smoked cigarettes. They were all cute. They headed down the river with absolute confidence that they would get where they were going.

T om Wolfe's transition from non-fiction to the novel reached its pinnacle with the publication of A Man in Full, *his critically acclaimed and best-selling story of Atlanta real estate magnate Charlie Croker. In this excerpt, selected by Wolfe, Croker is entertaining guests — looking to shore up a crumbling empire — at his 29,000 acre quail-shooting retreat in southern Georgia, a place called Turpmtine.*

Tom Wolfe

Excerpted from
A Man In Full

It was Friday evening, and the master of Turpmtine, Charlie Croker, was presiding over dinner at the burled tupelo maple table Ronald Vine had devised for the Gun Room, which was the show-piece of the plantation's new Gun House. Logs blazed in a vast hearth, fashioned by Ronald out of Georgia limestone, casting Charlie and his thirteen guests — fifteen, if you counted Serena and Wally — into a pattern of firelit glows and deep shadows. The flames sent highlights flickering up the long barrels and ornate chase-worked clasps of a parade of shotguns, many of them classics from the so-called Golden Age of Shotgunning, Dicksons, Bosses, Purdys, Berrettas, L. C. Smiths, the lot, priceless pieces that lined the entire room, all four walls, rank after rank, encased in burled tupelo gun racks.

Up above the gun racks, between two rows of heavy tupelo cornice moldings, ran an array of stuffed boars' heads with fantastic curving tusks and stuffed coiled diamondback rattlesnakes with their jaws agape, their fangs erect. A boar's head, a coiled diamondback rattlesnake, a boar's head, a coiled diamondback rattlesnake — they alternated, creating, in Ronald's phrase, "The Frieze of the Unfriendly Beasts." Each boar, each snake, was a masterpiece of taxidermy, and they were Charlie's beasts. He had killed or captured them all with his own hands out in the fields and swamps of Turpmtine, a fact he fully intended to impart to his guests, given a halfway natural opening.

Four black maids in black uniforms with white aprons had just finished serving the first course, turtle soup, under the supervision of the butler, Mason, an old black man who stood, erect and watchful, near the kitchen door. The turtle soup gave Charlie an idea.

"Hey, y'all!" he boomed out over the hubbub of conversation around the table. "I want'chall know sump'm!"

He said it so loudly that even Lettie Withers, the Atlanta *grande dame* who was seated on his left, stopped talking to Ted Nashford, the surgeon and chairman of the board of the Emory University School of Medicine, in whom she seemed to be taking such a coquettish interest. Even old Billy Bass stopped telling the bawdy story with which he obviously hoped to shock Lenore Knox, the wife of the former governor of Georgia, Beauchamp Knox, who was just across the table.

"I want'chall to know," said Charlie, "that this turtle soup comes from turtles rat'cheer at Turpmtine. Uncle Bud caught every one uv'em. You know how he does it? He ties a line to a bough hanging out over the water and baits the hook with chicken. When the bough bends, he knows the turtle's struck. Turtle don't come any better'n Uncle Bud's." Then he surveyed the table and beamed.

Putting it into words would have been beyond Charlie, but he knew that the magic of Turpmtine depended on thrusting his guests back into a manly world where people still lived close to the earth, a luxurious bygone world in which there were masters and servants and everybody knew his place. He didn't have to explain who Uncle Bud was. He merely had to say his name in a certain way, and one and all would realize that he was some sort of faithful old retainer, probably black.

He had hoped that Uncle Bud's catching the turtles might somehow serve as a transition to just who had caught the boars and the rattlesnakes. But that wasn't happening, and so he leaned across the woman on his right, Howell Hendricks's second wife, Francine, and said to the man next to her, "Well, Herb, whattaya think a yer turtle soup?"

"Oh, it's delicious, Charlie," said the man, with a somewhat embarrassed smile.

Charlie beamed, hoping to coax a little more conversation out of him. But it wasn't forthcoming. Herb Richman was going to be a tough pigeon to bag, a hard one to mesmerize with the magic of Turpmtine. For a start, he was Jewish, which in Georgia meant that your paths weren't going to cross socially all that much. And he was so damned mild-mannered and polite. It wasn't going to be easy to put him under the Turpmtine Spell with the usual hearty, jolly, manly chatter. Nevertheless, Herb Richman was the pigeon he needed. This whole weekend had been created for the sole purpose of casting the Spell over Mr. Herbert Richman, who was known in the Atlanta newspapers as "the fitness center tycoon." Herb Richman was the founder of DefinitionAmerica, a network of 1,100 health-and-fitness centers, which he had started in Atlanta and then reproduced thick as shad throughout the country. He was looking for 360,000 square feet of prime office space to create a new corporate headquarters. With luck and the Turpmtine Spell, that might mean seven floors and more than $10 million a year in lease income at Croker Concourse, a financial and public relations coup that would impress even the workout people at PlannersBanc with their "niche focus" and all the rest of it. Practically every big weekend at Turpmtine had its pigeon, a term Charlie had said out loud only once, to his first wife, Martha, who had found it distasteful. So he had never dared utter it at all to Serena, although he had told her exactly why he had invited Herb Richman and why he would be paying so much attention to him. Turpmtine might not be, strictly speaking, an experimental farm, but it had paid for itself many times over in terms of bagged pigeons, a point he didn't quite know how to get across to those small-brained niche-focused motherfuckers at PlannersBanc.

Charlie continued to beam at his pigeon. Herb Richman wasn't much of an advertisement for DefinitionAmerica, which promised its thousands of members sculpted, high-toned, sharply defined bodies. He was only forty-four but already running to fat. His head popped up out of his blazer and polo shirt like a bubble. His skin was pallid and pasty. A few strands of hair the color of orange-juice stains skimmed back across his otherwise bald pate. His extremely pale hazel eyes gave him a look that was at once eerie and washed out. He looked sleepy. It occurred to Charlie that he himself would have presented a better picture for such a firm, even at the age of sixty. Charlie was wearing an open-necked khaki shirt that brought out the girth of his neck, the width of his shoulders, and the massiveness of his chest. Casual dress was very much the fashion at the grand plantations these days, even at dinner, except for a few spreads in South Carolina owned by Northerners who were infected with British customs.

"I want to make sure you meet Uncle Bud tomorrow," said Charlie. "Uncle Bud's a walking history of Georgia plantations. He's been here at Turpmtine since a long time fo' I ever was. His folks were all Turpmtine Ni— Turpmtine People from way back, when all you did here was, you harvested resin from the pine trees for naval stores and that sorta thing. I couldn't even begin to tell you how old he is. I don't think he could, either." Charlie shook his head with a salt-of-the-earth significance. "Uncle Bud."

"Sounds like an interesting man," said Herb Richman with a weak smile, great politeness, and utter lack of conviction.

The table's conversational buzz had now dropped badly, even though Charlie had managed to stock the weekend with enough loquacious, colorful, prestigious characters to impress Herb Richman, no matter what his personal tastes were. Down at the other end of the table, on one side of Herb Richman's wife, Marsha, he had put Howell Hendricks, the big, hearty, melon-headed CEO of Serry & Belloc, the second or third biggest advertising firm in the South. On the other side he had put Slim Tucker, the country singer who was one of the first music business figures to buy a South Georgia quail plantation. They had both been paying a lot of attention to Marsha Richman — who was such a pretty brunette that Charlie figured she *had* to be a second wife — but now all three of them were silently exploring their turtle soup with their spoons. The old ex-governor, Beauchamp (pronounced *Beacham*) Knox, who was sitting next to Serena, was doing the same. Even Opey McCorkle, the Baker County judge who could talk a raccoon out of a tree, had stopped talking to Ted Nashford's young live-in girlfriend, Lydia Something-or-other. In true Opey McCorkle fashion he had turned up for dinner wearing a plaid shirt, a plaid necktie, red felt suspenders, *and* a big old leather belt that went around his potbelly like something you could hitch up a mule with, but for now he had cut off his usual torrent of orotund rhetoric mixed with Baker Countyisms. So it was up to Charlie himself to put some life back into the proceedings. This he felt well primed to do. Before dinner he had downed a couple of glasses of bourbon and water — "brown whiskey," as opposed to the Yuppie Lite stuff that was in vogue in Atlanta these days, the white wine and vodka and so on — although he hadn't made an issue of the point, since Herb Richman had asked for white wine — and then he had brought out some of Uncle Bud's homemade corn liquor. The ladies had turned it down with appropriately terrified ladylike protestations. But naturally Charlie had to knock back a glass of it, despite the fact that it practically took the top of your head off. It stopped his right knee from aching, in any event, and left him feeling ... *loud.*

"Hey, Mason!" he boomed out to his butler, who was still standing by the kitchen door. "Don't we have any honest-to-God logs around here? All's I see in'eh's lightwood and kindling."

Mason, wearing an old-fashioned white cotton mess jacket and a black bow tie, came forward with a worried, slightly wounded look on his face.

"There's logs on'eh, Cap'm Charlie. '*Put* logs on'eh, just a while ago."

"I don't see nothing but *light*wood, Mason," said Charlie. "Go get me some *logs.*"

The butler hesitated, then averted his eyes and shook his head. He was a tall man with broad shoulders, now turning bony with age, who wore his hair parted in the middle and combed straight back in little marcelled wavelets.

In a whispery voice, as if they were getting into a subject that didn't bear discussing in front of the guests, he said, "Put too much wood on'eh, Cap'm Charlie, gon' th'ow out too much *heat.*"

Charlie understood. The problem was that it was warm outside, up in the high sixties even now. But Ronald had given the Gun Room a fireplace big enough to walk into, a fireplace so stupendous it clearly demanded a fire. The only way you could stand the fire on a day like this was to turn the central air conditioning on to the maximum, which Mason had done. Every now and then a frigid draft would sink from a vent overhead and make you feel as if your gums were congealing and your teeth were coming loose. If Mason put a full load of hardwood on the fire, enough to look appropriate for the hearth's colossal andirons, the fire might overwhelm the cooling system completely. But hell … you just had to have a roaring fire in a hearth that big.

In a now somewhat softer voice Charlie said to Mason, "Go on. Go ahead and get me some real logs."

"Yessir, Cap'm Charlie … but I 'on know …" Mason shook his head.

Serena spoke up from down at the other end of the table. "Please, Charlie." Then she looked at Mason. "We don't need any more logs on there."

Mason stared at her for a moment, then stared at Charlie with a pained expression. Charlie was also aware of the expression on his son Wally's face. Wally was sitting three seats away from Serena, between Doris Bass and Ted Nashford's little Live-in Lydia, and his eyes were going from Serena to Charlie to Mason, and he seemed to be shrinking in his chair.

Now Charlie glowered at his wife with resentment, three kinds of it. She was coming perilously close to countermanding his instructions to his butler. Not only that, if he knew Serena, she was capable of describing to the entire table the battle between the fire and the air conditioning, thereby making him look vain and foolish. And to top it all off, she was making Mason uncomfortable. Mason disliked taking orders from her or having her intervene in household matters in any fashion. Mason remained loyal to Martha even now, three years after the divorce. Charlie could feel it every minute Mason and Serena were in the same room.

Now Mason was standing there awaiting further instructions and a resolution of the conflicting opinions of Cap'm Charlie and his hot new cookie on the subject of the magnitude of the logs in the fireplace. Charlie was afraid to tell him to just do what he said and get the big logs, for fear Serena would jump in and bring up the matter of the air conditioning. Clearly a change of subject was called for.

So all of a sudden he gave Mason a big smile, and then he gave Lettie Withers a big smile, and he said, "You met Mason, didn't you, Lettie? You met Mason when you were here last time."

"I certainly did," said Lettie in the sort of smoker's baritone many older Southern women had from a lifetime of cigarettes. "It's nice to see you again, Mason."

"Fine, Miz Withers." Mason had the habit of saying "Fine" when he met people, regardless of whether or not they asked him how he was. At the same time, Charlie was impressed that he had remembered Lettie's last name.

"Mason's had a lotta good news since you were here, Lettie." Mason looked perplexed.

"Tell Miz Withers about your son and your daughter, Mason." Mason hesitated. So Charlie said, "Where's your boy now?"

"Georgia Tech," said Mason.

"Tell Miz Withers what he's studying."

"Electrical engineering," said Mason. His eyes were now jumping from Charlie's face to Lettie's face and back again. This recitation was making him uncomfortable, which Charlie realized, but he was determined to establish a point — and not for Lettie's benefit, either. Charlie's own eyes were beginning to jump from Mason to Herbert Richman.

"Electrical engineering *where?*" said Charlie. "Which school?"

"Which school?" The old butler looked at Charlie quizzically. "Georgia Tech?" It came out like a question.

"Naw, I mean the *graduate* school," said Charlie. "Mason's boy is in the graduate school, Lettie. He's already got his BS from Tech. He got that last year. In'at right, Mason?"

"Yessir."

"And now he's in the graduate school in the best engineering program in the South, if not the country," Charlie said. "In'at right?"

"Yessir."

"I graduated from Tech, too," said Charlie, "but they wouldna *had* ... *me* in the graduate school! I bet you don't doubt that, do you, Mason?" Yet another glance at Herbert Richman.

"No, sir." Mason's face was now twisted into a terribly embarrassed, tortured smile. "I mean, yessir, I speck they'd a had you if that's what you wanted."

"Naw, Mason," Charlie said, laughing, "unh-unnh. They're too smart for that at Tech! Now tell Miz Withers about your daughter. Tell her about Verna. Where's Verna now?"

"She's in Atlanta."

"What's she doing in Atlanta? She's a nurse, in'she? Where's she a nurse?"

"In the trauma center at Emory." Mason was now standing with his shoulders pulled forward and his hands twisted together at hip level, like a dutiful student.

"The trauma center at Emory," said Charlie. "That's a pretty important job, in'it, Ted?" He looked at Ted Nashford, the surgeon, on Lettie's left, then swiveled another quick glance at Herbert Richman, to make sure he was paying attention, then looked back at Ted.

"Oh, yes," said Dr. Nashford, "that's a very important job."

Charlie smiled. He beamed triumphantly. "I think that's great, Mason. You oughta feel very proud."

"Yessir," said Mason.

"And I don' just mean proud a your children. You oughta feel proud a yourself." He gave Mason a long, penetrating stare.

Mason comprehended what his employer now wanted him to say. "Yessir, but I speck — I couldna — couldna done it 'thout you, Cap'm Charlie. You been mighty gen'rous."

"Aw, nonsense, Mason," Charlie said grandly. "All I did was knock on a couple a doors. You've got two fine children there."

Charlie turned again to glance at Herbert Richman, but in that same moment he noticed that Wally, all sixteen years' worth of him, was now slumped way down in his chair as if recoiling from something distasteful and looking anxiously toward Serena. For her part, Serena was giving him, Charlie, a look that expressed anything but pride in his benevolence toward his faithful black servant. In fact, the look was accusatory. About *what*, for godsake? All he was doing was making sure that Herb Richman understood how warm and tolerant and — and — and *enlightened* things were nowadays down here at Turpmtine. What was so bad about that?

An immense, cackling laugh broke out halfway down the table. Unmistakably ... Billy Bass. Billy's gangling form was thrust back in his chair, and his head was thrown back and his chin was pointing almost straight up in the air. He had the sort of laugh that was so profound, he would lose his breath. He was a big, tall, untidy man with a paunch and drooping eyelids and wattles like a hound and thinning gray hair that always stuck out this way and that. Seeing him now, reared back in his khakis and looking like a big old aging Cracker, which he was, you would never know what a superb physical specimen he had been forty years ago when he was a senior playing end for Tech just as Charlie was starting off as a sophomore in the backfield. This particular old Cracker roosted atop a fortune. He was one of the few real estate developers who had been smart enough to sell his holdings in 1987, near the peak of the 1980s boom in Atlanta. Although Charlie hadn't known him when he was a boy, Billy had grown up practically next door, in Dougherty County, and he had grown up the same way Charlie had, dirt poor and common as pig tracks, and for years now he had been Charlie's great huntin'n'shootin'pal and a fixture, an endless source of good comic low humor, at these big weekends at Turpmtine. The entire table was watching by the time he finally got his breath back and rocked forward, tears of laughter streaming down his cheeks, and looked at Lenore Knox and roared:

"Did you say … a *ball* for AIDS? A … BALL FOR AIDS?"

As the former First Lady of Georgia, Lenore was an old hand at dinner table conversation who had dealt with practically every peculiarity known to that endeavor, but she seemed genuinely nonplussed by this one. She cocked her head defensively.

"I've *heard* a balls for AIDS," cried Billy, "but this is the fust time I ever knowed anybody that actually *went* to one!" *One* came out wuh-uhn; two syllables; in South Georgia, Billy's speech became even more Down Home than Charlie's. The key to his low humor was that he started laughing even before the first words left his mouth, and his laughter swept you along like a wave, no matter what he was actually saying. "I was born at the wrong damn time, Lenore! Hell" — *Hale* — "when I was growing up, if you got a venereal" — *vernerl* — "disease, it was a *stigma!*" Already he was looking away from Lenore Knox and toward the men at the table, as if rallying his troops for a salvo of male laughter. "If you got syphilis or the clap, it was a *dis*-grace." His eyes sought out Governor Knox's — the old Governor didn't know what to do, since his wife seemed to be the butt of the joke — and then they sought out Howell Hendricks's and Judge Opey McCorkle's and Herb Richman's and Charlie's and Ted Nashford's and Slim Tucker's. Charlie and Judge McCorkle were already laughing, because they were pushovers for Billy's brand of humor when he went on these dinner table jags of his. "I can remember plenty a fellows with vernerl diseases, but I don't remember anybody throwin' *parties* for'm!" exclaimed Billy, bursting with mirth. "I don't remember any DANCES! I don't remember any LET'S RAP FOR CLAP nights! Or LET'S RIFF FOR SYPH!"

"Or LET'S HOP FOR HERPES!" volunteered Judge Opey McCorkle, who was laughing so hard he could hardly get the words out.

"Or LET'S GO GREET THE SPIROCHETES!" contributed Charlie, who was now in the same paroxysmal condition.

"Or LET'S GO ROAR FOR THE CHANCRE SORES!" exclaimed Billy Bass.

"Or LET'S PAY OUR DUES TO THE PUSTULAR OOZE!" exclaimed the judge.

"Or LET'S GO HUG A DYIN' BUGGER!" cried Billy, who was gasping for breath and weeping with laughter at the same time. "Now — now if you get AIDS, you're some kinda saint! — and they give banquets for you! Everbuddy goes dancin'!"

"Glory ME — I got da HIV!" sang out the judge, who had his mouth open, his eyes wide, and both hands flopping in the air up by his ears, as if he were a minstrel performer. This started Billy and Charlie laughing even harder.

"They never used to give lepers banquets for being LEPERS!" shouted Billy. "They put BELLS around their necks so people could hear 'em coming and stay OUTTA THEIR WAY! Maybe they could do that with all these characters with AIDS!"

"Yeah," said Charlie, " 'cep when you went to New York or San Francisco or one a those places, Christalmighty, you wouldn't be able to hear yourself THINK! It's bad enough in Atlanta!"

Billy and the judge redoubled their laughter, which pleased Charlie, who was afraid that up until then he had fallen behind in the rounds of wisecracks. Oh, this was the real thing! This was vintage manly humor deep in the huntin'n'shootin' atmosphere of Turpmtine! This was the sort of good times among men that the Gun House and this Gun Room had been built for! "Let's Rap for Clap!" "Let's Riff for Syph!" "Let's go hug a dyin' bugger!" Jesus, Billy was one funny old sonofabitch! This was letting it all hang out down here below the gnat line!

Charlie surveyed the table, to enjoy the sight of the rest of the party caught up in the rich manly humor of Turpmtine. In fact, what he saw surprised him. Howell Hendricks had a grin, or the beginning of one, on his big face, but his eyes were not laughing. They were jumping anxiously from Serena to Dr. Ted Nashford's young

Live-in Lydia to Veronica Tucker, who was sitting on the other side of Herb Richman. Billy's wife, Doris, was laughing heartily, but Serena was once more staring accusingly at him, Charlie, and Wally had slumped so far down in his chair and rolled his eyes so far back in his head — he had embarrassment written all over him. Live-in Lydia was staring across at Ted Nashford with her lips parted, as if waiting for a cue as to which way to turn them, up or down. Ted's expression was like Howell Hendricks's: a smile topped by a pair of small, anxious eyes. Charlie had heard Lettie Withers's smoke-cured laugh braying when it had all started, but now she had settled back into her chair with an apprehensive look. Slim Tucker, who wanted to prove he was a natural-born plantation-owning type, had on a big grin, but it was frozen. Marsha Richman, sitting between Slim and Howell, was staring morosely across the table at her husband. And as for Herb Richman —

Herb Richman's fat face looked numb. He was returning his wife's stare with a look that seemed to say, "Well, here we are, and there's nothing I can do about it right now."

What the hell was going on? This was Turpmtine! Not only that, this was the Gun Room at Turpmtine, the very bastion of male camaraderie! What was wrong with these people?

Suddenly a reedy voice piped up from down at the far end of the table: "Why don't you just nuke 'em all, Dad?"

It was Wally. Charlie was stunned. He had no idea what he was talking about, but he sensed revolt. It was in the boy's very tone, which began with a lilt of levity and then swooned into a quaver. The table went stone quiet. The sound of a log burning through and collapsing with a crunch on the hearth seemed like an avalanche.

"Nuke who?" said Charlie. There was his son, shrunken back in his chair, staring like a raccoon transfixed by headlights, his mouth slightly open.

"All the people with AIDS." Not even the pretense of lightheartedness now. Nothing but a sixteen-year-old boy thoroughly frightened by his own audacity.

"Nuke 'em?" asked Charlie. "Why nuke 'em?"

More tremulous than ever: "Because that way the ones that don't die, you can see 'em coming, because they'll glow in the dark."

By the time he reached *glow*, his young voice was close to a sob of panic. Every dinner party's worst nemesis, stricken silence, seized the table.

Then Judge Opey McCorkle forced a country laugh and turned to Charlie and said, "Charlie, damn if your boy ain't bad as you! 'Nuke 'em!' *Heh heh heh heh heggggggggghhhhhh!*"

The judge's intervention gave everybody the opportunity to release the tension by joining in the laughter. Everybody but Charlie; he couldn't even feign a smile. Finally he pulled himself together and looked toward the kitchen door and roared out:

"Mason! Bring these folks some more turtle soup!"

About
The Public Library
of Charlotte
and Mecklenburg County

With more than 1.7 million books, magazines, and other materials, the Public Library of Charlotte and Mecklenburg County serves a population of more than 600,000 in a rapidly growing region. More than three million times annually, patrons visit PLCMC's twenty-three locations. In 1999, library staff answered 1,361,624 research questions; in the same year, the library's computers were put to use almost 300,000 times, and public programs numbered 11,225.

Through its resources, service to the community, and innovative programming, PLCMC continues to win regional and national recognition for excellence.

With this book, the library introduces an innovative new project, Novello Festival Press, which will publish the work of emerging writers and celebrate the literary legacy of our region.

Biographical Notes

AUTHORS:

Jerry Bledsoe is a former newspaper columnist whose true crime books include *Death Sentence: The True Story of Velma Barfield's Life, Crimes, and Execution*; and the nationally acclaimed *Bitter Blood*, which reached number one on the *New York Times* best-seller list.

Joseph Bruchac is a Native American story-teller and author who has written more than forty books for children and adults. His works include *The Wind Eagle and Other Abenaki Stories* and *Bowman's Store: A Journey to Myself*.

Will D. Campbell is a Baptist minister and former civil rights advocate who lives near Nashville, Tennessee. He is the author of sixteen books, including *Covenant, Soul Among Lions*, and *Brother To A Dragonfly*, which was a National Book Award finalist.

Fred Chappell, a national and international award-winning writer, is the poet laureate of North Carolina. He is the author of two books of essays and eleven books of poetry, as well as eight novels, including his most recent, *Look Back All The Green Valley*.

Pat Conroy first gained national attention with his memoir, *The Water Is Wide*. His highly acclaimed and best-selling novels include *The Prince of Tides*, *Beach Music* and *The Great Santini*. He lives in South Carolina.

Walter Cronkite has been a journalist for more than sixty years. A former war correspondent for United Press International, he gained national fame as anchor of the *CBS Evening News*. He is the author of a memoir, *A Reporter's Life*.

Hal Crowther is a widely published columnist and winner of the H.L Mencken Award. He the author of *Unarmed But Dangerous: Withering Attacks on All Things Phony, Foolish and Fundamentally Wrong With America*. His newest book is *Cathedrals of Kudzu*.

Clyde Edgerton is a novelist, essayist and part-time musician from North Carolina. His books include *Raney, Walking Across Egypt, Killer Diller, In Memory of Junior* and *The Floatplane Notebooks.*

Sandra Y. Govan teaches American and African American literature at the University of North Carolina at Charlotte. Her essays have appeared in numerous journals and anthologies, including *My Soul Is A Witness* and *Father Songs.*

David Halberstam was a war correspondent in Vietnam and won the Pulitzer Prize for his reporting. His books include *The Best and the Brightest, The Children* and *Playing for Keeps: Michael Jordan and the World He Made.*

Robin Hemley is an award-winning novelist, essayist and short story writer who teaches creative writing at Western Washington University. His most recent book is *Nola: A Memoir of Faith, Art, and Madness.*

Jody Jaffe is a former newspaper reporter who combined her journalistic expertise with her love of horses to write three mystery books: *Horse of a Different Killer, Chestnut Mare Beware,* and *In Colt Blood.* She lives in the Washington, D.C. area.

Nanci Kincaid, a Florida native who now lives in Arizona, is the author of two novels, *Crossing Blood* and *Balls.* She has also written a critically acclaimed collection of short stories, *Pretending the Bed Is a Raft.*

Charles Kuralt, the late CBS News correspondent who was known for his poignant stories about ordinary people, is the author of several books, including *Charles Kuralt's America, Southerners: Portrait of a People,* and *Life On The Road.*

C. Eric Lincoln was a native of Alabama. Prior to his death in early 2000, he was a novelist, poet, essayist and scholar who also held a divinity degree and was a Fellow of the American Academy of Arts and Sciences. His books include *Coming Through The Fire: Surviving Race and Place in America,* and *This Road Since Freedom.*

Jill McCorkle is the author of a book of short stories and five novels, including *Tending to Virginia* and *Carolina Moon*. Her work has been selected four times for the *New York Times* Book Review list of Notable Books of the Year. She lives in the Boston area, and has taught most recently at Harvard University.

Frank McCourt, who worked for many years as a writing teacher at Stuyvesant High School in New York, won the Pulitzer Prize for his best-selling memoir, *Angela's Ashes*. His latest book is *'Tis*.

Tim McLaurin is a novelist whose books include *The Acorn Plan, Cured By Fire* and *Woodrow's Trumpet*. His first memoir was *Keeper of the Moon: A Southern Boyhood,* and his current book, also a memoir, is *The River Less Run*. He lives in Hillsborough, North Carolina.

Reynolds Price is a native of North Carolina. A member of the American Academy of Arts and Letters, he is the author of numerous novels, essays, plays, works of poetry and memoir. His novel, *Kate Vaiden,* won the National Book Critics Circle Award in 1986.

Dori Sanders is the author of the international best-seller, *Clover;* a second novel, *Her Own Place;* and the cookbook, *Dori Sanders' Country Cooking.* She considers herself first and foremost a South Carolina peach farmer, and is currently at work on a family memoir.

Gail Sheehy is the author of *Passages,* one of the most widely read books of our time. As a contributing editor to *Vanity Fair,* she has written extensively about political figures including Margaret Thatcher, Saddam Hussein and Mikhail Gorbachev. Her latest book is *Hillary's Choice.*

Lee Smith, winner of the O. Henry Prize and the Robert Penn Warren Prize for Fiction, is the author of ten books, including *Black Mountain Breakdown, Fair and Tender Ladies, The Devil's Dream* and *News of the Spirit.*

A.J. Verdelle, author of *The Good Negress,* is a native of Washington, D.C. She holds degrees in political science and statistics, and is currently a lecturer in the humanities and creative writing program at Princeton University.

Ashley Warlick is a novelist whose first book, *The Distance from the Heart of Things,* won the Houghton Mifflin Literary Fellowship Award. Her most recent novel is *The Summer After June.* She lives in South Carolina.

Tom Wolfe first gained national renown as one of the fathers of "new journalism," with such books as *The Right Stuff,* which won the American Book Award. More recently, he has won acclaim for his best-selling novels, *The Bonfire of the Vanities* and *A Man In Full.*

EDITORS:

Frye Gaillard is the author of seventeen books, including the national award-winners, *If I Were A Carpenter: Twenty Years of Habitat for Humanity* and *The Dream Long Deferred.*

Robert Inman is a screen writer, novelist, and newspaper columnist whose books include *Coming Home, Dairy Queen Days, Old Dogs and Children,* and *Home Fires Burning.*

Amy Rogers is an award-winning magazine writer, columnist and editor. She was contributing editor for *An African American Album, Volume II.* Her books include *No Hiding Place: Uncovering the Legacy of Charlotte-Area Writers.*

Photo Credits

Jerry Bledsoe by Erik Bledsoe

Joseph Bruchac by Carol Bruchac

Will Campbell by Judy Newby

Walter Cronkite by Peter Liepke

Clyde Edgerton by Marion Ettlinger

Robin Hemley by Beverly Hemley

Jody Jaffe by Jerry Bauer

Nanci Kincaid by Steven Meckler

Jill McCorkle by Michael Mundy

Frank McCourt by Gasper Tringale

Tim McLaurin by Lance Richardson

Dori Sanders by Layne Bailey

Gail Sheehy by Gasper Tringale

Lee Smith by David G. Spielman

A.J. Verdelle by Marc Norberg

Ashley Warlick by Piper Warlick

Permissions

Index